EMBRACING
THE ELEPHANT

EMBRACING
THE ELEPHANT

a novel by

Lori Hart Beninger

On Track Publishing

San Jose, California

For information regarding permissions, contact us at:
OnTrackPublishing.com
San Jose, CA 95124-1008

Library of Congress Control Number: 2012940688

   1. California Gold Rush 1848-1849 Fiction,
   2. Fathers and daughters Fiction, 3. Sailing Fiction

Cover photo: "Isabella on the Balclutha" by Tiffany O'Brian
Butterfly and a Dog Photography

Cover photo re-imaging: Anda Beninger

Book and cover design by Longfeather Book Design
LongfeatherBookDesign.com

ISBN 978-0-9856897-0-4 (softcover)
ISBN 978-0-9856897-1-1 (hardcover)
ISBN 978-0-9856897-2-8 (electronic)

To the resilient, persistent child in all of us

CHAPTER 1

March 25, 1848

WHEN THE CITY OF NEW YORK DISAPPEARS behind a curtain of late-season snow I am thrilled. The voyage has begun. The steamer trip from Boston was only a stutter step. Now I am on my way. Soon I will be with Papa.

I am less pleased as the snow turns to sleet and I am driven below decks. It is foul-smelling and crowded there and I know almost no one. Had this been my home in Boston, a blustery day would have been enjoyable with my cousins and me playing games and telling stories and making mischief on the staircase. However, my cousins are still in Boston and the ship's staircase is hidden and probably forbidden and the only children close to my age are the ones with whom I travel and they are not very playful.

Once hailstones pound the decks and the ship tosses and rises and then plummets into gigantic troughs of waves I retreat to my bunk in terror. I expect to be shattered. I want to find the captain and beg him to turn back. The violence of the voyage has turned the stomachs and bowels of my fellow passengers to water and all joy wanes.

Then I think of Papa and I resolve to clutch the sides of my berth until the storm passes and say nothing of my fear to the captain or anyone.

As the storm abates, the wind remains. Today the rain and ice are gone and the decks are dry and I can keep my footing for the first time since we sailed from New York Harbor. I am glad there is this wind for it speeds the ship steadily forward even though it invades every seam and gap in my clothing and makes my body erupt into gooseflesh. I hope this is the kind of wind that can blow ships to the farthest points of the earth like the North Wind which Mama told me about. Papa lives in one of the far points of the earth.

"Good morning, Miss. Fine freezing day isn't it?"

Mr. Boyle stands before me: Mr. Boyle, the thin and weathered sailor who discovered me on the front-most deck watching as a little steamer towed *The Pelican* into New York Harbor from the channel at Clark's Wharf. Mr. Boyle, who ordered me to leave that deck because of its danger: snow slick, its railing open to the sea. Mr. Boyle, who grabbed my hand when I gave him no response and, with a snort, led me back to the larger deck, his blunt fingers clenched so tightly that I nearly cried out as I slid across the boards behind him.

"Where are your parents?" he barked once we stepped onto the proper deck. I remained quiet. "Why aren't they watching you?" I looked down at my shoes, biting at the walls of my cheeks.

He squatted before me and tilted his head to catch my eye. "Ah, I see. I'm a stranger and you're not allowed to talk to strangers. Is that it?"

I nodded, avoiding his gaze. Of all the advice with which Aunt Margaret peppered me in preparation of this journey the warning against talking with strangers was the most repeated.

"Well this'll be fun," he said. "Four."

I frowned because I could not fathom the significance of the number he had spoken.

"I'm guessing you're ten years old; am I right?" the sailor asked. I shook my head. "Fifteen then?" I was more emphatic in my denial as his guess was well past the mark. "Then you must be twenty. And don't try to tell me you're any older 'cause I won't believe you."

"I am eleven," I said.

He smiled in triumph, showing squared and yellowed teeth. "I told m'self I could make you talk before I'd asked four questions and I've done it in three. But don't you smile about that as it's a small victory. Now I must divine your name and that'll be harder. What's your name?"

The wind answered the sailor's question and I gasped. Of course it could not have been the wind, I knew that. However, since I distinctly heard my name above the noise of the ship, I turned to look for the source only to find the Reverend descending upon us, his wispy hair flaring atop his head in a corn-silk halo.

"Guinevere, what are you doing here?" the Reverend shouted as he neared. "I've been looking everywhere for you. Mrs. Dunsford has given me a terrible scolding for having lost you while still in sight of land. She worried that you might've gone overboard when we left the pier or…or worse." His eyes were fixed on the sailor during this speech as if to accuse *him* for my wandering. "I'm the Reverend Dunsford. To whom do I have the pleasure of speaking?" He did not sound as if he found it a pleasure and did not offer a greeting hand. Instead he stepped behind me, his thumbs pressing hard against my shoulders.

The sailor stood tall. "Boyle. Eamon Boyle, chief mate of *The*

Pelican," he said as if in challenge.

"Yes, well I must get this young lady below. So good day, Mr. Boyle," the Reverend said, turning me swiftly away from the sailor.

Ah, but now Mr. Boyle was no longer a stranger; introductions had been made. I wriggled from the Reverend's grip. "Guine," I shouted over the wind and the clang of rigging. "My name is Guine. Pleased to meet you, Mr. Boyle." I was joyous even as the Reverend grabbed me once more and spun me toward the cabin.

"You know you're not to talk to strangers. Why were you talking to that man, Guinevere?"

"I was not talking to him, sir. I was listening."

Now with the snow and sleet and hail and proper social introductions behind us, I am again on deck and, to my way of thinking, free to respond to Mr. Boyle's salutation of "Good morning, Miss. Fine freezing day isn't it?"

"Good morning, Mr. Boyle. It is indeed a fine day."

"What brings you out here?"

"I hope to find a place to read," I say, displaying the book I hold.

"Out here? You'll freeze your…you'll freeze."

"I do not wish to be below anymore. It smells there," I whisper.

Mr. Boyle nods and sighs and I am relieved that I do not have to explain further.

"And how is the Reverend, your father?"

By his tone I am certain Mr. Boyle does not care how I answer his question; he is only being polite. I am amused that he could think me related to the pale Dunsford family with their faces and hair the color of buttermilk. "The Reverend Dunsford is my guardian," I reply. "I am traveling with his family to California where my father lives. My father is a doctor in San Francisco and I am to join him. Dr. Harold James Walker." I puff with pride as I state my oft-repeated news: I am to join my father.

"May I ask you something, Mr. Boyle?" I continue. The Dunsfords remain below, suffering with seasickness, and I crave company. "How long is the journey to San Francisco? And why do we sail into the morning sun? San Francisco is to the west. Why are we going east? I should think, at the very least, we would be sailing south."

I hope Mr. Boyle's smile is an indication of his pleasure at my questions. "We sail until we catch more favorable winds and the current, to the east. It'll help our speed. Once there we'll quickly move south, 'round Cape Horn, then north to San Francisco. Given a few stops along the way I think it fair to say that you'll be with your father by September."

I am disappointed but not surprised. Six-month duration is exactly what my aunt and uncle told me I would face. I glance at the novel in my hand and vow to read slowly so as not to finish all of my books before reaching my destination. I have brought many, but six months is a very long time.

"What is your book?" Mr. Boyle asks.

"*The Adventures of Robinson Crusoe.*"

"A shipwreck book? On an ocean voyage?"

Uncle John thought it a strange choice too. "It was handy," I say.

"Well enjoy it Miss. And try to keep warm." Mr. Boyle nods, touching the brim of his cap as he turns to leave.

"Will you tell me about the ship, please? How big it is, how old, and what things are called? I have heard that ships have unique terms for even the smallest of objects." I only mildly care about these things, but do not want him to leave.

He nods. "I'll give you a tour if you like, as my duties're light at the moment."

I eagerly accept his offer even though I believe such a task will take almost no time. From where I stand, I am able to see everything from one end of the vessel to the other. There is little except a clutter of cages and barrels and bales and ropes and piles of canvas. The ship hardly looks bigger than Uncle John's barn. It is far less tidy.

For the most part, I am right—there is little for me to see. To prolong the tour, I point and question while Mr. Boyle repeats the strange terms that describe the features of the square-sailed ship: the masts and scuppers and bilge pumps and things like that. There must be a hundred different types of sails on the ship. We visit the deck house with its workshop and chart house, mess, and galley. The galley is my favorite as it is warm.

Then he indicates the places that are forbidden: the forecastle where the crew sleeps, the dangerous forecastle deck where I have already been, the quarterdeck for crew and captain only, and the hold with its ever-shifting cargo stacked to the rafters. He says I am never to venture near these places. Since they comprise more than half of the ship I find the restrictions disappointing. I do not say this aloud, as I do not want Mr. Boyle to think I did not enjoy his instruction.

"You ask a lot of questions," Mr. Boyle notes as his tour concludes. "Do you mind if I ask you one?" I nod. "Your accent quite clearly makes you a Bostonian. How did your father come to be in California?"

"Her manners are superb, Harold, but she will not bend to rule,"
Aunt Margaret wrote, demanding I read her nearly finished letter,
instructing me to search the dictionary for any words I did not
understand. I understood every one. I believe my aunt hoped that
the threat of telling Papa about some unruliness might change my
behavior. She made it clear that this was not the first time she had
complained to Papa; Aunt Margaret liked to make things clear.

She was especially clear after the "carriage incident."

I did not think the carriage incident was bad. After all I had
not damaged the rig or the horse. Unbeknownst to my aunt I had
harnessed the beast several times already during the preceding
months, each Sunday before the drive to the elder's house.

The stable boy thought it strange that a girl wanted to know
how to do such things, but he agreed to teach me anyway. He asked
for nothing in return except that my aunt and uncle not be told.
I thought that a fair request although sometimes I brought him a
piece of pie or other sweet saved from supper the night before, just
to let him know how much the lessons were appreciated.

I always arrived at the barn well before my aunt and uncle,
donning old boots and a heavy overcoat I kept hidden in one of
the horse stalls. I found the clothes in the attic and decided they
were well suited for keeping my dress and shoes from spoilage;
it would not do to step among the congregation with something
more than dust on my person. The garments once belonged to
Cousin Clarence, but I did not think Clarence would mind my
use as he was away at university and far too tall for them anymore.

Despite great effort, one Sunday Uncle John discovered me

standing on a stool to fit the harness and slip the bit into the horse's mouth. Much to my surprise he was pleased and even said so at the time (although he did not talk to his wife about it and requested that I not mention it either).

Apparently readying the carriage and driving it to the banks of the Charles River were completely different matters.

Often in the summer, when the city of Boston steamed, Papa and Mama and I went to the Charles where the river breezes cooled us. We would spend the day on a blanket in the short grasses that grew along the river's edge, dining on Mrs. Schrader's fine food as we watched sailboats and skiffs go by, and I would listen to Mama's tales.

"This grass is like the grass that grows in the ruins of the old abbey, near the village where your father grew up," Mama said as she ran her palms over the tops of the blades.

"Take me there," I begged. This was our game.

"Ah," she said, "it is really your father's tale to tell." She smiled, stroking Papa's hand and urging him to speak of his native land.

Despite pleas from both Mama and me, he refused. "Your mother is much better at tales than I." This was his usual response.

"I am just a lad," Mama began, pretending to be Papa, using her best British accent (which Papa told her was atrocious). "From my house, I walk the road to Mrs. Stoneman's cottage with its thatched roof and warped door. The road continues on to the next town, but I do not take that road. To the far side of Mrs. Stoneman's is a cart path carved through the meadow which leads to a hill that rises to the north. At its crest are trees that look like huddled monks.

"The path is surrounded by grass and divided down the

middle by a row of the same. Oh, not grass such as this," she said, her eyes closed as she ran her hand over the blades again, "but tall and dancing." I closed my eyes to see it too.

"I follow this path for more than three miles as it wends up the hill; although they…*we* do not measure distance in terms of miles in England.

"For the better part of an hour I walk until I reach those hilltop trees. I'm somewhat breathless from the hike and so I pause, turning to look at my village now miles away. The roofs of the cottages below cluster around the church spire and sheep graze in the surrounding fields. Each parcel of land is separated by low stone walls crisscrossing the green countryside. There is smoke coming from every chimney to ward off the chill of the spring day.

"Once rested, I turn again and walk through a shallow valley to the Sutton's farm beyond then onto the next hill.

"From that new summit, I look upon a place that pulses with emerald light. It is a beautiful valley with clusters of oak and hawthorn trees at its edges and bright grass, just like this, spread across its floor. Rising from the grass is a once-great abbey, its ruined arches standing tall like giant sentries, the roofs and walls in rubble at their feet. The grass is the abbey floor now and it has been that way for three hundred years. It is magical and hauntingly sad."

I traveled hundreds, perhaps thousands, of miles with my mother on that and most other days. Sometimes her tales came from books, sometimes she recast stories heard in her youth or, at times, she invented her own. Her words transformed any surrounding into great halls or palaces, lush English or Irish fields, or the sandy shores of some distant land. To hold bedtime at bay, I begged for her tales of the grand and mythical: an enchanted prince who lived in a castle east of the sun and west of the moon (having been blown there by the infamous North Wind), princesses, flying horses, and Christmas ghosts. I wanted the stories to never end.

It was early winter the day I took Uncle John's carriage to the Charles and nothing was as I remembered. The Charles River looked dead, its trees without leaves, the grasses yellowed and crusted in a thick coat of frost. The river was not the deep French blue of summer. Instead it was a dull slate color with dirty gray ice clinging to the banks.

A few hours later, Uncle John and the constable found me shivering with cold in front of an abandoned anonymous boathouse, staring toward the distant harbor. Well that was how Uncle John described the scene to Aunt Margaret in his attempt to gain the most sympathy possible for me. I do not remember having shivered very much despite the icy locale. I did not feel much at all except disappointment.

Aunt Margaret sent me to my room without supper that night and her letter to Papa was dispatched the next day, with a postscript.

When I was called into the parlor less than a month later, my aunt was vibrating with excitement. She had her own story to tell.

"Do you remember that day you stole the carriage?" she asked as I held my breath. "Well the very next day a dear friend from church told me about a Presbyterian minister from Lowell who is taking his family to China where the people are in great need of God's Word. Their ship is to make a stop in San Francisco.

"So I wrote to this reverend of Lowell, the Reverend Dunsford, that very day to explain your plight, Guinevere. And do you know what happened?" I shook my head. "He has replied! You should be very grateful, Guinevere, as this is a tremendous opportunity. The Dunsfords have agreed to be your guardians, your escorts to San Francisco."

Uncle John groaned from his favorite chair, although I did not think long on his reaction. I was ecstatic.

Aunt Margaret let me read the Reverend's letter. It contained many biblical quotes along with details of the family's planned journey from Lowell to Boston then onto New York where their chosen ship was to depart. The Reverend provided instructions on what personal items I might take and the size of the luggage allowed. He bragged about not having paid full fare for some of his children, who ate little and would share beds. The cost for nine Dunsfords would have been too prohibitive had he not been such an excellent negotiator.

I found none of those particulars interesting at all. It was the latter part of the letter I remembered best:

All pleasantries aside, Mrs. Whipple, you must excuse me for I am compelled to advise you that such a journey is fraught with peril. It is of some comfort to learn that our captain is reputed to be an able, God-fearing, and temperate man. However, the voyage itself I am told will take six months, possibly longer. We will sail into some of the most treacherous waters God, in His mystery, has seen to bestow upon the earth and we will make landfall in foreign and exotic places. I have great trust that the Lord will see us safely to our destination, but I know not what trials He may lay before us as we journey. My family and I count ourselves blessed to have this opportunity to deliver the Word of God to the unenlightened and have put our full faith in the Lord.

"If I Rise on the wings of dawn, if I settle on the far side of the sea, even there Your hand will guide me, your right hand will hold me fast." —Psalm 139: 9-10

Although we will not make San Francisco our home, my family and I look forward, with great anticipation, to visiting what will soon be our country's newest territory. Conclusion of the war with Mexico can only bring great prosperity to this glorious nation that stretches from sea to sea.

As you have been most persuasive in your argument that it is in the best interests of the child to be with her father, you may be assured that Mrs. Dunsford and I will do our utmost to deliver her safely unto Dr. Walker.

My wife and I look forward to meeting you and Mr. Whipple in late February when we will travel to Boston to gather the young miss and make our final preparations to sail. Until then, please know that you, Mr. Whipple, and young Guinevere are in our prayers.

Your humble servant,
The Reverend Donald Dunsford,
Lowell, Massachusetts
January 24, 1848

As I finished the letter, Aunt Margaret continued chirping. I did not hear her words, but for the first time in several months my emotions and hers were mirrored.

I tell this tale to Mr. Boyle, who sits quietly and asks no questions. As the ship's bell peals he finally responds: "I must be going, Miss."

As he stands and walks away, I realize I have told him why I am going to California but not why Papa is already there. My lapse is not surprising as I do not know the answer.

CHAPTER 2

May 2, 1848

THE FOURTEENTH BIRTHDAY CELEBRATION for Lizzie and Matthew, the oldest of the Dunsford's seven children, is modest. Mrs. Dunsford requests that the cook put molasses on the duff served at evening meal (which does not improve the taste much) and barely contains her own excitement as the twins open the brown wrappings of their gifts: matching brick-colored woolen scarves. The gifts are a mystery. Why would Mrs. Dunsford give a winter gift when summer is fast approaching? And how has she managed to create the mufflers without the knowledge of my cabin mates or me? Given our cramped living conditions, secrets are a rarity.

Despite the Reverend's original plan, the Dunsfords and I are not among the main cabin passengers. At any hour of the day or night those travelers may be found talking and gossiping among themselves, writing journals and letters, smoking and playing card games. There is little room between beds as excess luggage and cargo crowds the room, stacked against the ship's hull under the starboard portholes. I do not know how anyone manages to sleep there. In fact I do not recall ever seeing anyone actually sleeping as I pass through the main cabin.

Instead, Uncle John secured two private cabins for our

voyage. The Dunsford males (the Reverend and, as testament to his reverence, Matthew, Luke, Mark, and John) have one cabin and the four Dunsford females (Mrs. Dunsford, Elizabeth called Lizzie, Mary, and Anna) and I share the other. As two-year-old Anna sleeps with her mother, the rest of us have berths to ourselves. However, "to ourselves" means merely that we do not share a mattress. There are no curtains to draw for privacy and, therefore, each of us knows everything the others do in this space that is little bigger than a wardrobe. Well not everything, I suppose, as Mrs. Dunsford has managed to knit in secrecy.

Lizzie keeps no secrets. She is fond of expressing her every thought openly and often. She wants to return to Lowell where she has friends and interests and stability in the sense both of expectations of life and the surface beneath her feet. She complains that the sailors and other passengers are "coarse," that she never feels clean having to bathe in seawater, that the food is atrocious, and the scenery monotonous at best. No land graces the horizon. There are neither trees nor birds on the ocean: a fact she finds distressing.

I cannot disagree with Lizzie's complaints, but that does not make them any less irritating. Mrs. Dunsford does her best to quiet her daughter, assuring the girl that she will make many new friends, that the ship will stop in exciting ports along the way, and that China itself will be a great adventure. God will protect them in all things, she says. His plan for them is great.

The two youngest girls are much like my younger cousins: they fuss sometimes, but are easily distracted with dolls or a story or a stroll around the deck. No, it is Lizzie that fills the cabin with her unhappiness.

Lizzie is not the only problem, as I believe Mrs. Dunsford herself is terrified of this voyage to China. She has not said as much, but the more we are together and the more of her conversations I overhear the more certain I am of the fear. She describes God's great plan for the Dunsford family with the same reverential words the Reverend uses, but her eyes dart left and right as she speaks and her voice has a breathless quality. My Cousin Alfred does the same when telling lies.

Weather permitting, I spend most of my waking hours on deck and it is Mr. Boyle's company I seek. I am learning much about *The Pelican*. To test that growing knowledge he created a game in which he points to an object on the ship and demands its name. If I reply correctly, he gives me a copper penny. If I fail, I must give him a penny and he tells me the correct term for the next time. I was cautious of the game at first as I brought very few coins and the Reverend has charge of the larger portion of my money (which I doubt he will give me to play games). As it happens, my memory is good and Mr. Boyle has already paid me several pieces of copper. It is a fine way to pass an afternoon if he has time during his busy day. If not, I perch on a nondescript bale lashed beneath the quarterdeck to read and keep my own thoughts or watch the unceasing activities of the crew. I wish I had known how boring this voyage would be so that I had brought more books. I have finished reading my third novel already.

The Pelican herself requires constant attention and the sailors are never idle. Mr. Boyle and the second mate, Mr. Sterbenc, move from "stem to stern" (an expression Mr. Boyle has taught me) hundreds of times each day, setting the crew at a feverish pace of labor, inspecting the work or drawing attention to a forgotten detail or the next assignment. Sails and ropes are mended, rigging checked, and decks scrubbed. The sailors scramble nimbly up and down the ship's height and length without regard for her pitch and roll, even in rough weather. I admire this for I have not yet mastered the trick of walking a straight path on the deck. I have abandoned all attempts to skip rope on the ever-tilting surface and, since I seem to have outgrown that activity since last summer, I gave the rope to Mary as soon as she overcame her seasickness.

I am impressed with the undertakings of the crew, but not with Mr. Sterbenc. I find no better word to describe the man than "mean." He is the meanest man I have ever encountered. Whereas Mr. Boyle raises his voice to spur the crew on, Mr. Sterbenc raises his fist. He kicks the sailors when the quality of work is not pleasing. Heads are smacked for the smallest of errors or omissions. Buckets of water, if in his path, are knocked over and the errant sailor is pummeled with abusive language as he lowers the bucket into the sea to be refilled. Mr. Sterbenc does not talk to passengers; he certainly has never spoken to me and that is to my liking.

"This is Sterbenc's first time with Captain Watson and I hope it's his last," Mr. Boyle confides when I ask him about the mate's behavior. "He'd just as soon flog a man as talk to him. He has no business being on a ship like this. Better if he joined a clipper's crew; they expect that kind of man there. Why, he was once nearly strung up by some of his men."

"What does 'strung up' mean?"

Since he grimaces and sighs before responding, I suspect that Mr. Boyle did not mean to be so open with his words. "Hung," he mumbles. "Hung by the neck."

"I thought only murderers or incorrigible thieves were hanged," I say, my opinion of Mr. Sterbenc plummeting even further.

"And hellish mates." Then Mr. Boyle shakes his finger at me. "Don't you dare tell the Reverend I told you anything about Mr. Sterbenc, do you hear? He'll want to string *me* up for talking of such things to a child." He squints and tries to suppress an impish smile. "It is your fault, you know. You can cast spells to make a man talk just like that magician in your books, can't you? That Marlin fellow? No, a marlin's a fish. What was his name?"

"Merlin," I laugh.

"Well I'll resist your bewitching and speak no more of hangings or Dick Sterbenc." He crosses his arms and composes his face into an implausible frown. He does not mention Mr. Sterbenc again for the entire day.

"Mr. Boyle says the sky will be clear tonight and he has access to a telescope," I announce at the mess table. "Please, sir, may Matthew and I go on deck after supper to see the stars?"

The Reverend has become reluctantly tolerant of my acquaintance with Mr. Boyle. Initially he warned me against talking to a "common sailor." However, when I assured him that Mr. Boyle was an officer of the ship he had no further argument along that line. Still, he reasoned, my father would not be pleased to hear of this "friendship," emphasizing the word as if Mr. Boyle were a scoundrel, possibly a murderer.

"I believe Papa would view Mr. Boyle as the best teacher I could have with regard to ships: an experienced seaman." This argument was received with surprising success. Truth be told, I do not think my claim valid. My father has never expressed any positive opinion of sailors, officer or no. However, by the time the Reverend might verify my contention the voyage will be over and the issue behind us.

The "friendship" became more acceptable to the Reverend when Matthew chose to join us. At first I thought the boy had been put to the task by one or both of his parents. He made excuses to approach: Mary wanted to know if I had seen her hairbrush, his mother was not feeling well and wished everyone to stay away from the cabin until suppertime, his brothers wanted to hear the story of Robin Hood again at my convenience. However, once he began to ask pertinent questions, I came to realize that his interest in the ship was genuine. I do not mind his company as he is far more pleasant than his twin, Lizzie. In fact, the more I come to know him the less I find him like his sister at all: he is uncomplaining and polite and soft-spoken (his only unfortunate feature being the ugly red spots that cover his face).

My announcement about the telescope is well received around the table; all of the Dunsford children want to see the stars. I am discouraged, as I would prefer to view the heavens without a crowd. "I am sorry, but Mr. Boyle did not invite everyone," I say. "He only invited Matthew and me. I cannot presume that he would welcome anyone else."

"That's not fair," complains Luke, the Dunsford's second son (or perhaps it is their third son. I often confuse Luke and Mark since they are close in age and look so much alike). "Mother, she and Matthew shouldn't be allowed to go if we can't go! It isn't polite! Didn't your mother teach you to be polite? Where is your mother, by the way? You never speak of her. What happened to your mother?"

I forget the night sky and the promise of stars. Finding my lips suddenly numb and the words in my mind scattering like startled beetles, I stand and leave the room.

Papa warned of his intention to tie mittens firmly on my hands. When I continued to scratch at the rash despite his admonition he threatened to lash my wrists to the bedposts, his voice tense with irritation.

Instead Mama requested that I be allowed to sleep with her. She would keep an eye on me and make sure I did not cause my skin to bleed. We will distract each other, she said, keep each other from scratching; weather the measles together. Besides, she reasoned, Papa would not need to run between rooms to tend us if we were both in one bed.

Papa relented.

Mama and I lay side by side trying not to touch, pushing the covers away. It was mid-September and Boston's summer had lingered. No breeze lifted the lacy curtains to relieve us. The air was thick and heavy as if the room had been stuffed with damp, felted wool. Our cotton nightgowns showed pink where the cloth touched our moist bodies.

Papa visited occasionally, but there was little he could do. He made a ritual of dipping a towel into the water-filled basin that stood beside the bed, wringing it thoroughly before applying its coolness to Mama's forehead, neck, limbs. He stroked dark curls from her damp face. Then he did the same for me. More often, it was Mrs. Schrader who wiped the cooling cloth over us.

"Shall I tell a story?" Mama asked.

I nodded limply. I seldom turned down the offer of a story, but if she had not suggested it I would not have asked. I was already drowsy.

"It is Christmas morning and very, very cold outside. Mother and Daddy and I are to go into Boston proper for a special service at the North Church as we do every Christmas. Uncle James and his new bride, Jessica, are with us. I am fifteen."

Then Mama groaned, running a hand across the mound of her belly, a bulge of navel poking at the cloth of the nightdress. "Oh don't mind me, my sweet," she said when I raised my head to question her distress. "It's just the baby. Where was I?" she asked, shifting position, her face relaxing again into a small smile. "Ah, yes. There is a fresh dusting of snow on the roads so the city is white and quiet. The snow still falls, but only lightly.

"I am in a beautiful new dress of dark green velvet trimmed in a white lace that Mother ordered all the way from Italy. My bonnet is new too, and Mother and Daddy have given me a rabbit-fur muff that tickles my nose when I put my face into the soft fluff; it keeps my hands wonderfully warm.

"Our sleigh awaits, the horse festooned with bells and pine-bough wreathes. He stomps his hooves and shakes snowflakes from his black mane, snorting plumes of white steam from his nostrils, proud and anxious to show off his finery to the world."

"The horse's name is Pilgrim," I added, contributing to the story I had heard so many times. "But you do not go near Pilgrim because only Grandfather Somersworth can handle him."

The bed shook slightly as Mama nodded her head. "Yes, he is very beautiful. Yet he is dangerous and difficult.

"The front steps are slick with ice, so we must be careful. Once in the sleigh, we cover ourselves with thick blankets and settle back as Daddy takes the reins and our journey begins. He drives through the neighborhoods to a long avenue sweeping past The Common, past all of the lovely homes and buildings of Boston. From there, he turns onto Back and then Salem; streets that become more and more narrow as we get closer to the middle of the old town. Everything is beautifully wrapped in a mantel of new snow.

"The church appears before us from the white mist of snowflakes, peaceful and splendid in red brick with white trim, the steeple rising grandly into the gray sky.

"There are dozens of stable boys waiting to take the horses and carriages and sleighs to a warm shelter once we have alighted at the church entrance." She added this part after I repeatedly asked about the fate of the horses when the worshippers go inside.

"The church hall is bright. Some light comes through the windows that reach high above us, reflecting off of the bright white walls. Most brilliant are the hundreds of candles glowing in graceful brass chandeliers which are draped with boughs of evergreens in honor of the season.

"We enter our box and Daddy sets the brassier near the center and begins the task of feeding more coal into its hungry mouth. He started it burning at home, but I am afraid it has been ignored as we traveled through the avenues. And now, when we hope that it will bring much needed comfort in the cold church, the coals have died. He pats his pockets, frowning his fatherly frown, looking for a lucifer to relight them. Then he remembers: they are in a tin at home, useless to us there.

"However, a young man in the adjoining box offers to help. He is slender with fair hair and the most amazing blue eyes I have ever seen. His hands, long-fingered and graceful, reach into his waistcoat from which he pulls a slim match, offering it to Daddy. He smiles and then, for the first time, turns those wondrous eyes upon me. They sparkle in the candlelight and I am smitten. I believe that what has really happened is that fairy dust has sprung from those very eyes and spread over me, turning my brain to mush."

"It is Papa."

"It is," she sighs, echoing my whisper. "He is there with a group of friends celebrating the holiday."

The story usually ended there as Mama allowed the memory to play to its finish in her mind of mush. When pressed, she says that she cannot remember much of the day after meeting my father. She was too in love to hear the service, too enamored to remember having talked with anyone. She certainly was too young and timid to have spoken with the young man.

In our sickbed on that late-summer day, she said nothing of her timidity or her love. She rested one hand protectively on her belly, her voice flat and tired. "Including the dazzling Miss Munro," she whispered.

That is not as the story had ever ended in the hundreds of tellings. I had never heard of the dazzling Miss Munro. I raised my head, blinking with surprise, opening my mouth to ask about this intruder, the room vibrating as if a rock had been thrown through a pane of glass.

Her eyes were closed tightly although I knew she was not asleep. I laid my hand beside hers on the mound of her stomach. Her sadness that day seemed much like those times she spoke of my father's absences when he was called away in the dark to visit the ill. "He is a good doctor and I am content with that," she usually said, although I did not hear contentment in her voice. It was the same when she uttered the name of Miss Munro.

I leaned my face close to her swollen stomach and whispered to the baby, requesting it to roll or nudge or tickle Mama, as that usually made her laugh with delight. Perhaps if the baby moved it would chase Miss Munro and all of her sadness from the room.

The baby remained still. My eyes closed.

It was dark when I next awakened. Mama was not beside me.

A dim light hovered in the hall. She was standing at the doorway, braced against it. "It is too soon," I heard her whisper.

Papa suddenly emerged from the darkness, approaching quickly and leading her back into the room. He said nothing and I could not clearly see his face in the sputtering light of their candle. Their shadow (for it looked as if they were one) writhed on the walls of the room. He moved with urgency as he guided her back onto the bed. Then he rushed to my side, gathering me in his arms, carrying me to my own bedroom to lay me in the cool sheets. "Stay here, Guine. I need to help Mama. Go to sleep."

I stumbled twice from the room at the urgency of their whispers, punctuated by Mama's groans. Papa ordered me back to bed where I lay awake, listening to the worrisome noises.

Despite my growing alarm, I dozed.

It was still night when I awoke to find Mrs. Schrader beside me in her nightdress with a lacy cap that covered her graying hair.

During all of the time she had lived with us, I had never seen her in nightclothes. A basin of water was now in my room and she dabbed the wet cloth over my forehead, absently making shushing sounds. "Go to sleep, little one," she murmured.

Again I did, itching and tossing and burning with fever. But Mrs. Schrader was in her nightclothes and something about that was not right.

Then it was daylight and Uncle John bathed my face with the cool cloth. Uncle John, who had never been in my room, had never ventured past the sitting room or the dining room when he and Aunt Margaret and Cousin Clarence visited.

Is Mama better? Where is Papa? Is Cousin Clarence here too? Who is Miss Munro? He brushed my queries aside and continued to swab my forehead. "Go to sleep, Guine."

Thoughts of those days and the strangeness that followed were never welcome, but I could not keep them away. They were like mice scurrying around corners of a room, hovering in the background, venturing forward to nibble whenever they pleased. Every day I shooed them away, but they would not leave.

"Your mother is...gone," Uncle John announced, his sad eyes diverted and blinking. "I'm so sorry, Guine. I'm so sorry. Your mother was a wonderful woman.

"She and your baby brother are both gone." He sounded both hesitant and determined. "The baby was not yet ready. It wasn't due to be born for a couple of months yet. She wasn't strong herself. This was the first baby she had been able to carry since you were born. She had lost so many already.

"Childbirth is a difficult thing for even the strongest of women. Thousands of women..." his voice trailed away, the unfinished thought hanging in the room.

Somehow I knew he was trying to make me feel better, chatter my pain away, cover the void with words. But I did not feel better.

"I've lost my little sister," was Aunt Margaret's response to those who asked, as if my mother had been a lovely necklace that my aunt misplaced; of great value but ultimately little import.

Papa said nothing.

As for me, I felt a ripping in my chest that grew each day. It was as if the big hook the stable hands used to grapple hay bales had found purchase in my body, tugged each time I entered a room where my mother had walked. I wanted to ask Papa if someone could die of a wound that does not bleed but will not heal. However, he was in no mood for questions.

Two weeks later, my tenth birthday passed without notice. By Christmas, Papa stopped seeing patients and we moved to my aunt and uncle's house in Brookline. Papa was seldom there. When I did see him he was not really there. Two months later, he left for California.

Papa said there were too many memories in Boston, but I did not understand. Perhaps he knew a way to leave thoughts in a place where they were never found again. Maybe the mice could be caught and taken to a field someplace far away where they no longer needed attention. Or maybe, for Papa, the creatures would stay in Boston.

I swat at those mice as I lean over *The Pelican's* railing. A brisk wind carries sea spray across the decks and I taste the salt on lips which are raw from the exposure of the last several weeks. My fingertips are split too, and I have torn pieces of skin from around my nails. I concentrate on these little wounds.

The water is invisible in the dark as it laps against the hull of the ship, hiding the myriad of monsters I fear may knock at her underbelly. I doubt the water or the creatures would be visible to me even in the daylight, as I see only the shocked faces of the Dunsfords' when I turned to escape Luke's question: "What happened to your mother?"

What happened to my mother? She has passed; she is no longer with us. She is in heaven; she is with God. She is gone. I know the proper words, the polite words, but will not give them voice.

In the morning I find the crocus have sprouted, pushing pale stalks through the seams of the burlap pouch where I have them hidden. I am certain they cannot live all the way to California. I had hoped that having the bulbs in the dark of my portmanteau, inside the burlap, might allow me to keep them from knowing the spring and foil their urge to flower until they were safely transported. However, they have outwitted me and now may wither and die. They will not make it to their new home. They will cease to be the "little adventurers" of my mother's tales, the first flowers to poke their heads above the ice and snow each spring.

I solemnly carry the bulbs on deck and look for Mr. Boyle. But he knows nothing of plants except that they are for eating and for landlubbers. He insists he cannot help and knows of nowhere for the flowers to be planted. "You'll find no dirt here. My job is to make sure there's no dirt on this ship," he says. "Although I'll wager you'll find plenty under some fingernails."

I think this is one of the least helpful suggestions I have ever heard and I ignore him.

"What happened to you last night? You didn't want to see the stars?" he asks.

"I'm afraid all of the others wanted to come too. Since you said the telescope was fragile and the slightest scratch might earn you a good thrashing, I did not think you would want them there. Mark and Luke are quite rough, and the others, except Lizzie, might be too small to hold it."

"Well I doubt Miss Lizzie would've been there."

"Why?"

"Oh, me and her don't get along. I angered her good last week. Came upon her quarreling with the youngest boy. Which one is that? John? She was threatening to toss one of his toys overboard. Well I couldn't have that, now, could I? So, I grabbed her arm. Just in time too. That little tin soldier'd be at the bottom of the ocean if I hadn't. I took the toy from her, handed it back to the boy, and let go. I didn't say a word, although I would've like to. She cast me one of her haughty looks and stomped off.

"She needs a good thrashing, that one. I'd do it myself, but I figure the Reverend might not like that. It's certainly crossed my mind. I've seen her misbehaving many times."

So have I, both in Boston and on the ship. On more than one occasion Lizzie slapped or punched her younger siblings, careful to avoid the notice of her parents. Once I overheard her threaten them with greater harm if they tattled, leaving them quaking at the sight of her. I suspect she is angry at having to go to China and I tell Mr. Boyle so (although I do not mention my similar suspicions about Mrs. Dunsford—that would be like gossiping and I like the woman far too much to spread hearsay).

"No excuse," Mr. Boyle declares and departs with an apology for the peril of the crocus and an aside that I am free to invite the others to see the stars when the weather again permits.

Later in the day, he delivers a small wooden bucket filled with sawdust and wood shavings from the carpenter's shop. If he has any say in the matter, this is as close to dirt as anything I will get on *The Pelican* prior to our arrival in Rio de Janeiro.

CHAPTER 3

June 13, 1848

MY FATHER WROTE TO ME of Rio de Janeiro in one of the three letters he sent during his voyage to California (all now tucked away in my portmanteau which is in the small cupboard at the foot of my berth).

April 11, 1847

My dearest Guine,

I hope this letter finds you well and behaving yourself for your aunt and uncle.

I have found the voyage difficult, at best, given my strong unease with sea travel. I have always had this proclivity (ask your aunt or uncle what this means if you do not know already). The illness happens every time I venture on a ship, even the very first time I sailed to Boston those many years ago. Hope for the future causes forgetfulness, apparently, as only after the sickness once again makes its assault do the memories of it return. There have been few days when I have felt well enough to venture on deck and I certainly have been in no condition to be of help to others. If your Uncle James harbors any designs for me as a doctor aboard one of his ships, he will be disappointed.

At the moment, I am once again on land (thank heavens). What a strange land it is! Rio de Janeiro is our first port—and I have found it to be the most exotic of places. The colors assault the senses: the bright sea that surrounds the city, the dazzling expanse of sky, the astounding birds, the colorful dress of the people, and certainly the skin of the people so different from our pale, subdued Bostonians.

Fortunately, I have found solid ground and civilized food at a local inn while staying here. I want to spend as little time as possible on that infernal boat which, although safely anchored, still pitches and rolls like a drunken fool. We are in port for only two days longer and I am already loath to give up these quarters.

I must close this letter and ready it for delivery to the captain of a ship bound for Boston, whom I met yesterday. He was less than optimistic that I will find the next leg of the voyage any more enjoyable. However, he assures me that my current route, around Cape Horn, is superior to a journey across Central America. While exceedingly unpleasant, he declares that seasickness has no lasting ill effects—something which cannot be said for the dreadful fevers of the isthmus or an unfortunate plunge into some Panamanian ravine. He is certain that I am better off taking my chances with the longer sea voyage. I must trust that he knows whereof he speaks.

Remember to be a good girl and do as your aunt and uncle bid you. Your safety and wellbeing are uppermost in their minds, as in mine.

Affectionately,
Papa

When first I received the letter, I rushed to Uncle John's library to study the maps he kept rolled in a corner. Surprised at the distance between Boston and Rio de Janeiro, I was even more startled that Brazil was so far from California. Papa had been gone nearly two months at the time he wrote the letter, yet what remained of his journey promised to be longer still.

Now with the prospect of land upon us I can hardly wait to see this place of colors about which Papa wrote. The captain has announced that *The Pelican* will make port within two days.

In the hope that I may sight land before anyone else, I remain on deck the entire first day of our approach. However, it is Mr. Boyle who sees the peaks that rim the horizon and I am rewarded only with a nose and lips angry with blisters which Mrs. Dunsford smears with cooking grease she begged from the cook. The rest of the day I imagine I smell of fried pork.

Early the following morning *The Pelican* quickly converges on the Brazilian coast along with dozens of others ships, sails swollen in the breeze. The ripples and wakes that surround the vessels sparkle with sunlight as if the ships move on waves of diamonds.

Where New York whispered its goodbye behind a lacy screen of snow Rio shouts in the sunshine. There is nothing subtle about its brilliant waters or jagged silhouette. Barren hills of rock stand alongside mounds of land immodestly dressed in glossy shrubs and spindly trees whose leaves are like huge green feathers sprouting from their trunks.

"You did not tell me about the giant," I chastise Mr. Boyle as the ship draws even closer to the harbor mouth. Mr. Boyle casts me a quizzical look as I point to the bald rock jutting from the shore like a severed digit. "The giant that belongs to that thumb.

The giant that could reach out of the water and stop us from entering the harbor any time he desires. He need only pick up the ship and put it into his mouth, gnashing us to bits with his sharp blue teeth." I point to the distant mountains.

"You are a very curious child." Mr. Boyle snorts and elbows Matthew in the ribs for concurrence. "That is *Pão de Açúcar* which the English and Americans have named the Sugar Loaf. And that," he points to the large stone structure that guards the entrance to the harbor, "is the fortress of Santa Cruz."

Within the arms of the bay, framed by the jagged mountains, white palaces and mansions and cathedrals crown the hills that slope toward the water. As the land levels, a hodgepodge of bleached buildings with red-tiled roofs crowd to the water's edge. Swells from passing ships lick the foundations of structures nearest the shore. The harbor teems with vessels at anchor whose masts sway like a forest of leafless trees.

I bounce at the railing with excitement. Land! I have missed it more than I realized.

However, we are not to venture to shore the evening of our arrival. The officials of the harbor must complete their tasks before anybody or anything may leave the ship. First the Customs Boat to levy the taxes on our cargo, then the Harbor Master Boat to collect the fees for anchorage and, finally, the Health Boat to ensure that *The Pelican* carries no diseases—the Brazilians take no chances that cholera or other ills will sneak into the city from our decks. By the time the officials depart it is well past sunset and Captain Watson will launch no boats for shore as it will not do for crew or passengers to wander in a strange city at night.

The exception is Mr. Boyle. Claiming that he must find a dry

dock for the ship's repairs, he hops cheerfully aboard the Health
Boat as it departs for shore. Rio de Janeiro will be our home for
eight or nine days, he says, so that the copper encasing the ship's
hull can be caulked. *The Pelican* is leaking. Bilge pumps have been
manned day and night for nearly a month to save the ship from
sinking. When Mr. Boyle confided this fact to me we were still
weeks from land. I must have seemed alarmed, for he laughed and
explained that all ships have this problem, but most of them make
it to their destinations.

He appears quite happy to be in Rio (as he calls it) and waves
a cheerful goodbye from the Health Boat railing. I want to go
ashore with him, but I do not ask. I know the answer will be that
such a trip would not be proper. He never answered the question
I *did* pose: how was he to find a dry dock at this time of night? I
tried not to pout as I asked.

By early the next morning *The Pelican's* dinghies are kept in
constant employ ferrying passengers to this new shore that beckons
across the placid waters of the bay. For our return we must hire
one of the hundreds of barks that ply the harbor carrying people
and goods from ship to shore and back; but at least our passage
into town is free. The Reverend is happy about this.

We have our delays: it is difficult to get all of the Dunsfords
into the dinghies for the trip. It seems that Mrs. Dunsford is
afraid of heights and the distance from the ship's deck to an
awaiting dinghy below is more than she can bear. Finally, after
much coaxing, the Reverend accompanies her, standing on the
dangling ladder a step behind to prevent her falling. Rungs bow
while ropes squeak and strain with the couple's combined weight.
Mrs. Dunsford cannot manage to move her arms and legs in a

coordinated effort. Their descent is excruciatingly slow. At last stepping into the small boat Mrs. Dunsford abruptly sits and closes her eyes. She seems to like the water no more than she liked the height.

Once at the jetty, where we are to climb ashore, the ordeal continues. Being a short woman with a full breast and bottom and short stout legs, Mrs. Dunsford finds the stone quay a challenge. She struggles for some time to find purchase without sending herself over the side of the boat into the water. She reaches safety aided by two of her children pushing from behind. The Reverend straddles the gap between boat and pier, lifting her bodily to the steps. Kneeling until she has sufficiently gained her composure and balance, Mrs. Dunsford at last lifts her skirts, lumbering up the remaining steps to wait for her family.

With joy, the rest of us alight and wobble along the jetty toward a three-story building that faces the harbor. Now on dry land the Dunsfords teeter on the stone pier as if still on the decks of *The Pelican*, rocking from side to side, waddling like a line of ducklings after their mother. I too feel the sway and cannot help but laugh. Mr. Boyle warned us about "land legs;" it may be some time before the muddled sensation ceases.

The building before us looks important and well-tended, its façade laced with iron balconies from every upper window. When I ask one of the oarsmen about the structure he says that this is the Imperial Palace of Rio, the *Paço Imperial*. It is no longer used as the royal palace for that honor goes to a spectacular building among the hills. The *Paço Imperial* is now only a government office. To prove its continued importance, two soldiers flank the entrance. They are dressed in dark blue uniforms with intricate

silver trim at the cuffs and collars, their rifles held menacingly
across their bodies.

Most government buildings in Boston are far more imposing
than this Imperial Palace, so I turn my attention to what awaits
in the adjoining plaza: hundreds of tarps and multi-colored
umbrellas and tents from which a roar and hum rises and falls
like a pulse. This is the marketplace.

There is color everywhere. People clog the aisles between
stalls, their fashions and skins astonishing (just as Papa wrote).
Dressed as proper New Englanders, the Dunsfords and I look
drab in comparison. The Americans and Europeans, men and
women alike, wear silks and linens of yellow, pale blue, and cream
colors. The bronze-skinned natives sport wide-brimmed hats
perched on hair that is pure black without curl, their dress more
subtle in color than the fair-skinned among them, but far more
brilliant than the average Bostonian daywear. The black-skinned
women with red or yellow turbans wreathing their faces wear
bright shawls and ruffled skirts, multi-colored bands of cloth
wrapped around their waists and hips. Their male counterparts
may not be brilliantly clad, but the contrast of black skin and
white trousers is startling.

Soldiers and sailors mingle with the crowd walking two or
three abreast, sporting a variety of uniforms in gray, blue, scarlet,
yellow, and black; trousers of one color and jackets of another
with brass and silver buttons glinting in the sunlight. Most sport
a polished silver sword at their side, a bottle in hand.

Wares overflow the stalls: animal hides, woven baskets and
mats, vegetables, livestock, bolts of cloth. Birds of every kind
squawk from wooden cages: chickens, geese, and ducks like those

sold in the markets of Boston. However, among these are birds of the most fantastic plumage: bright red and green and blue and yellow, often all colors on the same creature, rivaling even the crowd in their splendor. Their beaks are as large as my fist, their eyes golden.

There are countless stands dedicated to food; the aromas make my mouth water. Familiar oranges, lemons, pears, and pomegranates are arrayed beside fruits I do not recognize: yellow sickle-shaped stalks I assume to be bananas (as I have seen the illustrations in Uncle John's books), gourd-shaped green fruit with a blush of pink, globe-like melons of every color, and one curious specimen that looks like an overgrown green apple covered with raised fish scales. I ask the Reverend and Mrs. Dunsford the names, but they do not know. They too have never seen anything like them. Neither Faneuil Hall nor the Haymarket boast the colors or smells of this marketplace and everywhere I turn is a new discovery.

Flower stalls overflow with blooms I cannot identify in colors I cannot name. Sounds buzz around me. I understand not a word that is spoken by the swarms of people passing by.

The booths closest to the harbor house the fish mongers, hawking oysters and sardines, shrimp and live fish kept in barrels of sea water covered in netting so that the creatures cannot escape. These I have seen in Boston so I do not linger.

Music pulses through the plaza: pipes, guitars, voices raised in song, drums (sometimes in accompaniment, sometimes alone) whose steady beats vibrate through the stones to my feet and echo through my body. Music is everywhere. Even when I cannot see the musicians I hear their song and match my gait to the rhythms.

I stop and gawk then twirl and turn, not wanting to miss anything. More than once Mrs. Dunsford comes to my side to pull me forward, urging me along.

She is again tugging my sleeve. "The children are hungry, Guinevere. You must move more quickly so that we may find someplace to eat," she says, her face drooping with heat and exhaustion. "I hope for a quiet little restaurant. Oh, I'm sure we'll find someplace.

"It's really maddening. Everyone keeps handing us things to buy and once we touch them, which we can't help doing as they're very forcibly thrust upon us, the sellers won't take them back! We've resorted to dropping them on the nearest table. Otherwise I fear we must pay for everything we touch. I should've brought a parasol, this sun is hotter than I expected for this time of year. Can you believe the things they sell here? Oh dear. Please hurry."

I linger over a vast array of fragrant spices. They are displayed in small burlap sacks wedged against each other like row upon row of ground gemstones. Reluctantly I turn to follow Mrs. Dunsford through the crowd.

We pass stalls with the familiar and stalls with the exotic. I am tempted to touch everything, to verify that it is real. Most tempting of all are the creatures displayed under a faded red tarp in the heart of the marketplace: monkeys.

I saw monkeys at the menagerie in Boston (where there was also an elephant and a bear). However, the creatures here are sprightlier than those that visited my hometown; they screech and bound from side to side in their cages. They are far more of them than were at the menagerie as well, some as small as a man's hand, others the size of a dog. Some have faces like lively old men, others like the elves of the books Mama read to me. Their cages are made of thin tree branches tied together with twine; their antics rock the flimsy structures on their bases.

I reach to stroke the wiry fur of one small copper-colored creature. It screams loudly and shows sharp little teeth, looking none too friendly and reminding me of Uncle John's barn cat only far worse. I quickly back away, stumbling into an adjacent table. The air fills with a chaotic music of clinks and jangles.

"Oh, I am terribly sorry," I exclaim, glancing around a table cluttered with pots and jars and bottles, glass and earthenware. Nothing seems to have broken and for that I am thankful.

The seller is a woman even shorter than Mrs. Dunsford with a brown face creased like the shell of a walnut. Her silver hair, shiny and straight, is wound around the crown of her head in a single plait. She wears no hat and her clothes are subtle shades of brown and tan, so unlike the brilliant colors worn by the crowd that presses around us.

She is smiling, pulsing her hands in a gesture of calm, her lips alternating between a smile and a crimp as she makes shushing noises. As she does not seem upset I relax and smile back at her.

Abruptly she turns to look through her wares, sorting and lifting the pots and bottles that litter her booth. Uttering a soft "Ah," she grabs a small earthenware jar from among the hundreds and dips her hand inside. Her fingers emerge covered in an opaque greenish paste which she proceeds to smear across the bridge of my nose.

In the excitement of seeing Rio and being on land again I have forgotten about my burned and blistered features and how awful I must look. Startled, I back away at the unexpected gesture.

However, I find the green paste has cooled and comforted my sunburned nose already and smells far better than the greasy pork fat Mrs. Dunsford had used. I step forward once more, allowing the gnome-like woman to continue applying the lotion.

Then she clasps a different bottle and shakes a white cream into her palm, grasping my hands and working this new salve into my fingers, concentrating on my split and broken fingertips and ragged nails. It is soothing and comforting and I close my eyes; for the first time in two months my hands ceased to burn.

"Thank you," I say, flexing my fingers and patting my cool cheeks. "Thank you."

"O*b-ri-ga-do*," the woman replies, speaking loudly and gesturing in a deliberate way. I believe she wants me to repeat the word.

"*Obrigado*," I oblige.

Nodding and smiling she says something friendly but unintelligible as I nod and smile too. Then with a wave, I turn to rejoin the Dunsfords.

Although there are hundreds of noisy shoppers and gawkers pressed into the narrow row between the vendor stalls there is no sign of the family. I am sure they are not far ahead and continue wandering from one side of the aisle to the other so as not to miss any of the sights. The row empties into a street filled with horses and carriages and other strollers. I find no Dunsfords.

The adjacent aisle is even more crowded, if that is possible. I press through a smothering array of skirts and petticoats, trousers and uniforms with their varying odors of sweat and soap, musk and damp clothing. I venture further along between the stands, my view limited, the crowd swelling. My heart begins to pound as if I have run a great distance. I see no one I know.

A fire-eater, like those that travel with the carnivals through Boston, has created a crush. The normally milling crowd is crammed together to watch the man's lips fill the air with flames like the breath of a dragon, hot and bright, gold and red. I search the spectators for the Dunsfords to no avail. The fire-eater extinguishes the last torch in his mouth and stands before the appreciative throng for applause. I do not see a single familiar face.

Amid the ovation, a small child emerges from a nearby booth dressed in the same multi-colored pantaloons as the fire-eater. However, it is not a child for its face and shoulders are powder white, a cap of black fur on its head. Its body and arms are black too, and a long black tail curls from an opening in the seat of its trousers: a monkey. Unlike the hissing, screaming monkeys in the cages this one behaves civilly. It circles through the crowd, thrusting forward a hat into which the on-lookers toss coins as if into the plate after a sermon.

I reach inside my skirt pocket for my pouch of coins as the creature draws near. When I attempt to drop a copper penny into his hat, the monkey grasps the coin, his bony fingers knocking briefly against mine. He makes a show of putting the coin between his teeth, biting down, then tossing it into the hat with a deep bow before moving on. I laugh, finding his comical waddle reminiscent of the Dunsfords walking down the stone quay. Ah, yes, the Dunsfords.

In response to a tug at my skirt I turn, hoping for a familiar Dunsford face. I find instead a boy, older than me, with skin the same color as the wizened woman with the lotions. But, unlike the woman, the boy's straight black hair is filthy and I smell a foul odor from his body even in the press of people. He wears a tattered shirt lacking any buttons or other closures and breeches that are stained and ripped, tied about his waist with a frayed rope, ribs protruding above.

The boy extends a skinny hand, palm up. I assume he has seen me pass a coin to the monkey and now wants one for himself. As I believe the poor child must be starving, I reach again into my pocket and pull out another coin, turning to drop it into his open palm. However, a different boy awaits me. It is the same body, but his look has changed from want to greed. He glances at the coin, then in the direction of my pocket, and I realize my mistake: he now knows I have more coins and where I keep them. I drop the coin into his palm and quickly turn to push my way into the crowd, back the way I came, away from the boy. He has said nothing, but I feel threatened all the same.

I am certain the Dunsfords have never ventured into this aisle and I should not have come here. Perhaps they turned down one of the streets that emptied into the plaza to look for a quiet inn in which to have a meal, just as Mrs. Dunsford had wanted. Perhaps I should go back to where they would have last seen me, wherever that might have been. Surely that is where they will begin a search. I hope they will begin a search.

It does not take long to reach the end of the row. I emerge onto the busy street lined with commanding buildings that flank a church, its steeple stretching a shallow shadow across the avenue. I do not see my guardians nor do I spot any of the other passengers from *The Pelican* from whom I might ask aid. No one looks familiar and no one is speaking English.

I am undecided where to turn, where to search next, unhappy

to be alone, worried that no one will find me and, at the same time, terrified that I will be followed by the filthy boy (for that is how I think of him). The Dunsfords must surely have noticed my absence by now. Perhaps if I go back to the jetty, I can wait for them there. The jetty should not be too hard to find again.

Glancing back, I see that the filthy boy has followed me and has recruited two other boys as well. I dart to the aisle where the monkeys are and plunge into the multitude, unsure if the boys have seen me. There are too many people; I cannot see my pursuers, but fear they may be close nonetheless. I push and turn and scramble through the crowd as quickly as I am able.

I know I cannot escape. At the end of the aisle, the throng will thin and I will have no place to hide. I need some other plan to find the Dunsfords and get back to the ship and be safe once more.

To my left is a vegetable stall, the wares displayed on wooden crates piled atop each other. I run to the booth and duck behind the crates, pulling my skirts tightly around me. I wait, looking through the slats of the boxes, trying to spot the ragged trousers of the boys as they pass. My breathing is rapid and shallow like a dog's.

Within moments, a shove at my shoulder and a sudden sharp inquiry informs me that the owner of the stall is not pleased that I crouch among his onions and cabbage. I must find another haven. Not wanting to venture into the aisle again, I run to the back of the stall among discarded boxes, smashed and wilting lettuce, and other garbage from both the vegetable seller and the stand behind his—a butcher. The severed head of an unfortunate chicken, its beak still moving, is tossed at my feet among other unidentifiable entrails and animal parts. I gasp and kick it aside, moving swiftly through the gloom between the stalls, among the slippery refuse. More than once I fail to stay on my feet, leaving a crash and tumble of noise and debris in my wake.

Too soon, the stalls end and I am once again on the street facing the impervious buildings whose barred windows offer no relief. There is the church. The church has no bars on its windows. *"My refuge and my fortress, my God, in whom I trust,"* our minister once quoted. Perhaps the filthy boy will not follow me into a place of worship and I will be safe there.

I run to the church fearing any moment that I will be overtaken by the boys, my arm grabbed, my skirt clutched. I hear the panting of the filthy boy as he looms behind me, feeling the heat of his breath on the nape of my neck as his shadow overtakes mine. I reach the door and, struggling with the thick heaviness of it, wrench it open and slip inside.

The entry is dark after the bright sunlight of the plaza. I shuffle quickly to one side, further into shadow, to lean against the cold wall until my breathing slows and I no longer feel the heartbeat in my ears. I wait, eyes closed, for several minutes. The door does not open.

Finally, breathing calmed, I open my eyes.

I have never been in a church before. The Presbyterian congregation in Boston met in the home of an elder. When I lived in Brookline with Aunt Margaret and Uncle John, they too worshipped in a private home. No more than fifteen worshippers gathered at any one time, so more space was not needed. There was always talk of building a church, but the congregation believed that the worshipping was more important than the location, so firm plans were never made.

Although Mama described it often, I had never been to the North Church. The Somersworth holiday tradition had ended after Mama and Papa married. I suspect it was due to Papa's reluctance to go, but Mama said that the family had become too scattered with Aunt Margaret and Uncle John in Brookline and Aunt Jessica and Uncle James in a township whose name I do not remember. However, given Mama's detailed description, I knew the North Church had been plain with pure white walls that reflected light from the clear glass panes of enormous windows. Grand but uncluttered.

This church is different. The walls and ceiling are crusted with lacy strips and ribbons of gold against an ivory background. On each side are tall doorways leading to three smaller chapels (any one of them larger than the elder's home), framed in carvings edged in gold. These gloomy alcoves are lit only by clusters of faint reddish flames which seem to float in the dark and glint dully off of gold-framed pictures and candlesticks that crowd the shadowed altars. There are statues everywhere, painted in vivid colors, the robes edged with gold. The haloes too are gold.

A barrel ceiling stretches several stories above, embedded with high windows just under the vaulted curve. Light pours through them and floods the church with a golden glow. Hundreds of rainbow stripes dance over the gilded walls as light shines through the crystal prisms of a dozen unlit chandeliers. It is grand.

My footfalls echo as I cross the stone floor toward the main altar and sink onto its lowest step. I am tired and feel very small. I so want not to be lost, not to be chased, not to be sunburned, not to be crusted with layers of salt that make my clothes chafe, nor fed tasteless food. I want no longer to be alone. I want Mama, but know that is not to be. I want to be with Papa and I want him to want me there.

The damage to my person is slight but widespread: the palms of my hands are scuffed and dirty, and one filthy leg of my pantalets is tattered, the stocking underneath striped with runners. The seam of my left sleeve has torn loose in the back, lace ripped from the edge of my petticoat, skirts covered in filth. My shoes are scuffed and my hair snarled, the ribbons missing.

Hearing footsteps I turn, surprised to find that I am ready to stand and run again if the need arises. With relief I see that it is not the filthy boy nor his friends. It is a priest approaching as one would a cat, unsure whether it will dart away. He is speaking, his voice soft and gentle, but I understand nothing of what he says, aware only that his words are shaded with concern, lifted in question.

He sits beside me. He is dressed in a dark robe that falls to his feet, a brilliant white collar at his throat, and a large silver crucifix around his neck. The body of Christ reposes peacefully upon the spar of the crucifix despite the nails and the thorns. I turn away, thankful that Presbyterians have no use for such adornment.

"*Francês? Espanhol?*" he asks. I shake my head. "*Inglês?*"

"English?" I question. "I am American, but I speak English."

"Ah," he nods, but ventures nothing more. Then, one finger poised as if asking me to wait, he rises and hurries behind the altar, exiting the church through a small door near the back.

He is gone for what seems a very long time. Finally, having tired of this latest abandonment, I stand and scream into the vastness of the church, the sound echoing and beating against my ears.

"I received a visit today from Mr. Taylor, John. You know the man. Guinevere's teacher." Aunt Margaret dabbed her napkin daintily at the corners of her mouth. "He dropped by to inquire after her as it seems she has not been in class this week. At all."

I lowered my head, looking at neither my aunt nor my uncle who sat at opposite ends of the dining table.

"Is this true, Guine?" My uncle asked, putting his own napkin aside. Supper was over.

Tempted at first to deny my absence, I demurred. I liked Mr. Taylor even though I found him boring; the lessons he taught were the same ones I had learned last year when I was in the downtown school. If I denied my absences, I would be calling him a liar and I did not want to do that. Besides, Aunt Margaret would only have had Uncle John take me before the teacher to make my claim in person. It would have been obvious who the liar was then.

"Yes, sir."

Uncle John dropped me at school every morning before he continued on to the government office in Boston where he worked. He was diligent in his duties and I arrived each day on time; I had simply stopped entering the schoolhouse. As he drove away, I walked across the lane, through the pasture and into a small stand of maples where I spent the school hours with a borrowed book. I could see when the students rushed through the door at the end of lessons which meant it was time for me to go back to my aunt and uncle's.

"You can imagine how embarrassed I was," my aunt sputtered.

"Poor Mr. Taylor thought you might be ill. Of course I had to tell him the truth. That you were not ill, simply a delinquent."

"Where do you go, my girl? I know very well that you arrive at the schoolhouse every morning, so where do you go after that?"

"Nowhere."

"What an incorrigible child! Go to your room this instant. Your uncle will be along shortly to mete out your punishment."

From the room that was called mine I could still hear their discussion. I could not distinguish all of the words, but Aunt Margaret's voice was raised in fury. I heard her say Cousin Clarence's name several times, assuming she was once again extoling his virtues. Clarence would never defy them as I did. Clarence was a model child. Clarence, Clarence, Clarence.

Eventually the commotion ceased and Uncle John lumbered up the stairs, his reluctance evident in his step. He knocked and I bid him enter, keeping my eyes to the floor.

"That man will never learn, will he?"

I glanced at my uncle. Man? Of what man was he speaking?

"He was a horrible teacher when Clarence was in school and he's a horrible teacher now. Can't tell the difference between a dullard and one dulled with boredom. Clarence used to fall asleep during the history lesson."

I laughed softly. This was hardly the punishment I expected.

"I shall talk to Mr. Taylor, have him give you different assignments from the others your age," Uncle John continued, sighing deeply. "Pick out a few books from my library which interest you. Perhaps you might read those aloud to the others or tell the class what you've learned from them. It might be more interesting for the other children too; certainly it could be no less so than the pabulum he serves now."

He came to my side, placing a hand gently on my shoulder. "You do know, however, that I must punish you? Your aunt will not give either of us any rest until she hears you whimpering. It cannot be helped. Turn around, please."

I did as I was told and Uncle John swatted swiftly at my bottom. It did not hurt, especially through my petticoats, but I felt my lips quiver and the tears gather nonetheless. Embarrassment, frustration, confusion clogged my throat. I did not utter a sound.

"Please, Guine, you must cry out. Even if it is just a little. Your aunt must know I have done my duty."

I refused. After less than a dozen smacks, Uncle John stopped. "This will not be the last you hear of this, my dear. Your aunt will have her way, you know."

He left then. I clenched my fists, determined not to cry. Instead, I screamed. The throaty animal sound was liberating. All tears vanished as I drew breath to yell again. I slammed my fists into the bed, giving full force to the effort.

When I was spent, there was only silence from downstairs.

This time there is no hesitation in the priest's approach as he rushes to where I stand, the ring of my scream replaced with the sound of his heels slapping on the stones of the floor. This new noise bounces throughout the church like a flock of birds that has taken flight. Crows, I think. That is what Papa would say. "Bloody papist crows," he had once barked in response to a newspaper item about the clergy who ministered to the new Irish immigrants of

Boston. "Picking over the bones of their stupid flock." My face flushes at the memory. Crows.

The priest shushes and fusses for a moment. Then since it is clear I am unharmed and calm once more, he motions to another who has followed him. The man comes forward and stands before me. He is a priest too, much older than the first.

"My English," the older priest says in a deep, heavily accented voice, pointing to his own chest. "Not good. I talk a little."

So we begin a difficult exchange that, due in large part to the patience of the priest, results in the understanding that I am not a local, cannot speak his language, arrived on a ship that is still in the harbor, and want very much to be on that ship again as quickly as possible. Each time we get closer to this conclusion, the older man seems excited with my responses. He holds his hands together as if in prayer, which I assume to mean that he has no more desire to have a stranded girl on his hands than I have to be that girl.

As the conversation draws to an end, I realize that a plan has evolved. I am relieved and can barely contain my joy: someone will walk with me through the Palace Plaza to the jetty and I will not have to brave the crowd alone. Everything will be set to right and I will not be robbed or stranded.

Finally, the older priest's face relaxes with resolution and I get to my feet. It is the younger priest who will accompany me to the quay.

It rained during the time I had been in the church and the air is now warm and heavy with moisture, the stones of the plaza slick. Many of the tents and umbrellas sag as rainwater pools in their folds. The few remaining clouds part so that the sun once again bakes the marketplace. Steam rises from the paving and umbrellas as if the market stands above a pot of boiling water. The rain has chased none of the crowd away.

No Dunsfords greet me at the stone jetty and there are no other passengers from *The Pelican*. The ship itself sways gently in the distance. "My ship," I explain to the priest, pointing at the ship and then to myself. Hailing a small square-sailed vessel near the shore, crewed by bare-chested men with skin the color of black olives, I am lifted aboard and the priest climbs in beside me for the journey. It seems that the blessings of the church pay my passage as the captain refuses the priest's coins.

The Pelican is the first ship at which the bark stops and, as I grab for the ship's ladder, I whisper to the priest using the only word of this local language I know: *Obrigado* (hoping it means "thank you," as I assume it does). *Obrigado.*

Although happy to be on deck and anxious to find Mr. Boyle and tell him of my horrible adventure in the market, I know my first duty must be to get word to the Dunsfords of my safety. They must be worried about me.

The ship seems to be deserted. When I finally find someone, it is the cook who tells me that Mr. Boyle has not yet returned and the captain has gone ashore and Mr. Sterbenc is in charge. I contemplate hiding in my cabin instead of approaching that man. The Dunsfords will learn soon enough that I am safe, when they return themselves.

That would never do, however. I must get word to them.

Mr. Sterbenc is on the quarterdeck and, since Mr. Boyle extracted my promise never to venture there without permission or escort, I call to him from the main deck. Initially he does not hear me (or chooses not to, I cannot be sure). Finally attracting his attention by waving my arms and jumping, I explain the circumstances as best I can in my loudest voice.

"What do you expect me to do?" he grumbles. He is a broad-chested man, the muscles of his arms bulging as he grips the quarterdeck railing. He is imposing and menacing and the last person with whom I want discourse.

"Someone should be sent to find the Dunsfords and let them know I am safe."

Mr. Sterbenc erupts with an ugly laugh. "I've no one to spare." His voice is rough and abrupt. "Half the crew's ashore on leave and the rest have work to do." He appears pleased with this report. "You're Boyle's pet, aren't you?" He glances at my spoiled dress and stockings.

"I beg your pardon?"

"Yeah, I thought so. The fancy-talkin' Boston brat." Mr. Sterbenc grins crookedly. I do not like the smile as it reminds me of Jeremy Franklin, back home, who likes to tease and torture the other children at school. "I've no one to spare," Mr. Sterbenc repeats and retreats to the helm. I find this very rude being that the ship is not moving and there is no need for anyone at the helm. I acknowledge that few sailors are on board, but that is no excuse for the man's ill manners.

I am at a loss as to my next action and pace the deck, my face burning more and more with each turn. It is hardly fair to leave the Dunsfords to think I am lost. It is not right. It is not right.

I exchanged my tattered and soiled garments for clean clothes before the family returned to the ship. I am more calm and resolved that the Dunsfords will hear no more of my plight than that I was lost. They will know nothing of the filthy boy and his friends or dead chickens or frantic dashes through the marketplace or Mr. Sterbenc. I was separated from them and wandered into a church and here I am. That is all. There is no need to worry them further; there is no need to share my terror.

The details of the Dunsfords' turbulent afternoon are relayed to me in a loud voice.

As soon as my absence was noted, the family retraced their steps down the aisle with the monkeys. When that proved fruitless, Matthew and his father scoured the marketplace, calling for me. Mrs. Dunsford and the other children settled in a nearby eating establishment where the younger ones enjoyed a meal (although Mrs. Dunsford herself was too sick with fear to take a bite). Unsuccessful in their search, the family returned to the pier hoping to send word to the captain, to ask his help. How they learned I was already on board ship is never made clear.

"Traipsing through that awful market! Gallivanting in decadent churches! You could have been killed or kidnapped and sold into slavery!" the Reverend shouts, veins pulsing on his forehead. "They condone slavery here, don't you know that! Every one of those Negroes you saw in the plaza is a slave. It is not like Boston! Did you see the scars on their bodies? Did you not take note of the anger and fear in their faces? You would not like being a slave, Guinevere, believe me."

I open my mouth to say something that might rescue me from his tirade, but he gives me no chance to speak. "There was a slave auction in that marketplace today, Guinevere. Horrible. Just horrible. A little girl of your age, nearly naked in front of the entire crowd, examined like livestock, sold to the highest bidder. It was sickening. This is a wicked and evil place. You had no business running off like that."

"I did not run off," I yell, raising my head and my voice to be heard. "You left me behind."

The Reverend gapes then sputters, his face darkening. Then he utters his edict: I am not to leave *The Pelican* for the remainder of our time in Rio. I might not even be allowed to visit land until we reach San Francisco.

Wanting to scream again, I instead lower my eyes to the deck, fearful that any more protests will only cause the Reverend to expand his proclamation. Still, I find the punishment unfair. I did nothing wrong. I did nothing more than get lost. It was not my fault. However, I say nothing as there seems to be no point.

I am miserable sitting among the Dunsfords at supper, none of them speaking to me. I see not one pair of faded blue eyes cast my way. They hide them well beneath those straw-colored lashes.

At least the meal itself is better than usual—fresh fish and vegetables grace our plates instead of the standard slop (as Mr. Boyle calls it). In addition, one of those green apple-shaped fruits armored with scales accompanies the other food.

I jab at the strange fruit's skin with my fork. I am more determined than ever to eat this oddity because the faces of the Dunsfords show their contempt for it. The stabbing is impractical so I palm the fruit and run to the galley seeking help from Cook, who cleaves the fruit with one swipe of his knife. "What is this fruit called?" I ask as he hands me the neat halves.

"Suga' apple," he says. "Don' eat dem seeds. Dey's poison."

It is the oddest fruit I have ever seen with smooth dense flesh and large black (and apparently poisonous) seeds buried deep within. There is not much juice, but the edible part is moist and delicious, grainy like a pear, tasting like custard. I like it.

"It is good," I announce as I re-entered the mess. "Would anyone like to try it?" I hold the uneaten half of the fruit toward the family.

The children cringe as if I hold a snake or something even more repulsive, wrinkling their noses. The Reverend looks away without a word, pursing his lips. Mrs. Dunsford wraps her arms around her nearest child and clicks her tongue in assurance that her darlings will not be required to try the strange fruit.

"I'll try it," Matthew says avoiding looking at his parents. "Thank you."

Handing the sugar apple to him with a warning about the seeds, I exit to the main deck without another word. I do not ask for permission to leave the table this evening as I do not want to take the chance that it might be denied.

The lights of Rio cast ribbons of gold and silver light upon the water, reminiscent of the shimmering decorations in the church. From the shore, the sound of music and the steady beat of drums carry on the breeze.

I wish Mr. Boyle were here, but he returned only briefly earlier this evening, spoke to the captain then rowed back to shore, his face split with joy. He certainly seems to like Rio.

I spit the last of the black seeds from the sugar apple into the bay (shamefully pleased at the vulgar gesture, briefly wishing I could have spit them in Mr. Sterbenc's face) before I throw the rind over the railing. It floats along one of the ribbons of light as if drawn to the shore, then fills with water and sinks.

CHAPTER 4

June 15, 1848

WITH THE MORNING TIDE the captain moves *The Pelican* further into the harbor to a dock where the ship will be repaired. All passengers are to find quarters in the city for at least the next week. This announcement does not please the Reverend and his protests clearly indicate that the unexpected cost will be a blow to the family finances.

Mr. Boyle returns to *The Pelican* in time to hear the remnants of the Reverend's tirade. Fortunately Mr. Boyle knows of several inns. One in particular, owned by an American woman, is clean and affordable and not far from the wharf where the ship will lay to. He agrees to lead us there and negotiate for rooms if necessary.

The Reverend expresses his gratitude and when I make the offer that some of the cost be defrayed with money he holds for me he becomes somewhat cheerful. Not that the gesture softens his attitude: I am to be confined to quarters even on dry land. Apparently I cannot buy my freedom that cheaply.

Mr. Boyle must dispatch his official duties before he can lead us to the inn, so we disembark (using the gangway instead of the "skimpy ladder" of yesterday—much to Mrs. Dunsford's liking) and wait. Clasping the bucket of crocus flowering in their makeshift soil, I wander to the far end of the pier to watch diving birds plunge into the bay. They are sleek and adept at their craft, their black beaks like daggers that jut from among the dark feathers of their heads. Most surface with a fish speared and wiggling.

"Kingfishers," Mr. Boyle announces, having come to fetch me from my perch. "Cargo's unloaded, tariffs assessed, luggage sorted. I'm ready to escort you to your new quarters, Miss."

"Will you be staying with us at the inn?"

"No, no, no," he rushes to answer. "I stay at the home of a friend when I'm in Rio." As we approach the wagon waiting at the far end of the wharf, loaded with luggage and Dunsfords, he says, "Ah see, you're the last to arrive. Once again off on your own. I heard about your adventure in the city yesterday."

"It was not my fault. I was looking at all of the new and wonderful things. What is the point of going someplace if you rush past it all without seeing everything? If I had been in a hurry, I might have missed something—something grand."

Mr. Boyle puts his hands up in defense. "I didn't scold you, did I?" Then, one finger under my chin, he turns my face upward. "What'd you do to your face?"

I reach to my cheeks. "Nothing. Why, what is wrong?"

"You don't look as terrible as you did. The blisters are nearly gone. You seem to be healing quick."

As we walk toward the wagon I tell him about the little Brazilian woman who smeared my face and hands with her lotions. "I want to go back to the marketplace and buy some of her creams. I know the Reverend will not let me go, but if I give you the money you could buy them for me, could you not?"

Mr. Boyle shakes his head. "I must return to the ship as soon as rooms are found. After that I'll have no time save for the repair. Besides, there are many women that sell magic potions in the marketplace. I'd not know which one to choose."

"Her booth is next to the monkeys."

"You saw monkeys did you?"

"Yes! They look like old men. However, they seem really mean."

"Of course they're mean. You'd be mean too, if someone locked you in a cage all day after you'd been swinging free through the trees your whole life."

Then I tell him about the tame one that belonged to the fire-eater. I do not mention the filthy boy or his friends. Nor do I tell him of Mr. Sterbenc. Even had I not decided to keep quiet about yesterday, Mr. Boyle needs no more reason to dislike the man. I do not wish to cause trouble.

The inn is two short blocks from the harbor in a narrow street that would be called an alley in Boston. The area is clean and the crowded, two-story buildings are in good repair. Rich yeasty smells waft from a nearby bakery. Although I cannot read the language, the signs hanging before the surrounding stores are shaped to represent products and services: a shoe-shaped board denotes the cobbler opposite the bakery; the image of a needle and thread adorn the tailor's shop next door. A butcher's shop, open to the street, and a store displaying dishes and brightly colored decorative platters proudly in its window face the door where Mr. Boyle leads us. He calls a loud "hello" through the open portal.

A tall woman soon appears wearing a plain dress covered with an apron, her chestnut hair held back from her face in a delicate netting of ribbons. She is slight of figure and rough of hands.

"Eamon!" she cries, rushing forward to kiss Mr. Boyle on the cheek. "It's so good to see you! How've you been? How're the lovely Ofelia and the children? I'm sure they're happy to see you."

"They send their regards," Mr. Boyle replies. "Mrs. Reynolds, this is the Reverend and Mrs. Dunsford and their children of Lowell, Massachusetts; and Miss Guine Walker of Boston. Have you rooms they might let? I shouldn't think they'll need them longer than eight days. *The Pelican's* in repair and accommodations are needed for the time. They're friends of mine."

"I've two vacant rooms," Mrs. Reynolds says, surveying her potential guests. "Each has only one large bed which will hold at least three, I'll wager. Some'll have to sleep on the floor, but I've extra mattresses." She tells us the daily rate and the Reverend silently calculates what the final bill might be. "The rooms are small, but clean. I serve breakfast and supper included in the price. And I can draw hot baths for an extra 5 cents each."

"Very reasonable, Mrs. Reynolds, thank you," the Reverend says smiling; I assume the calculation has gone well. "Alright children out you get. We'll be staying with Mrs. Reynolds for a time."

"And did I hear that someone was from Boston?"

"I am," I offer, hopping to the ground.

"Well so am I," Mrs. Reynolds says. "Oh, I haven't been there in quite a while, but Boston was my home when I first married. Where are you sailing to?"

"California. The Dunsfords are bound for China, but I am going to California to join my father, Dr. Harold James Walker."

Our baggage is lugged up the stairs and into the rooms we will call home for the next week. Straw mattresses are pulled from the attic, beaten and shaken with vigor to rid them of any creatures they may have attracted there. These are put on the floor of our respective rooms for those of us who will not fit in the bed. Mrs. Dunsford and I choose to sleep on the floor.

The window of our bedroom faces onto a courtyard shared by the shops that neighbor the inn and those on the street behind. The courtyard is divided into plots. Some, like Mrs. Reynolds', have gardens for vegetables; others are covered with flat stones on which perch brightly painted tables and chairs; flowers and fruit trees grow in others. There are no fences to divide the sections, yet each seems to have their own identity and demarcations. Together they form a vivid, if haphazard, quilt.

I place the bucket of crocus on the sunlit windowsill. The subtle purple and yellow and white faces seem pale compared to the bullying colors of Rio. The flowers have done surprisingly well and I now believe they might survive the voyage to California after all, despite their ordeal of strange soil in a strange land while blooming out of season (for Mr. Boyle says that June is an autumn month in the southern hemisphere).

For the next five days, whenever the family plans to venture into town, I beg Mrs. Dunsford to let me accompany them. Each day her answer is the same: "Guinevere, the Reverend and I are concerned that you'll get lost again and we simply can't take that chance. Your father would never forgive us were something dreadful to happen to you."

"But nothing dreadful will happen. I will stay by your side the entire time. Please, Mrs. Dunsford. Please."

"I'll ask the Reverend when he returns."

If she did, I never heard her. When I ask him directly I am told no. He says that if I introduce the subject again I will be sent to my room without supper.

The Reverend goes into the city every day to find a public place where he can lecture on the evils of slavery and extol the virtues of the Lord. He does not seem to mind that few understand his sermons. He is certain that reaching but one soul will justify the hours spent in the hot sun. Perhaps he is practicing for China where the chance of English-speaking peoples is even more remote. Upon his return in the evenings, his face is glowing with satisfaction beneath skin the color of a new radish.

He has never really left off preaching. He was too sick during the first two weeks of our voyage; however, once the weather cleared he began moralizing to a small gathering assembled on the main deck of *The Pelican* each Sunday morning at 9 o'clock. He dressed formally in his best black suit for the occasions, finally foregoing his hat when the wind kept threatening to send it overboard.

The first two services, on Palm and Easter Sundays, were well attended. However, by the third sermon only the most devout remained to hear him speak about the myriad of sins of which we might be guilty. Oddly enough some of those sins were the same ones for which Captain Watson had established ship rules: no fighting or swearing (this being a voyage with women and children); drinking and gambling would be tolerated only if everyone remained civil.

The Pelican's main cabin was set nightly with barrels and crates doubling as tables and seats for serious games of cards and dice.

There were frequent complaints from the family men among the passengers regarding the rowdy competitions that "kept the women and children awake." Quite often the criticisms evolved to shouts that lead to punches. To my mind, the fights that ensued were worse than any game had been, but I kept quiet since I suspected I would find no sympathy from the Dunsfords—the Reverend referred to cards as the Devil's tools. I think he felt the same about dice.

The Reverend's third sermon struck to the heart of the issue: gambling. Never before had I realized how many times the Bible spoke to the sin that was gambling and, once declaring his subject, the Reverend was determined to cite every pertinent reference (thus dashing all hope I may have had for a short speech). It was an impassioned sermon; one of his best, I admit. The Reverend trembled as he summoned the picture of Roman soldiers vying for the clothing of Jesus, his voice rising and falling with the roll of the ship and the force of his words: "*And when they had crucified him, they divided his garments among them by casting lots.*"

Not one of the gambling men was in attendance at that sermon, so it was no surprise that the nightly games continued despite the Reverend's heartfelt lecture.

The many biblical warnings about excessive fighting and drunkenness became favored topics of the Reverend on subsequent Sundays. Nonetheless there continued to be plenty of both on board. As soon as the weather turned fair the captain's rules about no fighting, no swearing, and only civil drinking went largely ignored, almost as if the moment the storms had calmed the ship itself became stormy.

The fist fights were not restricted to the adults of course—on more than one occasion Matthew stepped between his younger brothers to insist that they not beat each other bloody. The very day after one of the Reverend's "fighting" sermons, *Behold, how good and pleasant it is when brothers dwell in unity*, Luke sported a black eye earned at Mark's hand.

Far from being discouraged by his lack of influence on the ship, with new sins about which to lecture in this evil and wicked city of Rio de Janeiro, the Reverend's enthusiasm blossomed.

With the Reverend preaching in the city and the rest of the family there too, I am left to find my own amusements. I plot to escape every day, but the memory of the filthy boy has kept me obedient.

The first day of my imprisonment is not too difficult: I rid myself of salt and grime in a warm bath and, under the tutelage of Mrs. Reynolds, scrub my clothes and hang them to dry on a line fastened above her garden. I mend what I can, discarding the stocking and pantalets ruined during my adventure through Rio's market stalls. I shine my shoes which does nothing to stop them falling apart or pinching my toes. I wash and comb and tame my hair as best I can. I even complete a letter to Aunt Margaret and Uncle John which I later ask the Dunsfords to post for me on their next outing. I admit that the tone of my request is barely civil.

A local girl comes to the inn every day to clean and cook. She allows me to assist her bake bread, gather tomatoes from the garden, and slice vegetables and meats for the stews served at supper. Having never been permitted to do anything in a kitchen before, this helps pass the time although I suspect she would prefer

I not aid too much. She speaks only Portuguese (the language of Brazil), so I cannot confirm this.

Mrs. Reynolds is good company so I spend much of the time with her.

"I came to Brazil in '33; so that would be…yes, fifteen years ago," Mrs. Reynolds explains as she works in the garden. "My husband bought a coffee plantation here on a whim—he thought Rio might cheer me. We worked that for five years…until he died. Caught the fever and was gone so quickly, I… Well I was left a widow with a large property, twenty slaves, and a poor understanding of the ways of a plantation despite five years of trying. The locals won't labor on a plantation so I could find no workers to hire. I wanted to free the slaves, but the laws are too complicated. So I just sold the place, slaves and all. A fine New Englander I turned out to be, selling people," she says, shaking her head. "Then I bought this house. I had fallen in love with Brazil—I did not want to go back to Boston. There was nothing for me in Boston." Her gaze is distant and wistful.

"Why can't you go with them? The Dunsfords I mean?" Mrs. Reynolds asks, unpinning her dried clothes from the line and folding them into a large basket. "I know the Reverend has said you can't, but why not?"

Squashing bugs and digging useless holes with a hand trowel, I tell her about having been lost in the marketplace, emphasizing for the hundredth time that it had not been my fault.

"Ah, I see. Well it's very dangerous for a child, especially a girl, in any town. Here it's made more so because of the language. I understand their concern."

"I have promised to stay close."

"I've seen the way you are, Guine. When something catches your fancy, you see nothing else. You'd be distracted without meaning to. You're much like my son was." She pauses, folding her arms in front of her apron and staring at me for a few moments. "Do you like to draw?"

I confide that I have not done much drawing. When I was younger I once used colored pencils to enhance an illustration in a book from Uncle John's library. However, Papa had not viewed it as an enhancement and I had been smacked on the hands for defacing property not my own.

Mrs. Reynolds smiles and, balancing her laundry basket on one hip, reaches for my hand. "Come along. I've something to show you.

"Have you seen the pictures in the common room? The paintings on the walls?" she asks. I shake my head. I have been too preoccupied with my own thoughts and plots to have taken note of pictures. "Look at them and tell me if you notice anything special."

The paintings are lovely scenes from the countryside of Brazil. At least I assume they are of Brazil as the feather-topped trees appear in almost every one of them. The pictures are brightly colored, depicting a view of the sea or the harbor, workers toiling in the bright tropical light.

"They are very pretty."

"But do you notice anything?"

I shrug, feeling as I do in school when the teacher calls upon me to answer a question for which I have no answer. What does she want me to notice?

"There," she says, pointing to the bottom right of one of the paintings. "W. Reynolds. Willa Reynolds," she smiles. "That's me."

"You painted these? All of them?"

She nods. "And I have one I am working on now in the room just off the garden. Would you like to try your hand at painting? I have extra canvas."

I hesitate. I have never painted before and I am certain I will not do her canvas justice. When I say so she laughs. "Well no one is good the first time. You have to practice. Let's practice. It'll keep your mind off of the marketplace."

The small sunny room smells of something Mrs. Reynolds calls linseed oil. She removes the cloth that covers the canvas on which she is working. It is a painting that depicts the French doors of the room in which we stand. However, the room is not filled with art supplies and the garden beyond is not a riot of vegetables. Instead she has painted a veranda with a wooden table and chair, the grain of each slat raised and nudging through old paint. The veranda is surrounded with shrubs covered in purple and pink and orange flowers, and trees such as grow beside the mansions that grace the adjacent hills. Beyond that is the harbor with the giant's thumb jutting into a cloudless sky. It is nothing like the real view.

"One time on *The Pelican*," I say, "Mr. Boyle invited the Dunsfords and me to view the night sky through his spyglass. We spent the evening looking at stars and clouds of dust that pretend to be stars, like the one in the Orion constellation.

"Eventually, when the Dunsfords tired of the night's vigil and went below, only Matthew, Mr. Boyle, and I remained at the railing. It was then that Matthew saw that the wake of *The Pelican* was burning with greenish flecks of cool fire.

"'There are certain sea creatures,' Mr. Boyle told us, 'that keep the light of the sun trapped in their bodies. At night, they shine on their own. The ship's wake stirs them to the surface so that we can see them.'

"There were thousands of them and we watched for several minutes as the wake sparkled like the stars themselves. The sight raised gooseflesh on my arms and neck; it was eerie yet wonderful. A playground of beings not really hidden, only waiting.

"'They are mermaids swimming beneath us, the light of the stars glinting off their scales.' I said. 'They carry *The Pelican* forward, guiding us to Brazil and the safety of the harbor at Rio de Janeiro. Do you hear them chatter as they swim? They wave to us.' Matthew and Mr. Boyle said nothing at the time. I hope they liked the tale, but fear they may simply have thought me mad."

Mrs. Reynolds smiles. "I knew you would understand about my painting," she says, tucking a lock of hair away behind my ear and handing me a paintbrush.

The next several days become more bearable. I help with chores in the mornings after the Dunsfords have left for the day. Then Mrs. Reynolds and I retire to the little room off of the garden, energized with imagination and ultimately drowsy from the scent of linseed oil.

Sunday afternoon, one of the apprentice sailors from *The Pelican* arrives to announce that all passengers are to be on the dock early Tuesday morning to board the ship. *The Pelican* will set sail again on Wednesday at dawn. Even though I have enjoyed my time with Mrs. Reynolds, I rejoice at the news as I will once again be on my way to Papa.

Supper that evening is pleasant and I find it tolerable to listen to the Dunsfords talk about their daily sojourn.

"I thought she looked like a harlot."

"Luke! That is most unkind, young man—you're never to say such things. Besides, you know nothing of harlots other than what you have read in the Bible. Let us give thanks," the Reverend bows his head and says a long and thorough Grace. "*The thief comes only to steal and kill and destroy. I came that they may have life and have it abundantly.* Amen."

"They sold the most delicious looking pastries in one of the shops near that wine merchant, Dear," Mrs. Dunsford chirps, passing a bowl of potatoes across the table. "My mouth was watering simply to look at them. They were very expensive, however."

"She had red hair. What else could she have been but a harlot?"

"I wanted to try some of the coffee too, but I knew if I entered the shop I wouldn't have been able to resist the pastry."

"Not every red-haired woman is a harlot. Think of dear Mrs. Reynolds."

"Oh, and the bread looked interesting too, with different seeds sprinkled all over."

"Her hair's not red, it's… it's not the same. This woman's hair was…well I've never seen hair so red in all of Lowell."

After supper, Matthew and I engage in a game of spillikins in the common room among Willa Reynolds' pictures. We play several rounds and Matthew wins each time. He seems to know exactly which sticks to pick up without disturbing the rest and always selects a stick the color of which earns him the highest points. Since I cannot seem to win, I attempt to break his concentration as he studies the pile to make his choice. I make faces and even tickle him, but he does not falter.

Unlike the rest of his family, who even now continue their warbling from mealtime, Matthew is quiet; more quiet than usual. When I ask him why, he shrugs. "They won't let me explore the city. I have to stay near Mother and the children. I can't see what I want to see. Tomorrow will be my last chance and, instead, I will be forced to spend another wasted day wandering around the town."

When I ask what it is he wants to see he grins broadly. "Do you remember that large white structure we saw from the harbor when we first sailed in?" I shake my head as I do not remember it at all.

"It's an aqueduct," he says, his face lit with excitement, ignoring the fact that I do not know what he is talking about. "It stands several stories high. I've asked everyone I've met about it; well those that speak English at least. It was built nearly a century ago and is the source of all fresh water in the city. It flows from a river high in the mountains into fountains and cisterns throughout Rio de Janeiro. Every time you take a sip of water or draw a bath you're using water that has traveled miles and miles from the mountains over that aqueduct. It's amazing.

"But Father won't let me go see it. He says it's too far away and that I could get lost. It can be seen from nearly every street corner in the city, so I can't possibly get lost. I know exactly where it is." He sighs deeply and returns to his examination of the remaining pile of thin sticks on the table. "They never let me go where I want to go. I wanted to go the inland route from Boston to New York; but as soon as your uncle said that it would be faster and probably less expensive to take a steamer my parents didn't again waiver," he grumbles. "So many new roads are being built and new lines of railroad tracks laid throughout New England. But I couldn't see any of that. Not from a ship."

"Why does that interest you?"

"I want to build things," he says, his face once again brightening. "I want to build roads and bridges, tunnels and canals. And aqueducts. I'm going to be an engineer."

I smile for I like his enthusiasm. "Will there be opportunities to build things in China?"

"I imagine there must be, but I'll have to go to the university first."

"Are there universities in China?"

Matthew shrugs and carefully picks up another stick, waggling it at me with a smug look on his face. Even if I disturb none of the other sticks in the pile, he has calculated that I cannot amass enough points to beat him. Again. "I'll probably return to Boston and go to a university there. That's what I want to do anyway. If *they* will let me."

I gather the sticks to reset the game then, glancing toward the dining area where his parents chat with the other guests, I lean forward and whisper, "Let's go exploring tomorrow."

"Where?" Matthew keeps his voice low, suspicious.

"I will go with you to the aqueduct if you help me to find the lady with the creams."

"Really? But, Guine, we could get in trouble."

"By tomorrow night we will be packing to go aboard the ship

again. Even if they confine us to our cabins there is nowhere to go
on the ship. Please go with me. It will be our last chance. I am too
frightened to go into the city alone, but I could do it if someone
were with me."

With a cursory look at his parents, Matthew smiles and nods.
"What about Mrs. Reynolds?"

"She told me she is to meet the seamstress tomorrow just after
breakfast. She will not be here either."

The plan came together nicely. I am excited that I will not be
imprisoned on my last day in Rio.

"Wait," I say, grabbing Matthew's arm. "Has your father ever
struck you?" He shakes his head. "Do you think he would strike
me if he discovered our plan?"

"My father believes that God measures out all appropriate
physical punishments. If there is any striking to be done, God
will do it himself." Matthew pauses for a moment. "Has anyone
ever struck you?"

I dismiss the smack to my fingers for fouling Uncle John's
book and the padded punishment I received for skipping school.
Instead I tell him about the day of the menagerie.

I wanted to see the animals—I did not want to hear of the
menagerie afterward in one of Mama's "take me there" stories. I
loved those stories, but the menagerie had come to Boston. It was
so close and it would be a shame if I could not see it.

However, Grandmother Somersworth was adamant that
children had no need of strange, exotic creatures like tigers and
bears and elephants, so wild and gigantic and ferocious. Instead,
she insisted that her grandchildren (all except the two eldest) be
kept away. Our parents could expose themselves to danger if they

wanted, but her grandchildren would be safe at home. That was how it would be. Mama said that Grandmother was "formidable." At the time, I thought that word meant "mean."

I begged constantly, my pleas becoming more strident as the day approached. Papa was not as tolerant of my persistence as Mama and I was swatted sharply on the rump following one foot-stomping display. Nothing I did persuaded either of them to challenge Grandmother Somersworth.

The afternoon the carriage took everyone else to the menagerie, I watched their departure from the branches of the tree in front of Grandfather Somersworth's house. Cousin Alfred and I had climbed there just to spite them; we intended to make them sorry they had left us behind. We were going to live in that tree forever and never come down.

Even when the maid called us to supper, we refused to descend or even answer her (although Alfred complained of being hungry and acknowledged that we would have to devise some scheme for bringing food to our new home). She called our names several times, venturing into the yard until she stood below the tree, calling and calling. Finally, Alfred and I could no longer control our laughter at her plight. Hearing us, she looked up to find that we were quite high in the tree. So she screamed. Well, Alfred and I thought her scream even funnier, so we laughed harder. When she demanded we come down, I told her "No," and Alfred echoed my response.

The maid ran into the house to fetch Grandmother Somersworth. My grandmother emerged, storming across the yard to stand beneath our hiding place and yell for us to get out of that tree "this instant." I thought only of my righteous anger at being denied the menagerie visit.

"Only Papa can tell me to get down," I said. Alfred was silent beside me.

Grandmother Somersworth could not climb the tree or shake the branches, so I was not surprised when she went back to the house. In a while, she returned with a sweet smile on her face and her hands hidden behind her back. She called again, saying "Guinevere. Alfred. Come down, I have something for you."

By that time, Alfred and I were both hungry and I was tired of sitting among the hard branches and catching my petticoats on the twigs. We had been in the tree for some time and, I hoped, had made our point. So, Alfred and I scrambled down from the tree, anxious for the treat my sweetly smiling grandmother held.

I should have known that she was angry for she had called me by my full name, Guinevere; the name that preceded all punishments. We were not met with a treat—we were met with a willow switch with which we were lashed soundly. Grandmother had the maid do the whipping, but she supervised.

"When everyone returned from the menagerie that evening Alfred and I met them with faces streaked with dirt and the tracks of tears. Grandmother would let neither of us wash all afternoon so that our parents could see what dirty, wicked children we both were."

"Well I don't think we're wicked and I can't think why God wouldn't want me to see the aqueduct or you to have soft skin. I'll be ready tomorrow," Matthew says.

I fear he will change his mind by morning, but he does not.

The Dunsfords take a long time to ready themselves: Mary has misplaced her hairbrush again; Luke and Mark repeatedly shove each other preventing one or the other from dressing; Lizzie cannot seem to move at all; and Mrs. Dunsford makes up for Lizzie's sluggishness by spinning around the rooms, talking to herself, reciting aloud the long list of things she must purchase before the ship sails. When I suggest she write them down, she sputters "no, no, I haven't time for that" and continues her babble. The Reverend has long since left for his last sermon in Rio.

"I won't be going, Mother," Matthew tells her. "I don't feel well today and would like to rest." He did look pale, probably the result of having spent the night worrying about our fate after today. I barely slept myself, but I am convinced that the risk will be worth it.

My only concern is that the day will be half gone before the Dunsfords are finally out of the house. However, the clock in the common room reads only nine as the door closes behind them. Within minutes Mrs. Reynolds departs for the dressmaker's.

Leaving a hastily written note for Mrs. Reynolds, surmising that she will be the first to notice us missing (and hoping that in any case she will be sympathetic to our adventure), Matthew and I finally leave. We follow the road that rings the harbor as Matthew believes he will spot the aqueduct more easily from that vantage point.

"I thought you could see it from every street corner," I protest.

"Well not always. I think it will be easier to see this way."

"How far is it, do you think?"

"Maybe three or four miles."

I nod and skip a while to keep up with him. He already has an adult-sized stride. "What will you do when we get there?"

"Look at it. I want to see how it's constructed and what

material was used. I want to see the proportions and…oh, I don't know. Anything interesting."

None of it sounds particularly interesting to me, but I am happy to be away from my prison.

"There it is," Matthew exclaims, not far from where we passed the Palace and its marketplace.

The aqueduct is a towering white bridge that reaches across the town, looming above houses and shops, its dual levels of arches gleaming in the sun. From the perimeter road it is still far away and we must venture into the city to get near.

I disagree with Matthew, however, as it cannot be seen from nearly every street corner. In fact, zigzagging through the broad people-filled boulevards, we lose sight of the arches for blocks at a time. We must constantly search for an opening that accords a new view and suggests our next move. When the street ends or buildings obstruct the aqueduct from our sight Matthew anxiously rushes to the next block, almost sighing with relief when he sees it once more.

Then we are somehow past the structure without having come upon it and Matthew is agitated. He sprints several blocks, pulling me with him, before one of the lanes opens into a park where the aqueduct stands in its full glory. He sighs with relief and awe.

The aqueduct towers over all structures near it, higher than any building I have ever seen. It stretches the entire length of the surrounding park and into the city beyond.

Without hesitation, Matthew runs to the base and lays his hands on the plaster walls. "The Romans built these throughout Europe. There are hundreds of them still in use after thousands of years. I have read about them."

"Surely the Romans did not build this one. They would not have traveled this far and it is too new, is it not?"

Matthew laughs. "No, the Romans didn't build it and yes, it is too new. The Brazilians built this one or maybe the Portuguese; but it looks just like the Roman ones. Except the lower arches. I don't think I've ever seen the small arches on the bottom. I wonder why it's been built this way? Or why there are holes at the top like portholes on a ship?"

He spends several more minutes skirting the foundation of the watercourse, reaching as high as he can to estimate its height, knocking on the plaster-covered stone of the pedestals. "I wish I could climb to the top. The view must be spectacular."

"You do not share your mother's fear of heights, I see."

Matthew chuckles and shakes his head. "My mother fears a lot of things."

We trace the track of the aqueduct, looking for a way to climb, leaving the park behind. Soon the jumble of houses seems to absorb the arches as if by magic; densely built neighborhoods swallow it whole. Following its course becomes impossible and Matthew suggests we return to the park.

We retrace our steps through the neighborhoods. The houses are huddled together, crouching under a layer of grime, plaster crumbling from the walls in large pieces. The iron balconies, their rusty tears streaking the walls, are strewn with laundry and pots and children dangling dirty feet between the balusters. The windows of the dwellings are curtain-less and dark, the streets quiet. I suspect we are watched from behind those windows, although we see no one there. We had noticed none of this our first time through. I expect to see the filthy boy or others like him and glance around, hoping that a church is near. I do not see one.

A group of children run by us, kicking a ball made from leather strips tied with twine. Their laughter echoes eerily through the narrow street. We are lost. I am lost, again.

When a small herd of goats blocks the street we must pause. Exchanging a few words with the mistress of each cottage, the goatherd selects an earthenware pitcher from among several tied around his waist by thin cords. Holding his container beneath the animal, he milks then transfers the creamy liquid into a vessel each woman has fetched. He is handed coins and moves along to the next house. I have never seen such a thing: it is a clever way to deliver fresh milk. The goatherd pays no attention as Matthew and I pick our way around his animals, avoiding their dusty flanks. A little girl emerges from one of the houses, plucking curiously at my skirt.

Stumbling among the jumble of streets, we at last re-enter the park where the aqueduct stands. We do not linger. Recognizing the road where we first entered, in unspoken agreement, Matthew and I run through the avenues toward the harbor road. We do not pause and are distracted only once when I recognize sailors from *The Pelican* celebrating at an outdoor tavern. Agreeing that it is best to avoid anyone who might later betray our secret explorations, Matthew and I give the tavern a wide berth.

The marketplace is just as it was before: bustling with people and noise and smells, joyous and raucous and wonderful. Matthew immediately asks the location of the stall where the lotions may be found, but I suggest that we wander. I am tired from the run and I want to catch my breath and have something to eat. My stomach growls in agreement; it is well past midday. I have brought only a few coins this time which I dole out to make my selections: a small roll covered in seeds; squashed beans rolled into bite-sized spheres and fried as I watch; and a slice from an oblong fruit with spiked leaves, covered in massive scales of gold edged with green. The flesh of the fruit is bright yellow and very juicy, sweet and tart at the same time. Although the vendor repeats the name for me three times, I cannot pronounce it—evidently it has no English equivalent. I buy a second slice. Matthew has bread, a large wedge of cheese, and a pear.

We sit in a shady place on the hard stones of the plaza with our backs against the wall of the Imperial Palace as no formal seats are to be found. A juggler passes as well as a man selling toys and trinkets from a tray strapped around his neck. "I hope we see the fire-eater," I exclaim. "I would like you to see his pet monkey."

Several soldiers, like those that guard the Imperial Palace, are among the throng, their faces somber as they survey the crush of people. A guitar troupe stands close to the palace walls, their music loud and lively.

"Are you looking forward to living in China?" I ask, licking the grease and fruit juice from my fingers, my thoughts turning from the newness of Brazil to what might prove an even more exotic place for the Dunsfords. I have never questioned Matthew about China.

"I think only my father is excited about it." Matthew finishes the pear, tossing the core to a waiting flock of pigeons. "I would've been happy to stay in New England. I know my mother would have. But, there's no turning back now, I suppose.

"However, we should go back to Mrs. Reynolds'," Matthew sighs, glancing at the gathering clouds. The weather can turn suddenly in Rio. Mid-afternoon each day the sky grows dark and drops torrents of warm rain on the city, just as it did the day I sought refuge in the church. The Dunsfords have been caught by surprise several times in their explorations. Matthew and I agreed beforehand that we would be back at the inn well before the daily drenching.

Brushing crumbs from my frock, I lead the way to the aisle where the little brown woman sells her wares. I hear the monkeys screaming at the passers-by and follow the sound to the flash and glitter of bottles and jars that stand on the table of the gnome-like woman.

"*Bom dia*," I say as I approach, having remembered to ask Mrs. Reynolds how to say "good day" in Portuguese.

The little brown woman screams. She darts forward to clasp my face in both of her hands then embraces my arms, frowning and shaking her head and speaking the whole while in a strident manner. She clutches at Matthew's sleeve too, agitated and becoming more so when she sees the puzzled looks on our faces. What is the matter? What have we done?

Anxiously surveying the crowd, she shouts and gestures wildly, snatching at our arms and wrists, looking into our faces and continuing to shake her head. I am confused and frightened and understand nothing she says. What does she want?

I try to back away, but she simply tightens the grip of her small brown hands around my wrist. Strong; she is surprisingly strong.

A crowd has gathered in a semi-circle around us, their eyes darting between us and the woman. They do not seem hostile; they seem only questioning, puzzled at this display just as I am puzzled. "Matthew, what do we do?"

He shakes his head, surveying the gathering.

Then the group parts. Through the opening walk two of the Palace soldiers, rifles slung over their shoulders and bright swords dangling at their sides. The gnome-woman pulls us toward them, gesturing to us and talking faster than before. The soldiers look from her to Matthew and me, then nod.

"What did we do?" Matthew asks, pulling himself to his full height and squaring his shoulders. "Has she accused us of something?"

His questions are ignored as we are each grasped by a soldier. I struggle and kick at my captor's shins, but the soldier who holds me seems not to notice my efforts.

"Where are you taking us?" Matthew demands. "We're American citizens. We're innocent of all wrongdoing. Let us go."

Gawkers watch as the soldiers drag us through the market and into the street that fronts the harbor; no face is familiar. "Help us, please!" I bellow my innocence to no one in particular.

A woman, her child in tow, calls to the soldiers. Upon hearing their reply she shakes her head. An exasperated look on her face, she turns without further comment. Men approach asking questions; they nod in knowing response at the answers. Beyond expressing curiosity, no one ventures to help us further despite my loud assurances that this is a mistake.

I struggle and shout as we are dragged past the stalls of the fish mongers, away from the quay that stands before the Imperial Palace, pushed along the waterfront by our captors.

At the perimeter of the marketplace stands an enclosed coach shaped like a box, its windows barred. Two more solders stand beside it. My knees weaken.

At our approach the carriage door is opened by one of the "new" soldiers who smiles in a grandfatherly way and gestures for us to get inside. I am angrier at that smile than I have been at the rough handling received from his fellows and I kick viciously at his leg, grabbing the edges of the coach. The man's smile disappears and the rough handling continues.

Inside, the coach is unadorned and uncomfortable and humid, the benches of raw wood worn smooth by use. It smells as *The Pelican* had during the first week of our voyage. The door is slammed behind us; there is no handle inside.

I grab the bars that cover the window, shaking them and screaming to be let free; we must be let free. Matthew gently pulls me away from the bars, making shushing sounds.

"Stop shushing me!" I slap his hand from my shoulder as the wagon lurches forward. "What would soldiers want with us? Where will they take us?" Matthew does not answer. Slumping against the seat, I wedge my body into one corner. I bite my lower lip to stop its quivering, but cannot control my trembling limbs. "Why did she do that? What did we do?"

Without a word, Matthew rises and moves to the seat beside me, taking my hand. I do not slap him away this time.

Inside this little box, Matthew and I do not speak, staring through the rotting timbers of the floorboards as the cobbles pass beneath us, the coach vibrating in time to the slow rhythmic clop of the horses' hooves on the stones. The soldiers laugh and call greetings to others. I hear the Reverend's words again: "A little girl of your age, nearly naked in front of the entire crowd, examined like livestock, sold to the highest bidder." I envision being cast into a dungeon, dark and dank and crawling with rats, left to starve, no word to our respective parents. Papa and the Dunsfords will never know what has happened to us and we will die in obscurity. Or we may be sent to a workhouse to labor in factories and fed gruel and beaten when we resist, or sold to an undertaker where we must wash dead bodies and...

"I don't think they're soldiers," Matthew whispers, startling me from my gloomy disjointed thoughts.

"Why not?"

"They wear no medals. Soldiers always flaunt medals across their chests. These men have no medals at all."

I twist in the seat so that I can see him better. "Who do you think they are?" I whisper.

"I think they are the police."

Somehow the thought of capture by police seems worse than by soldiers, although I cannot say why. I have seen police in the streets of Boston, but have never met one before. "But what would the police want with us? We have done nothing."

Matthew shrugs and shakes his head just as the carriage halts.

I grab the bars again, peering out the window. There is little to see. We are in a small alleyway similar to so many alleyways of Rio. Nothing appears unique until my eyes happen upon the decorative platters in one of the shops. The inn! We are outside of Mrs. Reynolds' inn and my heart skips.

The coach door flies open and Mrs. Reynolds grasps me. As I alight, she tearfully demands to know if I am all right, if I am hurt. Once this brief personal inspection is complete, she turns to Matthew to ask his condition, hands caressing his face and arms as well. Then she tells us to go inside while she remains to speak with our escorts.

I do not hesitate to get away from the coach and the soldiers or policemen or whatever they are. I run into the common room, touching the backs of the chairs and tables that fill the space, clasping my hands, my knees bobbing in excitement. I am so happy to see the paintings, this room, this house—we are back; we are safe.

My joy disappears as Mrs. Reynolds enters. "Where have you been?" Her tone is icy.

"We went to the marketplace," I respond, dutifully looking at the floor.

"You may have been there when the police found you, but you were certainly not there this morning. *That* was the first place I looked.

"I was not gone more than fifteen minutes and I return to an empty house. Do you have any idea what might've happened to the two of you? I had the police looking everywhere for you! Where did you go?"

Matthew and I exchange a glance. This is not going at all as I had hoped. Mrs. Reynolds is far angrier than I expected. Her face is contorted and her lips, when not forming words of reproach, quiver as mine had done in the police coach.

"We went to the aqueduct," Matthew says, clearing his throat.

"The...the aqueduct?" Mrs. Reynolds holds her head as if it might not stay on her neck. "That is miles and miles and miles from here. What were you thinking? No, I don't care what you were thinking! Not only did you disobey your parents, your guardians, but you put yourselves in...horrible, horrible danger. Rio is not a safe city. There are any number of people who could've done you harm."

"We were mostly on main streets," I protest, thinking it best not to mention the time we wandered lost among the houses lining the aqueduct. "We stayed together; we were careful."

"You could've been killed, for God's sake," she yells and I think she has taken the words of my father and changed them to match her voice. "You're children. And well-to-do children at that. Compared to most that live here. If anyone wanted to do you harm, you would've been easy targets. Both of you."

Mrs. Reynolds' voice trails away and she pales, steadying herself against the back of a chair, swaying until I think she might fall. For a moment there is only the sound of the clock on the wall, ticking like a heartbeat.

"Go to your rooms. Now. And do not come down until you are summoned." Her voice rasps as if it has been locked away for years.

My limbs are heavy as I turn to the staircase. "What do you think she will do?" I whisper to Matthew from the bottom riser.

"I don't want you talking to one another!" Mrs. Reynolds follows us to the foot of the steps. "You are not to talk, to whisper, to make faces, or write notes or tap on walls. Nothing. Do you understand? Nothing."

We nod. Then she flees into the kitchen.

"You will go to your room and not leave until I tell you," Papa said. "I will not be argued with, young lady; do you hear me? Go to your room."

As I climbed the stairs I slapped each baluster. I was in no hurry.

I did not think I had done wrong. However, since Papa had sent me to the room that was called mine almost daily for the last several weeks, his words came as no surprise. He usually said it when I was making noise as I ran through my aunt and uncle's house, pretending to be the French princess. I rode a flying horse with the boy from County Mayo, all of us invisible. The day before, I had been only the horse.

This time I was not even in the house, choosing instead to trudge through the snow to the barn for a visit with the real horses. I liked the barn. Nothing lived there except the horses, Uncle John's dog, and the cat that belonged to no one. They never seemed to mind my noise.

The barn was warm, smelling strongly of hay and manure as always. I sought the cat in the corner of a horse stall where she had recently delivered kittens. As I approached she hissed and lashed a paw swiftly in my direction, claws prominently exposed. I backed away quickly, robbing her of the opportunity to slice another deep gouge in my hand as she had the last time I tried to touch her and her newborns. Instead of reaching again, I sat a few feet away from the young family, waiting for my presence to be accepted. But the mother cat stayed tense and watchful.

I climbed into the loft and ran to the end where a pair of wide doors hung open. The fields and fences beyond were blanketed with white. Gnarled trees reached into the gray sky; witches hands snatching at crows ripe for the cauldron. The witches intended to brew a potion of terrible power, strong enough to bring the dead back to life. I shivered at the thought.

Pulling on my gloves, I reached for a rope that hung near the open loft doors. I had seen the stable hands use this rope and the pulley to which it was attached to heft great bales of hay into the loft. Certainly I was lighter than a bale of hay.

There was a loop at one end of the line, like a stirrup. I inserted my foot into that loop and grasped the opposite strand of rope. Using my free leg, I pushed away from the barn to swing suspended in mid-air. I loosened my grip, allowing myself to drop a few inches. As the rope slipped through my hands I pushed against the barn again, swinging and twisting and falling all at once. I closed my eyes.

When I reached the ground, I wanted to try again. I ran through the barn to the ladder, climbing once more to the loft and hoisting the loop back to the opening.

Thus it went. Each time I dropped a little farther before tightening my grip to stop my fall. My hands burned beneath the woolen gloves. My pounding heart climbed high in my chest with each plunge. I deliberately swung myself further each time, pushing at the barn with my free leg. Swinging and twisting and falling.

I lost count of the times I ran through the barn and let myself fall. I was flying. I was invisible.

I did not hear Papa approach. Nor did I see him before he grabbed my arm, just as I reached the ground. He turned me roughly around, his face red and contorted.

"Guinevere! What are you doing? Did you not hear me? Why did you not stop when I yelled?"

I hung my head, squirming against the iron grip of his hand.

"You could have been killed, for God's sake," he yelled, shaking me. I made no response. "Look at me! Look at me when I speak to you! What were you doing?"

"Nothing." I kept my eyes on the ground.

He stood straight then and, when I glanced up at him, his hand was stretched across his forehead pressing both temples at once. Then he dragged the hand to his jaw. "Go to your room."

"I was only having fun."

"You will go to your room and not leave until I tell you. I will not be argued with, young lady; do you hear me? Go. To. Your. Room."

All afternoon I listen from my room at the inn for the sounds of the door below. I envision the Reverend flying up the stairs, two at a time, bursting in to admonish me with his Sunday voice, fists clenched. I fear he will put his principles aside and beat me with one of the umbrellas Mrs. Reynolds keeps in a tin cylinder by the door for her guests. I have no fear that punishment will come from Mrs. Dunsford. No, if there is to be a meaningful thrashing it will be at the Reverend's hand.

However, the afternoon passes and the Dunsfords return and I hear only Mrs. Reynolds' greetings from below, surprisingly cheerful.

At suppertime Mrs. Reynolds calls her guests' names, Matthew and mine among them. She is subtle; I doubt anyone but Matthew and I take note that she has never before called names at supper. We have been summoned.

I remain quiet at the meal, anticipating that Mrs. Reynolds will lower her fork at any moment, fold her hands in her lap, and begin her tale with a great sigh: "Well, let me tell you what Guinevere and Matthew did today…"

She does not. The buzz of conversation and noise from plates scraped and tapped with utensils eddy around me. My stomach churns. I do not attempt to glance at Matthew even once throughout the meal. My head is lowered whenever Mrs. Reynolds is in the room; I do not want her to see my face and be reminded of my transgression. I am not sorry that I explored the city. I am only sorry the police were involved and that we were hauled through the streets of Rio so ignobly.

"I've arranged for a cart tomorrow to take our belongings to the ship," the Reverend announces, spooning more stew onto his plate. "We must be ready no later than nine o'clock, packed and fully dressed. If you dally, we shall leave without you and you can find your own way to the ship." However, he smiles as he says this, appearing happy at the prospect of once again sailing. "Nine o'clock. Remember."

We retire early in anticipation of the next day's activities. I lay on my mattress for hours before finally sleeping. The more time that passes the more drastic I imagine my final penalty will be.

The next morning, the Dunsfords and I scour the house for stray toys and clothes, pack everything away and watch as our luggage is once again crammed into a mule cart.

"Would you like to take your painting, Miss Walker?" Mrs. Reynolds asks.

I shake my head and thank the landlady for her kindness in teaching me to paint. I do not believe I have done a good job as the colors became muddy the more I added. I confess this and suggest she paint something beautiful over my messy canvas.

As it appears that Mrs. Reynolds has not and will not say anything to the Dunsfords, I try to express my gratitude for her silence without actually speaking the words "thank you for not tattling on us." I do not know how successful I have been, but she smiles and hugs me tightly before we depart.

Cargo and baggage are still being loaded into *The Pelican* when we reach the pier. Men and mules labor with the ropes and capstans as they lower large pallets into the hold. The incoming cargo of calico cloth, fine furniture, and boxes of shoes from New York are replaced with lumber and barrels of coffee and sugar and other containers labeled in both English and Portuguese. The crew and stevedores glisten with perspiration despite a cool breeze that washes the dock. The work is hard and their patience with each other evaporates with their sweat. Perhaps it is good that I understand no Portuguese, although many of the words they yell are in English.

Mr. Boyle is among the men, barking directions and gesturing, whistling shrilly at the laborers and the sailors to focus them on their tasks. He takes scant notice of me, waving absently when I call to him.

I wander down the pier to watch the seagulls and diving birds again, trying to memorize the look of the harbor. How will I begin the tale of my visit to Rio? "There is a gentle giant that guards the entrance to Guanabara Bay…"

Soon I am summoned aboard. Our departure from Rio will not be until early tomorrow morning; however, this afternoon the ship is to be moved closer to the mouth of the harbor; she is now ready. I shuffle up the gangway and make my way to the ship's railing to watch the crew cast off, planting my legs in anticipation of her sway as she moves away from the pier. I turn to see Mr. Boyle standing behind me, his face reflecting the strain of his recent labors. He is waving to someone on the wharf.

"Is that your friend's family?" I ask, leaning on the railing for a better look at the woman and two children who stand below. The woman is dressed like most Americans: a trim bonnet, a dark blue dress that flatters her plump figure. However, I recognize that she is a local woman because her skin is a lovely Brazilian bronze, her hair black under the wings of the hat. She dabs her eyes with a lace handkerchief as she waves to Mr. Boyle. A girl and a younger boy, both neatly dressed in the American fashion, wave as well. "Where is your friend?"

"He had business to attend to."

"What are the children's names?"

"Adão and Elisabete. She is your age."

"My middle name is Elizabeth. Do you have children, Mr. Boyle?"

"I do. Four boys...no, five boys and three girls."

I tease him because he has forgotten how many children he has, but he does not laugh. "I see them seldom. That's the life of a sailor," he says. "There for the conception, seldom the rest. My eldest boy, Eamon, is married and has a child of his own. Never met my grandson, even though they live just up the road in Albany."

"Can they not sail with you some time?"

"This is the first I've ever sailed with children aboard a ship and I've been sailing since I was your age. It's not common."

"Do you like having children aboard?"

Only then does he stop waving, turning to look at me, contemplating the question for several moments. "Ask me when we've reached San Francisco," he says, turning back to the receding shore. He continues to wave until the three figures are no longer discernible from the pier. Then announcing gruffly that he must ensure the cargo is adequately secured, Mr. Boyle hurries to the hold.

I venture to the cabin to unpack my few belongings.

Like the rest of the ship, our cabin has been painted. The porthole is open to lessen the fumes, which are not pleasant like Mrs. Reynolds' linseed oil.

Briefly acknowledging Lizzie, who is on her bed staring at the ceiling, I climb into my berth careful to avoid the newly installed hooks that line the lower edge of the bunk. "What are these?" I ask, pointing to the strange fasteners.

"How am I supposed to know? I didn't put them there and they seem ridiculous to me as they're facing the wrong way."

She is right; they have been installed upside down. The same hooks, in the same position, line all of the bunks in the cabin. They cannot be used to hang clothes or curtains and I cannot fathom another use for them.

"Why don't you ask your beau?"

I frown at Lizzie. "I beg your pardon?"

"Your beau. Mr. Boyle. Surely he knows all about everything on this ship and would be happy to explain it to his little sweetheart." When I laugh, she asks: "What's so funny?"

"He is not my beau. That is really a silly idea. He is married and has eight children and one grandchild."

"You certainly don't understand the way the world is, do you?"

I wrinkle my nose and decide it is best to ignore her. I have doubts that she knows the way of the world either, but explaining that will serve only to rile her more.

The package on my bed, my name clearly printed on the brown

paper wrapping, is a surprise. It is oddly shaped and tautly tied with twine. As I lift it, the contents clunk like the sound of horses hooves muffled in snow. "What is this and how did it get here?"

Lizzie raises her head briefly and glances at the bundle. "How am I supposed to know? Maybe it's from your beau."

I make a face at her, but she has already turned her back to me. I tear the package open to find a little green bottle and two small clay pots. Selecting one of the pots, I slide its twine binding loose, lifting the wooden stopper. Inside is a greenish paste. I reach for the note that rests on top of the other items.

Dear Guine,

As you see, I found the woman with the lotions. It is hardly a wonder as your description was most accurate—next to a monkey booth. She remembered you well due to your poor burned face and knew exactly which concoctions you wanted. She would take no money for them; they are her gift to you.

She apologizes for having frightened you and Matthew when you visited her the second time. I am afraid this was my fault as yesterday morning, when I found the two of you missing, I expected you would have gone to see her since you spoke so often of the benefits of her creams. She had not yet seen you at that time. I was very frightened that I would not find you and I told her that you and Matthew had run away. I asked that she summon the police if you were to come again. I then went to the police station and reported you missing, panicked as I was for your safety. It is fortunate that the chief of police is a friend of mine and that you are American. Otherwise, they would not have been bothered with two missing children.

When I returned to her booth this morning, to thank her for the part she played in your recovery, she loaded my arms with these and wished you a safe voyage and a speedy reunion with your father (for I told her your life's story, I fear; as much as I know of it at least).

I too wish you a safe journey. I rarely have children staying at my inn; with you there I realized once again how I miss having a child by my side.

I know that you are not pleased with your painting, but I am happy to keep it as a reminder of my time with you.

Be safe my dear girl and enjoy your Brazilian potions. I hope your reunion with your father is all that you wish it to be.

Warmest regards,
Willa Reynolds

P.S. —The one cream you may not recognize is for Matthew. Eulalia (for that is the woman's name) noticed the spots on his face and thought it might help. He need use very little—this one pot should last him a long time.

Both the lotion and cream are there: the green for my face and the white for my hands. The remaining pot contains a substance that is nearly clear and very sticky. Surely, this is the one meant for Matthew.

I tuck Mrs. Reynolds' note into my portmanteau next to the letters from Papa, nestling the jars among my clothes so that they will not be bumped. Jumping to the deck I look for Matthew, silently thanking Mrs. Reynolds for her thoughtfulness.

CHAPTER 5

June 21, 1848

BEHIND *The Pelican*, Sugar Loaf glows copper in the light from the rising sun. I nod goodbye to the giant.

The first two weeks of the continuing voyage pass with calm seas and strong winds that are, unfortunately, blowing in the wrong direction. As the month of June ends we are not sufficiently distanced from Guanabara Bay as far as the captain is concerned (this from the Reverend who overheard a frustrated pronouncement from the quarterdeck).

There is a marked improvement in the food since our departure from Rio. The ship is now loaded with fruit and vegetables, a large variety of fresh and cured meats, eggs, milk, and good bread. It is much better fare than was available in New York apparently. It occurs to me that Cook, a freedman from that city, is not inept in the kitchen but that the materials with which he previously had to work were inferior.

After much badgering with questions, descriptions, and my feeble attempt to pronounce the unpronounceable word, Cook finally announces that the fruit I tried in the marketplace was probably pineapple, or *abacaxi* in local parlance (stating that Mr. Boyle would undoubtedly correct his pronunciation because Mr. Boyle speaks Portuguese so well). He then provides me with two slices for he has brought several of the oddly shaped fruit on board.

For the first time since our trip began we do not venture into open sea, hugging the coastline of South America instead. There is an abundance of sea life and birds that were absent in the depths: turtle and seaweed; crows, pigeons, and other birds whose names I do not know who come to rest on a yardarm for a time before resuming their flight. Whales occasionally spout only a few hundred feet from the ship and dolphin are plentiful. I seldom see the land itself, but it makes itself known.

One of our feathered visitors, an albatross, does more than rest: it flies into the rigging and thumps loudly to the deck, unsteadily waddling for a time, dazed and shaking its head. It will let no one near, squawking loudly and aggressively pecking at any who try. When Mark and Luke descend upon it, the bird leads them a chase around the main deck. Then, apparently tiring of human companionship, the creature hops to the railing and spreads its wings to at least a full fifteen feet, catching the wind and leaving us behind only a few feathers shy.

The seat below the quarterdeck where I used to read is no longer. It has been replaced with a barrel of fresh water, an ever-present cup hanging at its side from a stout piece of twine. I finally select the planked hatch covers as my new perch; a folded blanket borrowed from the cabin is my cushion. It is not nearly as sheltered from the breezes or as isolated from other passengers, nor is there anything against which to rest my back, but my choices are limited—the deck seems even more crowded than before.

I avoid Mr. Sterbenc. Not that I ever sought his company before, but I make a special effort now. If he approaches, I quickly cross out of his way. If I come upon him suddenly, I avert my eyes and scurry past him. I hear him chuckle at my evasions, but I would rather have him amused than near me.

I see little of Mr. Boyle although he nods and waves as he passes on his way to some business. There is about him an energy that is in direct opposition to the sluggish movement of the ship. He descends into the hold daily to check for leakage (of which, I have heard him say, there is none) or ensure the ballasts are well placed and that the cargo will not shift. He orders sailors aloft to test the soundness of a certain piece of rigging or the strength of a sail. Even when he stops to exchange a few words, his eyes dart over the ship as if fearful he will miss some detail of importance. He listens not to me, but to *The Pelican* as if she is singing to him in a voice I cannot hear. Sometimes he pauses mid-sentence to heed the tune.

The crocus finally cease blooming and I retrieve the bulbs from the sawdust, clean them off, and gently place them once more in their burlap travel pouch, wedged into my portmanteau beside the Brazilian potions. As I dump the damp wood shavings Mr. Boyle comes to stand beside me, watching closely to ensure that I do not drop the bucket overboard. He drums his fingers on his thighs as the last of the chips fall to the water below. He taps his knuckles on the railing as I ladle saltwater into the bucket and churn it to wash out the last bits of wood. Annoyed at his fidgeting, I accuse him of "dancing on a hot griddle" (one of Mrs. Schrader's expressions).

"Did your father write to you about Cape Horn?" he asks.

I nod. I have read that letter only once; it terrifies me. It is the lone one of the three missives I have not memorized. My father wrote that he was thankful just to be alive.

Mr. Boyle nods when I tell him this. "Cape Horn is a treacherous and fickle place. The ship needs to be ready to take it on. She's been 'round it many times before. So has the captain. But you can never be too prepared."

Mr. Boyle has been "'round the Horn" as well, once before. For many years, his sailing was restricted to junkets down the eastern seaboard of the United States, into the Caribbean and onto South America. However, there are better wages to be earned in the longer routes to China and India.

"What will it be like?"

He asks me to think about the worst storm I ever endured when in Boston then says it will be worse. He asks if I remember the first week of our voyage out of New York then declares that will be nothing compared with the Horn's winds and rains, the seas pounding against us, over us, churning around us in black fury. One minute all will be calm; the next, everything will be tossed about like straw.

"Can you take me there?" I ask, but Mr. Boyle does not know what I mean. I have asked him to play my mother's game before, but he usually describes things inadequately (although I admit that this time he frightened me more than Papa's letter). Mama was the only person I knew who could make everything real with her words. Even when she read from a book, her rendition was more vivid than when Mrs. Schrader or Grandmother Somersworth or anybody else read to me. When she retold the unwritten hand-me-down stories, I could see every blade of grass and every castle stone about which she spoke. My favorite was a story she created about an orphan boy, John Quincy, who joined a band of gypsies. She created the John Quincy stories when the books incited me to sneak candles into my room or lay awake for hours reciting the tales aloud from memory, imagining myself to be a princess or a pirate or whatever the latest character might be. I think she believed an ordinary boy like John Quincy would not capture my imagination quite as much and would lull me to sleep. However, I found John Quincy even more interesting than the fairytales. I provided details for the stories and suggestions for new escapades, all of which rendered me more awake than ever. As a prelude to the menagerie visit, I suggested that John Quincy sneak into the show and ride the elephant. After that Mama began the "take me there" stories—the ones from her own life that did not require or encourage my embellishments. Well not as often at least.

From the "take me there" stories I learned how she met Papa in the North Church, about her "spectacular" debut and the young men with whom she harmlessly flirted, and what dresses she wore to the events given in honor of my grandfather. These tales were even more vivid than the books and she quite forgot herself in the telling. No one could tell them better.

"You must be prepared too," Mr. Boyle cautions. "Did you see those hooks along the side of your berth? I had those put on all the bunks. It was an idea I had after I made the crossing. Mr. Hester, the sail maker, has sewn straps which can be attached to those hooks so you won't be tossed out of bed if the storms hit while you're sleeping. We'll give you the straps as soon as we sight Staten Land."

Then I remember another piece of Papa's letter: he had been strapped to his berth, still too seasick to move and too weak to hang onto anything. The ropes had cut him terribly, but he had been thankful for their presence.

"Is it always like that?"

"Always. It does not matter the month; there is no good season for rounding the Horn." Mr. Boyle shakes his head. "But you'll be fine. We will get through this, all of us."

His bravado is only mildly reassuring.

The sailor who came to Mrs. Reynolds' inn announcing *The Pelican's* imminent departure also warned us to keep our winter coats and gloves handy. I thought it very strange since the weather in Rio was so comfortable.

Now, I want to thank that sailor for those instructions—the further south we travel the colder it becomes. It is difficult for me to think of July as a winter month, but in the lowest part of the southern hemisphere it is. The temperature steadily drops a little each day. Lizzie and Matthew proudly wear the scarves their mother gave them in early May for their birthday. We had once thought her gift eccentric. Now, the twins are grateful for her foresight.

The most disorienting part of the journey is the sun: it rises late and sets early without a trace of cheer or warmth.

During one brief interval of daylight, as we pass through the Strait of Le Maire, I am awed at the mainland: cliffs soar above the sea for thousands of feet, battered at their base by huge waves. The jagged peaks further inland look like the fangs of a dog.

Storms pound *The Pelican* regularly, sending a few of the passengers to their beds and all of us huddled inside for warmth. I wear my coat and gloves even in the shelter of the cabins, often while under the blankets of my bed. When in the main cabin, I maneuver close to the captain's galley, as that contains the only stove in this part of the ship (not counting the one in the captain's cabin, which he does not offer to share). The deck house and, therefore, the mess benefit from the main galley stove, but time there is limited.

Still, Mr. Boyle says it will be worse. I can hardly imagine, but do not say so.

CHAPTER 6

July 30, 1848

THE STORMS WERE RELENTLESS once *The Pelican* passed
Staten Land. The Captain continued south until wind and sea
became more manageable and he could turn the ship west toward
the Pacific Ocean.

Within days of the turn, Cape Horn once again releases its
fury on the ship. All sailors are forced to remain on deck for
three days without relief, reefing and unfurling sails as the wind
demands.

As the sailors struggle with the sails above, below decks we
strap ourselves into our bunks, using the odd-looking hooks Mr.
Boyle had installed in Rio. The straps are wide, fastened in the
middle with rings that enable us to pull them tight. Still, even
secure in our berths, sleeping is impossible. With the worst of
the storms, anything not lashed down (including passengers) flies
into the bulkheads.

During the ordeal Mrs. Dunsford, although clearly as terrified
as the rest of us, displays a strength that surprises me. She clings
to her children protectively, often using her body to cushion
and shelter them against the buffeting. Each evening, assured
that her daughters and I are tightly strapped to our berths, she
braves passage through the main cabin to her husband and sons,

confirming their relative safety before hazarding a return. She does not complain, but I am certain that the body beneath her winter coat is more bruised and aching than mine.

Then comes a welcomed period of calm from the winds and driving rain. The Reverend utters a grateful prayer.

At last, after the three-day struggle, the crew will find time to eat, warm themselves with coffee, catch a brief nap, and tend to their bloodied hands, readying themselves for the next onslaught. And everyone believes there will be a next onslaught.

Below, we too appreciate the quiet but eerie change. Mrs. Dunsford recommends we get into our berths, cinch ourselves in, and sleep while we can. If we can.

I help Mary, tucking her beneath the quilt and attaching the bindings. The hooks on each berth accommodate three straps, although I only need two for Mary as she is small. She watches each move I make but says nothing. I tighten the binding across her chest, ensuring that her arms are free. She holds the strap tightly when I finish.

Lizzie settles her mother and Anna, the straps puckering the blankets and quilts like twine around a package. Anna's eyes close as she nestles at her mother's side. I do not think she is yet sleeping.

"You girls get in your bunks now," Mrs. Dunsford whispers to Lizzie and me.

Lizzie jumps into her bed and quickly attaches the straps. We have become experts with them. Grabbing the cabin stool and placing it beneath my berth, I step up.

Then the horror. The floor moves suddenly and I am violently thrown against the cabin door, my shoulder smashing into the handle, my head knocking against the wood above it.

For a moment I remain still, my ears ringing, my shoulder throbbing, my cheek pressed against the door. Then I realize that I am lying flat—in effect, the door has become the floor of the cabin. The ship is somehow lying on its side.

"Guine!" Mrs. Dunsford claws at her straps, trying to loosen them.

"No, Mrs. Dunsford," I finally say, clutching my head to stop the ringing, "I am all right, really. I am all right."

I stand as best I might on the canted door and leap toward my berth. I hardly remember getting into the bed, attaching the straps, and cinching them against myself. All the while, the ship stays in its awkward and unnerving pose, rocking with each new wave. Renewed and ferocious winds scream across the ship's hull. The calm is over.

Despairing cries echo from all over the ship, but no one in the cabin makes a sound. I glance at the two girls in the bunks opposite. They are held in place only by the grace of the straps: Lizzie with her eyes closed tightly, Mary staring at the underside of Lizzie's bed. Each clutch the strap at her chest, knuckles white, pursed lips trembling as are mine.

The calls for help outside carry over the howl of the winds. Then a sound vibrates through the cabin, silencing the other, lesser protests. It starts as a moan, then becomes a shriek, then a wail. With a shudder and a final scream from deep within her, the ship returns to its proper position. The storm continues to wail around us, but we are upright. Miraculously, we are upright.

We awaken to decks and railings blanketed in four inches of new snow. Ice crystals cling to the rigging in berry-like clusters and icicles hang from the railings, masts, and spars, glistening in the weak sunlight. I fear that frozen shards might crash to the decks at any time and on any passerby. It is beautiful in a sinister way: the sparkling white ice palace of a wicked queen floating on the sea.

The Horn is far behind us now. It took *The Pelican* twenty-three days to travel from Staten Land to the Pacific—a few hundred nautical miles that is traversed in less than ten days in normal waters, according to Mr. Boyle. The waters around Cape Horn are never normal, and we are lucky to have survived the journey at all.

The Dunsfords and I are the only passengers on deck at the moment. I am told that it is not customary for passengers to attend the funeral of a sailor, but the Reverend wanted the family there because the lad had been so young: only a year older than Matthew and Lizzie. Service is held on the main deck instead of the usual quarterdeck, for without the enclosed railing we would almost certainly slip on the icy surface and into the sea.

The Reverend delivers a moving eulogy: *And when the ship was caught and could not face the wind, we gave way to it and were driven along.* There is a heaviness upon the crew as the observance ends and they disperse to their posts.

The boy, whose name was Thomas, had fallen from his perch on the mizzenmast when *The Pelican* was laid on her side, floundering in the tempestuous waters during the Horn's tantrum. No one had wanted to send the inexperienced boy aloft. He was to stay at the lookout post for only a short time, just to give the others respite. There had been no other choice.

Mr. Boyle's voice is controlled as he imparts this news, but his face is drawn, the fair stubble on his chin dark in contrast with his pallor. As with all of the other sailors, his eyes are sunken and bruised underneath. His hands shake.

"The crew was…well I couldn't have asked for more," Mr. Boyle says, looking over waters whose calm belie the horror of the last several days. It had taken all of the crew's skill and strength to level the ship. By the time they had righted her, Thomas was gone from sight beneath monstrous waves. There was no opportunity to turn *The Pelican* around or launch one of the smaller crafts to rescue him. Either choice would have been suicide since the Horn would not cease its renewed vehemence for the sake of a single lad. Wave after wave washed over the ship, leaving the main deck flooded in water two feet deep, the scuppers overwhelmed.

"He's the one spotted that first wave during the calm. He's the one that called down to the captain," Mr. Boyle says. From his perch at the top of the mast, Thomas had sighted a wall of white water on the horizon already as tall as the ship, driven by the blast of some distant wind. He called the alarm. The captain ordered him down, instructed the helmsman to turn the ship to port and meet the surge at the bow—not dead on, but at an angle to slice through the wave.

The previously-welcomed calm became our foe. Without a wind, *The Pelican* could not be turned as the captain ordered, and was at the mercy of the current. The ship weltered sidelong into the path of the rogue wave.

The captain had wisely ordered life lines for the men on deck;

surely this saved their lives. It was a wonder not more had been lost, Mr. Boyle says. A miracle.

"He couldn't get down in time." Mr. Boyle runs the palms of his hands over his face. "He couldn't get down."

He is quiet for a moment, staring across the gray water. "He was the same age as my boy, Ciarán," he says, shaking his head as if to unsettle the image. "Captain should have gone further south. It takes more time, but it's easier, the further south. He'd never had trouble at that latitude before, but…Easy to know now, I suppose." With a heavy sigh, he looks at me, "And what about you? How've you fared?"

Although I think it may be trite to complain, I consider that Mr. Boyle might want something to distract his mind from imagining a son lost to the sea. "I am bruises all over. I hit my head on the cabin door." I show him the acorn-sized knot on the side of my head. "And I jammed my finger, reaching for something to hold. The straps helped a great deal." I do not divulge any more details of our ordeal below; they seem minor now.

"My wounds are nothing compared to Mr. Rathburn. He was in the main cabin when a barrel broke loose of its ties. He had already been thrown to the deck with one of the swells. Then the cask rolled over his leg before hitting the bulkhead and splintering. His leg was broken, but it could not be set until the pitching stopped. The poor man was in agony for several hours, screaming every time his leg was jostled in the least, which was quite often. He finally used one of the splinters from the barrel staves to bite on so his shrieks would not further disturb the children."

"His leg is set now, right?"

"Oh yes. The carpenter found two straight slats in the

workroom. He set the leg then fashioned a crutch so that Mr. Rathburn could get about the ship."

"Ah, good man," Mr. Boyle says. He grabs the railing and looks up at the masts. "Now that he's finished his doctoring, I'll get him to help Mr. Hester. We lost two topsails in the wind. Ripped right off the rigging as if they were handkerchiefs pinned up to dry. Dry." He sighs and shakes his head again. "There's five inches of standing water in the main cabin—I can't think how we'll get that bailed out. Seems some idiot forgot to close the hatch on the quarterdeck.

"She's sound," he muses. "She's not ready to give herself to the sea. The cargo hardly shifted, although I doubt that set of china will've survived. We had only to move a few of the ballasts to correct that list to starboard…" His voice trails off, but the idle chatter and the inventory of chores seem to help him regain his composure. We had passed Cape Horn several days ago, but storms continued to batter the ship until yesterday. No one had time to take stock before this. "All of the Dunsfords come through all right?" I nod. "What was in the barrel? The one that broke poor Mr. Rathburn's leg?"

"Sacks of flour."

"Ah." Mr. Boyle closes his eyes. "Flour. Covered in five inches of salt water for more than a week. If the sacks didn't bust apart, I'll have bags of cement. If they did, there'll be flour in everything. That'll be a fine mess to clean. Is your cabin dry?"

"Yes. Some of the standing water splashes in when we open the door, if the ship is rocking, but we are mostly dry."

Mr. Boyle stares at me for a long time, reaching to tuck an unruly lock of hair behind my ear to keep it from blowing into my eyes. Several times he opens his mouth as if to speak, but then changes his mind. Finally, he says "What were your aunt and uncle thinking? What was your father thinking?"

He looks away, brings his hands to his temples and rubs hard. "Do you remember when you asked me, when we left Rio, if I liked having children aboard? Well I don't. Children shouldn't be on a ship. Ever."

He rises abruptly and stomps toward the deck house, leaving me alone, shivering with cold and thoughts of the youthful Thomas whom I have never met.

Mr. Boyle finds more to do than make sails and bail out the main cabin. During the next week, sailors are more active than usual, swarming over the ship, scraping decks and railings, painting and scrubbing, taking wire brushes to the cleats and other pieces of exposed metal to eliminate any tarnish, applying grease and tar wherever needed, preparing oakum and tediously shoving it between exposed boards. Mr. Boyle is pleased that the ship has sustained no major injuries during the rounding, but the severe weather has still battered and bruised her as much as any of us.

It rains daily, but the winds hold and we move steadily north into warmer climes, the days lengthening again. There still is no normalcy about winter in August, but the daily improvements help.

Papa's letter spoke of such times and I pull the letter from my portmanteau to read his words again.

July 15, 1847

My darling daughter:

I am grateful for my life, although I do not know who to thank. I have been most certain, for the better part of the last four weeks, that I would be no more.

It is calm now, although raining. The winds are favorable and I am happy to be leaving Cape Horn behind. I hope never to see that monster again.

Hourly I requested the honor of death. More than once I thought my wish had been granted. But, alas.

I can hardly find the words to describe the terror that has governed the ship since we left Rio de Janeiro far behind—it has been as if all of the earth's wrath were concentrated at the bottom of the world, ready to plunge the ship and its inhabitants into the black cauldron of seawater that is churned, unstopping, night after endless night (for there is no day here); bending us, breaking us at its whim.

My body, weakened by the sickness that I have not yet overcome (with doubts that I ever will), is even still cut and bruised, rubbed raw and bleeding from the ropes that held me to my berth during the violence that accompanied us from Patagonia in the Atlantic to the Pacific Ocean. However, those same ropes were the only reason I was not dashed to pieces on the deck. I hated their presence, yet welcomed their safety. I loathed that my heart pounded at my ribs with the force of a sledgehammer, whilst knowing that its beat meant I was still living, albeit reluctantly. I cannot explain and perhaps you are too young and I should not try. Please forgive me.

Know that it has been the memory of your sweet face and your laughter that has helped me heal, now that we are in calmer waters—most welcome after the horrors of Cape Horn. You are safe in Boston and your father is alive in the Pacific; I can ask for no more.

Your always affectionate,
Papa

I find the letter less frightening upon reading again. Perhaps it is that I understand better the things about which he wrote. Perhaps it is just that now it is a common experience; something that Papa and I have both been through, even if not together. Except the sickness; I am glad that I have not shared Papa's experience of seasickness.

Mr. Boyle says that it is rare, but some people never get used to the sea. Almost everyone is ill the first three days of a voyage, even some of the sailors. But by the fourth day, as long as the seas are relatively calm, it is common for everyone to feel as if they have been on a boat all of their lives. My father just happens to be one of the rare ones.

In this instance, I am just as happy to be among the commonplace.

Lizzie is in love, or so it seems.

I first noticed a change in her after the storms of Cape Horn, after Thomas' memorial. Everyone on the ship took care to talk quietly and politely to everyone else. The gambling, although not ceasing, became cordial. The drinking resulted in tears and embraces rather than fisticuffs. Everyone and everything was altered, Lizzie most of all.

She abruptly left off torturing her siblings, instead taking mending and small pieces of embroidery onto the deck, spending hours sitting near my new reading post. Had it not been for the wind that whipped her light hair and the substantial shawl draped over her shoulders she could have been a young lady in a drawing room, sitting with needle in hand. Very little of the embroidery got done.

As the camaraderie of the shared nightmare faded and passengers and crew got back to their routines Lizzie did not. She remained quiet and wistful, a secret smile hovering at the corners of her mouth, a demur cast to her blue eyes. She brightened when approached by one of the other passengers or even her parents, slipping back into reverie as soon as the person's back was turned.

At the same time that Lizzie began her transformation, Mr. Boyle began to act strangely too.

Whereas I enjoy the new Lizzie, I am not at all pleased with Mr. Boyle. He is abrupt when he speaks, which is seldom, and intolerant of mistake made by the crew. He stamps his feet when he walks and mutters to himself as he makes his rounds of the ship.

When I ask him what is wrong, he shouts at me that I am to mind my own business and stop prying all of the time. I ask too many questions, he says, and he has no time for that; no time at all.

He develops the habit of interrupting conversations by walking into the middle of them and escorting at least one of the speakers away. Several times I notice him doing this with Lizzie. When the Cecchi brothers approach as she is sewing on the deck, soon Mr. Boyle happens by, throws his arm across the shoulders of each young man, and leads them to a different part of the deck with a tale I cannot hear.

Once, when Matthew came near to show me something he discovered in one of his books, Mr. Boyle was suddenly at our side taking Matthew by the arm and asking his opinion on the construction of a storm-protection device of some kind that Mr. Boyle had in mind for the next Horn approach. He is everywhere, reminding me of the sheepdog that Uncle John adopted who, in the absence of sheep, had taken to herding the cousins into tight groups, nipping at our heels if we ran away or bowling us over if we wandered too far afield.

Mrs. Dunsford has her own campaign of diversion with respect to Lizzie and the Cecchis. Most days she joins her daughter by bringing knitting or sewing onto the sunlit deck. She usually sits someplace between Lizzie and me, including me in her conversation. I listen for a while, then go back to my book as I soon lose track of the numerous branches of Mrs. Dunsfords' family (her favorite subject of conversation). Weddings and funerals and holidays in Lowell must have been confusing affairs with Crawleys (for that is her maiden name) and Dunsfords and other extended family assembling together in various locales. She claims the gatherings were so large that she once spent an entire day and did not speak with the same person twice. I fear this may have been because she completely forgot previous conversations, but do not say so.

Surprisingly, this parental vigilance does little to discourage the Cecchis. They are attentive to Lizzie and respectful of Mrs. Dunsford too. In the beginning, I cannot tell which brother is the more interested in the girl as they both seem to have plenty of time and opportunity to hover and roughhouse close to the sewing circle. Eventually the elder brother, Antonio, tires of the game and finds other pursuits. Roberto, who insists to all (except his mother) that he be called Robert, becomes the chief hoverer.

Robert is a square boy: square face, square hands, square shoulders. I think he looks like a pedestal. He is seventeen and anxious for a life in California.

"He was born in a town in Italy called Castellina in Chianti. *Castellina* means 'little castle,' isn't that wonderful? He was born in a little castle," Lizzie gushes one evening as we gather in the mess for supper. "His family lived in New York for ten years, but every time they thought they'd saved enough money to buy a farm, the price had gone too high and they couldn't afford it. Well his uncle was in California and wrote that there's much good farmland there and it's very affordable, so they sold everything in New York and bought fares to California. They're certain they'll find a farm there." I wonder when she will take a breath.

"Lizzie, I'm sure this boy is nice," the Reverend interjects, "but you will meet many other young men that will be better suited for you."

She takes a breath. "Why is Robert not suited for me?"

"He's Italian, dear," Mrs. Dunsford offers in a soft voice, patting her daughter's hand, exchanging glances with the Reverend. "That means he's Catholic."

I think of crows and the wedge of shiny black hair that often blows in Robert's eyes.

Lizzie pales and is silent the remainder of supper.

When the meal ends, I escape the mess. I feel sorry for Lizzie. Nothing more was said about Robert, but his presence was felt. I think of him as Guleesh dining in the halls of the French king, maintaining his invisibility as he carefully watches over the unhappy princess. Lizzie looks like a discarded stocking by the finish of supper.

Not wishing to be smothered by the sadness that would surely accompany Lizzie to the cabin, I stroll the decks, enduring the cold to gaze at the stars and the half-moon which glows like a debutante hiding behind a fan. One good outcome of surviving Cape Horn is that the Dunsfords have eased their rules, at least a little, and I no longer must ask permission to go on deck at night.

The Pelican has made good progress for several weeks and the Pacific Ocean is living up to its name: the skies are clear, the wind strong and steady and heading in the desired direction. The hours of daylight continue to increase as we journey closer to the equator. Cold; it is still very cold, but the weather warms every day the further north we travel.

The flirtatious half-moon reminds me of Mama. I see her standing in the doorway of our home in Boston, the glass beads of her dark purple gown sparkling like stars, my father placing a cape over her bare shoulders. The velvet cloak was black like the night sky with a dusting of light along the folds and drapes like the sweep of stars in the Milky Way.

My parents had plans to go to the theater; I was to stay with Mrs. Schrader. They did not see me in the shadows on the stairs where I pouted. I was most unhappy that I would not be going with them despite assurances that I would be bored at the play.

As my father turned to get his hat, Mama's cape slipped from one shoulder. She caught the wrap deftly, pulling it back into place. But when Papa turned again toward her, she deliberately let it fall once more, the round whiteness of her shoulder gleaming against the dark of her dress, the dark of the cloak. She raised the mantle slowly into place before lowering it a second time. Even in the half-light I could see her eyes crinkled at the corners, a smile on her lips, the single shoulder vibrant as it waxed and waned.

Finally, my father reached his slender fingers to clasp the cloak, gently raising it to its proper place. He nuzzled his nose against her cheek. "We shall be late. Come along," he whispered.

Then they left. I sat at the top of the stairs wishing I could hear the music to which they danced. For that is how it looked to me: a playful dance in the doorway. I wanted to go with them.

"Are you lost in one of your fairytales?"

I jump. It is Mr. Boyle who has come to my side without a sound. "How can you walk on this deck without someone hearing you?"

"I can't. The watch went by a quarter of an hour ago and you didn't move. I could've been an elephant and you'd not've heard me."

"Have you ever seen an elephant?"

He said no and asked if I had. "Yes, in Boston. Papa and Mama took me to see the menagerie when I was six. There was an elephant there. It was like nothing I had ever seen before. She was so large and made a sound like a bugle, only louder. I think there is not another animal on earth like an elephant."

The creature had been standing in the middle of a corral, cordoned off with velvet ropes, her back leg chained to a post.

She rocked back and forth as she shifted her weight from foot to foot. Her eyes were closed. I remembered thinking that it must have been lonely for her. In the midst of the crowd that had come to gawk, this uncommon creature was alone.

"Do you hate Catholics, Mr. Boyle?"

"How do you come to talk about elephants and Catholics in the same breath?"

I shrug. At supper, Lizzie had seemed as alone as that menagerie elephant despite the presence of her family. "I do not know. I was merely thinking. Do you? Hate Catholics, I mean?"

"I should think not; I am one. Although I can't claim to be a very good one." He leans against the railing and looks up at the stars. "Lizzie's found out the Cecchi lad's Catholic, I suppose," he says after a long silence. It is not a question. "I wonder which of their hearts'll be most broken. She's quite nice when she's in love, isn't she?"

I laugh as I nod in agreement. "Will you be back, now that Lizzie is not in love anymore?" I ask.

As he turns to me, the moonlight reveals a curious look on his face and I expect him to protest his innocence or make excuses for his odd behavior.

"You don't know that she's not still in love. Besides, I've you and Matthew to worry about, don't I? Mrs. Dunsford's not yet mindful of that, is she?"

"I beg your pardon?"

"You and Matthew. Isn't he your sweetheart?"

I wrinkle my nose and shake my head.

"Well I stopped by Mrs. Reynolds' the morning *The Pelican* was to leave the wharf. All of you had left already, but she told me that you and Matthew had run away in Rio the day before and she sent the police after you."

"We were not running away! We were exploring. We were coming back on our own."

Mr. Boyle asks where we had gone and, when I tell him, he is not pleased. He rants about the location, the distance from Mrs. Reynolds' house, and the dangers to which we opened ourselves.

"I know. Mrs. Reynolds already said all of that."

"Well it's true. You should pay attention and not think adults are just being cautious and stupid." He shakes his head and blows air from his lips like a horse. "You are certain that you and Matthew're not going to run away together? He's not your sweetheart?" I shake my head for the hundredth time. "Well I'd best hear nothing different in future. I've already given orders to the watch never to let two children on deck together after dark. There'll be no youthful swiving on my ship."

"What does that mean? 'Swiving'?"

"Oh, for…never mind," he sputters. "I'm sorry. You're never to repeat that, do you hear me? That word is not to come out of your mouth. The Reverend and your father'll have my head."

"But what does it mean?"

"It is an expression my father used. It means…well, it's not very nice, but it means…kissing and such; much more about the 'such.' It's not polite and certainly's nothing a young lady should know about."

I think it is too late for that, but say nothing.

"So, I'm turning in before I get myself in more trouble. I just wanted to be sure the watch does their job. Most of the men'll do as I ask. But, I fear there're one or two would gladly dump the boy in the sea and take his place."

I am certain he means Robert Cecchi rather than Matthew.

I nearly ask why he has such concern for the doings of the children on board, given that he does not care for their presence in the first place. However, I remain silent since every question I have, every sentence I form seems too harsh and accusing. I am afraid he will simply be angry with me and stop talking. I have missed talking with him.

"I've a daughter Lizzie's age, you know. One your age too," he says softly, answering the question I did not ask. "I hope that someone is watching out for them back home, doing what I'm doing now.

"Except the bad words part…I don't want any daughter of mine knowing such things."

CHAPTER 7

August 4, 1848

WE WILL NOT STOP IN Valparaiso, Chili as my father had. We are to anchor at Callao, Peru. Mr. Boyle calls it the armpit of Peru then speculates that this must make the beautiful Lima the lowered shoulder of the Andes. I compliment the poetry of his description for which I receive a snort in reply.

I will never learn anything about Callao and neither will the other passengers. Soon after signaling the port captain of our presence, the ship is met by the customary officials breathless with tidings: the city is swarming with half-mad newcomers. There are rumors that gold has been discovered in California, so now the world wants to go there.

When pressed, the administrators admit this to be an exaggeration. Instead of "the world," it is only several hundred strangers who are in the city now although more arrive every day seeking passage on any ship that might take them north to the new American territory. The hotels and inns and boardinghouses, up to the boundaries of Lima, are at capacity. With formal shelter no longer available (or affordable, as the prices have risen astonishingly overnight) the hopefuls erect tents in the city common areas or sleep in the streets and doorways. With the rising population, city officials fear outbreaks of any number of diseases. There is grave concern that the streets will soon be sloppy with filth (which Mr. Boyle thinks is an exaggeration too as the streets were sloppy with filth the last time he landed here, or so he says).

The Reverend reveals this at supper as we lay anchored in the shelter of Callao's inlet; Mr. Boyle confided the news to him.

"Gold in California!" the Reverend repeats. "Can you imagine? The ink of the treaty with Mexico is hardly dry! Our newest territory will be a great boon for America." He is so excited that, had I not known his whereabouts for the last several months, I could believe he made the discovery himself.

"The officials are hesitant to let us dock because ours is one of the few ships actually bound for San Francisco and they think we may be overrun with emigrants. Mr. Boyle was none too pleased with that news as it will be harder to unload the cargo without docking," the Reverend continues, puffed with importance. "The Captain and Mr. Boyle rowed into town this evening to assess the situation." They will be there for a day or two, to augment our supplies and seek out the owners of the Callao-bound goods *The Pelican* carries—the dock workers have already left for California so these owners must be willing to unload the cargo themselves.

Captain Watson and Mr. Boyle return the next day and go straight to the captain's cabin with Mr. Sterbenc, Cook, and the carpenter in tow. They emerge a few hours later in high spirits. Cigar smoke belches from the cabin and chokes the corridors with a pewter-colored haze. I am astonished to see Mr. Boyle slap Mr. Sterbenc on the back, both of their faces bright with drink and camaraderie.

That night after Mr. Boyle once again goes ashore with a

small troop of men, the captain gathers everyone in the main cabin.

"We will be taking on more passengers," he announces, another cigar in hand. "Over the next few days, there is much work to be done to accommodate this. It will be an inconvenience for all of you, I'm sure, and for that I apologize in advance. We will work on the second-class cabins first, ensuring they all have four bunks. Then the women and children and their families will be moved there for the remainder of the voyage. No extra charge."

He receives a hearty cheer from the family men following this announcement.

"Next, additional bunks will be added in the main cabin. I ask your cooperation for the carpenter, Mr. Lopes, and his crew— they will endeavor to accomplish this quickly.

"As compensation, just prior to setting sail from Callao, each of the remaining main cabin passengers will be given a keg of rum," he declares, then motions for one of the sailors to raise a small barrel over his head in demonstration. "I would distribute them sooner, but we want everyone fit to *move* out of the way while construction is on-going." A great deal of laughter follows this statement.

Then the chaos begins. Mr. Boyle and his crew arrive the following day with a flat boat filled with lumber and straw, barrels of nails, and other building supplies. Once the materials are on board, the hold is opened and the crew lifts several nets of cargo onto the flat boat which then returns to shore.

Almost as soon as the lumber has touched the decks, the carpenter begins to build. Five additional men are hired for the work, all of them small, wiry men with dark skin like the Brazilians, speaking a language I do not think is Portuguese. Fortunately, the carpenter speaks their language well. They attack the second-class cabins while the sail maker Mr. Hester stuffs straw into canvas bags for use as mattresses.

The flat boat returns, again filled with provisions: barrels of food and fresh water, large hunks of cured meats, live chickens and pigs. Cook growls instructions for the storage with an enthusiastic goodwill that belies his roar.

Two days later, the main cabin is transformed. Where once there had been fourteen well-spaced berths there are now sixty-four bunks, two wide and two high with additional bunks capping off each end of a row and barely room in between for the passengers to walk. In the days that follow, those of us in the cabins adopt the habit of opening our door only slightly and calling a warning before swinging it wide so as not to hit someone just emerging from bed.

On the 'tween deck, under the forecastle, more berths are constructed. Cargo is shifted to accommodate this request. Since the excess cargo of the main cabin was stowed there as well, I imagine the hold must be more crowded than ever. Using a narrow stairwell behind the captain's galley, I venture below for a closer look, but am soon escorted back to the stairs by one of the sailors I often see with Mr. Boyle. He stays at the foot of the steps to ensure that I return to the main deck. I have the impression that the man was forewarned that I might undertake to be there.

Three additional crew are hired to help Cook. The meals, which had gradually lost wholesomeness since our stay in Rio, improve once more. Abundant and hot, the food causes no complaints while we are in port.

The sound of sawing and hammering and swearing fills the days, ceasing only for the Reverend's weekly sermon in which he chooses to speak of Jesus' original profession and the benefits of industrious labor: *Is not this the carpenter, the son of Mary and brother of James and Joses and Judas and Simon?*

Mark and Luke stay out of the way by playing in the rigging and, for the first time, nobody seems to mind. The boys find sticks from the rubble and transform them into swords. Having nearly been thrown overboard by an overly enthusiastic Luke, John decides that marching his tin soldiers in the safety of the cabin is a better choice than playing with his brothers. Mary is usually content to have me or her mother read to her or to join her littlest brother at his play. Anna is the most difficult to keep entertained and out of the fray. Walking on deck is dangerous enough, what with all of the activity, but Anna wants to run, to climb the stairs, to swing from the railings or the rigging as her brothers do. When Mrs. Dunsford needs a rest from the child, the task of keeping Anna corralled falls to Lizzie and, once in a while, Matthew.

Lizzie accepts her duties with regard to Anna gracefully. She was only mildly changed after the announcement of Robert's conflicting religion. The day following the suppertime declaration he approached her as she stitched at her perch on the main deck, as usual. She was cordial, also as usual, but there was a reserve about her that he soon noticed. He tried again the next day and the day after that, but eventually withdrew, as his brother had before him. He only occasionally advanced thereafter. They were civil with each other and were still seen speaking near the railings at times. I expected tears, but perhaps the romance was not as serious as Mr. Boyle and Mrs. Dunsford had first supposed.

Gold (or rather the rumor of gold) brightens the mood of everyone on *The Pelican*. The frenzy of activity has a zeal to it that was not there during repairs of the ship after Cape Horn. I do not understand it fully, although gold figures frequently in my books. There is talk on board of little else as everyone goes about their labors. I think about gold often too, wondering what Papa thought when he heard the news that gold was near at hand. Without reward, I scour my books once more for some clues as to the power of this mysterious stuff.

The day the new passengers come aboard is startling. They are mostly male, from young men to ancient fellows; I count only five women among the hoard. The vast majority speak only Spanish (for I have learned that this is the language of the ship's carpenter). Some appear well-to-do; others look to be struggling in life. Some cart their possessions on their shoulders. Many carry packages crudely wrapped in hides that cannot conceal pickaxes and shovels tied with thin ropes and bearing some kind of mark that identifies the owner. These bundles seem to be precious to those who have them and are protected diligently. Any one of these hopefuls might be rich in the gold fields of California within months and I believe it is this thought that buoys their spirits for they enter the ship jostling and laughing.

I watch from the open door of our compartment as the newcomers file into the main cabin, letting eyes adjust to the dim light before finding their way to an empty berth. The night before, the captain recommended that all of the existing passengers stay in their cabins or berths while the new arrivals board and get themselves settled. This was to prevent any misunderstanding about occupancy.

Their numbers seem endless, their reception from the existing passengers cool in contrast to the amity among them. The kegs of liquor were doled out that morning, but as none have been opened none of the rum's warmth is yet felt.

Where once there were only a dozen inhabitants of the main cabin, there are now more than sixty; more continue to board. After inspecting the receipts each has in hand, the sailors direct another twenty or so into the hold, to the newest bunks under the forecastle. As my count inside the main cabin extends, I squeeze through the throng to the deck and the crowd there.

From relative safety behind a water barrel, I end my tally at one hundred and sixteen new passengers. Including Cook's latest assistants, *The Pelican* now carries one hundred fifty-nine souls, passengers and crew.

As soon as the last man steps on deck, the ladder is raised, railing secured, and the order given to weigh anchor. A deafening cheer rises from the new passengers as *The Pelican* surges forward, starting maneuvers in the harbor that will take us to the open sea once more. We never came close to a wharf.

"Poor dears," Mrs. Dunsford exclaims as I re-enter our cabin. "They've spent weeks trying to get passage, the Reverend told me."

She speaks to no one in particular, but Mrs. Dunsford often does this and I do not think long about it.

"Not many have brought their wives, so I suppose they don't intend to stay in California long," she notes, idly combing Anna's hair, trying to prevent the child from running out to the decks. "I wonder where they came from? I don't think any of them speak English. Guinevere, have you heard any of them speak English?"

I shake my head. "Some of the sailors speak Spanish; at least enough to order the others about."

"Surely they must speak English in California; although it has been a Mexican territory…Does Mr. Boyle speak Spanish, do you think? He seemed to get along quite well in Brazil, didn't he? He must spend a lot of time there. Hold still, Anna. The more you wiggle, the more it will hurt."

Our cabin door and the porthole are open, allowing a scant breeze to pass through; the day has become warm. I volunteer to take Anna onto the main deck and into the fresh air to run. It has taken hours for the passengers to come aboard and I am as restless as the child.

The deck has never been so active. Many of the new passengers are at the railings, watching as the shores of Peru fade to a blue distance. The rest are lounging on the hold coverings, for that is to be where they will sleep. In the bright sun, they talk and laugh among one another, one man singing as he strums a battered guitar that quickly goes out of tune in the humidity—he does not seem to mind and neither do the others around him. Several pause and smile or laugh as Anna sprints among them, waving her arms and giggling at her freedom.

With the hatch covers thus occupied, once again I realize I must search for a new location in which to read.

CHAPTER 8

August 13, 1848

THE GOODWILL AND HIGH SPIRITS that accompanied *The Pelican's* new passengers does not last more than a day. That may be because a number of them are immediately seasick as we pull out of the shelter of Callao's inlet. Even though the original passengers were just as ill when we left New York, the living conditions under which we find ourselves after Peru make it all the more obvious and contagious. There are too many people and no place for anyone to go to hide their sickness.

Sailors swab the decks every fifteen minutes or so and gather many buckets of seawater with which to wash down the hull of the ship at regular intervals. To accommodate our greater numbers, some prudent person had ordered construction of a new ship's head. Even so, both heads are usually occupied by ill passengers or crew members. Wait times are long and often the railings must serve.

Mr. Boyle's insistence upon clean decks creates a great deal of work for the crew. In one passing moment, when he has time to say anything to me, Mr. Boyle complains that most of the new passengers have never seen a ship before, let alone been on one.

As Mr. Boyle predicted, within three days the queasiness passes for almost everyone. However, that does not improve conditions. Once they are well again, passengers adopt the past-times in which the original travelers had indulged from the beginning of the voyage: drinking, smoking, gambling, and fighting. Now the numbers make it impossible to ignore or sleep through the noise.

The captain gave his introductory reading of the rules the first evening, painfully translated by the carpenter, Mr. Lopes, who was the most fluent among the crew in both English and Spanish. I say "painfully" because the poor man is shy and has a soft voice (except when instructing his crew on building a berth) as well as a pronounced stammer which is obvious even to those of us who understand no Spanish. He is constantly urged to speak louder and, when he does, the stammer becomes more obvious. I was bored following the captain's original delivery of the rules in New York; I am nearly spent by the end of the two-language version.

Again, the instructions go unheeded.

I keep to the cabin more than before; it is the only place where I can read without interruption. Plus, with the door closed, it smells better than anywhere else on the ship.

I still venture on deck at odd intervals for I find that I miss the sky and the breeze and the chance to simply lean against a railing and think about San Francisco and my father. Finding spare space or getting to the mess or the head is like running a gauntlet: dodging reeling bodies; stepping around groups of men huddled over barrels converted to dice tables; avoiding pools of vomit that stink like old cheese and smell sweetly of rum. English and Spanish curses are thrown across hands of cards while whoops of encouragement and dissatisfaction in multiple languages surround every fistfight. There seem to be many more of the latter, as everyone presses together. Mr. Boyle and, surprisingly, Mr. Sterbenc try their best to keep the peace, but they are sorely outnumbered.

With unabashed joy, the Reverend discovers that attendance at his sermons soars. He is soon preaching from the quarterdeck (with permission from the captain, of course) overlooking a main deck that is packed to capacity. It does not seem to matter that the majority of the Reverend's words are a mystery to this congregation. With hats removed and heads bowed, they nod at the sound of Jesus and Mary's names, palms pressed in prayer or raised to the sky whenever the Reverend speaks of God, a response of quiet fervor at each "Amen." One look at the Reverend's face or the way his belief lifts his shoulders seems to convince everyone of the glory of God. Well, perhaps that is not true for the still-seasick passengers who pale when the Reverend intones: "*The Lord on high is mightier than the noise of many waters, yea, than the mighty waves of the sea.*"

It is unfortunate that such respite happens only one day each week.

The families of original passengers eat in the mess still, but everyone else lines up for each meal at the galley entrance to be handed a plate of food that is taken back to a berth or a customary spot on the hatch covers. This speeds each mealtime considerably, but means a wider area for the sailors to clean.

Ten days out of Callao, *The Pelican* once again crosses the equator, this time without calls to watch for the line. On the journey south much was made of the crossing—the sailors shouting for everyone to keep an eye open for the equatorial line across the ocean's water, so as not to miss it. By day's end many of the passengers swore they had seen a line. I had not and thought the others were lying, ultimately pleased that Mr. Boyle agreed with my theory that the entire affair was a hoax (although he did not bother to say this until after the "line" was well behind us). Thankfully this second crossing gives rise to no such nonsense.

The Pelican swelters at night and bakes during the day now that August has taken on its usual summer traits. The days are at full length and the skies darken only occasionally for a brief, warm downpour. The deck passengers bear the drenching well, steam rising from their blankets and coats once the sun peeks through the clouds again. Fortunately it has not rained after sunset so everything dries quickly.

Even in the early morning hours, our cabin's porthole is opened wide to let some heat out and air in. The few ladies on board carry fans.

The Pelican is anchored for a time while her small craft is dispatched to a town called Acapulco to replenish our freshwater supply (which has run short sooner than expected). We do not linger once the additional barrels are delivered to the ship and, after the crew and passengers endure another harangue from the captain about washing and laundering only in seawater, we quickly leave the port behind.

I am finished with sailing. I have nothing left to read, having gone through my books at least six times each including the novel that Papa ordered from England just before he sailed for San Francisco: *Oliver Twist*. It is my new favorite, but still I am tired of the Artful Dodger and his mates.

Only the sunsets break the monotony now. They are more beautiful than any I remember. I could watch from the porthole in our cabin (except when the ship tacks directly into the sun). However, the porthole viewing seems too restricted. So each evening I brave the crush of people at the railing as rays strike the clouds with gold, tinting the crests the color of a ripe plum. Bright rose chases the gold, slowly fading to gray as the sun disappears into the smooth blue line of ocean. The spectacle is so different from the sunsets in Boston where the city and its trees darken to silhouette against the glow.

It was a strange February day for Boston. It was unseasonably warm, causing the snow to soften and rivulets of water to form in the streets and splash up behind the carriages in dirty clouds.

We arrived late at the pier. Papa quickly hugged me and kissed my forehead and repeated that he would be back. For the hundredth time, he told me to be a good girl. Then he said a brief goodbye to Aunt Margaret and Uncle John before boarding the ship, assuring them that he would carry their blessings to Uncle James in San Francisco. I could tell he was anxious to go; not happy, just anxious.

We had spent the previous evening in argument.

"Why must you go, Papa?"

Dropping the last of the shirts into his trunk, Papa turned. "You will be safe here with your aunt and uncle."

"But why?"

He covered his face with one hand for a moment. When he looked up, his eyes were red. "I have to go. There are too many memories..."

"But why?"

"Dammit, Guine, stop whining. We have been through this before. You will be better off with your aunt and uncle and I do not wish to hear another word about it, do you understand?" I reluctantly nodded. "There is a good girl. Your cousins made no fuss when your Uncle James left for California, did they?"

I could not remember, as that had been a year ago. Alfred complained to me often that his father was away, but perhaps he had said nothing to Papa.

"You will have ponies to ride and your cousins to play with," Papa says. "You like your new school do you not? You have made new friends? What more could a little girl ask?"

Mama, I thought; I could ask for Mama. Or him.

Papa would not listen and would not change his plans; certainly he had no intention of changing his plans for me. We spoke no further that night, no word at all.

The following day, as his ship sailed through Boston Harbor, I waved until I could see Papa no longer. Uncle John finally took my hand and pulled me away, promising a lovely dessert with supper.

On the return to their house I asked to ride on the box so as to see the coming sunset. I climbed next to Uncle John and settled myself as he clicked his tongue and snapped the reins. Aunt Margaret complained that she would be on the seat all by herself, but I could tell she was only pretending to pout.

The setting sun was blinding as it hovered over the trees and houses of Boston, but I did not mind. I briefly closed my eyes to avoid the glare, pretending to be somewhere over the English Channel, fleeing from France, riding a magical horse that could soar farther and faster than any bird. I opened my eyes as the sun washed the clouds a bright golden pink, the sky above still bright and blue in the fading light. It promised to be a near perfect sunset to my mind.

It was certainly a perfect time of day to be riding an invisible creature. A call of "Hie over cap!" and I knew that my magical steed could bound beyond Boston and fly past New York heading for Pennsylvania. How many leaps would it take to get me all of the way west, all of the way to San Francisco? I could be there before Papa if I tried.

As the colors faded from the sky, I closed my eyes again, flying higher and faster on the fairytale animal. I pictured the wind blowing my hair behind me in long shimmering waves, blending with the tail of the horse. I flung my arms wide, ready to yell the words that would signal my horse to bound across the countryside, leaping ever west. Perhaps if I stood just as he jumped, he would carry me further and faster. If I stood, I would be less of a burden.

I stood, sure of my footing, sure of the power of the horse.

Then I was in Uncle John's arms. He had stopped the carriage and was holding me, stroking my back, making soft shushing noises as if I were a spooked and nervous animal. I was vaguely aware that he turned to the seat behind and snapped, "Be quiet, Margaret." It was the first and only time I heard my uncle speak sharply to his wife. I nestled closer into his winter coat, the soft wool caressing my face.

I did not remember the carriage moving again nor arriving at the house in Brookline. I did remember Uncle John handing the reins to Lester and carrying me inside, up the stairs and into the room that was called mine. I was quiet, but he did not stop making his soothing sounds. He set me on the bed and gave instructions for my shoes and stockings to be removed and for someone to prepare me for bed. The room darkened as he left.

It was Uncle John who brought the bowl of soup, placing the tray in front of me as I sat propped against a pile of pillows. The lace of my new nightgown, a gift from Papa, scratched against my throat. Uncle John sat straight-backed in the chair he had pulled to my bedside, urging me to eat. I did not eat, nor did I look at him or speak to him; I did not think I could. He stayed until greasy yellow dots formed on the surface of the soup. Then he took it away and had the fire stoked.

Hovering outside the door Aunt Margaret asked him what was wrong with me; what was wrong with that child? I did not hear his response.

He returned to sit again in the chair after shadows had swallowed everything else in the room. He said nothing to me this time, which was alright. I could see the glow of his pipe in the darkness, smelling of cherry pie baking in the oven. I liked the smell of Uncle John's pipe. Sometime later, he left again when I did not respond to the sound of my name. The room became colder after that.

The sounds of the house drifted up the stairs: a clink of plates cleared from the supper table, doors closing, the creak of floorboards. My aunt and uncle climbed the stairs and went to their rooms, one of them stopping to listen at my door for a moment before moving on. I remained still long after that, waiting for the house to quiet.

Sometime after moonrise I swung my legs to the floor, retrieving my coat and shoes and grabbing the comforter from the bed. I dressed and eased down the stairs to the kitchen, through the door that led to the backyard, across the snow to the barn.

The horses stomped and snorted at my intrusion. They soon recognized me, quieting once again. The sheepdog woofed softly as he ran to my side, his body wiggling, his tongue sopping my face. He normally slept in one of the horse stalls, toward the back. I headed there.

Uncle John found me in the morning with one arm thrown across the body of the sheepdog, my face buried in the sour stink of his fur, the comforter muddy with paw prints. As Uncle John approached, the dog lifted his head in acknowledgment and thumped his tail loudly on the hay that lay beneath us.

Aunt Margaret started her first missive to my father that morning.

I believe I know what to expect of the voyage from this time forward because of Papa's last letter.

September 10, 1847

My darling Guine,

As I write this I stand at the railing to watch the ship sail into San Francisco Bay. Yes I am actually upright and in the fresh air for I have refused to stay abed on the last days of the journey. The weather has been most temperate and calm, for which I am thankful. As you can imagine, I am anxious for this voyage to end.

I have ventured on deck at least once each day during the past week. My legs are weak and my clothes hang on me in copious folds, but the sights have given my heart such joy that I find I can no longer stay below. This ordeal is almost at an end.

I first made the effort to be on deck when the ship neared the coast of Mexico. What a wild and rugged place Mexico appears to be: tall mountains covered with jungle that march all the way to brilliant and pristine stretches of beach. At times, the cliffs fall directly into the sea without benefit of sand. It is very like Brazil in its beauty.

Then came the coast of Lower California, as dry and inhospitable a place as ever I have seen. The lush green of Mexico was behind us and there was nothing save bleached hills and deserts with only the occasional shrub close to the ground and wanting for water. I saw little except dry earth that reached inland for several miles before finally climbing to faded blue mountains, wreathed in clouds. My first thought was horror: can all of California be like this? I was assured that only the southernmost part of the territory is of this nature.

Once past the island of Santa Catalina and a large "pueblo" that bears an exceedingly long name (thankfully shortened to "Los Angeles"), the coast began to assume a much more pleasing character: long stretches of white sands, majestic cliffs with waves washing their bases and dark green trees at their crests. Beyond, the land is lush and green, trees covering the mountains that stand a short distance inland. I sense a rugged calmness like nothing I have seen in New England. There are few towns; the land is mostly wilderness.

Yesterday we stopped briefly in a cove near the town of

Monterey to gather mail for delivery north and pay the tariff on the goods we carry. It is heartening to know that the money no longer goes to the Mexican government since Monterey is a U.S. possession now. It still bears the look of a Spanish town: white-washed adobe buildings and red-tile roofs. It was the capital of Alta California during Mexican rule. There is talk that it is being considered for the new capital if and when California becomes a state. I cannot imagine that a town so small would qualify; surely there are better choices.

Now with the sun setting behind the ship, the entrance to San Francisco Bay is at our bow. What a magnificent sight! The captain says that a military explorer by the name of Frémont christened this "The Golden Gate" and I certainly understand why. The north headland rises from the sea at least a thousand feet, covered in grasses of gold that glow now in the sunlight.

The southern face is no less beautiful, but seems diminutive in comparison. Miles of sand dunes culminate in ivory cliffs capped by trees that look as though they have been soundly beaten, grappling for a hold, their gray branches torn by the winds.

I am told that there are two forts on either side of the entrance, but they must be waiting in ambush as I cannot yet see either of them. The town of Yerba Buena, rechristened San Francisco, lies inside the bay on the southern promontory, but I cannot see that as yet either. It is also a Spanish town, but different in character from Monterey in that the dwellings have been built among the town's many hills (or so your Uncle James has written).

I am anxious to see your Uncle James and offer what services I may in this new place that is now America.

I close this letter, my sweet, sweet daughter, determined to post it the moment my feet strike land. Oh, what a heartening thought that is—land. At last. At last.
I hope this finds you safe and happy.

Your loving,
Papa

The captain announces that we are but two days from San Francisco and, if the winds hold, will make port on October 8th. *The Pelican's* passengers react with a resounding cheer followed by speechless quiet. California is no longer a faraway mythical place to talk about and speculate upon. The day after tomorrow we will be there—I will be there. I have imagined hundreds of possible scenes during the past several months, but few are satisfying and I discard these endless plays in the hope that whatever happens will be better than anything I might invent.

However, the vagaries of the voyage are not yet over. The day we are to sail into the San Francisco Bay, the temperature drops and we are surrounded by fog so thick that sailors sent aloft can see no more than fifty feet in front of the ship. It is as if she magically returned to the coast of Patagonia. We can sail no further. The word is passed among the passengers: we will anchor not far from some islands called the Farallons and pause for the fog to lift. San Francisco must wait until tomorrow.

Even though I suspect it will not make the time pass more quickly, I pace the decks, squinting through the fog for a glimpse of the elusive land, leaping in a silly game between the puddles of pale light thrown by midday lanterns. This delay is the most tortuous of the voyage.

At the sound of a deep cough, I turn. It comes again from across the water, hoarse but loud at the same time.

"Sea lions," Mr. Boyle says, stopping by my side. "They live on the Farallons among the birds. They are trying to get comfortable on the rocks."

"What is a sea lion?" I ask, imagining a lion with fins or a mermaid's tail.

"No sea lions at the menagerie? No pictures in your uncle's library? Well, have you ever seen a seal in Boston Harbor?" I nod. "They look like that, only at least twice as big."

He rests his forearms on the railing and stares into the fog for some time. "You'll see your father tomorrow."

It is a simple enough statement, but it causes my stomach to flop. I am excited yet worried that Papa may have forgotten me or will not be pleased to see me. I again imagine different greetings we will give each other, then dismiss them all as nonsense or inadequate. I want to keep myself small for reasons I do not understand.

"Promise me you'll not get yourself arrested in San Francisco."

"I was not arrested! Mrs. Reynolds said they would not have even bothered with us had the chief of police not been a friend of hers."

"Well that's certainly true. He's a *very* good friend of hers."

There is something in his tone that reminds me of Mama and Papa as they stood in our doorway in Boston preparing for the theater. In the fog I imagine Mrs. Reynolds dancing with a swarthy gentleman in a policeman's uniform.

Mr. Boyle shakes his head and clears his throat. "Things won't be the same without you onboard."

"So you do not mind having children on the ship anymore?"

"No! I hate having children onboard! I've not had a night's rest for months and don't expect that to change, what with the Dunsfords here all the way to China." He clears his throat again. "No, it's you that's made it different. You are a curious and somehow lovely child. To whom I've lost a lot of copper."

"Not a lot. We have not played since Rio."

So he points to a heaver and a scupper, a windlass and the backstay, and a dozen other objects and features of the ship. I correctly call the name of each.

"It is good that the Captain is to pay me that bonus tomorrow."

"What bonus?"

"Ah, you know all of those new passengers? Well…" He drops his voice to a conspiratorial whisper then explains that most of the new passengers have paid passage four times what it cost for the rest of us to travel from New York. Four times as much for less than a quarter of the trip. Those sleeping on the decks paid less, but not much. Expenses were totaled: the new construction, the rum used to bribe the old passengers, and the additional food and water (which cost more than in New York regardless of the "incentives" the officials of Callao offered for *The Pelican* to take some of the masses off of their hands). Despite those costs, Mr. Boyle, the captain, Mr. Sterbenc, Cook, and the carpenter will each clear a very healthy profit.

CHAPTER 9

October 9, 1848

THE FOG LIFTS in the late morning hours and Captain Watson hazards entrance through the strait into San Francisco Bay. The headlands to the north remain shrouded in clouds. Beneath the haze, the lands lay brown and rocky. Only a few stubby bushes are there to break the monotony. These cliffs are not the glowing golden mountains Papa described. Straight before the ship is a small island that looks like a discarded pile of rocks. San Francisco Bay is nothing like the harbors of Boston or New York, Rio or Callao. It is empty and wild.

As *The Pelican* passes the headlands, her cannon speaks and her sails are struck so that she drifts on the tide into the wide harbor. Within an hour, a puny boat with three men struggles through the choppy waters to meet the ship.

"Gone," a harried sailor says as he lumbers aboard and ploughs through the crowd to the captain's side, panting from the effort and announcing his name as Jepson. He is to be our pilot since the harbormaster is not available; he will guide us through the bay to the cove.

Everyone has deserted San Francisco, Mr. Jepson declares. The rumors of gold are all too true. The rivers at the center of the territory sparkle with it. Sam Brannon's *California Star* carried the story last March, two full months after the initial discovery. The newspaper's owner himself shouted the news as he paraded through town holding aloft a bottle filled with the metal. Nearly every man and woman soon departed to grab their share.

There will be no customs officials or health inspectors to demand taxes or fees—they too have gone in search of their fortunes. It is very confusing now that the territory belongs to the United States. Nobody knows what to do. The only reason the pilot himself was not hunting gold was that Mrs. Jepson threatened to pummel him if he did. Besides, he need not dig for riches as his wife was already making her fortune renting cots and selling meals to arriving crews and passengers who found themselves merely passing through town.

Mr. Jepson guides *The Pelican* past sandy hills, beyond a rocky promontory that falls abruptly into the mud flats on the north peninsula of a little cove that he calls Yerba Buena. Rising above the mud, San Francisco is a village at best; a windswept settlement with little more than a dozen structures huddling in uneasy permanence at the water's edge. Fewer than a hundred buildings cling to the rolling dunes above. They look like they were dropped directly from the sky. Crudely erected tents crouch among the shrubs in numbers far greater than the buildings. There are no trees, no cobbled roads—only sandy gashes where the avenues might one day track.

Once in the cove, Mr. Jepson bids the ship farewell having first gained permission to hang a wooden sign announcing prices and giving directions to his wife's establishment.

"Passengers will be ferried ashore," the Captain announces. "Those without luggage will go first so as to clear the way. I expect an orderly exit."

It does not go well. The ship is anchored more than 100 yards from the shore; but instead of waiting for the dinghies, several men jump from the railings, pick axes in hand, struggling to the beach. Most lose their treasured tools somewhere between the ship and the mud of the cove. They scream about their loss and the frigid temperature of the water.

Even as the boats are lowered many more men leap into the bay, thus setting "order" at naught. Soon they are begging to be hauled aboard lest they drown. The oarsmen scowl and curse as they pull some jumpers into the crafts, using paddles to beat the remaining away to prevent capsizing the boat. Most take their proper place in line after a wet climb to the deck. None are lost as far as I can tell.

I scour the shoreline for Papa, bouncing at the railing as the ship empties. One dark-haired man waits on the beach. Papa does not have dark hair.

Mr. Boyle has already told me that we are scant weeks from our originally scheduled arrival and Papa will know that the ship is in harbor if he asks at the customs house. Surely he has checked every day; surely he knows *The Pelican* has arrived. I am baffled by his absence from the shore. Perhaps if I ask Mr. Boyle for the spyglass I will have a better chance to spot him. But Mr. Boyle is below, readying the cargo for removal. I scour the shore again. Still only the dark-haired man waits.

Regardless, arrangements begin to transport me to the town. Mr. Boyle has found my trunk among the cargo and carried it to the deck. He and the Reverend will accompany me to the beach then search for my father.

The other members of the Dunsford family will remain on board as there is no need for them to go ashore: as soon as the ship is made ready to sail they will continue to China. As Mrs. Dunsford cries and embraces me, Matthew awkwardly pats my back. I drop a brief curtsey to Mark and Luke who, in response, nod their heads in what presumably passes for a bow. None of us know what is proper and expected in these circumstances. I do not know quite what to do, as I find myself daubing at sudden tears. The two boys run off as soon as they can, leaving me to hug the youngest children and tell them to be safe and well and enjoy China. And I mean it. Saying goodbye to the Dunsfords is certainly harder than I expected. I may not see them again.

I do not seek Lizzie. She disappeared below shortly after Robert Cecchi and his family had reached the beach, having waved after their small craft as it scudded through the waves all the way to the shore. Though she tried to hide them, the tears I expected long ago flowed down her cheeks.

Descending to the dinghy, where Mr. Boyle and the Reverend wait with my portmanteau and truck, I settle myself in the prow. The progress to shore is slow as the Reverend is plainly not skilled with the oars. I see no sign of Papa and find myself short of breath at the realization of his absence. Surely he will be here soon; surely he will come to meet me.

"Guine!" the dark-haired man shouts and waves as the dinghy nears the shore. "Guine!"

It is Uncle James. He left Boston more than a year before Papa and, although I do not remember him well, it can be no other. His enthusiasm for my arrival is evident even across the water. Once Mr. Boyle lifts me to the relative dryness of the sand I run to my uncle, clinging to him, calmed by his presence, relieved that I am not forgotten.

"Ah, Doctor Walker," the Reverend breathlessly remarks, having slogged through the mud flats and shifting sand behind me. He holds out a hand in greeting.

"No, no. Sorry," my uncle stammers. "I'm James Somersworth, Guine's uncle. You must be the Reverend Dunsford. My sister wrote that you and your family were escorting my niece." Loosening his welcoming grasp, Uncle James shakes the Reverend's hand, thanking him for his kindness in accompanying me to San Francisco, saying any number of other polite things.

"Where is Papa?" I ask, reluctantly separating from my uncle's embrace.

Uncle James is rumpled, his hair and side whiskers untidy, chin scraped raw from a hasty shave, clothes and shoes powdered with dirt and sand. The creases and wrinkles around his eyes match those of his bedraggled jacket.

Of course he is probably horrified at my appearance as well. I am dressed in my best clothes, but I am short of presentable. I could not brush the salt rings from the waist and underarms of the dress, the back stretches tightly across my shoulders, the waist hikes under my ribs, and the sleeves no longer conceal the bones of my wrists. Though recently washed, my hair hangs in thick ropes rather than curls, weighed down by the salt residue. The soles of my shoes separate where the stitching has worn through; already I feel the seep of sand through the broken seams. I smooth my skirt and hope Uncle James does not notice or, if he does, is forgiving.

"I must apologize for my brother-in-law, Reverend. He had every intention of meeting his daughter's ship, but was called away quite suddenly." Uncle James' voice is tight and I hear the lie in it. "But I shall take the young lady straight away home and get her settled. How was your voyage, Guine?"

"Long," I respond, unable to speak more. It is not right or fair to have come all this way only to land in an ugly town on an ugly beach which smells of brine and rotting things in the salty flats. Without my father to greet me. Remembering my manners, I continue: "But, the Dunsfords were excellent company, Uncle, and took really good care of me. I appreciate all that they did. Thank you, Reverend."

"Thank you so much," Uncle James says, sounding far more sincere than I had. "I have a man here to help. He can take you anywhere in the town you wish to go. I can recommend one or two inns, although they will be nothing like the inns of Massachusetts." He waves his arm in the direction of the city with an apologetic smile.

"No, sir, thank you," the Reverend says. "We shan't be staying. My family and I are bound for China and the mission there. We are to leave as soon as the ship has sorted its cargo and is ready to sail again."

Uncle James stares at the Reverend, his mouth slightly agape, his brow furrowed. "For your sake, I hope that's true. I'm afraid that the new standard has been for entire crews to desert their ships once they hear of the gold fields." He waves his hand again, this time at the three ships anchored in the harbor not far from *The Pelican*. "Those ships—abandoned, empty, every one. Going nowhere."

"You must be Dr. Walker," Mr. Boyle declares as he approaches, carrying my portmanteau and reaching his free hand toward Uncle James.

Uncle James again makes his apologetic introduction.

"Oh." Mr. Boyle's tone is disapproving. He glances between me and my uncle, his mouth soundlessly working like a beached fish. I expect him to grab my hand and return to *The Pelican* without further discussion. Finally, he turns once more to Uncle James. "Well I'm Eamon Boyle, chief mate. I met Miss Guine on the ship."

"Ah, the first mate of *The Pelican*? I've cargo aboard her," says Uncle James, reaching into his coat pocket for a packet of papers which he unfolds and hands to Mr. Boyle. "I have lighters, a wagon, and a few men to unload her. Can you assist?"

Mr. Boyle glances over the thick fold of papers. "You've the lion's share of the remaining cargo it seems."

"I can boast to being the largest shipping agent in San Francisco at the moment, although the assertion is somewhat dubious in that there are very few of us."

With a familiar snort, Mr. Boyle continues discussing the particulars of the cargo with Uncle James, the details of duty shifting their focus. I believe I have been forgotten, like the ships that bob in the cove. As the conversation continues I shiver in the morning air, the dialogue circling around me like the rush of dried leaves in a cold whirl of wind.

"I don't suppose that's news to you, Harold. I really don't know how you've managed," Uncle James laughed. "Living with my mother when she was younger and in good health was trial enough."

We sat on the veranda at my grandparent's home in Boston. No, that was no longer correct as it was now *our* house, mine and Papa and Mama's even though Grandmother Somersworth lived there still. We had moved to the house last year, after Grandfather Somersworth passed away. His passing left the dwelling empty and incomplete like a gown on the dress form in Mama's sewing room. I found his ghost everywhere, etched into the walls and echoing in each creak of the floorboards.

Papa and my uncles were smoking cigars, the smoldering stink of the tobacco dissipating along with the heat of the day in the breeze that wafted from the bay. My aunts and Mama had retired after supper to the parlor as they always did when the family gathered. I did not want to go with them, however. I wanted to see the fairies that danced in the summertime like bright skipping points of light along the marshy bank of the creek below the house. I would not see them if I went inside.

I sat at Papa's side on the cane settee, trying to keep my head below the level of the cigar haze, tucked under Papa's arm and straining to see through the mist of the lowlands where the fairies were. Papa would let me remain only if I was still; it was always so difficult to be still.

"Anne takes care of it," Papa said. "It is her mother, after all."

"When do you sail, James?" Uncle John asked. Uncle John always seemed to be the one to steer a conversation away from any unpleasantness (and Grandmother Somersworth was an unpleasant subject, becoming more so each day). I could not remember ever having heard Uncle John say anything bad about anybody except perhaps "those idiots" in Congress. Even then, by the end of the discussion he would have found something redeemable in their actions or opinions. An optimist, Mama called him.

"The fifth of July. We shall go out with the fireworks."

"Why the devil have you chosen California, James?" Papa asked. "There is nothing in California except…well, Californians and Mexicans who speak only Spanish and bow to that tyrant in Rome. I for one can do without—we have enough Papists here in Boston already."

"The Catholics are a hard-working lot," Uncle John asserted. "The ones here, at least. Uneducated, true, but I believe that is due more to a lack of opportunity than a lack of ability."

"They have done little for California," Papa countered. "The entire territory boasts of no industry except cattle. The length of it has no town that is even a fraction of the size of any on the East Coast. I doubt the population approaches what we have in Boston alone, despite their penchant for gaggles of children."

"Oh, I too have read Dana's book," Uncle James interrupted. "But perhaps you missed the part where he says that it will take only an industrious people to make California grand. I'm convinced that it will be the gateway to the Orient someday. It can't long remain part of Mexico, given 'Manifest Destiny' and all of that nonsense the President is so set on. And America needs a shorter route to the Far East and her riches. Oh, certainly the path has been improved since we acquired the Oregon territories; but from what I've been told, the San Francisco Bay is a far superior port to anything north of there. Once in American hands, it will be the next big trade center, I'm certain of it. And I want the Somersworth Trading Company to be there first. Or nearly first."

Uncle John chuckled. "You should go into politics, James; your words are compelling. If I didn't know better, I'd swear that you'd followed in your father's footsteps after all. You could even surpass him, I'll wager. Why, you could be on the floor of the Federal Senate, urging this expansionist agenda President Polk favors."

"One remaining politician in the family is more than adequate, John," Uncle James sighed, smoke wreathing his head. "I had enough of that talk all through my childhood. I was ecstatic when Margaret married you: Father had a fellow statesman in the family and the pressure was off of me."

"What about you, Harold? Have you ever thought of going into politics? You're a logical man with strong opinions and a fine way with words however sparse they may be at times," Uncle John urged, fiddling with his cigar.

"That is not the life for me," Papa replied abruptly. "I am horrible with crowds, I have no skill with extemporaneous speech, and I cannot imagine the Americans accepting a Brit as their representative—too many are still alive who remember 1812. If nothing else, Americans have long memories especially here in Boston.

"Besides, I have not the patience to listen to endless debates, compromises of every ilk, inclusion of unrelated rubbish simply to get some bill passed. Thank you very much, but I prefer my scalpel—clean, efficient, and quick."

"Oh, I think you're wrong. Being in politics is a bit like being married actually," Uncle John said, causing both of my uncles to laugh heartily. He turned once again to Uncle James. "Jessica will miss you, surely."

"Heavens, no. She's tired of being pregnant all the time. She can't wait to see her feet once again. Mind you, I am certain that in two, maybe three years, she shall so long for my company that she'll pack up the children and move to San Francisco of her own volition."

The conversation continued to rumble over my head, turning and twisting among subjects I did not understand nor care about. But Papa did not shoo me away and I would not have left for any reason; I had not yet seen the fairies.

The Reverend returns to the ship with Mr. Boyle, a pat on my head and a quick "Godspeed" as his hasty farewell. He has discharged his duties in my regard and I believe is anxious to be on his way.

Mr. Boyle says that *The Pelican* will be in port for several more days. He assures me that he will come to my uncle's lodging for a proper goodbye long before she sails.

"Where's Papa," I ask again when Uncle James and I are alone. "Why is he not here?"

Uncle James sighs and looks over the waters of the bay as if to find an answer there. "Come along. Let's go to the warehouse—it's not far from here. I'll make you tea. I'll have something stronger. And then we'll talk about your father." He reaches for my hand and the portmanteau; my trunk can wait on the beach until his hired man finishes unloading *The Pelican* cargo—it has been placed well above the tide line and will be safe for the time being.

The Somersworth Trading Company storehouse is not far from the shore. It is small and cramped with all manner of boxes, crates, barrels, and bales, a few narrow passageways separating the neat stacks. It looks like a much tidier version of *The Pelican's* decks.

Just as the warehouse is filled to capacity so is my uncle's office. It is not much bigger than one of the ship's cabins with a desk and two chairs crowded along one wall and two large cabinets on the other. Books and ledgers are neatly arranged on every surface and a small stove stands in one corner. The window above the desk offers meager light which may be due to the position of the window but just as easily might be from the gloominess of the day.

Motioning for me to take a seat, Uncle James puts a kettle on the stove, retrieving a tin of tea and some cups from the desk drawer along with a bottle of whiskey. Then he sits in the other chair. "I had forgotten how much you look like your mother," he says, smiling. He sighs and leans forward, elbows on knees, head bowed and countenance suddenly as woeful as the day. He opens his mouth many times, but it is several minutes before he speaks. "There is just no easy way to say this, my girl. I've rehearsed several possibilities over the last few weeks and one reason never seems any better than another. My sister should never have sent you, Guine. Your Aunt Margaret was wrong to have put you on that ship, exposing you to needless danger.

"Your father does not mean to stay in California. He just needed some time to…sort through his life, to get away from the gossip and pettiness of a close-knit community like Boston. He intends to go back; he *will* go back, eventually. He was just…lost."

Yes, I knew. Every day for months he wandered into rooms, seeming not to remember why he had entered. He picked up surgical instruments and stared at them before setting them down and wiping his hands on his trousers as if something dirty had rubbed off. He was startled when people spoke to him and answered all queries with a blank stare or a wordless grunt. Lost was as good a description as any.

"It was a tragedy," Aunt Margaret confided to one of our kindly neighbors, "but should Dr. Walker not get on with his life and take care of his child and his mother-in-law?"

Uncle John urged us to move into the house in Brookline where he and my aunt could watch me, leaving Papa to focus on his career and the new clinic and whatever else he needed to do. Papa was reluctant at first, changing his mind soon after forgetting to fetch me from school one day. His decision may have been due more to having the headmaster send the constable to our doorstep than anything else. He gave the old Somersworth house, together with an increasingly addled Grandmother Somersworth, over to the care of Aunt Jessica and her brood. It was to have been a temporary arrangement, but he left for San Francisco less than three months later.

"I think he wanted to return the moment he got here," Uncle James explains. "I believe the only thing keeping him was the fear of another voyage, another six months of illness. I hardly recognized him when he arrived; he was skeletal."

There was little work for a white doctor in San Francisco. The majority of the population, which had been little more than 500 souls at the time, spoke no English and already had their own doctors and remedies for ailments. When word came in early spring that gold had been discovered in the mountains my idle father caught the fever along with the rest of the population of the city. That is what they call the madness, Uncle James says: "gold fever."

"The entire town is quite deserted. Everyone has run off. The only people left are those passing through and those that can make a living from the transients. There's little help to unload cargoes and I can't muster a crew, save for those ships that ferry the new miners and their supplies up and down the river. Even then I must keep their wages high just to prevent desertion."

The throb of the kettle interrupts and Uncle James busies himself with preparing tea. I remain seated, my head leaden and pushing down into my shoulders.

"He's quite good at it, you know," Uncle James continues. "After only a few months of panning he returned with sacks of gold piled onto some scrawny little mule he acquired. He needed little for himself, he said, and wanted the majority shipped back to your account in Boston. We have no banks in California. But when we learned you were on your way, he decided to invest the gold here. As of September, both of you own several parcels of land throughout the city and are partners in the San Francisco branch of Somersworth's. I suppose I'm going to have to change the signage to 'Somersworth and Walker.'"

"September?" I ask, my throat tightening. "He was here in September?" In September he must have known I was close at hand. He should have stayed to meet the ship; he should have been here to greet me. "Why is he not here now?"

Aunt Margaret's letter had arrived sometime in June or July—nearly seven months after it had been posted, Uncle James tells me. Since the letter had not been addressed to him, he had learned of my voyage only when my father had re-entered the town last month laden with gold dust and nuggets. Only then had the letter been opened; only then had they learned of my approach.

"Margaret wrote that the ship was to arrive in early September.

When it did not your father became impatient and nervous, expecting the worst. He railed at Margaret for having put you in danger. There were few people in the world at whom he didn't rail. Waiting around did him no good: he paced and stared, forgetting things. His temper flared at the slightest inconvenience. Your father and I have been friends for a very long time, Guine, but I hardly recognized this person he had become.

"We had many long and loud conversations. Most of the loudness was directed at Margaret, of course, but not all. We did agree on one point, however: the mountains are no place for a young girl. You were born of station and manners and should not be subjected to the wild.

"He shouldn't have left you with Margaret in the first place. Jessica would have welcomed you. Your father thought she had her hands full, what with our nine children *and* your grandmother. Your father is a brilliant man, but sometimes he can be really thick-headed."

"When will he be back?"

"I don't know. He says it's getting harder to leave the claim site for fear of some squatter taking over. He has left you a letter, which I stupidly forgot at the boardinghouse. Perhaps that will explain things for you." He does not sound convinced.

"They're coming to California in droves, Guine, these gold hunters: from South America, the Far East, Australia and islands in the Pacific. By land and ship—hundreds every day. We see only a fraction of them here. Sometimes they land in San Diego or Monterey. The ones that come overland, from Mexico and Oregon, head straight for the Sierra Nevada; the mountains.

"Once word reaches the East Coast, if it hasn't already, I

imagine there will be even more. Nothing an American likes more than a new conquest and easy riches." My uncle sighs deeply. "It's what I wanted, but I had no idea it would happen so quickly." He shakes his head and hands me the tea, pouring some whiskey into his own cup. "Well I'm a little rusty. What exactly do eleven-year-old girls do with themselves these days?"

"I am twelve," I say, sulking. "My birthday was over a week ago."

"Well happy belated birthday," Uncle James says, toasting with his teacup, clinking it gently against mine. "I welcome your company my lovely niece."

He seems sincere although I have little doubt he too realizes that my father has deserted me, my aunt and uncle do not want me, and there is not another ship bound for Boston in all of San Francisco. Perhaps I will swim to *The Pelican* and stay with her as she sails to China. Except that I cannot swim.

"I know that I could keep your clothes and shoes in better order than they are at the moment," I say, nodding in my uncle's general direction, not raising my gaze from the floor. "I am handy with a brush and a needle and thread. I will try not to be a nuisance to you, Uncle."

Uncle James ignores the rudeness of my statement. "No nuisance, Guine. You're most welcome here, although I have little to offer. Conditions are primitive and help is hard to find, but I'm sure we'll manage. I *truly* will enjoy having you here. I miss my family very much.

"I'm renting a room on Stockton Street while I have my own house built on the hill. Oh, I mean *that* hill," he points out the window to the rocky bluff which borders the northernmost edge of Yerba Buena Cove, above the dunes. "There are so many hills in this town I suppose I shall have to be more specific until you learn where you are. It's called Loma Alta, but we newcomers have dubbed it 'Goat Hill' as you need to be a goat to climb. It accords a great view of the harbor, however. So I bought a plot of land and there you have it."

Construction of the house has not begun as there are no longer any good carpenters in town, all of them having joined the quest for gold.

"You intend to stay in San Francisco, then?"

Uncle James pauses and leans back in his chair, breathing the office air deeply, a smile playing at the edges of his mouth. I cannot imagine what he sees as he looks about the room, but it pleases him. When his eyes crinkle mischievously, I am reminded of Mama. They look alike, brother and sister. "There's nothing about California that I don't like, except that my family isn't with me. Your Aunt Jessica won't think of coming until she knows there are good schools and paved streets. Those seem to be the prerequisites. Actually, I don't think I can expect her until your grandmother is…better. A voyage is out of the question for Mother, and Jessica wouldn't think of leaving her with Margaret.

"Someday I'll let you read the letter your aunt wrote once she learned Margaret had put you on that ship. Jessica was furious. Had Margaret told her you were leaving she certainly would've stopped it."

I am silent as we finish our beverages and leave the warmth of the office, trudging through the dirt to the boardinghouse where Uncle James lives. He converses brightly, pointing out various landmarks and street names to help with my orientation. "We have a public school just down that road at Portsmouth Square. I hear it's the first public school in all of California. I'll enroll you next week."

The boardinghouse on Stockton Street looks foreign to the landscape: a squat gray clapboard, surrounded by a white picket fence, dropped in the middle of a sandy field. A similar dwelling stands nearby, but otherwise only dunes stretch for blocks on all sides, the hilly landscape littered with hundreds of hastily assembled calico tents. No trees or other vegetation grow there.

Mrs. Llewellyn, Uncle James' diminutive landlady, meets us at the door, kissing my cheeks in the European fashion. In a lilting accent, she brightly announces that she welcomes the company of another woman. She shoos Uncle James away and leads me to the kitchen where a large copper wash tub sits like a throne in one corner. She ordered the tub from the east, she announces, and it arrived only last week. She has used it once and declares it to be the most wonderful of appliances. Then she bustles with preparations for my bath, recruiting me to surround the tub with hanging bed linens ("for privacy," she says).

Mrs. Llewellyn is like a bird, flitting through the house, gathering what she needs, chattering about the important and the mundane. Her laughter rings like silver bells. The kitchen seems to brighten and spin as she dances purposefully across the floor, each step a blur.

She is French Canadian, having been in America for eighteen years since meeting and marrying the Bear (as I come to think of her soldier husband—she refers to him only as "my 'usband" and describes him as "big like a bear"). Mrs. Llewellyn followed the Bear from New Orleans to Florida then Texas as the conflicts, his duties, and commanding officers changed. Florida was nice, she says, although damp like New Orleans. She did not like Texas at all: too hot and dusty. Then, nearly three years ago, the Bear was ordered to California when war with the Mexican government seemed assured.

I learn all of this within five minutes of arriving. I think she has greatly missed having a "woman" with whom to talk.

The Bear was briefly assigned to quell a small revolt of Americans north of San Francisco. However when the real battle flared near the pueblo of Los Angeles, for the first time in their marriage, she could not accompany him. When the Americans assumed control of the Presidio to the north he "ordered" her to stay in San Francisco where not a single shot had been fired. Los Angeles promised to be a full-scale war; skirmishes were a lot different than a full scale war. He would not allow her to be in danger.

"I did not like that 'e thought 'e could decide for me. *Mais*, it was good." When the fighting concluded in Los Angeles, the Bear was stationed at the port of Monterey which is only two days' ride south from San Francisco.

Now, Mrs. Llewellyn will not leave this city. Never in all of her travels has she loved a place more. She will stay here and, if the Army will not keep the Bear close, he can resign his commission, she says ("that is if 'e still expects to be my 'usband"). She will not go back to the confines of the old society—in the United States or in Canada. This is her home. She likes it here.

"We will get boots, tomorrow per'aps," she trills as she darts around the kitchen. The priorities upon arrival are a bath and unsalted clothes, she insists, and offers me used clothing gathered from various townspeople. "Shoes are not practical in San Francisco. Laces are too 'ard to keep clean and the…the… the little 'oles allow dirt and sand to be inside. Boots are best. Your shoes are so tattered; we shall burn them and buy dainty slippers to wear in the 'ouse. I know just the man who can make them. Provided, of course, that 'e is still in town; no one knows when the gold fever strikes."

As Mrs. Llewellyn prattles, she heats large pots of water, fetching towels and soap, constantly in motion. She does most of the talking as I can think only of Papa's absence and I doubt Mrs. Llewellyn would be interested. When I mention Uncle James' plan to enroll me in the public school, Mrs. Llewellyn's mouth drops and her laughter soars once more. Alas, my uncle's information is terribly out of date: the public school has closed. The teacher, a Mr. Thomas Douglas of Yale (although it might have been Harvard, she could not remember), left a month ago to seek his fortune in gold. Even the School Board followed shortly after. The hunt for gold had trumped education: no teacher, no School Board, no classes. Some of the town clergy have started private instruction, but there are no Presbyterian schools as yet.

I express my concern that I will have nothing to do in San Francisco; however, Mrs. Llewellyn does not agree. I can help my uncle with his books, she says, which will strengthen my mathematic and penmanship skills. She herself can always use help with her English, except she fears that my accent and rapid delivery might pose a problem. She is used to the soft drawls of Florida, Louisiana, and Texas, not the harsh New England tongue. I bristle at the "'arsh" adjective, but cannot deny my Boston roots.

She tells me I may start a garden in the backyard next spring.

Tomatoes will not grow as there is not enough hot weather even in the summertime, but Mrs. Llewellyn is certain that anything else will flourish. Plus, there is always laundry to do and clothes to mend.

"Do you not have others to do those things?"

Mrs. Llewellyn halts suddenly although the room seems to whirl around her for a few seconds longer before it stills. "Others? Do you mean servants? Ah, *oui*, we 'ave servants, with usual times. But these are not usual times. No one is in town."

The landlady empties another pot of hot water into the tub, her manner clipped as she says, "I can pay you, if you wish."

"No," I falter, "that is not what I meant. I do not ask wages. I just…well, it is different in Boston," I let my voice trail away, not certain what I have said to anger the woman.

"I know." Mrs. Llewellyn's voice softens. "It is different in Montreal and New Orleans as well. It will be much the same 'ere someday I suppose. Always there 'ave been master and servant. But now, the servant 'ave a chance to *be* the master; their 'ard work may be rewarded tenfold. 'o can blame them?

"*Mais*, for now, everyone does their own work. And gets 'elp where they can. I *will* pay you. It will be the least I can do for the 'elp. And I promise not to ask you to empty any chamber pots."

I pull the makeshift curtain closed, strip off my clothes, and step into the tub as Mrs. Llewellyn resumes her friendly chatter, her ire already gone.

I cannot understand why Mrs. Llewellyn chose this ugly town to love, but decide to ask at a later time. I relax until the milky water turns cold along with my hopes about San Francisco and Papa.

CHAPTER 10

October 29, 1848

EVERY NIGHT FOR A WEEK after our arrival I dreamed of *The Pelican*: the lulling sway, the timbers groaning, the stomp of the night watch over my head, and the lapping of the waves against her hull. I was not frightened—it was not as if I dreamed of rounding Cape Horn or suffering the attentions of Mr. Sterbenc or any other horrible thing—but I awoke dizzy, unsettled, waiting in bed for several minutes while my uncle's room took shape and my memory returned.

That week I did not leave my bed and I covered my ears with a pillow to fend off the sounds of the house. I told Uncle James and Mrs. Llewellyn that I had a fever and aches, but I did not really have either of these. I doubt they believed me anyway, but they cooed sympathetically, at least for a time.

When I can no longer pretend to sleep through the noise and bustle of the house nor keep my mind blank enough to pass the time in bed, I rise.

Mrs. Llewellyn has eight guests including Uncle James and me. Three of her residents work for the United States government: a surveyor, the new postmaster, and a man who is investigating the broken tariff situation. The others include a land-claims lawyer, an assayer, and a man who is lobbying for office as police chief or sheriff. I am not certain to whom he lobbies since Mrs. Llewellyn insists that most city officials are off hunting for gold. Uncle James grumbles that this man is "not much more than a common gambler and an opportunist." However, Uncle James hastily acknowledges that it is none of his business. I eventually meet all of these boarders at the meals Mrs. Llewellyn serves promptly at six each morning and evening.

It is not a large house, but the landlady organized it wisely by turning the parlor into her own room and constructing a wall down the middle of each bedroom. (I hesitate to use the word "wall." Widely-spaced boards, standing on edge, with calico tacked across them hardly qualify as "walls," if you ask me.) There were two bedrooms originally, now divided into four. New doors were cut so that no one need enter the room of another to get to his bed. The same was not done for the windows—each is "split" in two by the dividing wall, so that opening the window of one room opens the window in the adjoining room. Footfalls and snores carry easily through the calico and the gaps. Candlelight from one boarders' room glows into the other as if through a curtain. It is very intimate, even if one does not wish it so.

Each half-room is furnished with bunks nailed to the framing of the wall along with the calico. A braided rug, a straight-backed chair, and one small bureau with four drawers complete each room. My hand-me-downs from Mrs. Llewellyn and the few remaining items of my own pack easily into the bottom two drawers of the bureau.

Uncle James is one of the earliest risers and is often the first at Mrs. Llewellyn's breakfast table. He eats quickly and rushes out of the door to the warehouse or to meet ships and shop owners alike, stopping only to kiss my forehead if I happen to be awake and dressed.

Cured of my "fever," I accompany Uncle James to the warehouse where I read manifests aloud while he writes the list of goods and figures in his ledgers. When he suspects that the count on the paper does not reflect the inventory in storage, we venture to the warehouse and sort through the crates and boxes, spending the afternoon counting shoes or bolts of calico, barrels of sugar and coffee or bags of grain brought by the ships. We eat our midday meal by the shore, watching the many small crafts that ply the harbor. Uncle James knows them all by their outline and rigging. He knows their names and the names of their captains too.

Only one ship sails through the narrow strait and into the bay in October, announcing itself with a volley of cannon fire just as *The Pelican* had. Its arrival recreates the chaotic scene of *The Pelican's* landing so exactly that I nearly laugh aloud: men careening overboard and racing up the narrow beach on their way to the gold, stumbling over one another in their haste.

The Pelican remains in port. Despite all efforts of Captain Watson and Mr. Boyle, the entire crew including Cook, the carpenter, the sail maker, and Mr. Sterbenc ran off to hunt for gold the moment they received their pay. Apparently that bonus money was not enough. Now there are four abandoned ships in Yerba Buena Cove.

With no crew to sail her and no men that may be conscripted to do so, the captain, Mr. Boyle, and the Dunsfords convert *The Pelican* into their own private hotel. It is ideal in many respects:

there is no rent to pay and the galleys and heads work well enough. There is access to the town with its fresh food and water, however cumbersome it is to row back and forth from the shore each time. Matthew and his father are not yet adept at piloting a dinghy but they certainly make every attempt. Mrs. Dunsford has not yet overcome her fear of the ship's lengthy ladder, but everyone tries to convince her that it becomes easier with time.

It seems neither the Dunsfords nor I are going anywhere. At least the Dunsfords have a reason. I have only a letter from my father that unsatisfactorily explains my predicament.

September 30, 1848

My lovely daughter,

If you are reading this, then your ship will have safely arrived in San Francisco and you are with your Uncle James in that unique little hovel he calls home. I pray this is the circumstance.

Happy birthday. It is difficult to believe that twelve years have passed since the day you were born. It is even more difficult for me to fathom that you will soon be a young woman. I try not to think of it as I wish I could stop time and keep you as a babe forever. However, I know full well I shall be doomed to fail were I to try.

I hope you are not too angry with me—I attempted to stay in San Francisco to await your ship; but as the date of your scheduled arrival passed, I was overcome with visions of the dangers you faced from the moment your aunt set you on that path. I thought I would go mad.

As I am sure he will have explained, I have left you in the capable hands of your uncle. He has far more experience than I in raising a child, especially a daughter. I had hoped that your Aunt Margaret's motherly instincts would have prevailed on your behalf, but James assures me that they were never present even with her own child. My ears still smart from the lashing he gave them upon hearing that I had left you in Margaret's "care." Your presence in California speaks volumes for James' wisdom.

But that does not address the issue you and I must face. To be quite blunt, my sweet girl, you cannot live with me in the conditions in which I find myself. My home is a tent at the side of a fast-moving creek, surrounded by trees and grizzly bears, mountain lions and Indians. When I run short of supplies, I travel to a miner's camp which is a half-day's journey on my newly acquired horse. I take with me a stubborn little mule. The horse was named Fuego by his original owner. It means "fire" in Spanish, but he hardly lives up to the moniker. The name I call the mule is better left unsaid.

I know this decision will not please you, but I expect you to make the best of it with your uncle. I have certainly not forgotten your penchant for contrary behavior (of which I was reminded by frequent letters from your aunt). However, having you with me is simply too dangerous to contemplate. That you have survived one perilous adventure does not render you fit for yet another.

Write to me. Assure me you have safely survived your journey. Give me surety that Mrs. Llewellyn's atrocious cooking has not made you ill. Forgive me for my frailties and poor judgment of your aunt's character.

> *With great affection,*
> *Papa*

As my father correctly surmised his letter is not to my liking. He outlines his reasons for keeping me away, but I have as many to justify why I should be at his side. So, I compose a letter of my own which I will dispatch in care of the general store in the Sonoran Camp where it will be held until Papa visits to replenish his supplies.

He argues that the mountains are too wild, yet I have seen both bears and doglike creatures called coyotes fishing in the mud flats of Yerba Buena Cove. As long as they are left alone they do not bother with people, but run into the hills above to enjoy their meals in peace. Certainly the grizzly bears and mountain lions of which Papa writes will behave no differently.

He lives in a tent, yet I am living in little more than a tent. I have seen calico pavilions among the San Francisco hills that accord as much shelter and privacy as Mrs. Llewellyn's walls.

There is gunfire from somewhere in the town nearly every day, usually from the gambling hells where, according to Uncle James, cheating is not taken lightly. Arguments frequently erupt among the men queuing all the way across Portsmouth Square from the Post Office whenever a new ship brings a bundle of mail. Those disagreements nearly always prompt unspeakable words in many languages as well as split lips and bloodied noses. How much less civilized could the Indians be than the men who impatiently await a favorable turn of luck or a word from home?

I argue with my father in my letter, emphasizing that I am nearly grown (which I know is stretching the truth) and can care for him. I have learned to cook (more from Mrs. Dunsford than Mrs. Llewellyn—Papa is right about the food at the boardinghouse). Daily I fetch fresh water from barrels delivered to Mrs. Llewellyn's door. I gather kindling from the chaparral above the town for heating and cooking. I dust; with the wind keeping a steady supply of fine dirt seeping into the house, my efforts are never-ending. I sew a little when asked. I do not wash laundry, but I do help Mrs. Llewellyn tie the bed linens and her guests' dirty clothing into tight, reeking bundles that she then carts to a lagoon north of town to be laundered by some Californians who work there. They do not iron, but nobody in San Francisco does—it is the style of the city to be rumpled, I think.

San Francisco is still without a school teacher, so life in the mountains cannot possibly be less helpful to my formal education. I would do whatever schoolwork Papa set me to—he need only ask.

I argue all of this carefully in my best handwriting. I think my reasoning is thorough.

I post the missive and wait.

Ribbons of light from *The Pelican* ripple across the water as Uncle James rows the tiny skiff to meet her. The ship's ladder is already lowered in anticipation of our visit. We are joining the Dunsfords for a Thanksgiving celebration.

Rain has been pelting us since we left the boardinghouse. I sit in the stern of the tiny boat, huddled beneath an umbrella, and try to keep myself and the basket of Mrs. Llewellyn's bread dry. I pat my skirt pocket for reassurance that Papa's latest letter is still there and dry as well. I do this every few minutes. I have not yet read the letter. I am afraid to read it.

Mrs. Llewellyn was invited too, but declined to join the festivities as she is waiting for the Bear. He has been granted a 30-day leave and, not certain when he will arrive, she wants to be where he can easily find her. She is more restless and excited than usual.

Uncle James and I are more wary than excited about this meal: it will be the first holiday for the Dunsfords since Lizzie has been gone.

It was earlier this very month that Lizzie first went missing. Prior to breakfast one morning, Mrs. Llewellyn's house was shaken by pounding on her door. Mr. Boyle, the Reverend, and Matthew were on the porch with a frantic plea: they needed my uncle's help to find Lizzie. She had last been seen at 10 o'clock the evening before, but a morning's search of the ship had availed them nothing. The Dunsfords were convinced that the girl had met with foul play for they found the ship's ladder lowered but none of her belongings taken.

Mr. Boyle could not convince the family that the girl had left the ship of her own volition: only someone already on board could have lowered the ladder. His belief was that she had run away with the Cecchi lad. The Reverend would not hear of this. He insisted that Robert Cecchi had been a harmless infatuation and that his daughter would not have run off with "that boy." Besides, the Cecchi family had left long ago for their new home to the north.

Uncle James gave Mr. Boyle's theory some credence when he dispatched his hired man Alonso to check with the harbormaster about any ships that may have sailed in the previous twenty-four hours. The Reverend was clearly not pleased with this, but as he had asked for my uncle's help I did not think there was much he could say.

All volunteers, which included several of Mrs. Llewellyn's guests, were organized by Uncle James into pairs and given instructions. He wanted them to search the areas of the city that were most likely to contain men of an unscrupulous nature. Therefore, Pacific and Broadway Avenues were foremost on the list. All of the gambling hells would be scrutinized as well, which would take some time as there were a great many of them.

There was much speculation about who the culprits might be. Many suspected *The Pelican's* South American passengers or someone from the crew who, having been attracted to the blonde girl, returned to the ship for their dastardly purpose. Some suspected others of San Francisco's new arrivals whose reputations for "high crime at every opportunity" were already well established in the city. The latter were the denizens of Pacific and Broadway.

Before the searchers left, Uncle James assured them that the welfare of a little girl would rally the good and honest people of San Francisco to the cause. By that he meant most of the population of the city, despite the influx of criminals. Still, he recommended that everyone carry a weapon. When it became apparent that neither Dunsford carried anything deadlier than fingernails, he paired himself with the Reverend and Matthew with Mr. Boyle. He was adamant that I remain with Mrs. Llewellyn and under no circumstance follow them. I expected as much.

"Who are the Cecchis?" Mrs. Llewellyn asked as the front door closed firmly behind the search party.

I told her of the boy born in the little castle in Italy who had the misfortune of being Catholic. I spoke of the flirtation, mentioning how pleasant Lizzie was after she had fallen in love with Robert. I told Mrs. Llewellyn about Lizzie's tears on the day *The Pelican* made anchor in San Francisco.

"Where was the family to go?"

I could not remember. Lizzie had told me, but her rapid and breathless descriptions had left little time to commit such things to memory. Besides, it had been of no interest to me at the time. "Somewhere north of the bay, I believe."

"I think we should 'elp Alonso, no?" Mrs. Llewellyn said, her dark eyes narrowed and focused on something not in the room. "Will you join with me?"

I was overjoyed and told her so, although I had reservations. "I know Uncle James said they would be safe, but he did insist upon carrying weapons. It could be dangerous."

"Well not where I mean to go," she said with a smile, then pulled a small pistol from the drawer of her china cabinet. "But to be certain…," she said as she confirmed that the gun was loaded before slipping it into her skirt pocket. "I think we will be fine. Come along. Grab a coat and your boots, my girl. We have lovers to find."

As we made our way to the cove and the shops along Montgomery Street, Mrs. Llewellyn freely expressed her scorn at the Reverend's shortsightedness about his daughter. "I defied my family to marry. My father could not understand why I would want to marry someone without family, or education, or wealth (and a Protestant, at that)."

She had met the Bear while visiting relatives in New Orleans where he was stationed after an Army skirmish with Indians or marauders or something she could not recall. She liked his uniform and his manners and his immense height and how he called her "ma'am" even though she had been only seventeen ("...because 'e is from Kentucky and they are very polite in Kentucky"). They were married after only fifteen days of courtship.

Her father offered the Bear money to annul the marriage, probably realizing that it was fruitless to duel with a military man of his proportions. She herself had been offered anything she wanted if she would leave him. Independent of one another, both she and the Bear had declared "no" to each proposition.

"My father was very angry. I think no one 'ad ever told 'im 'no' before. Even me." Mrs. Llewellyn laughed.

We found no lovers in our search of San Francisco, but we did find the Cecchis—Antonio and his father—and they were looking for Robert. The boy had run away last week from his new home, north of the village at the entrance to the Sacramento River. The family was certain they knew his purpose: *la bionda*, Lizzie, was the only person on Robert's mind from the moment the family had left New York Harbor. Everyone suspected the boy had returned to San Francisco (or sailed to China if need be) to be by her side.

"Pardon me, Mr. Cecchi, but you are Italian, no?" Mrs. Llewellyn asked. "This means that you are Catholic, yes?" Antonio and his father nodded in answer to both queries. "What were Roberto's intentions for Miss Dunsford?"

Neither Cecchi seemed to understand the question.

"Did he want to marry 'er?"

The Cecchis nodded in unison without the slightest hesitation.

"Then, we go to the Mission," Mrs. Llewellyn announced. She turned to me. "But first, we find your uncle so 'e and 'is men are not killed in some 'ouse of ill repute looking for the girl."

We happened upon Alonso first, returning from the harbor office to deliver the news that no ships had departed last night. Of the two small vessels that were to leave that morning for Stockton, the passenger lists had been checked and the harbormaster's aides dispatched to each. No blonde girl was on either ship and, after questioning each passenger, nothing suspicious was found. The harbormaster was most cooperative; the kidnapping of a little girl would not be tolerated.

Alonso's news was met with nods by the Cecchis and Mrs. Llewellyn; the Mission it was to be. The four of us climbed into the wagon with Alonso to search for my uncle and the others. It did not take us long.

"I know you find it 'ard to believe, Reverend. But the boy is missing, Lizzie is missing, Guine saw 'er crying on the day the Cecchis departed, and Mr. Cecchi assures me that 'is son wants only to marry the girl. So I believe they will 'ave gone to the Mission in the 'ope to marry. It seems simple enough to me." Mrs. Llewellyn explained, once we encountered Uncle James and his party.

Only when my uncle assured him that the others would continue the search within the town limits did the Reverend concede to a visit to the Mission. He did not yield gracefully, however, and there was little conversation as we traveled through the named streets of San Francisco to the wide, well-worn road that led to Mission Dolores. I could almost hear the Reverend fuming.

The Mission complex was surrounded by fields in their last days of harvest and grasslands that stretched toward oak trees huddled on the hills behind. Although the outbuildings were decaying, the stout church was well tended. The white walls and squared pedestals of its columns looked sturdy enough to stand for hundreds of years.

Lizzie and Robert were at the head of the stone steps, a priest at their side. I thought perhaps they had been waiting for us. She was dressed in a cornflower blue dress which did not fit her well: her slender wrists dangled below the cuffs, the skirt hovered far above her worn shoes. The ill-fitting dress did not matter; she was beautiful. I recognized her loveliness and for the first time understood what had attracted Robert to her even in New York. Robert himself, his face tense and uncertain, stood squarely at her side, one arm protectively clasped around her waist. By contrast, Lizzie was calm and smiling brightly.

Upon seeing the couple, the Reverend roared. When Robert stepped forward to announce that he and Lizzie had indeed married, the Reverend's face purpled. He ignored the boy, turning his wrath on Lizzie. He called his daughter a Papist whore and lashed out at the Catholic church for its indulgent rituals and beliefs, lambasting "that devil in Rome," spitting his fury until he could speak no longer, his voice hoarse. Finally including Lizzie's new husband and the priest in the circle of his spite, he demanded that the marriage be annulled, screaming that Lizzie was a child and had not obtained his permission. A brief smile passing over her features, Lizzie lowered her eyes, but not her voice. "I am not a child, Father. My marriage cannot be annulled as I am no longer a virgin. The marriage was…well, Robert and I…last night."

The Reverend paled, swaying as he stared at his child. His shoulders slumped. He looked deflated. "I shall have your things brought and thrown to the steps of this wicked place."

"I don't want my things. Nothing fits me anymore," Lizzie held out her arms, her exposed wrist bones demonstrating her claim. "Please, Daddy. It's my wedding day."

"You have chosen your new family and are no longer a part of mine." The Reverend turned away from the couple as he spoke.

We left Lizzie and the Cecchis staring after us in bewilderment and tears. When his father was not looking, Matthew waved to his sister, his face pursed and his eyes tearing. I suspected my face had been much the same that day I waved goodbye to Papa so long ago in Boston. I felt many of those same emotions as we retreated from the Mission.

During our return journey, the Reverend outlined his campaign of exclusion: he had only two daughters now. The rest of his family had better understand that and follow his lead.

When delivering the invitation to the Thanksgiving meal, Matthew confirmed that his father had firmly held to his principles in the interval since the marriage. Each of his brothers and sisters are petrified to speak Lizzie's name for fear of an outburst from their father. Tears are strictly forbidden too. The Reverend watches them all constantly to ensure that no communication is conducted with Lizzie. He will not let any of them frequent the Post Office; only the Reverend himself may make that trip. He distributes all "acceptable" mail by his own hand and is suspicious of any outbound letters, demanding the right to read them before they are posted.

As a result, the rest of the Dunsfords have become stealthy. At my uncle's suggestion, I act as intermediary between Lizzie and her family; all correspondence comes through me. Dozens of letters have already passed between Matthew and his sister, Mrs. Dunsford and her daughter. Except for the first letter, suggesting the plan, I do not write to Lizzie at all nor she to me. We have less in common now than ever before.

Uncle James and I climb *The Pelican's* ladder and rush to the main cabin door, seeking shelter from the rain. We cannot anticipate the family's mood, but if the gloom around us is any indication the evening will be long.

The ship is greatly altered since her abandonment—all to the better, to my mind. The bunks in the main cabin have been removed and much of that lumber sold in town, fetching a nice price since the citizens of San Francisco are in a fit of development. Construction on dozens of new structures has begun throughout the city. These buildings are in various stages of completion. Many seem frozen in time for weeks awaiting a stable carpenter who knows how to treat the rare and expensive commodity of milled lumber which has been shipped from the East Coast at great expense.

In an effort to make San Francisco look like a real town and protect their patrons from the ever-present dirt (which has turned to a sticky mud since the start of the rains), several of the merchants along Montgomery began to lay boards as walkways in front of their shops. Most of the planks went missing by the next morning and that effort was soon abandoned. Mr. Boyle suspects that a close look at any new construction will uncover road sand on much of the materials.

The few city officials left in town decided that formal wharves were in order, given San Francisco's new-found popularity and activity. However, dock construction is slow since city funds often run low (according to Uncle James) and it is difficult to keep the laborers' attention off of the goldfields for very long. Despite this, there is already evidence of a rudimentary pier at the foot of Clay Street and another further south in the cove.

The Dunsfords have made *The Pelican* as much like a home as possible. Each of them now has their own "room," the second-class cabins having been assigned to each. Mrs. Dunsford took charge of the cooking, converting the first-class cabin into a convenient pantry and using the captain's galley as the main kitchen. Anything that had not been stolen by the sailors prior to their desertion was moved from the deck house and safely stowed closer to hand. Captain Watson maintains his previous cabin and Mr. Boyle keeps to his old quarters in the deck house, preferring the additional privacy—he no longer has to share the cabin with the apprentices or Mr. Sterbenc and claims to be content with that even if it is a little inconvenient to cross the deck at mealtime.

Removal of the bunks has left the main cabin of *The Pelican* open for almost any purpose. Not *all* of the timber was taken from the ship: three newly built trestle tables and benches stretch across the main cabin deck where the family, the Captain, and Mr. Boyle take their meals and where Mrs. Dunsford's pie business flourishes.

Mrs. Dunsford began baking small pies, both sweet and savory, for sale to the shop merchants in town not long after the family's abandonment in San Francisco. Each day she arises at dawn to bake dozens of pies. The boys cart boxes of pastries from ship to the stores as their mother acts as negotiator. Each pie fetches a good price and Mrs. Dunsford is always able to sell every one. All residents of *The Pelican* seem quite happy with this arrangement as she uses the proceeds to buy only the best foodstuffs both for her next-day baking and meals for her extended family. Mrs. Dunsford is an excellent cook.

Despite Lizzie's absence (in fact, I suspect *because* of Lizzie's absence), Mrs. Dunsford insisted on this Thanksgiving meal. The Dunsfords, as most New Englanders, annually celebrate the occasion back home. She believes there is no need to abandon the tradition just because Californians might not be able to spell "pilgrim."

The turkey is courtesy of Mr. Boyle. He made a rare land sojourn the previous day, braving mud and the poison oak that covers much of the hills near the Mission among the oak and madrone trees. Turkeys freely roam the countryside and, with Matthew in tow, he hunted for the Thanksgiving centerpiece. The story told at the supper table is that he shot two birds, which was as much a surprise to him as anybody. Mrs. Dunsford is stewing one of them in preparation for tomorrow's pies; a bonanza she does not want to squander.

The bird chosen for the roasting is a large one which Mr.

Boyle estimates to be nearly twenty pounds (although my uncle thinks fifteen a more realistic guess). Even plucked and trussed, it could not fit into the galley oven. Mr. Boyle solved the problem: he placed a broad board across the bird's sternum, had Mark and Luke hold the board in place, and jumped on it. After two tries and much whooping encouragement from the boys, Mr. Boyle successfully flattened the bird enough for the oven. The roasting began.

Of course there is much to laugh at in this anecdote, but I am disappointed. In times past, Papa and I had a tradition of pulling the merry-thought bone every Thanksgiving. Now I assume the bone has been rendered useless by Mr. Boyle's actions.

With this new thought of my father, I pat at my skirt pocket again, satisfied with the soft crinkling of Papa's letter.

We sit at one of the long tables amid a quantity and variety of food that rivals anything seen on a Somersworth board. Alongside the roasted bird are three types of vegetables, biscuits, a squash pie, and cranberry relish. The cranberries traveled from New York on *The Pelican* in large barrels because, Mr. Boyle informs everyone, they are commonly used to prevent scurvy. While this is good news, I doubt anybody is thinking of disease prevention as we gorge on the delicious meal.

"I've enough surplus army tents for...well for an army. Yet I can't keep Sam Brannan in pickaxes and shovels, or your father in...calamine lotion!" Uncle James exclaimed, rubbing his forehead then flinging his hand out to the side, flapping the letter he held there. "Is that how you pronounce it? Calamine lotion? What the devil is it? And what does he use it for? He orders gallons every time I hear from him."

I shrugged as I had never heard of calamine lotion.

The dining table was littered with correspondence brought from the Post Office only that morning. Mrs. Llewellyn let my uncle use the table for such things as long as everything was cleared well before meals. With the heavy rains, it was more convenient for him to set up a temporary office at the boardinghouse than to hazard the hills to the warehouse.

It was not yet time to join the Dunsfords on *The Pelican* for their Thanksgiving feast. I was reading in one corner, near the window where the light was best. It was a cumbersome book, *The Last of the Mohicans*; cumbersome only because the author used unfamiliar words and I had no dictionary to aid me.

Matthew and I found this book and others in an abandoned ship from Australia, *The Ariadne*. We explored each of the ships (their number now grown to nine), looking for anything useful that we could haul to *The Pelican* or Mrs. Llewellyn's. At first we worried that we were stealing, but the more Matthew and I discussed it the less it seemed so. The original owners had not thought enough to take the things with them, after all.

We were sometimes astonished at what the deserters left behind. We loaded our dinghy with trenchers and tin plates, pots and pans, tools and ship-repair supplies, all potatoes that had not yet sprouted ugly pale tentacles, several partially-filled liquor bottles (for Captain Watson), and the books. Mrs. Dunsford quickly confiscated one of these books, a novel titled *The Fortunes and Misfortunes of the Famous Moll Flanders*. She threw the volume overboard before we could read a single page. Apparently she knew the novel by its reputation and refused to have a child of hers, even an occasional child like me, read such a thing. Other than that, it had been a productive day.

However, we found no dictionary during our explorations. So I struggled through Cooper's novel, confused and guessing at definitions as the author described the ancient New England landscape and the rigors of "frontier" life. I wondered what he would have thought of California.

"You have a letter there from Papa?" I asked, suddenly understanding my uncle's question about lotion.

"I wondered when you'd realize that I had."

"Is there one for me?"

Uncle James waved an unopened letter and smiled. As I reached for the envelope, he snatched it playfully away, handing it to me after a few additional mock evasions.

"I don't think you should read it now," he said, the lines at the corners of his eyes deepening. "What if he remains steadfast? Then you'll be very unhappy and ruin your evening at the Dunsford's. Why not leave it here and open it when we return?"

I turned the letter over several times, debating. Uncle James did have a point: what if Papa continued to insist that I stay in San Francisco away from his mysterious existence in the wild? This letter was his response to my carefully crafted arguments; I held Papa's answer in my hand. Did I dare hope that he had agreed that I could join him?

Still, I decided not to read the letter until after returning from the Thanksgiving feast. It would not do for me to mope through supper at any bad news I might read. I could pretend that his answer was favorable, at least through the party.

I tucked the letter into my skirt pocket and went back to my book until it was time to go. It was no easy feat to keep my hands from roaming to that pocket.

"Who is Miss Munro?" I asked, having found that name in Cooper's book.

"In that book?" Uncle James asked. "I believe there are two Miss Munros in that story."

"No," I said, "the one Papa and Mama knew."

"You mean Georgette? Georgette Munro? How do you know that name?" My uncle blinked, but did not convey anything else in his face.

I told him Mama's story of the Christmas Day when she met my father. Uncle James would have been at the North Church that day too; surely he would know of Miss Munro.

"She was not your mother's favorite person," Uncle James smiled. "She was a girl your father knew from long ago."

"Was Papa in love with her?"

Uncle James shrugged. "I don't think so. Although he may have been for a short time. She was certainly in love with him."

"Until he met Mama?"

"Well I don't think quite then. Annie may have fallen in love with your father that Christmas day, but I think he only thought of her as my baby sister for several years. He and I were the ones that forged a friendship first—he discovered I could get him the newest and best quality surgical instruments from Germany, for a reasonable price, and I found that he played a very fine game of chess.

"He was a struggling young doctor when we met…good even

then, but more given to charity work than making money. It was
the challenge of the work that enthralled him. I can't tell you how
often we had to stop him from discussing the details of a surgery
right in the middle of a meal, his face aglow with awe and wonder
at the complexities of his craft. We didn't understand most of
what he said, but he was...he was lost in the labor.

"Jessica and I used to invite him to supper every Friday just to
be sure he'd eaten at least one decent meal that week. We ate at
your grandparents' house, since your Aunt Jessica and I didn't have
much money ourselves at the time. The folks always served enough
food for a legion. What were a few additional mouths to them?

"Fridays, Father invited his political and business cronies,
probably in the hope that I could make some important contacts
for my business, which I usually did. He would've preferred me
in politics, but if I wasn't to join him in his trade, he wanted me
successful in mine.

"So, there we were on a Friday night with three, sometimes
four other couples talking politics and exports, manufacturing and
construction contracts, or some such thing. We tried to keep away
from medical topics, because of your father.

"One night, Harold brought Miss Munro with him to supper.
We'd met her at the church, of course; I think she'd dragged him
there that night. We'd seen her at other times too, although I don't
think he was serious about her even then. I never did hear the story
of how he came to be with those particular people on Christmas
Day. In a church no less. Miss Munro and her companions always
seemed so much less serious than he. It was peculiar.

"Nonetheless, he asked permission to bring a guest one Friday
and I told him yes.

"Your Aunt Jessica was not pleased. She already knew your mother's feelings for Harold and didn't think Annie would be happy to have him bring 'that woman' into the house. I had no idea. Dim, Jessica called me; positively dim."

"Was she pretty? Miss Munro?"

"Yes, she was quite beautiful actually. In a siren sort of way. Do you know what that means?" I shook my head. "You will someday. She was charming. I believe she hoped your father would propose to her, but he never did. She married a very rich man eventually, a good deal older than she. Her husband was a contributor to that clinic your father hoped to start, in South Boston. Closest Harold ever got to a political career, I think. Your father was so dedicated to that project.

"Anyway, Annie was insufferable that night. You should've heard her when she talked to or about Miss Munro. My God, your mother could be cruel in the nicest way. I don't think Miss Munro knew how badly she was being insulted. At every turn. And Annie only sixteen or seventeen." Uncle James turned to me. "Why do you suppose she mentioned Miss Munro to you?"

I shrugged again, remembering the shock of having the unknown woman invade my mother's story.

"I'm sure Annie would have seen Miss Munro—or, rather, Mrs...what was her married name? Simmons? Oh, I don't remember; but I'm sure your mother would've seen her occasionally over the years. That sort of thing can't be helped in a small place like Boston. Everybody knows everyone else in Boston. Perhaps she'd just seen her recently and been reminded."

Perhaps. I patted the pocket of my skirt again, satisfied with the rustling. I wondered if I should ask Papa about Miss Munro, suspecting that I would not.

"A toast! To the best cook in San Francisco!" Mr. Boyle raises his cup to Mrs. Dunsford as everyone cheers and claps in appreciation of the Thanksgiving meal that has been devoured. She blushes at the compliment, but seems pleased.

No one raised the subject of Lizzie all evening. Mrs. Dunsford came close one or two times, but caught herself midsentence and changed topics. She often tumbles thoughts together as a matter of course, so the Reverend did not seem to notice. He spent the evening waxing about some worldly evil of one kind or another to whomever would listen. It fell to my uncle to be his audience until Matthew rescued Uncle James with the offer of a chess game.

As the evening continues, Matthew and I are elected to clear the table. We are just beginning this task when the door to the main cabin opens. A thin man, wet from the rain, steps inside. He removes his hat and shakes some of the droplets from his long coat, passing his hand over a beard darkened with moisture. More water drips from the ends of his long hair where the hat provided no shelter.

Everyone at the table pauses, curious and waiting for the stranger to introduce himself and explain his presence at this family gathering.

Instead, the stranger looks around the room until his amazing blue eyes fall on me.

"Papa? Papa!" I run to this man dripping in the doorway, burying my face in the wet-wool stink of his coat. Eventually, he succeeds in pulling me to arms' distance, strokes my face and hair and gazes at me as if I am something foreign to him.

He is certainly foreign to me and I finger the grizzled beard and the dripping strands of his hair, caressing the weathered angles of his face and trying to reconcile these features with the man to whom I waved goodbye so long ago.

"Harold," Uncle James is standing respectfully apart. "Welcome back."

I introduce my father to everyone and set a chair by the table for him and fill a plate with the remnants of the meal, urging him to sit and eat. Whenever he ventures a hesitant bite I watch him lift the fork to his mouth just as Mrs. Dunsford watches Anna as she eats. I reach for his sleeve and touch the beard once more, then the hand he uses to grip the table. When I realize my constant caresses are bothersome, I grasp my hands tightly as if in prayer. I do pray; I pray that he will not suddenly disappear.

As if my father were a warming hearth, the Dunsford children cluster around. Luke asks the first question, but that is only the beginning: How much gold did you find? Does the gold sparkle in the rivers as everyone says? Why do they call it "mining" when there is no mine? Have you seen a grizzly bear? Are there Indians where you live?

Papa chuckles at their enthusiasm and answers each query with patience: gold does not sparkle; panning is the word for what he does and "prospecting" might better describe the work. Yes, but the bears keep their distance for the most part; and yes, but the Indians keep their distance as well.

"How long will you be in California?" Mr. Boyle asks. He is staring into the bottom of his whiskey glass, swirling the remnants absently.

"I have not decided."

"Will you go back to the mountains?"

"Most of the miners close their claims in winter. There is generally too much snow for them to work. I have done the same."

"But you're going back."

"Yes, I suppose. In the spring."

"What about Guine?"

For the first time, Papa turns to Mr. Boyle. "I am terribly sorry. I have forgotten your name. You are…?"

"Boyle. Eamon Boyle. Chief mate."

Papa glances around the cabin with an air of distain, grabbing the edge of the table again. "Chief mate of this ship?"

"She'll sail again." There is an edge to Mr. Boyle's response that I do not like, as if he and Papa are fighting.

My father squeezes the table harder as the ship rocks with the swelling tide.

"But surely you don't intend to take Guine with you when you return to your claim," Mr. Boyle persists, watching with amusement as my father holds the table's edge.

"Your concern for my daughter is touching, Mr. Boyle," Papa rises to his feet, swaying briefly. "I am tired from the journey." He turns to me with one hand outstretched. "I'm afraid you and your uncle will have to come with me, as I am certain that the sailor who rowed me here has long since returned to the faro tables where, I have little doubt, he will already have squandered the money I paid him."

I grab his offered hand and rise, anxious to remain with him and equally as anxious to stay and comfort Mr. Boyle for reasons I cannot explain.

With calls for safety and general good luck from the Dunsfords, I wave to Mr. Boyle as my father, Uncle James and I leave the warmth of the main cabin and descend the ladder for the journey to shore, up Clay Street and to our room at Mrs. Llewellyn's.

CHAPTER 11

January 23, 1849

SAN FRANCISCO SWELLED in the winter. New ships arrived weekly disgorging passengers and crew into the city. Miners came down from the mountains since many of their claims were snowbound just as my father had said. Papa assured us that not everyone traveled to San Francisco: most awaited the spring thaw in the inland towns that had sprung up along the Sacramento and San Joaquin Rivers. However, enough of them stayed in San Francisco to push the limits of the city's hospitality. "Hotels" were erected overnight: wood and canvas monstrosities accommodating fifty men in a room lined with tiered planks on which they slept head to toe (I peeked in on the Parker Hotel, near the abandoned schoolhouse, just to see what this new type of hotel was like). Food establishments flourished since none of the miners or deserting crews had places to cook. The gambling hells never closed.

I am no longer permitted to walk to the Post Office in Portsmouth Square by myself, and I must avoid Broadway and Pacific Avenues altogether. I usually arise early and accompany Uncle James to his warehouse. From there I meet Matthew for a day's exploration among the abandoned ships. On days I do not rise in time to go with my uncle, I carry Mrs. Llewellyn's tiny pistol as I walk to the cove through the raucous streets. Only Mrs. Llewellyn knows I walk alone.

Papa has not changed much since Boston except that he is thinner. I do not think he is happy in San Francisco; he never says anything, but I can tell. He paces the floors of the boardinghouse and makes excuses to be somewhere else. He refuses to be introduced as a doctor and requests those who know to call him "Mr. Walker." I caught him once kneeling before the dusty trunk that stands in our bedroom, lightly touching the shiny surgical tools that line the top tray, but he never takes them out.

He sleeps on the floor of the room we share with Uncle James and raves about how much more comfortable the floor is than the rocky ground of his campsite in the Sierra. I know what he is doing, but he cannot dissuade me so easily.

I never read his last letter and, in fact, forgot about it entirely until Mrs. Llewellyn handed me its bleeding pages along with my newly laundered skirt. Even though the pages were illegible, I know now that they contained Papa's refusal to have me live with him on his claim. I might not have been surprised at his appearance on *The Pelican* at Thanksgiving, but the evening would have been less enjoyable had I read the letter beforehand.

Regardless, I press my case at every opportunity. When he returns to the "hills" I want to go with him.

Mr. Boyle is as restless as Papa. He mends and scrapes and swabs *The Pelican*, but he talks of nothing except the sea. From Thanksgiving until Christmas he often crewed on ships that sailed the bay and up the Sacramento River to Stockton. While expressing some satisfaction with this, he declares that river sailing is nothing like the open sea. As of New Year's Day, he was made captain of *The Rebecca*, a small craft Uncle James acquired to deliver new miners and supplies to the diggings or bring wintering miners back to San Francisco. That seemed to please Mr. Boyle (or rather Captain Boyle), but he did not lose his frown completely.

There was no snow at Christmas and the Dunsford children and I were disappointed. Snow does not fall in San Francisco according to my uncle. He once said it might when hell freezes over, although I was not sure what he meant. He announced this upon his return from the center of the city where he had spent the evening gambling. He emptied his pockets of coins and bags of gold dust, then pitched into bed with a drunken giggle, making his cold prediction for the underworld before saying: "It could happen; this *is* San Francisco and the hells are plentiful."

During his previous leave, the Bear taught Matthew and me how to use firearms in the hills behind the Mission where turkey and rabbits are plentiful. I practiced firing a few pistols and rifles, but Mrs. Llewellyn's little gun remains my favorite because I do not find myself bruised and sitting in the dirt from the recoil. It will not kill game, the Bear said, but it will stop any man that tries to grab what he should not. By the time the Bear returned to his troop after Christmas, I was adept at hitting targets and reloading the little single-shot pistol. Using some of the Bear's other weapons, Matthew shot several rabbits for his mother's pies. I never hit anything that moved.

At least twice every week Mrs. Dunsford invites Papa, Uncle James and me to supper on *The Pelican*. It is a wonderful opportunity for one of her great meals, but it is also a time for passing letters from Lizzie and collecting the ones Mrs. Dunsford

or Matthew have written in return. As far as I know the Reverend
is none the wiser.

Papa seldom accepts the invitations to supper. He does not
like being on the ship as it rocks and sways during the meal. I
suspect that he does not care much for the questions Mr. Boyle
asks him either, although he never says so and is adept at politely
avoiding most of them whenever the two men cross paths.

Tonight both he and Uncle James refused the offer of a meal
in favor of an evening of gambling, so I go by myself. Papa does
not like the gambling hells particularly, but he often accompanies
Uncle James to "keep him from harm." I am not sure if the harm
comes from the drinking or the gambling or both and Papa does
not explain.

I readily accept when Mr. Boyle offers to walk me home from
The Pelican after supper, as the sun set hours ago. The streets are
shrouded in fog which whispers around the cocoon of light from
our lantern, but we are well acquainted with the path to Mrs.
Llewellyn's.

"Matthew told me that the Reverend has found a ship that
will be sailing for China," I say to Mr. Boyle, having exhausted
most of my other news. "But Mrs. Dunsford has refused to go."

The lantern highlights the smile on Mr. Boyle's face. "Yes. I'm
ashamed to say that I've overheard those conversations."

"Ashamed?"

"Well I could've gone to the deck house, couldn't I? But I
didn't." He shakes his head. "That Mrs. Dunsford. I wouldn't have
thought it in her to defy her husband. She told him he could go
if he wished, but she and the children liked it in San Francisco.
She's nearly saved enough money for one year at the university

for Matthew. She made it very clear that the Reverend wasn't to touch that money for fare."

"You would not like it if she left would you? You would miss her cooking."

"Well yes I would. But I'm going to miss that anyway." His smile disappears. "Guine, I'm leaving. Your uncle's hired me and Captain Nelson for another of his ships now that we can muster a crew. I'll be leaving for New York in a month or two. As soon as the ship's fitted out."

I stop walking, a heavy flutter in my chest. It is true that ships are leaving San Francisco Bay again. Sailors who once deserted are returning to the city because of the winter-locked mines. Most do not intend to return in spring, having found the work of mining harder than they expected. Many are anxious to go home or resume seeking their original destinations. Most are no longer able to live in California without a new source of funds as it is expensive here. For that reason, although ships are still abandoned once they make port, several have sailed out of the bay in the last few weeks having found tarnish on the strait that is now commonly referred to as "The Golden Gate."

"I need to be sailing, to be back working. I need to see my family, meet my grandchild. Maybe grandchildren, who knows. I've enjoyed my time with the Dunsfords and you and your uncle, but I must be moving on. These past months have been…grand and horrible all at the same time."

We must have begun walking again for we soon come to Mrs. Llewellyn's. I have said nothing, hoping Mr. Boyle will reveal his announcement to be a prank. Instead he talks about the "new" ship and all that must be done to make her worthy to sail, how it cost very little money to buy her since her previous owners were on the other side of the continent and quite done with her, that Captain Watson quit drinking the moment the opportunity for a new ship came along (which was a relief as Mr. Boyle was tired of playing nursemaid to his captain, he said). By the time we reach Mrs. Llewellyn's porch, I already hate the "new" ship.

"I'll leave you here, Miss. Will I see you tomorrow?"

There is no opportunity to answer as my father and Uncle James stumble toward us from the road, my uncle's voice bellowing through the fog. He is singing although I do not know the tune and cannot understand the slurred words. Mr. Boyle rushes to help my father, who has one of my uncle's arms slung across his shoulder; Mr. Boyle does the same.

"Well hello Mr. Boyle. I didn't see you there. Of course I can't see anything through this infernal fog. 've we made it home?" Despite his condition my uncle is polite.

"You're not far now."

"Good. That's good. I'm tired and I fear I've lost all of my money."

"No, James, I have your money," my father responds. His words are not slurred. My father does not drink much or often, even when he keeps Uncle James company.

"Oh, good man, Harold. Did I tell you, Mr. Boyle, that my wife won't be joining me any time soon? I received a letter from her today. It seems my mother is well."

"Which means that she is healthy and as impossible as ever," my father murmurs.

"...and my daughter, Rebecca, has a beau. He asked for her hand in marriage. Can you imagine that? That young man has a great deal of pluck; my Rebecca's still a child."

"She is nearly sixteen, James."

"No, that can't be possible. She was a baby when I left."

"She is sixteen."

The trio stumbles onto the porch, my uncle forgetting how many steps there are. "Jessica wants to know what I think of the young man. How can I know? I've never met him. She describes him in the letter, but I can't grant my permission if I don't even know him, can I? She can't expect me to give my daughter away to a stranger."

They turn sideways to slide through the front door and the movement seems to make my uncle dizzy. "She's not coming, you know."

Mrs. Llewellyn meets them, fully dressed, lighted candle in hand. It is not the first time she has seen my uncle in this condition; it is not the first time any of us has seen my uncle so drunk. She leads us to the door of our bedroom and opens it. Papa and Mr. Boyle prop my uncle on the edge of his bed while Mrs. Llewellyn removes his coat and Mr. Boyle removes his boots. My uncle laughs at these amusing ministrations.

Then lunging forward, Uncle James grasps Mrs. Llewellyn's face in his palms, pulls her toward him, and kisses her fully on the lips before his hands fall to his sides, chin drops to his chest, and he flops unconscious onto the bed. Covering him with a blanket, Mrs. Llewellyn ushers Mr. Boyle and me into the dining room to join my father who had left just as the kiss began.

"I apologize for my brother-in-law, Mrs. Llewellyn," Papa says. "He received bad news today. Well the news was actually good, but he received it badly. It was not what he hoped to hear."

"There is no need to apologize for 'im, Doctor Walker. 'e will not remember anything tomorrow." Mrs. Llewellyn lights a candle for us and retreats to her room.

I am disappointed to hear that Aunt Jessica is not coming. Uncle James was convinced that his last letter, which described the beauty of California, the wonderful weather, and his desire for her presence, would overcome any trepidation she had about the rutted roads and the lack of schools.

"He is afraid he will never get Jessica to move here once Rebecca is married and starts a family," my father offers by way of explanation.

"Mr. Boyle is leaving," I say, although I know this statement has no context and nothing to do with my uncle. Even with the activities of the last few minutes, Mr. Boyle's announcement is still uppermost in my mind.

My father stands and offers his hand to Mr. Boyle. "Yes. Well good evening, Mr. Boyle. Thank you for your help. You were present at a most opportune time. Nonetheless, I apologize that you had to see my dear brother-in-law in such condition."

"No, Papa. Mr. Boyle is leaving. He is sailing for New York."

"Oh? Oh. Well when will that be?"

"We'll set sail in a month or two. The ship's still being fitted out. That takes time," Mr. Boyle says.

"Will it be *The Pelican?*"

Mr. Boyle snorts. "Lord, no. That's become the Dunsford Home and Pie Factory."

"Ah, yes. Well I wish you all the best. My daughter will miss your company, I am sure."

"Doctor Walker…" Mr. Boyle hesitates, glancing first at me

then Papa. He clears his throat. "Mr. Walker, I'd like to...I don't want you to take this...well my intentions are good and...San Francisco isn't the type of place for your daughter. She's told me you're unhappy that there're no schools to send her to and there are too many...what's the word you used, Guine? 'Miscreants.' Too many louts and miscreants.

"I'd be happy to act as her guardian if you want to send her back to Boston. We're sailing to New York, but I'd get her to her aunt in Boston. Her Aunt Jessica. I'd make sure nothing happens to her along the way."

I am too surprised to respond. Papa stares at Mr. Boyle, mouth agape.

"I know she just got here and the two of you haven't seen each other in a long time. But..."

"Mr. Boyle," my father's voice is low and even. "It is out of the question."

"I just thought that it might be..."

"I do not care what you thought, Mr. Boyle. She is a child. She is a girl. And you are...a sailor." Spite colors his words.

"Mr. Walker, I have a daughter..."

"Then tend to your own child, Mr. Boyle, and leave mine bloody well alone. If you think I would entrust the life and safety of my daughter to a...to you, you are much mistaken."

Mr. Boyle draws breath as if to speak again but does not. His face has gone quite red. He looks from Papa to me and back, then nods curtly and leaves the boardinghouse, the air crackling behind him as if there had been a lightning strike.

I can think of nothing to do or say. I want to run after Mr. Boyle, to assure him that I will be happy in San Francisco with

Papa, but that I will miss his company and would enjoy sailing with him were circumstances different. How those circumstances might be different, I do not know, but it seems the right or at least the polite thing to say. And it is true; I enjoy his company more than anyone else's.

Instead, I am frozen in the middle of Mrs. Llewellyn's dining room, the flutter in my chest and stomach causing my eyes to tear.

"What kind of fool does he think me?"

"Papa, Mr. Boyle is a friend of mine."

"And you wish to go with him?

"No."

"Then what difference could it possibly make that he is a friend of yours? He is a common sailor."

"He is an officer on his ship," I snap, using the same argument I used with the Reverend aboard *The Pelican* so long ago.

"Much the worse; he assumes the color of authority."

I do not know what Papa means and say so, but receive no response. Instead, Papa begins pacing the dining room.

"However, perhaps there is some merit to the overall idea. I mean, look at you: consorting with sailors, looking like a ragamuffin, running the streets of San Francisco like a common urchin. There is no proper school. You have no pretty frocks; there *are* no pretty frocks to be found here. If I could find someone to accompany you…

"This is a horrible place for a child. At least back in Boston you would be safe and with family. You could live with Jessica this time…at least Boyle was right about that. You would have a regular school and proper children with whom to play, surrounded by your cousins. You would still have your Uncle John's influence and, when the time comes, he can introduce you into society. I am certain, if nothing else, Margaret would plan a spectacular debut for you.

"If I could find a nice woman to accompany you...Perhaps Mrs. Llewellyn knows of someone in town..."

He paces the floor, speaking half to me and half to himself. More words tumble forth from him than I have heard since Thanksgiving. He crosses beside me numerous times, taking little note of my presence, wafting his plans into the air like bubbles that rise and burst with each new thought.

I want none of his plans. I want the words to stop.

"You left me!" I scream as I hit him. I pound the heel of my fist into his back as high as I can reach, feeling the solid blow to his ribs under the flannel shirt. The thud of the strike is satisfying; much more so than the mattress at Aunt Margaret's. The blow vibrates through my hand and down my arm. "You left me!"

His words become a buzz, surmounted by sounds like waves echoing in my ears. I pull my fist back and strike again. I knock his arms away as he grabs at me. I twist from him, then dive forward to put the full weight of my body into each blow that falls.

"You left me."

He grabs my wrists and I kick his shins, hoping to hear a snap or a cry of pain. I hear neither. I wiggle my hands loose from his grip and slap, open handed, at whatever part of him I can reach. Over and over again, I want to feel the sharp sting as my hand meets flesh. I like the smacking sounds. I want to hurt him.

He manages to snatch my flailing arms once more and hold them. My kicks cease to strike anything solid.

When I can no longer break free from the grip he has on my

wrists, I lunge my head into him, a belch of air leaving his body as I hit. The flesh of my lip splits on the buckle of his belt. Blood oozes into my mouth as he drops my wrists. Sharp pains stab at my knees as I fall to the floor. Sinking beside me, Papa traps my arms to my sides in the vice of an embrace. I can barely breathe as he begins to rock me. We sit on the floor of Mrs. Llewellyn's dining room, Papa holding and rocking, his grip gradually easing as I calm.

"You left me." The words emerge in a snap of bubbles mixed with blood and tears.

"I…I know." He keeps rocking.

CHAPTER 12

February 19, 1849

PAPA AND I FOUGHT the rest of the month and into the next. Oh, I did not hit him again (and I felt bad about having done so in the first place). That night was never mentioned, although he ceased threatening to return me to Boston. Once I stopped crying, he cleaned me up and examined my split lip, pronouncing it not worthy of stitches; there would be no long-lasting damage. We did not speak to each other much at all for several days, but that did not mean we were not fighting.

Once we did commence conversation, we engaged in discussions and arguments which had me teetering. Just because Boston was no longer an option did not mean he would entertain the idea of taking me to the mountains. He repeated all of the arguments he had used in his original letter and I countered with the ones I had written in mine.

Finally, he agreed I could go upon one condition: I must pretend to be a boy. This meant I must have my hair cut off and wear trousers. I believe that he hoped I would not agree to these conditions.

"Why do I have to pretend to be a boy?"

"It is dangerous for a girl in the mountains."

"Mrs. Reynolds said that towns are dangerous too. It seems it is not safe anywhere for a girl. Why?"

"I do not know that I can explain it to you. You have seen the way men beat each other in the streets? Well they do the same, and worse, to women. Women are usually smaller and men take advantage of that—like animals that hunt smaller animals. It may not be to our liking, but that is as it is."

"But even as a boy, I will be smaller."

"It is worse for a girl. As a girl, they will seek you out."

I did not understand fully even with this explanation, but Uncle James and Mrs. Llewellyn, Mr. Boyle and Mrs. Reynolds, the Reverend and Mrs. Dunsford had all said the same at some point so I had no choice but to believe it was true. For some reason, I also thought that Mr. Sterbenc might agree with them. I cannot fathom why my mind had conjured that thought.

So my hair was shorn and Mrs. Llewellyn found suitable boy's clothes among the neighbors and shops of the town. When he first saw me with my boyish mop, Papa derided the scheme as something incredible, from a Shakespearian play.

I practiced behaving like a boy. However, when I tossed my head or laughed or flipped my hand in some small gesture, my father once again forbid me to go, convinced that no one would believe me to be male.

He paced the tiny bedroom at Mrs. Llewellyn's, reiterating the dangers of the Sierra. "There will be hunger and there will be cold," he said. "You will encounter wild animals and wilder men. In this rugged terrain, the slightest misstep could mean injury or death to either of us."

"I will be careful and do everything you tell me."

"What will I call you when I introduce you as my son?"

"I like the name Henry."

"Would you answer to the name Henry?"

"Of course."

But I did not. For several days, Papa surprised me by saying "Henry" to catch my attention, to which I never responded.

"Well your constant chatter will be a clear indication that you are not deaf, so we cannot use that as an excuse."

"How about 'John Quincy'?"

"Who the devil is John Quincy?"

"He is a boy about whom Mama used to tell me stories."

Papa winced as he always did when either Uncle James or I mentioned my mother. "You think you would answer if I called you John Quincy?"

"I would try. I know the name well. I will try."

That was a failure too. Instead, I suggested that I be John Quincy but use the nickname "Quinn," hoping that it sounded more like my real name. This proved to be a success.

Still it seemed that every other day Papa changed his mind and presented some new obstacle.

Uncle James never changed his mind—not once. He thought it was a bad idea from the beginning. Mrs. Dunsford and Mrs. Llewellyn agreed with him. Mr. Boyle did as well, although he would admit no concord with my father.

"I suppose you believe that *you* could resist her incessant arguments and tantrums were I to leave her here?" my father bellowed one evening after supper when Uncle James tried once more to convince the two of us that I would be better off in San Francisco.

"Me? God, no. She is an independent child, Harold, just as

Annie wished her to be. My own children are no better. Boston sensibilities prevail."

I bristled, angry that Papa accused me of throwing tantrums and that both he and my uncle thought it appropriate to talk about me as if I were not in the room.

"But, really, Harold, what good can come of having her there, dressed as a boy, watching her father scrape together a living from a few sparkling rocks. She'll have even less chance of an education and no polite society whatsoever."

"Shall we visit the dens of iniquity that abound in this city to sample the 'polite society' of which San Francisco boasts?" My father's face had turned a deep red color as he barked his words. "James, what would you have me do?"

The room throbbed from their exchange as they turned to me. I had heard no question directed my way, but it seemed they were waiting for my response. "I want to be with Papa."

That was the end of the debate, although I was the only one happy about the outcome.

Today Papa and I leave San Francisco. We are accompanied by Papa's horse, Fuego, and the not-to-be-named mule (who is laden with so many supplies that I fear he will topple over). I say my goodbyes to Uncle James and Mrs. Llewellyn, but it is much the same as it was yesterday when I bid farewell to the Dunsfords and Mr. Boyle. I make short work of it as I am so excited and they all look too sad.

For Papa the first leg of the journey is the worst: an eight-mile ride on a scow from Yerba Buena Cove to Contra Costa, the eastern coast of the bay. He endures this with a pale face and knuckles that bulge white as he grips the railing. His consolation is that there will be no more water travel until we cross the San Joaquin River, which he says is miles and days away.

I think Contra Costa is much prettier than San Francisco, perhaps because it has trees. Other than the shredded cypress that cling to the cliffs near the Presidio to the north and the hunched oaks that cluster around Mission Dolores to the south, San Francisco boasts not a single tree. There are stunted shrubs among the sand dunes, but little else. Trees may have grown at one time, but those were made firewood long ago. Even the distant mound of Angel Island and the tiny isle that rises just beyond Yerba Buena Cove have vast bald spots where trees once stood. In contrast, sturdy evergreen oaks cover the hills of Contra Costa.

Beneath a stand of these lovely trees, near a gap in the steep coastal mountain range that rings the bay, we make camp the first night of the journey. Papa builds a fire and we dine on some of the many meat pies provided by Mrs. Dunsford. Papa erects a large piece of canvas that he calls a "lean-to," assuring me that it will keep us dry were it to rain and prevent spiders and other bugs from dropping on us from the trees as we sleep.

Papa is gently snoring almost as soon as he lay down. I do not sleep easily, but I am uncertain whether it is because of my joy or the distant howls of coyotes and the numerous plopping noises of those unseen bugs that hit our canvas shelter.

Angels lived on the canopy above my bed. That is what I told Mama. I could hear them flutter their wings and whisper as I tried to sleep. They did not visit every night, but often enough for me to know they were present.

Mama and Mrs. Schrader took the canopy down the day after I told her about the angels. I hoped to see some of them scampering across the pleated stage. Instead, as the pale cloth was lowered, I found a dozen little moths lying motionless on its surface. Their patterned wings were beautiful, but they did not look at all like the angels of my storybooks. I touched one of the bodies, hoping it would fly away and I might see its flutter. Instead, the gray dust from its wings powdered the linen and my fingertips. Each weightless body was stiff and motionless. I was disappointed—I had so wanted angels.

"It is wonderful that you have a good imagination, Guine. But there is a difference between imagining and believing," Mama said.

"How will I know?"

"The difference? Ah," she said, shaking her head. "I wish I could say that you'll know in your heart, but that's not true. Didn't your heart tell you that these little lovelies were angels?" She swept her hand in the direction of the dead creatures and I nodded. "I wish I could say, 'if you can see it, then it's real.' But that's not true either. There are many things in the world that you can't see, but are very real: like love and loyalty, patience and forgiveness. So many things."

"Do you believe in angels?"

Mama laughed. "Yes, I believe in angels and yet I have never seen one."

Papa did not believe. He said that angels were the stuff of fairytales—rubbish. "Annie, by the time she is grown you will have filled her head so full of nonsense about flying horses and enchanted castles that she will not have the vaguest idea what to expect in the real world," Papa sputtered over supper the evening after the canopy had been returned to its place. I was unprepared for the vehemence of his response when I told him about the moths and the angels. "If you must tell her stories, can you not find ones that are…real?"

"As I recall, Harold, most of the books in her nursery are yours, from your childhood. Were you not read tales just as tall when you were small?"

"I was never encouraged to believe them."

"And neither is Guine. Why do you think I showed her the moths—I could've remained silent and let her believe she was hearing angels, but I didn't."

Papa put down his fork and turned to me, quite intent. "Do you really believe in angels?"

What satisfactory answer could I give him? I could tell by his voice that he would be much happier were I to say that I did not believe. But I did not want to lie to him—he got very angry whenever I lied to him.

"I like the stories," I finally said.

My response seemed to satisfy him because we returned to our meal without further discussion except for one brief declaration: "Rubbish," he said. I was not sure if he referred to the angels or my evasion.

The next day Papa rises early, strikes our camp, and helps me onto Fuego's back. He takes care to stack the bedrolls and blankets behind the saddle in response to my complaints about the soreness of my thighs and bottom from the short ride of the day before. While the padding is an improvement, the aches do not go away altogether. I am certain I have blisters and am fearful that my skin will scar like the hide of the little mule. I had tucked the remainder of my green Brazilian potion away in one of the packages on the mule's back, but I do not want to trouble Papa to find the jar now; he is impatient to go.

As it happens, that first night is the only one spent in the open. Most evenings we stop at one of the *ranchos* nestled in the brown valley beyond the oak-covered mountains. The California families Papa met on his previous trips welcome us and feed us and make us beds in their stables or on their verandas. They have no room inside their homes as there are already many people living there. They seem pleased with the opportunity to meet *Senor* Walker's son on Papa's fifth passage through their lands. I am the son who has come all the way from America. They are not yet used to the idea that they are now from America too.

Most of the families speak only Spanish, but Papa has acquired enough of the language to converse a little. The meals are lively and friendly, even though I remain ignorant of the subject of conversation. Papa translates when he can, but even he admits that he does not always follow their chatter.

After the evening meal, Papa sits by the large hearths so that each family member may approach to "speak" with him about ailments. They point to various parts of their body and Papa asks questions in his halting Spanish, aided with hand gestures from both parties. He peers into gaping mouths and puts his head to chests or stomachs, drumming his fingers along abdomens or spines, gently prodding their necks and jaws. He daubs rashes with a pale sticky substance or gives them a spoonful of a dark elixir he retrieves from large bottles that are packed carefully on our mule. He warns the Californians to stay away from this or that, shaking his finger as he speaks. Then he smiles and gently shoos them away, welcoming his next patient. He leaves a cup or two of the remedies with each family upon our departure in the morning.

"What is that lotion, Papa?" I ask one evening as we settle in the shelter of a stable.

"Calamine lotion. I put it on the rashes they get from the poison oak."

"Does it help?"

"Not very much. But if I keep them busy lathering their skin with it they have less time to scratch." He already identified the poison oak to me as we rode, warning me to stay away from it so as not to have my skin blistered and itching.

"What about the tonic? What is that?"

Papa smiles. "It makes them feel better, usually the older people. It is mostly molasses. There is a company in the East that will mix it with bitter herbs so it is no longer sweet. I tell them it will give them more energy. Surprisingly, it often does."

"Are you the only doctor here?"

"I'm not a doctor here. Lotions and molasses potions do not a doctor make."

"But you treat them."

"Do not begin a sentence with 'but.' I will not have you speaking like an untutored waif. You know the rules."

"How do they know to come to you?"

"It was an accident. Literally an accident. My very first trip, as I got off the ship in Contra Costa, there was a horrible incident. One of the local...oh, I do not remember what the owners of the *ranchos* are called, but it was his son. The father owns most of the land there on the eastern shore; a man named Peralta. The son had come to pick up cargo from the ship, but his wagon overturned in the mud and slime. He was nearly crushed under it. I helped. I saw no reason to leave the poor man when I knew what to do. I set his broken bones, cleaned and stitched up the cuts. I did what I could.

"Word travels as quickly in these wide-open spaces as in Boston, I fear. Upon my return to San Francisco, it seemed that people in every *rancho* in the valley had heard of me and were calling on me for medical help. *Rancheros*, that is what they are called; the *rancheros* are the owners. I did not, and still do not, have enough Spanish to explain to them that I no longer style myself a doctor."

"Bu...You are a doctor."

"No. I *was* a doctor. I am no longer."

I do not understand, but the tone of Papa's voice indicates that he wants to speak of it no more.

"Of course, I trust no one who asserts himself as a doctor in this territory. I met a Philadelphian last year who claimed to be a physician. Not a doctor like Dr. Franklin, mind you, but an actual physician. When I asked about his schooling and practice, it seems he had read some ancient rubbish about how to treat ailments and fancied that he could do that as well as the next man. So he called himself a doctor, charged people to misdiagnose them, then applied medieval methods to the illness. Even claimed that he bled people to health. Absurd. I wager that we will find his tent in Stockton even still, unless he has killed someone with his barbarism. In the latter case, he has probably been tarred and feathered and chased from the town."

"Or strung up?"

"I beg your pardon? Where did you hear that expression?"

I do not want to tell him that Mr. Boyle had introduced me to the phrase, so I say that a sailor on *The Pelican* had used it once. "Well you are not to use it again. What have I taught you?"

"If I am to speak English, I must speak it properly."

"Precisely. Therefore, you will not use slang."

We cross the valley in two days. During the daylight hours, we stop only for water and an occasional midday meal supplied by our hosts of the evening before. The little corn bundles that Papa calls *tamales* are my favorites.

Other than the *ranchos*, there are no towns or other settlements. I see fewer people than cattle, the latter of which are left to graze among the abundant wild oats and other brown grasses that cover the land around us. Unlike the green hills of Massachusetts, Papa says the hills and valleys of California are green only for a few months in the spring; most of the year they are winter dead or summer scorched. The cows do not seem to mind.

We meet several fellow travelers, most on foot. All are headed in the same direction as Papa and I: east where snow-laden peaks hover in the distance, even taller than the immense mountains that form the immediate borders of the brown valley through which we pass.

This afternoon, the third day of our journey, we reach the summit of the valley's border mountains and look upon a vast plain that stretches to the horizon where the white-capped crags appear no closer than before. Papa points to a small dust cloud in the lowland to the north and announces it to be the town they now call Stockton. Before sunset, we enter this town after having descended from the high hills and crossed the broad San Joaquin River on a ferry crowded with men and horses and gear. The river trip was short so Papa was not troubled too much.

Stockton looks even more temporary than San Francisco: I see not a single building. Instead there are hundreds and hundreds of tents, wagons covered in canvas, and rickety coaches laid out in rows. Even the stores are canvas, with hand-painted signs tacked to their tent poles announcing the goods or services which are to be found inside: "Claims Office," "Post Office," "Blacksmith," "General Store." More than one proclaims "Gambling" or "Spirits."

More crowded and bustling than Portsmouth Square, Stockton reminds me of a dusty Rio without the colors. Jangling harnesses and shouts of greeting and bargaining mingle with churning clouds of dirt. The people, mostly men, seem to be made of leather and stone with faces half hidden beneath slouch hats and untamed beards. They look like the giants of my picture books, their voices booming like thunder.

We ride through the bustle, away from the river, and approach a woman standing by a wagon with a sign tacked to its side stating "Hotel." In smaller letters at the bottom, I read "$5/Night (Two Bales) and $5/Meal." The final dollar figures are only the latest in a string of numbers painted through, increasing each time. Behind the wagon are dozens of hay bales lined up in several rows, end to end. Beside the wagon is an enormous woman talking with a rangy man in the disheveled dress of a miner. I have seen many like him in the streets of San Francisco with their filthy canvas trousers and red flannel shirts under ill-fitting jackets of indescribable color.

"Five dollars? I can get a whore for five dollars!" the man protests.

"Yeah, honey, that's right. An' five minutes later, you'll still need a place to sleep for the night," the woman responds, slapping playfully at the front of the man's coat. "You hain't been here long have you? Things cost more in California than anyplace on earth! Gold fever don't come cheap, I tell you."

"Are you the proprietress of this fine establishment?" Papa asks, sliding from Fuego's back and turning to help me from the saddle.

"Mr. Walker! It's mighty nice to see you again," the woman proclaims loudly, turning away from the miner. She enthusiastically shakes my father's hand then turns to me. "And who have we here?"

"This is my son," Papa says. "John Quincy Walker. He is called Quinn." It is a game we play—Papa uses this phrase every chance he can, gently reminding me of the charade. "He has come from Boston, by sea, to aid me in my search for riches. Quinn, this is Mrs. Schwartzman."

"Pleased to meet you, Quinn. Welcome to California, young man," the woman says, narrowing her eyes to see me better and extending her hand. Once I realize I am to shake that hand just as a man would, the woman's grip proves firm. "Whoa, you're gonna have to toughen this boy up, Mr. Walker. He's got hands like a girl."

I fear I have failed my first test and quickly shove my hands into my coat pockets, glancing at Papa, hoping not to hear him once again announce how ill-advised it is to have me with him. He has threatened to take me back to San Francisco three times already: twice when I complained about the saddle and once when I squealed as a mouse ran across the foot of my bedroll. I had not screamed; it was just a little squeal. The mouse had startled me.

However, Papa is smiling. "With time, Mrs. Schwartzman, with time. Have you room for my son and me? We shall be staying only one night."

"Heavens, you do speak proper, Mr. Walker. 'Course. I'll move ol' Krajewski and let you two have bales by the cook wagon in back. That way you're out of the road dust and, if it rains, you an' the young man can duck for cover under the wagon. It's as far from the necessary as I can get you too."

"We are obliged to you, Mrs. Schwartzman."

"Sure, Mr. Walker. Always happy to have gentlemen stayin' in my establishment."

There seem to be little *but* gentlemen in Stockton, just as it had been on *The Pelican* and in San Francisco. I count fewer than a dozen women in the town. I see no children.

"Quinn, help me unpack the mule. We will put everything by the bales and you can watch over them while I find a stable for the beastly animal and Fuego."

"I do not think him beastly, Papa. May I give him a proper name?"

"What proper name would you give him?"

"I want to call him…Guleesh."

"What kind of a name is that?"

"Guleesh was the boy from County Mayo who rescued the French princess from a terrible marriage. He was invisible and rode an invisible horse. Then he fell in love with the princess and was really nice to her until she fell in love with him too."

I expect Papa to refuse. "Very well then. We shall have an Irish mule. How fitting. He shall be Guleesh."

I pat the bristled gray hair of the mule and whisper the new name in his ear.

"Stay here while I stable the animals."

I sit on one of the bales Mrs. Schwartzman assigned to Papa and me, watching the townspeople whirl among eddies of brown powder that rise from the road and block the sunset. It does not seem to matter that it rained only yesterday; the ground is already parched and restless like the people. Everyone is in purposeful motion, the noise and bustle a startling change from the quiet of the journey thus far.

Once inland from the bay, I had hoped to find snow. Instead, there has been only rain interspersed with warm sunny days. February weather was never like this in Boston. There, when it was not snowing, it was gray and cold. Papa warns that I will have my fill of snow in the mountains. It will be as cold as Boston, he says, but without the parlors and hearths and stoves for refuge.

He has spoken little of the Sonoran Camp, his answer to all of my queries is usually "You shall see." It is not very satisfying, but I can pry no more from him.

"Eh, mate. What're you doing here all by yourself?"

The man had walked to my side without my notice, planting a leg on the bale beside me. I try to rise, looking around for Papa or Mrs. Schwartzman, but he blocks my movement. He is huge and I see no way around him.

"Nobody should be left lonely. What's your name?" he asks, leaning forward until I choke on the smell of strong soap, drink, and smoke that clings to him.

He has an accent like my father's but not as refined. Australian I surmise; I have heard their speech before in the shops and streets of San Francisco. Uncle James says that a lot of ships arrive from Australia every week bearing fortune hunters. There is an area on the cove-end of Broadway that the San Franciscans call Sydneytown because of the growing population of Australians there: it was one of the reasons I was forbidden from venturing down that particular avenue.

"I suppose you're not to talk to strangers, is that it?"

I nod. He is a handsome man with blond hair to his shoulders and sky-blue eyes. Unlike most of the others, he is clean-shaven and his clothes, although dusty, are tidy. Still, the heavy whiskey fumes and cigar smells are off-putting.

"Well, let me introduce myself so we won't be strangers no more. I'm Colin Hurley." He thrusts a calloused hand toward me.

I look at the hand, then into his smiling face, and begin to tremble. His words are friendly and he has a charming smile, but the intensity of his gaze reminds me of the filthy boy in Rio. I quickly try to shoo those thoughts away.

"You know, it ain't polite to refuse a man's hand. Some men would take real offence at that; might get sorely angry. Not Colin Hurley, mind you, but some."

I swallow and reach out my hand.

"There's a lad." His handshake is firm. Then he clasps my wrist and turns my hand over, stroking my palm. "Ah. Soft, pretty hands." One finger reaches to stroke my cheek. "What's your name, boy?"

I swallow the prickling sensation that has started in my throat, just behind my nose. I glance around again for Papa. "Quinn," I whisper, unable to stop the trembling in my lips.

"Quinn? That all?" Colin Hurley leans closer.

"I am Quinn Walker." I can barely hear my own voice. Colin Hurley has heard me, however, and bows his head near my ear, his breath tickling my neck.

"Quinn Walker. Who are you waiting for, Quinn Walker?"

I clear my throat and will my voice to be still. I can no longer raise my eyes to the man's face for fear my head will tremble. "I am waiting for my father. He is stabling the horse and will return shortly." I try to sound firm as I do not want the man to know how much he frightens me.

Colin Hurley's coat hangs open, a revolver tucked into his sash. When I see this, I slowly move my hand to the pocket of my coat where the little pistol Mrs. Llewellyn gave me lays. It was given as a gift the evening before I left San Francisco as she repeated much the same words her husband had used: it will stop any man from grabbing what 'e shouldn't.

"Will you take a walk with me, Quinn Walker?"

It is an unmistakable sound, the cocking of a revolver. During the Bear's instruction, I heard it many times as it was made ready to shoot. The noise was nothing like the sharp ch-chunk of the shotguns and the weak click of the little pistol that was now close to my fingers. The revolver made a series of sharp metallic ticks. "The solid sound of a Colt," the Bear had said. I hear that sound now, beside my ear.

Colin Hurley has heard it too and stops whispering. He raises his hands slowly and straightens his back until he is standing tall, arms in the air. He takes his foot from the bale and moves one step away from me. Mrs. Schwartzman stands behind the bale with a Colt in her hand.

"You keep your filthy hands off a this boy," Mrs. Schwartzman barks at Hurley.

"No harm, ol' woman. I was just tryin' to be friendly," Hurley objects, his bright smile in place everywhere except in his eyes. "He looked lonely sittin' there all by hisself."

"You take your friendly elsewhere, you hear?"

Hurley glances around. For a moment I fear he will drop his arms along with his smile and challenge her.

Instead he tips his hat and turns to go, shouting over his shoulder, "Pleasure to meet you, Quinn Walker. Maybe we'll see each other about."

I almost yell "I hope not" as he tosses one last ugly glance toward Mrs. Schwartzman before weaving away. However, I judge it imprudent to irk the man further. I keep my mouth shut. My heart calms as the Australian disappears into the crowd.

Mrs. Schwartzman un-cocks the gun and slips it into her skirt pocket. "Damn Australians is all rabble. I don't rent bales to 'em. Can't trust a one."

"I see 'em all here," she continues, looking around at the crowd at the boundaries of her hotel. "See that big man over there," she points to a brown-skinned giant perched on one of the hay bales near the road. "He's from the San'mich Islands. You know where the San'mich Islands is?" I shake my head. "Yeah, me neither. But they all look like that. Big. Kanakas, they call theirselves. Bigger than any men I ever seen. They're nice, though, quiet and polite unless you get on their bad side. I seen one crush the fingers on a man's hand with just one a them big paws. They don't gotta shoot you; they just hug you to death."

Her heavy body shakes the bale as she sits beside me. "I seen my first Chinaman last week. Ooee, that was somethin'. No bigger than a child with hair hangin' down his back in a skinny braid, yaller skin. I didn't even know what he was; I had to ask one a my guests. I heard about Chinamen, but I hain't never seen one afore last week.

"I rent bales to men that used to be sailors mostly, from all over the world. 'Cept I don't rent to Australians. 'Course, I don't rent to the Mexicans or the Californios or the ones from South America neither. They don't make much trouble, 'cept twixt theirselves, but the whites don't like 'em. If my husband were here, he'd be makin' target practice a most of 'em. 'This here's America now,' he'd say. 'All them others need to stay in their own country.' How long you been in California, boy?"

"I arrived in San Francisco last year on October 9th; the ship left New York on March 25th."

"Well that's quite a trip, hain't it? My husband and I sailed here more than a dozen years ago, you know, only from New Orleans, not New York. Well not to here—we sailed to Oregon. Traveled across Panama. Had a devil of a time in that hell hole.

"We's from Missouri. Lost our farm in '35. Tornado up and tore everything to pieces. Everything. I lost my boy, my house, livestock. He was about your age, my boy. They never found Mr. Foster, and the whole Swan family was killed; poor babies got blowed across the prairie along with my son. Everything gone.

So we just left. Abraham wanted to go west, but didn't want to meet no Indians, so we made the trip down the Mississippi to New Orleans and hopped on a ship, just like you. We carried mostly nothin'. We had mostly nothin'." She reminds me of Mrs. Reynolds, in her garden talking about her life in Boston. I cannot think why, as this woman is nothing like Mrs. Reynolds.

"We'd a probably lived in Oregon the rest a our lives if it weren't for the gold. Abraham couldn't get to it fast enough once he heard. I hain't seen him since. I tried to follow him, but once I got here to Stockton, I lost him.

"I never liked farmin' anyway, but I can cook and these miners'll pay good money for a decent meal. So I'll just wait here until that son of a...until my dear husband finds me. Then I'll tan his hide and take his money, if he's got any, and throw him to the dogs. I'm bigger than that old runt anyway."

"Will you wait long for him?"

"Ask me another. I don't care if he never shows his skinny little ass again."

Just then, a potential guest arrives at the wagon and Mrs. Schwartzman leaves to greet the newcomer and bargain with him about a bed. Papa returns, tossing Fuego's saddle on top of the pile of goods removed from Guleesh's back. "Are you hungry?"

I soon discover that Mrs. Schwartzman is almost as good a cook as Mrs. Dunsford. Papa is not shy about praising her food, declaring that $5 is certainly a good bargain for a meal this fine. He suggests I enjoy mine as I am not likely to get anything better for several days.

Stockton does not sleep at night and neither can I. Whereas the noise and gunshots from the hells of San Francisco had been a distant rumble, Stockton offers these almost next door (although, of course, there are no doors). Stumbling and cursing, laughing and yelling, men come and go from Mrs. Schwartzman's hotel at all hours.

"There's two reasons that horse will never beat mine in a race…"

"Yeah, why's that?" This slurred question is followed by silence as the first speaker struggles to remember even one of his horse's superior traits.

"I told him to get away from my gold or I'd blow a hole in him bigger 'n Georgia."

"Then what'd he do?"

"Well he run off right quick now, didn't he?"

"…pulled out a nugget twice as big as my head, it was."

"You couldn't carry a nugget that big."

"The hell I couldn't…"

Many of the conversations are in Spanish so I cannot understand them, but judging by the smeared words I assume the subject matter and level of drunkenness to be much the same.

In my sleeplessness, I toss and turn until Papa comes to sit on the bales beside me, running his hand over the short crop of my hair. "It will be quieter from now on. Stockton is the worst for noise."

I nod, enjoying his touch. I have already decided to tell him nothing of Colin Hurley and hope Mrs. Schwartzman does the same. I do not want to create yet another opportunity for him to regret bringing me with him. I certainly do not want him to know that the journey might turn out to be no less dangerous for me as a boy than as a girl.

CHAPTER 13

February 28, 1849

IF PAPA RUES MY COMPANY, he does not say so. I suspect as much by the expression on his face when he wipes dirt from my cheeks or bundles me in blankets at night. The farther into the mountains we ride the less we say to one another. Even my inquiries about the identification of birds and trees and plants cease. Most of the time, Papa answers with "I do not know" anyway.

We left the smoky morning fires of Stockton and followed the San Joaquin River. Most of the other travelers headed north where the goldfields were proven. Instead, we traveled south through the center of the California territory, out of the grasslands that surrounded Stockton, away from the tents and the noise, and into the quiet of the foothills leading to the jagged mountains.

The snow-laden peaks kept their distance. Midday, just as I was about to complain about the lack of progress toward the snow, our path was blocked by yet another river. Surprisingly, Papa seemed pleased with this obstacle.

"This is the Estanislao River," he announced, "although some are calling it the Stanislaus. It had yet a different name before that, but I do not remember that one. This will lead us most of the way to the Sonoran Camp."

We followed this wilder river into a country of rocks and

coarse brush and ever more vertical terrain. Clusters of oak and madrone remained but among them sprouted pine and hemlock, crowding to the water's edge: tall upright trees reflecting the sheer bluffs that surrounded them. There were more trees than I had yet seen in California; there may have been more trees than in all of the countryside around Boston.

Eventually we crossed this river too. Papa chose a slow-moving stretch choked with cattails and reeds in which to urge Fuego, belly-deep, through the cold stream. Guleesh tugged at his lead and strained to keep his head above the flow. I pulled my legs high above the saddle so as not to get my boots wet.

From there, Papa said, we keep our winter shadows pointed toward the Estanislao until we reach signs he knows will lead to the main road and into the Sonoran Camp.

However, there were few shadows. A leaden sky hid the sun and showered frozen rain as we rode. Papa draped a blanket over my shoulders for warmth. By the time he sighted a dry overhang of rock for the evening campsite, the blanket was sodden and smelled like Uncle John's dog after swimming in the creek.

To augment the outcrop of our shelter Papa fastened the canvas of the lean-to over pine branches he propped against the cliff. We had only hardtack and cured meat to eat, as we were too exhausted to make a proper meal. The fire was comforting and I put out my bedroll facing the flames, curling my back into Papa's lanky form to sleep. It was the first time all day I was warm.

By the third day, Fuego and Guleesh are struggling through snow to their knees. Only patches of frozen brown fodder between the snow drifts offer nourishment for the poor animals; the crisp grasses of the meadows are far behind. When Papa is not looking,

I share my hardtack with them. I must soak it in tea to eat it, but Fuego and Guleesh crunch the heavy wafers easily.

"Are there Indians here, Papa?" I ask. I have visions of Cooper's angry Magua behind every snow-laden bush. I completed *The Last of the Mohicans* before leaving San Francisco (which was good since Papa would not burden the animals with any of my books), but the vivid images of ambushes and scalp trophies are still fresh in my mind. The wild loneliness of this place must be the cause of such thoughts. I would like to see Indians, but want to do so only from a great distance.

"Yes. The Digger tribe lives here," Papa says, "although I believe that is the name the whites have given them. Their Indian name escapes me for the moment, but I will think of it. They have ventured into my camp a few times. They are small, very dark men (almost as dark as Negroes) with broad, flat faces. They travel on foot in bands of two or three. I have seen none of them on a horse and I have seen none of their women. They wear almost no clothing and have tattoos on their faces and chests, but little additional adornment. They want to trade skins and tobacco for pots and metal utensils mostly. They are very primitive sort—not at all like the Indians of the East. They are slow to speak and seem rather dull.

"Miwok," he says after a long pause. "That is their tribal name, Miwok. There are many Indians of a different sort in the Sonoran Camp, but those are usually referred to as Mission Indians. The Mission Indians are the ones whom the Spanish conquered. One cannot say 'civilized,' although I am certain that was the intent of the Spanish. These people have adopted an odd assortment of clothing—you shall see. Whatever their dress, they comport themselves abominably."

I want more details of these mysterious people. However, Papa claims he does not remember anything more and we lapse into silence. Papa has not mastered the art of taking me on journeys to new and different worlds. Perhaps the fact that he is physically taking me on such an excursion keeps him from speaking.

"My claim is up there," Papa points to a bluff of green granite that rises ahead on the other side of the river. "There is little doubt it is still covered in snow. The Sonoran Camp is this way," he says, turning Fuego south.

There are no other travelers on the path Papa chooses, even though we spot fresh evidence of boots and hooves and wagon wheels in the newly fallen snow. Smoke wreathes the tall pine branches like blue tulle and Papa announces that we have only a few miles left to go. He taps Fuego's flanks firmly with his heels.

He hardly needs to urge the animals as they seem to sense that shelter and warmth are near, lifting their heads and hastening their pace. They bray to each other as I have not heard them before. Guleesh, who left off teasing the horse for several days in favor of concentrating on his footing, bites at Fuego's tail once more. Food, a bed, a roof; I want nothing more and believe the animals feel the same.

Still we ride another hour as the light around us dims. Finally, I become aware of tents peeking from behind trees, glowing from the golden light of candles and lanterns that blink inside. Their numbers grow as we climb the hill and come closer to the Sonoran Camp. They look like fireflies, the twilight creatures of summer. I had whispered "fairies" the first time I saw them by the marshy bottom of The Common and my mother had laughed. It is too cold for fireflies here, however.

My musings are quickly dispelled by shouts and gunshots that ring out among the trees. Papa pulls the horse to a stop in front of a dark squat building. I suspect we have arrived at the general store where Papa says we have been invited to stay with Mr. and Mrs. Ellison until the snows melt and a better idea presents itself.

"It seems the miners are no less exuberant than ever," Papa says, acknowledging the commotion as he dismounts. "You will do well to avoid the east side of town. That is where they congregate; that is where the majority of the saloons are located."

We are greeted by a man with silver hair clubbed like the patriots whose pictures graced my schoolbooks, his face ruddy and lined, the lantern he carries bright and cheerful. "Harold! Welcome back. Come in, come in. You're just in time for supper. I've made stew and it's nice and hot. A fitting end to your journey; a fitting end to a snowy day. Did you bring this horrible weather with you? We've been enjoying clear days for weeks. Pity you get this for a homecoming."

"Michael, this is my son John Quincy, called Quinn."

"...*Quinn*. And you, young man, need to call me Mike since your father won't. Michael is the name my mother called me just before she boxed my ears." I shake the man's proffered hand, more comfortable with the gesture than I was in Stockton. I have taken care over the last few days to roughen my hands by gathering wood. I hope that Mr. Ellison does not note the softness that Mrs. Schwartzman had.

"This young man will call you Mr. Ellison," Papa says quickly. "I do not intend for him to adopt that horrid American custom of calling one's elders by their given names."

"...*given names*. Quinn, you need to remind your father than we horrid American's whipped the British in two wars already and could do it again, if the occasion presented itself."

Papa and Mr. Ellison continue their banter as I drift into the store, following the scent of freshly baked bread and Mr. Ellison's promised stew, my mouth watering and my empty stomach grumbling about its plight. Light glows through the open door of a room near the back, casting the piled contents of the store into sharp silhouette.

"I see your boy already knows where to go. Come in through the back after you've sheltered the animals, Harold."

I find a kitchen even smaller than *The Pelican's* galley. There are cupboards and shelves and a little pipe stove nestled in one corner, warm and cheerful, and a small table set for two. The delicious aromas have my mouth watering in anticipation of a proper meal after days of hardtack and jerked meat.

A woman stands before the stove, her hands folded over the apron at her waist. She has Mrs. Dunsford's ample figure, golden hair swept to the top of her head, and large, trusting eyes the color of my grandmother's jasperware vases.

"Quinn this is my wife, Kathy. Mrs. Ellison to you, I suspect. Kathy, meet John Quincy Walker, called Quinn."

"Pleased to meet you," I say, shaking Mrs. Ellison's hand, eager to display my masculine manners.

"Pleased to meet you too, Quinn," Mrs. Ellison says. "Your father tells us you sailed from Boston last summer."

"No ma'am, I sailed from New York, last winter, but I am from Boston."

"...*from Boston*," Mr. Ellison whispers, the soft words only seconds behind my own, as if in echo. When next he speaks it is full voiced: "You will have to tell us about your journey sometime. But now, how about a bowl of my fine stew?"

"Yes, please, sir."

"...*please, sir*. What great manners you have, Quinn. I can tell you're your father's child, even though your accent is different." Mr. Ellison pulls a stool from under the table and motions for me to sit as Mrs. Ellison prepares two more bowls of stew.

"Here you go, Quinn." She puts a steaming bowl of chunky stew and a large slab of bread before me. I want to bury my face deep in the bowl.

"Thank you, Mrs. Ellison."

"Oh, don't thank me, Quinn. Mike is the cook in the family. I bake, it's true. Baked that bread as a matter of fact. But anything real good that comes out of this kitchen is from my husband. I would be a lot thinner if we depended on my cooking," she says chuckling. We sit as Papa comes through the back door, stomping the snow from his boots.

The Ellisons chatter through the meal, imparting news of the town. Little of it makes sense to me as I know none of the people about whom they speak. No one asks me to participate and I am thankful for that as I cannot answer much with my mouth full. I devour two bowls of the thick stew and several slices of doughy, butter-slathered bread.

"You may not want to stay long, Harold. Could be dangerous for your boy here. I wrote you about that epidemic that started just before Christmas," Mr. Ellison announces. "Men dying everywhere. Had to clear a tract northeast of the town to bury them all. At least half with no name to bury them with; most of them have no families here."

"Has anyone identified the disease?" Harold pauses, a spoon halfway to his mouth, a frown creasing his forehead.

"...*the disease*. No, but we've lost hundreds already and the deaths aren't slowing much. They're still dropping."

"What are the symptoms?"

Mr. Ellison describes the dying men: they complain of shortness of breath and aches deep in their bones, then their teeth fall out and they turn yellow before fever and convulsions take them to their graves. Mr. Ellison describes it as a slow and painful death that he does not wish on a dog. "Everybody is afraid to get near anyone sick. They won't touch them for fear they'll catch the disease and die. Most of these fellows died alone in their tents and we didn't find them until days later when somebody complained they hadn't been seen in their usual drinking hole or something. Those of us brave enough to risk it wore gloves and covered our faces with kerchiefs. So far..." Mr. Ellison knocks quickly on the tabletop.

Harold lays his spoon on the table. "You cannot get that disease from touching anyone, Michael," he says. "I will make some inquiries tomorrow, but by the description you have provided those men had scurvy. It does not come from others; scurvy is caused by bad eating habits. That is certainly no surprise given the terrible food on which most of them subsist."

"...*them subsist*. Scurvy?" Mr. Ellison puts his own spoon down. "I thought only sailors got scurvy."

"It used to be common among sailors because they could not get fresh fruit or vegetables for months at a time. But even the navy knows what causes it now. These idiot miners do not eat well or regularly, they live in deplorable and filthy conditions no better than the lowliest of sailors. I will wager it is scurvy—which is preventable. Do you carry citrus here in the store, Michael?"

"You mean oranges? We have some oranges from the last delivery," Mrs. Ellison responds when her husband turns to her for the answer. "Not many, though. How many will it take?"

Papa shrugs. "I should think two or three every week for every man, woman and child in the town will do. At the very least."

"Then we will need to stock more, as I'm sure they'll be in demand once the miners find out. Can your brother-in-law get them quickly and send them, do you think?"

Papa shrugs again. "I know nothing of his business, but he will get them if he can."

"Cranberries," I say, finally setting my spoon alongside the bowl I have wiped clean with the last slice of bread (but only when Papa was not looking). "Mr. Boyle carried big barrels of cranberries on *The Pelican* to prevent scurvy. If there are any left, perhaps Uncle James can buy some from the Dunsfords."

Papa turns to me, his frown deepening, the air of the kitchen brittle with his disapproval. He forbade me to speak of or see Mr. Boyle after the night of the offer to escort me to Boston. Actually, what Papa said was that he did not want to hear Mr. Boyle's name or find out that I had seen "the man" again. I continued to see Mr. Boyle as often as I could before we left San Francisco; I simply failed to disclose that to my father and, until this moment, had not uttered Mr. Boyle's name in Papa's presence.

"Yes," my father finally says. "Yes, cranberries will do well."

"...*do well*. How do you come to know so much about scurvy, Harold? You're no sailor; you've made that clear."

My father pauses, glancing at me and gripping the table as if he were on the deck of a ship. "I used to be a doctor. In Boston."

"...*in Boston*," Mr. Ellison echoes in his strange whisper. "How is it, Harold, that we have known you for nearly a year now and you have never mentioned this phenomenal fact?"

"It is of little consequence. I have not practiced in more than two years. I do not consider myself fit to be called a doctor anymore." Papa's reply does not invite questions and the Ellisons comply, exchanging a glance more knowing than puzzled. "I need to get Quinn enrolled in that school you mentioned, the one with the Irish schoolteacher."

"She's not Irish," Mrs. Ellison say. "She married an Irish farmer, John Moylan, after his wife died, but I think she is Polish or something. Nice man, Mr. Moylan. He had two children already and he and Beth had two more before he died. That was a couple of years ago. She started the school soon after that to make ends meet, you know. A few of the folks in town," she smiles at her husband, "built her a real nice school house. It's not much, but it's right on her property in the apple orchard and easy to get to. Trades her teaching for food or supplies from the locals. She's from the East and was trained there as a teacher. She's a real good teacher, I hear."

"Does she take money? I have nothing to trade, but I do have gold."

"...*have gold*. I'm sure she'll strike a bargain with you, Harold. Your child here won't be uneducated just because of living in the wilds of California."

"Then we shall pay a visit to Mrs. Moylan tomorrow."

"...*tomorrow*. Tomorrow is Saturday, Harold. And her name isn't Moylan anymore. She married some Russian trapper just last year. I'll be damned if I can pronounce her new name. We just call her Miss Beth."

I can barely keep my eyes open as the warmth of the kitchen and the lull of the voices wraps me. Mr. Ellison shows Papa and me to a crowded little storeroom just off the kitchen where we are to sleep until those mysterious "other plans" become evident. Clearing places on the floor, Papa and I spread our bedrolls.

"Papa, why does Mr. Ellison repeat what is said to him?" I ask after the Ellisons wish us good night and take the lantern to the loft above, to their bed.

"Ah, you noticed that did you? Well I cannot say why, but I imagine it helps him to concentrate on what is being said. It certainly seems to have prevented him from developing that annoying American custom of interrupting. It is an odd habit, but I suppose it serves him well as a judge: he hears what is said, remembers it, and ensures that the jury comes to a fully informed verdict."

"Mr. Ellison is a judge?"

"Mr. Ellison is a lot of things. In these California towns they have gentlemen who serve as mayor and municipal judge when needed. *Alcaldes* they are called. Mr. Ellison is the *alcalde* for the Sonoran Camp although his services have only occasionally been called upon thus far. I imagine that will change with the town growing so rapidly."

Papa suspects the day will come when Mr. Ellison will be called upon to drop all other employment save his civic duties. At the end of autumn last year, the Camp was already double the size of the prior year. This coming summer will bring even more new immigrants, Papa is certain.

"Now go to sleep. Tomorrow, there is much to do about this scurvy business."

Saturday Papa spends the day visiting sick miners, returning to the Ellisons' only to rail against the horrible conditions in which he finds them (though I cannot think why since he himself anticipated the conditions only last night). With Mrs. Ellison's permission, he sends me on a treasure hunt through the store for provisions he suspects might be close to hand. At least half of the time, I return empty-handed and he begins a letter to Uncle James comprised mostly of a long list of needed supplies.

"I've been thinking of calling a meeting of the town elders to talk about putting up a hospital," Mr. Ellison announces.

"I suggest you do so quickly," Papa scoffs, "before your 'town elders' die of scurvy or go back to their claims at the thaw." I suspect by his tone that my father does not believe the Sonoran Camp boasts officials able to make such an important decision.

"You know, Harold," Mr. Ellison says, "we could build a tent at the back of the store once this blasted snow stops falling. It would be two rooms: one where you and Quinn can sleep and the other for a hospital. Everybody in town stops in for supplies now and then, even the sick ones. I could just send them to you back there. We could fit it out really nice for you. Until we get a proper one built, that is."

"You would be inviting every disease known to man into your store, Michael. I do not think that very wise."

"...*very wise.* You said we couldn't catch scurvy by looking at them."

"It will not stop at scurvy. Once the town learns you have opened a hospital you will have consumptives and chancrous reprobates and any number of men with the most despicable diseases. To say nothing of gunshot and knife wounds. Have you forgotten already what we saw in our tour of the Camp?" Papa shakes his head. "No, I've seen that sort of thing before: open a clinic and one finds that the population is sicker and more in need of help than ever imagined."

"...*ever imagined*. Therefore, you believe it is ill-advised to help at all?"

Papa stares at the list before him although I do not believe he sees it. "I cannot save them all," is his soft-spoken reply.

"You can only do what you can, Dr. Walker," Mr. Ellison claps a hand on Papa's shoulder. "I never did believe that a doctor can save everybody; you just have to help people out a little. Isn't that what your oath says?"

"Let us get past this current crisis, Michael. We can talk of the future some other time."

That ends their conversation, but I notice that Papa glances toward the back of the store many times in the days that follow. Mr. Ellison takes note as well, but says nothing more to my father. However, he proudly introduces Papa as the Sonoran Camp's new doctor at every opportunity despite my father's repeated protests.

When not foraging through the dark corners of the Ellisons' store, I explore any part of the Sonoran Camp I can without my father's knowledge. I am careful to avoid contact with the miners themselves. Mr. Ellison is happy that these "Argonauts" return to the Sonoran Camp from their claims each weekend, as they crowd into his store for provisions. I find their numbers stifling and their demeanor daunting. I want to observe them, but prefer to watch from a distance or a safe refuge as most of them are filthy and loud and drunk.

The streets of the Camp, which all slant upward from the store, weave and meander through the pine and oak trees. There are no straight roads or level walkways although the paths themselves are clearly marked by muddy ribbons through the snow. It is good that the hilly conditions in San Francisco prepared me for climbing.

My explorations come to an abrupt end Monday when I am to be enrolled in school. Early in the morning, Papa and I slog down the road toward the farms that spread west outside of town, plumes of steam rising from our mouths and nostrils in the brisk air. We do not go far before the school comes into sight on the edge of a wintering orchard near the top of a rise. The schoolhouse itself is made of calico tenting atop rough-hewn half-walls on pilings a few feet above the ground. A belching stovepipe rises from one corner of the "roof." Some of the tents in San Francisco were built like this: half building, half tent.

Papa surveys the structure, pausing before a door that hangs crookedly from worn leather straps nailed to the framing. I half expect him to abandon his quest and return to the store, as he does not altogether approve of a woman teacher who he also suspects to be Catholic. Finally, he knocks.

Mrs. Ellison had described the teacher, Miss Beth, as a lovely woman with fair skin and fair hair and eyes the color of the sage that grows wild around the Camp. This was after Mr. Ellison claimed that he could not recall what she looked like and asked that his wife provide the description. The woman who answers the door is beautiful and I understand Mr. Ellison's deferral to his wife.

"I am Harold Walker," my father says, bowing slightly to the woman. He seems flustered. "This is my son, John Quincy, called Quinn. I wish to enroll him in your school if you have a vacancy."

"Of course. Welcome, Quinn. Please find a seat while I speak with your father." Miss Beth's voice is soft and refined as she welcomes us into the schoolhouse.

There seems to be plenty of room for me for the inside of the structure is more spacious than I thought it would be. I count only ten students, both boys and girls, of varying ages. They are seated at trestle tables like the ones Mrs. Dunsford had on *The Pelican*. There are six tables, three on each side of the room, the children on benches facing front.

I sit on the nearest bench, hoping that the children will turn around and resume whatever it was they had been doing before I arrived. They stare and whisper as if they think I am something strange. I hope they do not see through my disguise.

After a few minutes, Papa's business with Miss Beth is concluded and he departs.

"Children," Miss Beth calls for attention. "I would like you to meet John Quincy Walker, our newest student who has come all the way from Boston, Massachusetts. He prefers to be called Quinn. Please stand and introduce yourselves to Quinn, then perhaps we can look at the map to see where Boston is located. Let's start with you, Fiona."

A little blonde girl in the front row stands. "I'm Fiona Moylan." Fiona is about Mary Dunsford's age. She sits and the girl next to her rises. "I'm Ráichéal Moylan." Sisters, I assume, as they looked much alike and much like Miss Beth.

Each child stands and announces themselves: Joe Crump, Jacob Stallmeyer, Frank McGillvray, Billy and Jimmy Fassberg, Aileen and Jack Moylan, Aldridge Turner. I hope I can put each name with its proper face when the time comes.

"Children please put your books on the table," Miss Beth instructs. "Quinn, we share the books here so I will need to know how well you read in order to assign you a partner. Take a look at the books and pick the one you think is best suited for your level. Then read a little of it aloud, please. Don't be embarrassed as we are all learning."

I shuffle along the center aisle, glancing at the various McGuffey Readers that lay on each table. All of the books are well worn with cardboard showing through the frayed cloth of covers darkened with use. Miss Beth's collection only goes as high as the sixth level; I was through the sixth level two years ago.

I pick up the sixth-level book and thumb to the content page. I pass up the poetry and the Rip Van Winkle story: these might entertain the younger students, but the three older boys in the class, the ones who look to be my age, might think ill of either choice. This will be the first time I have been in the presence of boys pretending to be one. My palms are already damp. What would a boy elect to read?

With joy, I find an excerpt from the book that brought Uncle James to California: *Two Years Before the Mast*. I begin to read: "*It is usual, in voyages round the Cape Horn from the Pacific, to keep to the eastward of the Falkland Islands…*"

Once I finished reading, Miss Beth gently took the book from me and handed it to a girl of Lizzie's age, the eldest in the class; a pretty girl with long black hair and eyes the color of a dove. "Perhaps I have some other books at home that you could read. In the meantime, please share this book with Aileen."

Miss Beth dismisses the class for a short time in the late morning so that the students may "stretch their legs." At the announcement of recess, there is a great rush for the door and I barely have time to button my coat before one of the older boys grabs my arm and urges me to follow. I dart after him and his companions, reminding myself again how important it is that I act as they do. The secret to staying in the Sonoran Camp at my father's side depends upon my vigilant imitation of these boys. I would have liked to remain with Aileen, but that is not to be.

The boys throw snowballs as they run. My Boston cousins and I engaged in many such contests, so with some relief I hastily fashion a large missile and throw it at the closest of my new-found friends, striking him squarely behind the shoulders. With a whoop, the boy shakes the snow from his coat and sails his own shot my way which I easily deflect with a raised forearm.

"Not bad, Boston. They must have snow there!" The boy yells over his shoulder as he races through the orchard to a gnarled oak that stands some distance from the school. He scales its trunk to sit in the lower branches where the other two boys await. They motion for me to follow. I am not a stranger to tree climbing, but it proves more difficult to gain a purchase than I expect. My assailant reaches forth his hand and pulls me partially up where I can grab hold and climb the remainder of the way to a low perch. He is nearly identical to my reading partner, with thick black hair and gray eyes, and I assume this to be Aileen's brother, Jack.

"I'm Jack," he confirms, "and this is Jimmy and that's Aldridge, in case you forgot."

"I'm John Quincy, but I prefer to be called Quinn."

"I guess nobody likes bein' called John. My name is John Patrick, but I'm called Jack. Your name is John Quincy, but you're called Quinn."

"I have an Uncle John," I say, although I immediately regret it. It is not polite of me to dash his theory at the first hearing. I must find camaraderie with these boys, not discord.

Jack shrugs. "Does everyone from Boston sound like you?"

"I beg your pardon?"

"Like that: 'pahdon.' Like it's got no "r" in it. You read real good, though" he says, before I can respond. "I liked that story with all the sailors all over the ship. Usually when one of us has to read, it's somethin' awful. When it's Fassberg's turn, all you hear is snorin' from the whole class."

Jimmy Fassberg protests, reaching out to push Jack.

"I made that trip," I brag quickly, wanting to prevent a fight, wanting these boys to accept me. "Only I traveled in the other direction: around Cape Horn to the Pacific Ocean. That is how I arrived in California from Boston."

As I hoped, they ask me about the voyage. I relay the details of the rounding and the storms. I tell them of being dashed against the cabin door (except that it is a cabin I shared with the Reverend and my friend, Matthew, in this telling), the death of Thomas, and the ghostly ice that covered the ship, sparkling in the low-lying sunlight at the far end of the earth on the day of Thomas' memorial. I provide the most vivid details, hoping that I take them there as well as my mother might have. They say not a word as I speak, my tale interrupted only by the ringing of the bell Miss Beth uses to summon us together again.

"Was there more?" Aldridge asks, as we scramble down the tree to the ground.

"I was in a marketplace in Rio de Janeiro, which is in Brazil. I was captured by the police and put into one of their wagons."

"Will you tell us about that tomorrow?"

I nod, pleased. With the books I have read and my own travel adventures, I think there may be many tales to tell. "Oh, yes. I can also tell you about the giant that guards the entrance of Guanabara Bay."

"What do you think of Miss Beth?" Jimmy asks as we trudge through the snowbound orchard back to the schoolhouse. Jack and Aldridge have run ahead already. "I really like her and think she's so beautiful. Don't you? I think she has a great bosom, but Jack doesn't like me talking about her bosom, 'cause she's his stepmother, you know. I think Aileen has a great bosom too, but Jack thumped me real good last time I said that. Knocked me right to the ground and split my lip. So now I just think about them all the time, but I keep my mouth shut."

I wish he would keep his mouth shut now, as I do not want to hear him talking about Miss Beth's bosom. I heard such talk from the sailors on *The Pelican* when they thought me out of earshot. Jimmy Fassberg seems to think I *want* to hear his prattle, which somehow makes it all worse.

"I would come to school every day just to see Miss Beth's bosom. Even Sundays."

I stop and turn to face him directly, my face burning with embarrassment and a building anger. I want to slap him, but cannot recall ever having seen one boy slap another. I believe they are more likely to throw punches at each other. However, I do not want to punch Jimmy for fear he will return the compliment.

"Then, perhaps you should heed what Jack says and keep your mouth shut." I turn abruptly and stomp the remainder of the way to the tent-school.

"Guinevere Elizabeth. Come in here, please."

Mama was in the parlor, a piece of embroidery forgotten in the hoop on her lap. Her voice was firm and the use of my full name never bode well.

"I have news that you slapped a boy after school yesterday, young lady. Please explain yourself."

For decorum, I kept my head lowered. However, I was not in the least embarrassed or sorry for what I had done. "It was only Jeremy Franklin and I slapped him because he tried to kiss me." Jeremy Franklin was one of the older boys at school and he was a lout (if I correctly remembered the definition of that word).

"Oh my."

"He does it to all of the girls," I blurted, wanting Mama to understand that hitting the boy had been justified. "He made Frances Carter cry last week. When he is not grabbing girls to kiss them, he is jumping out from bushes and knocking books from our arms or pulling our hair. He is an evil boy and deserved to be slapped. I told him that if he did it again I would tell my father and Papa would cut his arms off because he is a doctor and knows how to do that."

"Guinevere!"

"Oh I know Papa would never do such a thing, but Jeremy Franklin does not know that and I want him to stop being so mean to everyone."

"Guinevere," Mama said, shaking her head but clearly in a more forgiving mood than when first I came into the room. "My sweet, even if Jeremy Franklin is evil, as you say, you must learn another way to deal with him. You cannot slap people."

"But you slapped Papa."

It was a mistake. As soon as I had uttered the words, I regretted them. Mama was as surprised and speechless as Jeremy Franklin had been after the slap: eyes wide and mouth open but silent.

She *had* slapped him. I had seen her do it in this very room the week before. It was long past bedtime, but I had awoken to raised voices and ventured downstairs to investigate. Raised voices were not usual in my house.

"...accompanied me, you know," Papa was saying. They had not closed the door to the parlor and every word carried clearly to the top of the stairs (although I did not stay there long, making my way to the foyer to crouch beneath the round table staged at its center).

They were standing. Papa was dressed in his formal vest and trousers, cravat askew, jacket neatly folded over the settee. Mama was in her nightdress and lightest robe. The house still sweltered from the day even though it was well past midnight.

"You know perfectly well that I can't be seen in public these days. I'm as fat as a cow and my face is covered in blemishes. None of my gowns fit and can't be made to fit. There's not enough material in the world to cover this…this lump that is my body." She slid her hands under the swell of her belly to emphasize the point.

"Then I go alone. I must be there, Annie. These people are donating hundreds of dollars for the clinic and I am to be the chief physician. How would it look if the major stakeholder did not show his face? You know how I hate these functions, but as the daughter of a politician you also know how fundraising is done."

"She was there, wasn't she?"

"Annie, please…"

"I suppose she's as beautiful as ever."

"Annie, she is the wife of our largest and richest donor."

"What has that to do with her beauty?"

"What has her beauty to do with anything? Annie, you are being hysterical."

That was when she slapped him. Then she turned abruptly and left the parlor, passing me cowering under the table. The chandelier jangled as she stomped up the stairs. Only moments passed before a door was slammed from above, further endangering the chandelier.

Papa did not move, his shoulders slumped, his brow furrowed. Finally he strode to the sideboard with its ever-present decanter from which he poured a glass of whiskey.

I took that opportunity to vacate my hiding spot and creep back to my bedroom where I cried myself to sleep, my parents' pale and angry faces troubling my dreams.

"I know, my sweet," Mama was saying. "I should not have

done that. Your father is working very hard for this new clinic and I need to be less selfish about his time. I must learn patience. I too must learn better ways to deal with issues than to slap people. Especially your father."

Still, I could not bring myself to regret having slapped Jeremy Franklin. He was truly an awful boy.

The stories became my entrée into friendship with the boys. The tales seemed to keep them from realizing that I could not run as fast as Jack (although none of the others could either), or throw a rock as forcefully and accurately as Aldridge, or scramble through the branches of the trees like the diminutive Jimmy. I attempted to follow their every move, but suspect they were not impressed with me. Jack teased that I would have to talk my way out of a scrape as I certainly was no fighter. Still, they did not turn me away and for that I was thankful. Perhaps they recognized my shortcomings but did not care.

I entertained them every day at recess, repeating favorite stories upon request: the almost true accounts of my voyage from Boston, the legends from my books, the tales that were written nowhere, passed down to me from Mama. I took them to Brazilian marketplaces and for rides in police wagons, to Sherwood Forest and the deserted island of Robinson Crusoe, to the kingdoms of the Celtic tales and the halls of Camelot. I avoided the romantic stories when, after hearing the tale of Guleesh, Jack announced that it was stupid: there were no such things as invisible flying horses and princesses did not fall in love with poor country boys "even if they are fine-looking Irish lads like me," he said, convulsing with laughter.

After school we usually went our separate ways, home to our chores. The Ellisons found tasks for me around the store: I stacked small sacks of beans and flour and seeds (as I could not lift the larger bags), dusted shelves, fetched water for the barrel and kindling for the stove. When she had a particularly stiff batch of batter, Mrs. Ellison would ask me to lend my "strong young arm" to her efforts to stir it. Papa usually whickered at this request.

Papa helped in the store too, for persistent snow at higher elevations kept him away from his claim. If someone came in with an ailment or injury however, Mr. Ellison would pull Papa away from his efforts and introduce the new arrival and ask if there was something the "Doc" could do for the poor soul. Papa would frown at Mr. Ellison, but always took the person and a lantern into the storeroom for an examination. When they inquired into the cost, Papa told them what they owed and said they could leave the money with Mrs. Ellison behind the counter upon their departure. Once the patient was gone, Papa would ask Mr. Ellison to stop calling him "Doc." Mr. Ellison said he would if my father would call him "Mike." Papa did not, so "Doc" it continued to be.

Mrs. Ellison kept a running total of Papa's account and we used the funds to buy things for ourselves from the store. At the end of each week, if he had more than $100 there, Papa asked Mrs. Ellison to apply the difference to the account of someone else in town who had been making a good effort but continued to have trouble paying their bill down.

At least once a week, my friends and I found time to explore the creeks and meadows below the Sonoran Camp where the

snow had already disappeared. Jack taught me the names of most
of the plants and insects and both he and the others were quick
to find the most irritating uses for them: dropping beetles and
worms down shirts or launching great handfuls of wild-oat seed
pods at each other. Jack said this was the best time of year for
the wild oats as the pods would dry and drop their seeds when
summer approached, making them impossible to throw. As for
now, the little missiles were hard and green and stuck to almost
anything. Aldridge nearly always won the seed-pod battles. I
certainly preferred being pelted with the sticky pods than having
worms and beetles on my back. Whenever I was assaulted, I was
careful not to squeal or scream or behave too much like a girl
(even though Jimmy screamed once when Jack dropped a mouse
down his shirt and the creature scampered around his body for
almost a minute before Jimmy was finally able to free it).

Because my friends had a lot of chores, it was easier to help
them than to find exploration time. Unfortunately, I was abysmal
at much of the work. When attempting to milk the Turner cows,
I coaxed no more than a cupful of milk into the pail (although I
did get a nice stream into the dirt once). Jack announced that I
would never be any kind of a man if I could not handle a teat any
better than that.

Jimmy's father was the blacksmith, which seemed odd since
Jimmy was so small while his father was one of the biggest and
strongest men in the Sonoran Camp. The blacksmith shop was in
the part of town into which Papa forbade me to venture, so I could
not help Jimmy with his chores very often. When I did go there
I was careful not to be seen by anybody other than my friends, as
I did not want word getting back to Papa.

Jack had traps set in several places between his farm and the bordering creek. He visited those traps every day as he almost always had at least one rabbit to retrieve. The bounty kept his family in stew meat and Jack had a fine collection of rabbit hides. One time he caught a skunk in the snare and we had to stay away for two days until the smell subsided. Once retrieved, he said the meat was still good as the cold weather had kept it from rotting. Only in the summer months would he discard the skunk carcasses, as a few days of hot weather never did the meat any good. Skunk meat was not bad to eat, he declared, but I did not want to try it. I could not imagine eating anything that could smell that bad. I wondered how he knew whether it had rotted or not.

CHAPTER 14

April 16, 1849

WINTER FLEES the Sonoran Camp. Less than a week of slush and sticky mud mar the roads before the sun bakes them into passable shape. Overnight, leaf buds appear on the deciduous oaks and white sprouts stipple the branches of the Moylan's apple trees. The smuggled crocus bulbs I buried by the back steps of the Ellisons' store peek through the semi-frozen dirt in a colorful array; there seem to be more of them than I remember from Rio. When I show the dainty flowers to Jack and tell him of their journey from Boston, he leads me down the mountain into a densely forested area where wild iris bloom. There was no need for me to have brought flowers to California, he says. As spring progresses there will be thousands of flowers to admire in the meadows near the Estanislao, including a blue flower shaped like a spearhead that he calls lupine: his favorite. Then he threatens to punch me if I mention to any of the other boys that he likes flowers. He only told me because of the crocus.

As spring fledges, my friends' responsibilities increase. There are fields to be readied for planting and newborn livestock to tend and a myriad of other tasks that require their attention. The chores assigned by their families are far in excess of anything Papa or the Ellisons ask of me.

With my friends otherwise occupied, I take to wandering the town and the surrounding woods on my own, exploring the creeks and rivulets that crisscross through the countryside like laces on an old shoe. I must be careful around most of the waterways as they are punctured with deep trenches that miners have dug and never bothered to fill. Mr. Ellison and the other town elders check these holes every few days to ensure that no "drunken sot" has fallen in and broken his neck, or drowned when the holes fill with water from the spring run-off. One or the other is a common occurrence and I wonder why the elders do not organize an effort to fill in the holes. The creek that splits the Sonoran Camp in two, Woods Creek, is the worst for these unnatural cavities, but Sullivans Creek comes a close second for danger.

The little creek that borders the Moylan property, however, is free of such hazards as no one has ever found gold there. This untouched creek is where my friends and I spend most of whatever free time we have.

The town itself is getting rowdier according to Mr. Ellison. Both he and Papa constantly warn me to stay away from the eastern section where gunshots can be heard at all hours of the day. This is especially true on Saturdays and Sundays when most of the miners return from their claims to spend their money and replenish their supplies.

Mr. Ellison says that professional gamblers and roving bands of men, having failed at mining, are often in town now "stirring up trouble," preying on the miners. Most of the trouble is found in areas that teem with Europeans, Australians, and Americans where the men isolate themselves in their dull army tents, leading their solitary lives. Mr. Ellison calls these men "Saxons."

On Saturday mornings Aldridge and Jack and I venture into the bustle of the lively Mexican section of the Sonoran Camp to sell apples and milk.

The Mexican encampment is not like the Saxon camp. It is as colorful as the marketplace of Rio. There are a few *adobe* buildings, but most of the houses are tents covered in gaudy hangings of silk and cottons, flags, *serapes*, and shawls. Laundry flutters from the tent poles and rich, spicy aromas waft from the cooking pots that stand before almost every home. Children run and play in the mud and dust of the aisles between the pavilions, for there are wives and whole families there.

Jack questions why it is called the Mexican encampment since there are miners from Peru and Chili, Central America, California and Spain here as well as some of the Mission Indians. Initially he suggested we start calling it the Spanish encampment since everyone spoke Spanish. However, he changed his mind because that made it sound as if only Spaniards lived there and that was not correct either.

Whatever it should be called, the boys had been visiting the encampment every Saturday for almost a year. Jack lugs a sack of apples from his orchard (or the cellar, until a new crop became available) and Aldridge hauls a bucket of milk. The two of them started their enterprise last summer when Jack noticed that the Spanish-speaking townspeople were reluctant to venture into the Ellisons' store because of threatening glares from the Saxons. Mr. Ellison was always nice to them and had learned a little Spanish himself, but still they stayed away.

Since Jack spoke Spanish and was the better of the two boys when it came to mathematics, he was the negotiator when they went to town. He always sold all of the apples he could carry and the entire bucket of Turner milk.

When I told them of the goatherd in Rio, Aldridge appeared the next week leading one of his father's cows and carrying an empty bucket. Once at the encampment he milked the cow dry and made more than twice the money he had the week before. Following this success, I requisitioned Guleesh to transport several sacks of apples, tripling the number available. By the time we headed home that day, each boy's pockets were heavy with silver and gold coins and all of our stomachs were bloated with fried dough and *tamales* the Mexican women gave us for our efforts.

The worst of the scurvy epidemic has passed. Papa refuses to take any credit for its abatement and says the disease had likely run its course because of the fresher food available in the spring. A mule train of provisions from the lowlands arrives every week, now that the snows have receded and the roads are less sloppy. The store is stocked with an abundance of produce. Mrs. Ellison continues carrying oranges and as many fruits and vegetables as she can buy from farmers like the Moylans or order from the growers in California's big valley.

Plans for a tent house where my father and I are to live go forth. Once the ground thawed, Mr. Ellison and his friends erected the foundation and the half-walls and posts that will support the canvas roof, tying the structure into the back of the general store itself. In fact, the annex (which looks just like the schoolhouse only bigger) has an entrance directly into the store. Another entrance is added as well: a flap that leads outside for access to the well and the privy. The Ellisons must enter our tent now and exit through the flap in order to get to the necessary themselves.

Mr. Ellison was strangely quiet about the hospital, but the tent house is nearly the size of the main store and is certainly more room than Papa and I need. I am certain Papa made the same observation.

In mid-April, following a brief visit to his claim site, Papa announces that the snow is melted enough for him to resume panning. He spent the early part of the month building a sluice box to help with his work: an ugly wooden contraption that uses the power of the rushing river to aid in the search for gold. Most of the successful miners are using them now, he says.

Other miners kept to a regular week, returning to the Sonoran Camp on Saturday and leaving again Monday morning. Papa does not fancy that kind of routine, and so he promises to return two days for every six spent at the claim. This arrangement is just odd enough to keep his schedule different from everyone else's. It was difficult for me to track until he gave me a calendar that Uncle James sent with the last shipment of goods. Every time he leaves, I count the six days and circle the date he is to return.

I beg to go with him to the claim, of course. I enumerate all of the benefits he will enjoy with me there: I could gather wood and cook meals and wash clothes even if I did not prove effective at panning.

Papa proclaims that it is out of the question. My education has been interrupted long enough and I am not to miss any more school. I may accompany him once, for two days at the end of April, as long as it is a Saturday and Sunday and, therefore, will not interfere with the regular school week. Under no circumstances will there be any long-term camping in my future. Still, I rejoice at the progress I have made in my quest to stay as close to my father as possible (although I have no intention of completely abandoning my petition).

The delivery mules that arrive near the end of April are loaded with more supplies, Papa's trunk, and an unexpected bonus: an oven and cooktop that Mrs. Ellison ordered from the East Coast over a year ago. It arrives in pieces as the load had to be divided among the mules. Several days are required for assembly. Papa and I benefit from the presence of the new appliance in two ways: not only does Mrs. Ellison bake more, but the old stove is installed in our new tent house. Stoking it every night with wood gathered from the surrounding forest I sleep snug and warm, as the springtime weather continues to be cool.

To my delight, Uncle James tucked as much reading material into Papa's trunk as it would hold. Among the surgical tools and medical texts are the novels I carried from Boston, those books and periodicals Matthew and I scavenged, and some I have never seen before. Accompanying the shipment is a letter addressed to me.

April 11, 1849

Dear Quinn (I hope I spelled that correctly):

How are you? I am fine. So are my brothers and sisters. Mother sends her regards.

I still explore the abandoned ships in the harbor and found several books that I thought you would like. I asked your Uncle James to send them along. I hope you like them.

There are so many abandoned ships in the cove now that San Francisco's alcalde approved having the oldest ones stripped

*of usable materials then "scuttled" (a word Mr. Boyle taught me).
I made certain I had gone over all of them before that happened.
Not all of them are empty. Several ships have people living on
them just like my family and me.*

*Your uncle continues to help us with letters from Lizzie. In
her last one, she says that she is well and likes her new home and
family. She is expecting a baby in August which she thinks will
be good because then she will have someone to talk to in English
since they mostly speak Italian where she lives. She has learned a
lot of Italian, but misses speaking English.*

*Mother cried when she read about the baby. She was still
crying several days later and Father demanded to know the
reason for her tears. Mother couldn't say, of course, but she threw
a pie at Father and we had a big mess to clean.*

*We all miss Mr. Boyle. We miss the captain a little, but
he was mostly asleep in his cabin when he lived with us. On
the other hand, Mr. Boyle was always around cleaning and
repairing the ship and teaching us about her. Now the ship is
falling into disrepair ~~a little~~, because my brothers and I do not do
the job as well as he did.*

*The owner of The Pelican did not want her anymore so your
Uncle negotiated for us to buy her for very little money. We had
Mr. Jepson, the harbor pilot, sail the ship to one of the new piers
where Father arranged for some men to come aboard and strip
all three of her masts from the decks. Once the masts and sails
were sold, Father recuperated all of the money spent on buying
her. The ship looks strange now and, of course, we will have to
stay tied up to the pier from now on because she cannot be moved
anymore. But Mark and I dragged the gangway up from the*

hold and put it in place and now people come to the ship to buy Mother's pies. We ~~row~~ do not have to row into the town anymore just to sell the pies.

Father continues to write to the Ministry, but they have not responded. He was pleased when Reverend Woodbridge from New York arrived at the end of February. I believe Father thought the two of them could work together to start a vigorous ministry in San Francisco. However, less than a week after arriving, the Reverend Woodbridge left for the lands north of the bay. I think he believed that San Francisco did not need two Presbyterian ministers. Father was quite miserable for several days. Actually, he is still miserable and talks about it often.

Mother has saved enough money to send me to a university when I am 18. She insists that I write to some of the schools now to find out what I need to do about my education in the meantime. The public school in San Francisco remains closed although some of the religious leaders conduct classes in other places. Father will not let me attend the school of a rival church. He tries, but I have already surpassed the level of the courses he is able to teach. I have found a few engineering books on the ships, and am trying to understand those on my own. Your Uncle James introduced me to an architect who lives in town, but the man is so busy with building that he hardly has time for me.

Most of the miners have left San Francisco once more so the town is again deserted except for people who have just arrived and those who started restaurants and hotels and gambling houses (which is why there is so much building). We have some restaurants now that are owned by Chinese people. Some call them The Celestials. We like their food and Mother tries to have a meal there at least once every few weeks. Father goes to the restaurants to learn their language, but most of them are too busy to talk to him.

Your Uncle James continues to come to The Pelican once a week for supper, but he did not have news of you the last time. He had a letter from your father about a scurvy outbreak and a long list of supplies that were needed. I hope you don't catch the scurvy.

I would like to hear about your new home in the mountains when you have time to write to me.

I must close this letter now as Mother needs my help. Write to me soon.

Your friend,
Matthew

P.S. —I apologize for the mistakes in this letter.

Reading the letter, I am reminded of the warmth of *The Pelican's* main cabin, Mrs. Dunsford's pies laid out on the trestle tables, and the noise of the Dunsford children clamoring among the rigging. Of course there is no rigging now and I wonder what the children, especially the boys, do at play. What would Mr. Boyle think of his ship stripped of her glory and function?

I stuff the letter and a handful of biscuits into my pocket alongside the little pistol I still carry. My friends are busy today, but I do not want to mope around the Ellisons' store, thinking of *The Pelican*. It is a good day for exploring even if I am on my own.

On my way to the creek (which has become my preferred playground), I pass the Moylan farm. Jack is clearing shoots and vines from the furrows around the apple orchards. He waves as I pass. I know not to ask him to join me when he is busy with farm tasks. When I asked him once before, he barked his refusal, launching a tirade against his stepfather, the trapper. It seems the man has not yet returned from winter quarters and, therefore, cannot attend to any of the heavy chores that fall to Jack. Not that Jack thinks his stepfather could do any better were he around. His stepfather is not a farmer, has never been a farmer and, in Jack's opinion, knows little about growing things. As I return Jack's wave I wish for his company.

I am tempted to follow the creek to its southern end where, according to Jack, I will find another river the size of the Estanislao. That is several miles away and could take all day and I have never been that way before. I am tempted, but fear I will get lost.

However, if I follow the deer trail that hugs the creek upstream, into the hills, there is a waterfall where Jack and I hiked only a few weeks ago. I choose that direction, since the waterfall is breathtaking and I know the way.

Even in the few weeks since Jack and I were last on the creek, the forest has changed: new growths of ferns dot the banks and a variety of bugs skirt the surface of the water wherever it widens and pools. There are still patches of crunchy snow in the shadows and the path itself is slick with mud. I grab at the low branches to keep myself from falling. I try walking to the side of the trail, but the ground there is covered in pine needles and oak leaves, blackened and shiny from winter and even harder to traverse.

"Do you remember your mother?" I asked Jack when we hiked last time. My memories of Mama had begun to blur and that frightened me.

"I don't remember her really. Mostly I remember what my Da used to say about her before he died. I remember she used to sing, though, and sometimes I think I can hear her voice. She used to sing songs to me and Aileen all the time."

"Aileen and me," I corrected. It had become a habit, rectifying the grammar of the other children. I knew they found it annoying, but I could not help it as Papa's lessons were well engrained. The older children ignored me most of the time anyway.

"She used to teach us Spanish," Jack continued. "I still remember most of it. 'Course I get to speak it all the time in the Mexican camp so I suppose I didn't learn all of it from her."

"Why did she teach you Spanish?"

"Because she was Spanish. Californian. She was born here, but her parents came from Spain," he explained. "I think they still live somewhere in the lowlands, but I never met 'em. They didn't like that she married my Da. He was a sailor on a merchant ship that landed in Monterey. His tour ended while he was there and he decided to stay. Met my mother at one of the *rodeos* the Californians have all the time. He said she was the most beautiful *senorita* he'd ever seen and made up his mind to marry her right then. But her parents didn't like him, 'cause he wasn't rich and he wasn't Spanish.

"Da used to say that Aileen and me looked like her."

"Aileen and I."

"Even to the eyes. Da said that she had eyes the color of graylags or a comin' storm, dependin' on her mood," Jack laughed.

"What are graylags?"

"A type of goose that Da remembered from Ireland. They might live in other places, but not in California."

I tried to remember the exact color of my mother's eyes.

The waterfall had been frozen in places that day, thick icicles hanging in clusters the full length of the cliff, water moving in a trickle over the spikes. I shivered at the sight and Jack laughed again. "We sometimes swim here. Even in the summer, the water's so cold it'll freeze your stones off. We climb up that ledge there," he said, pointing to a thin slab of rock that ducked behind the cataract, "and we dive through the water into the pool below as far away from the falls as we can jump.

"Last spring the water was rushin' real hard and…well I slipped and fell right below the waterfall. It was so strong it held me for a long time under the water. I thought I was gonna die." He hesitated. "But I decided I wasn't gonna die and finally made it out. You should'a seen Aldridge and Jimmy's faces. *They* thought I was gonna die.

"Now, until high summer, we swim in that slow spot downstream instead of here. You know the one we swam in last week? Well, you would've been swimmin' in it if you knew how to swim, I guess."

Today, I continue on the path as Jack and I had done before, following the steep and rocky terrain bordering the creek itself, leaving the deer trail a half mile back where it veers away from the water. I can already hear the roar of the cataract, louder than last time.

Then the waterfall is before me. Water shoots over the green granite cliff, plummeting fifty feet to the stream below, the creek churned to a cloud of mist and splash. I close my eyes and feel icy needles of spray pepper my face. It is as if I am on the deck of *The Pelican* when the wind is high and the skies cloudy.

Vibrations from the roaring stream echo through my body like the pulse of the train my parents and I took to New Hampshire every summer. Except that we did not travel that last summer, because of the baby. The summer before she...I shake my head to scatter the unbidden thoughts.

I want to go beyond the waterfall, climb to the top of the granite wall, and explore the land beyond. The day is still early and nothing beckons me back to the Sonoran Camp. I have heard no accounts of the lands above the falls, so that adventure will only add to my arsenal of tales.

I climb. The first twenty feet are the hardest. I grab at rocks sticking out of the green wall to pull myself up, searching for crevices where my feet and hands will not slip. Finally, I reach the ridge and tug myself over its lip. The rest of the way I must still use my hands to pull myself upward but the going is less steep. Rock crumbles and slides to little piles at the base of the cliff, but I find decent footing all the way to the top. I pull myself over the last ledge and, sweating with the effort, look around.

To my right is a swatch of grassland surrounded by stunted manzanita and madrone. In the middle of the field amid a circle of low stones is a single buckeye tree, spears of creamy flowers adorning the dark foliage of its spreading arms. To the left, beyond the creek and below the ridge, stretch undulating hills dense with pine and oak. Even the meadows that I know lay at the bottom of the creek near the Moylan farm are hidden in the dense greens and blues the forest. The Sonoran Camp is only a few miles away, its location obvious from the haze of blue smoke that hovers above it. Beyond is the snow-blanketed backbone of the Sierra Nevada. Somewhere in between is Papa's claim.

I sit on a downed log, watching turkey vultures cross the sky in teetering circles. As I reach for the biscuits in my pocket, Matthew's letter falls to the grass at my feet.

The Pelican is gone for all intent and purpose: what is a ship without sails or masts on which to rig those sails? Mr. Boyle is gone, back to New York and his family and his grandchild. There will be no ship to sail even if he returns.

Matthew and Lizzie will celebrate their fifteenth birthday in a few days. Matthew will leave in a few years to go back to Boston.

I run my hands along my belly trying to imagine what it feels like to swell with a new being as Mama had and as Lizzie does now. However, I have not the imagination for that.

I am not hungry anymore and must wipe my eyes before I return to the edge of the cliff to begin the steep descent. I do not want to be here anymore; I have no desire to explore the land further. I cannot stop the flow of memories today, just as I cannot stop the flow of the creek or my tears. I want to go home. I want a soft bed and a warm bath and a pretty dress to wear.

I descend the cliff, slipping twice and sliding a few feet. When I reach the ridge of rock that marks the last of the climb, I cautiously swing one leg over in search of a foothold. I find a node of granite and test it with my foot. I lower my body until all of my weight is on the rock as I swing my free leg to find the next step. There is a bulge of rock below and to the right. I step on this stone and stroke my hand along the granite face to find the best place to grab. Clutching at a small fissure in the rock, I release the ledge. My upper foot slips and I swing away from the wall. Trying desperately to pull back into the cliff, I crash into the stone and feel my teeth knock together. Then I lose my handhold and plummet down the steep rock face into the rubble below.

I take stock of my injuries before opening my eyes: my head pounds, my jaw aches, and I cannot move the fingers of my left hand. I can barely draw breath and when I do pain stabs into my left side. There are other aches, but they are minor. I can move my toes, my legs, my right arm, and my neck. I am not dead as I do not think death would hurt this much. I groan with each of these exploratory movements; I cannot stop myself.

I remember little of the journey from the granite wall to wherever I am now except the pain that stabbed me with each step my rescuer took. I was carried in and out of the trees from shadow to sunshine to shadow again, ending in gloom, a sudden plunge into darkness deeper than the woods. I was lying on the ground. New agony began as my limbs were moved and pressed and turned and prodded. I was offered drink, a sour brew like tea, and then the pain went away.

When next I open my eyes there is only a single shaft of light, beyond my reach, shining overhead, dust floating in brilliance. Everything else is black. The dark surrounds me with a closeness I can feel.

Then there is more light and I squint against the glare. I see that I am in a round room with walls made from hundreds of curved staves—like a roughhewn barrel. The new source of light floods in from a gap in the walls: an opening covered by a hide which has been pushed aside so that someone may enter. Beyond the opening huddle other dwellings: huts like inverted cones of sticks. This scene disappears as the flap falls back into place and my vision contracts once more into the beam of light.

A woman kneels by my side, humming the strange tune that I heard before when the pain was the strongest. She carries the smell of wood smoke with her. A Mexican woman I think, then change my mind as she leans into the beam of light: Mexican women do not paint dark stripes on their chins or wear necklaces of shells and feathers. Indian. I shiver, recalling the tales I know.

The woman smiles and offers me a bowl. Though I shake my head, she is gently persistent, helping me to sit, holding the bowl to my lips. It is broth; it is good. When I have drained the bowl, she points to my injuries and speaks to me as if to explain what is wrong and what she has done. I cannot understand the words, but the pain points me to the places she has tended.

When he enters, the man must stoop low to cross the threshold of the hut. He looms over me, blocking the chimney where the beam of light pours in. When he speaks his voice is rough and strident, in sharp contrast to the woman's. I am afraid of him. He does not speak to me, but the words he has for the woman are harsh. I understand nothing of what he says, but I know he is berating her. He points to me, but the woman shakes her head.

"Get up," he says. "Your legs are unhurt. You can walk so you can leave."

"You speak English?" Despite my fear of this man, I am elated at this discovery. The man grunts his affirmation. "Where did you learn English?"

"I worked for the white man for two years. The mill."

"You speak it well."

The man shrugs. "You cannot be here."

"But you brought me here."

"Not me," he points to another man who has entered the hut too. "This stupid boy brought you. Her son is as stupid as she."

I bristle at the insult to my rescuers. Neither the woman nor her son respond, and I know they have not understood his words. "How do I thank them?"

"There is no word."

"I beg your pardon?"

"No word. The Miwok have no word for 'thank you.' That is a white word. The Miwok give, they do not talk about it. Now get up."

"But I have nothing to give her," I say. The man shrugs.

Since I have no other avenue, I say the English words "thank you" to the woman. She has remained kneeling, her back to the angry man and the younger one who stands behind him. I hope she understands. "What is her name?"

"Why? You will not see her again."

"Please, what is her name?"

He says something very fast and I cannot understand the word.

The woman starts at the sound of her name, glancing quickly between the man and me. I ask the man to repeat it, but he will not. "What does it mean?" I ask, hoping the meaning will make the word easier to recall. I have read that all Indian names have meanings.

The man hesitates and I see his sneer in the low light. "Moon on a stick."

"I beg your pardon?"

As if sensing the subject of our conversation, the woman leans forward and draws a figure in the dirt floor of the hut with her finger: a quarter moon with stars a few inches from each point. It looks like a spindle has pierced the crescent.

The angry man speaks again. "We tell stories of when the heavens are like this. She likes these stories. She likes to think of the moon as a toy. It looks like a toy. She is a child."

"She chose her name?"

The man grunts and I smile at the thought that both this woman and I have chosen our names (although mine is certainly not as entertaining as "moon on a stick"). "What is your name?" I ask the man.

He does not answer, growling again at the woman before leaving the hut. The woman sighs and reaches gently for me, gesturing me to my feet. Even with the man gone it is clear that I cannot stay. "*Nanyawyn*," the woman says slowly and points her thumb in the wake of the angry man. "*Nanyawyn*."

I struggle to my knees. My injured arm has been wrapped from knuckles to elbow in a mat woven from sticks. I press this to my aching ribs to keep the pain from pushing another groan from me. I do not want this woman, this Miss Moon-on-a-Stick, to hear me groan any more than she has already. I want to be strong and brave for the woman who has risked the anger of Nanyawyn to help me. Of course, maybe "Nanyawyn" is not his name; maybe that is a name Miss Moon has chosen for him, good or bad.

Outside the shadows are long. There is not much daylight left.

In the open air I see the woman and her son better. The boy may be Matthew's age, dressed only in a breechclout and moccasins, his chin and throat, chest and arms darkened by the same stripes and bold patterns that mark his mother. Miss Moon wears a skirt of animal hide, a separate pelt over her shoulders that is cinched at the waist with a woven belt. Both wear their hair loose, brushing their shoulders in bristling black strands. Their skin is very dark.

There are others now gathering to gawk at me, the stranger in their village. Men and women, old and young, stare and point and giggle. They are small in stature, slight of build, with the same dark skin and thick hair as Miss Moon and her son. They are dressed like Miss Moon and her son too, except the young children who wear nothing.

I am uncomfortable with their attention. I do not find them frightening as most of them are smiling, the children with open wonder on their round faces. Since Papa told me that only the men have wandered into his camp, perhaps it is that they have never seen a white person before. When one of the youngest steps forward and strokes my unbound arm, I know that I am a curiosity to them. Miss Moon shoos the child away.

Nanyawyn soon returns, carrying a rifle and two poles taller than he. Although the weapon bothers me, I am glad to see that he carries no rope with which to bind or hang me. I think he is probably capable of doing either, as his irritation does not seem to have abated any in the fresh air. I reach cautiously for my own little pistol only to realize that my clothes are gone. I now wear a loose fitting garment, a rabbit-fur blanket slung across my shoulders. My lips and knees tremble and I turn to plead with Miss Moon to let me stay instead of turning me over to this man.

"Walk," Nanyawyn barks.

I take a step only to pull up as my ribs angrily react. I weave as my head and jaw throb with renewed pain. I move again with no change in effect. "Too slow," he says as he lays the sticks on the ground. A pelt is attached between the rods: it is a litter. As he orders me to sit on the pelt, I anticipate that both he and the boy will carry me down the hill. I am grateful that the boy will be with me and the man's hands engaged with something other than the rifle.

"Can I touch him?"

"May I touch him," Papa corrected, "and, no. Can you not see that there are ropes all around to keep us away?"

They were beautiful velvet ropes and the crowd obediently stayed behind them for some reason I could not understand. They were flimsy after all and even I could have gotten by them.

Papa had lifted me so I could better see above the heads of the other spectators to glimpse the creature displayed behind the ropes, beyond my reach. This was the animal I had longed to see since the day Grandmother Somersworth ordered my thrashing. The menagerie was in town again and I wanted to see the creature that Cousins Clarence and Rebecca had described with enthusiasm after their visit: the elephant.

When she told me I could go this year, I begged Mama to find every book about elephants that Uncle John might have in his library. She read the descriptions and I studied and stroked the illustrations, trying to imagine how the wrinkled skin, the smooth tusks, the nose at the end of the curious trunk would feel beneath my fingers. I wanted to pet it as if it were one of my uncle's dogs or horses.

However, with the elephant before me at last, I was not allowed near.

"What is its name?"

Papa looked around for a sign, but found none.

"Is it a boy elephant or a girl elephant?"

"A girl, I believe."

The creature was chained well away from the ropes, a shackle attached to its back ankle. She stepped from one front foot to the other and swung her head from side to side, her eyes closed. I thought she was dancing and I swayed in rhythm with her and hummed a tune in time to her tempo.

"Papa, she is sad."

"No, Guine, *you* are sad because you cannot touch the animal. She has no feelings at all. She is an animal. Do not think that this creature has the same thoughts and feelings as you do. It is scientifically proven to be impossible."

"No Papa you are wrong, she is very sad. She misses her family."

"You are a curious child," Papa sighed and shook his head as he moved away, toward another exhibit. Not wanting to leave her behind, I stared over his shoulder at the dancing elephant.

I enjoyed the rest of the menagerie with its monkeys and lions. There was a bear whose ankle was chained much as the elephant's, gnashing and roaring in a way I could not imitate. I tried to make the sounds of all of the wonderful creatures as Papa and Mama and I walked past the cages and displays. However, it was the elephant that enchanted me and I repeatedly begged to return to her.

We did return just before closing, in time to hear its trumpeting: a mournful blast that thundered through the menagerie grounds.

Several in the crowd covered their ears, some backed away in fear. Her trainers grabbed at the bridle that circled her head, speared the flesh behind her front leg with a cruel, hooked rod, and snapped a whip at her face. If they intended to pacify her, I was certain that they were not doing it correctly. She reared onto her hind legs. She was a giant and could easily have crushed either of the men who desperately worked to quell her tantrum. She did not.

The solitude that bellowed forth from the beast rumbled through my own body and I was again certain that Papa was wrong. This singular animal among the circling crowd was lonely, I was sure of it.

I believe I will vomit. Since I doubt my ribs will withstand the heaving, I force myself to keep the Indian soup in my stomach and stay seated on the litter. The transport is preferable to walking, but I am still jarred with every step. I sit because being prone is worse.

The boy and Nanyawyn have argued continuously since leaving the Indian village. Rather, Nanyawyn has loosed a steady snarl of words as they walk. The young man says nothing and I am tempted to speak for him even though I understand none of what Nanyawyn has said.

"What does your name mean?" I ask, trying to deflect some of the Indian's wrath and take my mind off of the queasy feeling in my stomach, the dizziness, and other aches. Most of all I want Nanyawyn to stop yelling at Miss Moon's son.

The Indian snorts at my question, but does not answer.

"What is his name then?" I ask, gesturing to the boy. This

time Nanyawyn makes no sound at all. "This will go faster if you talk to me."

"Why?"

"My mind will not be on my discomfort and I will not have to ask you to stop, as I need to do now." I lean over the edge of the litter and retch, my ribs protesting. "I am sorry."

"Man Walking," he says, once I stop being sick and we again begin to move. "I have a longer name, but few white men can say it. So I am Nanyawyn and that means 'Man Walking.'"

"Miss Moon called you Nanyawyn too. So that must mean that Indians cannot say your full name either."

"Miss Moon?" His contempt for the name I have called the woman is evident.

"His mother whose name I cannot pronounce."

The Indian sighs impatiently. "He is Kalelenu. It means 'Runner.' He has a longer name too, but Kalelenu is good." The boy glances over his shoulder at the sound of his name.

"Do you want to know my name?"

"No."

"Why are you so angry?" I am irritated. My questions are harmless. "I have done nothing to you."

"Nothing?" Nanyawyn halts and sets his end of the litter on the ground. I grab the poles to keep from rolling backwards into the dirt as white starbursts of pain blind me. "Nothing? Your white face in our village could bring death to the Miwok. There will be no mercy if a broken little white girl is found among us. We will be slaughtered. Miwok are slaughtered for less."

Kalelenu puts down the other end of the litter and I relax my grip, the pain subsiding. Nanyawyn begins to pace. His fists

clench and clouds of dust rise around him like smoke. His eyes
narrow above his broad cheekbones. "We keep to ourselves and
yet we are slain. Our weapons are not for war, only for hunting,
yet we are killed. We once lived anywhere but now we live only in
these mountains. And still white men follow us, wanting more.
Our deer are chased away so that we have nothing to hunt. The
white man brings cattle and horses and mules to graze where deer
once were. But, if we hunt the white man's animals, our hunters
are killed and the meat taken and our people starve. They even
take our…" he grabs the hair at the crown of his head, pulling it
with a jerk as if that gesture will bring the word he wants to his
lips. "…our hair. Why? White men take everything. They kill
everything and leave the Miwok nothing." His voice is a hiss more
frightening than a shout and his words echo in the rustling leaves
as if the trees share his anger.

"I have done none of those things." My voice wavers.

"Your people do. And your people will come to look for you."

"I would explain that you helped me."

"They might not listen." Nanyawyn shakes his head. "It is
better if you died by the water. That I told the woman and this
crazy son of hers."

He breathes as if he has run a great distance, but the tirade
ends as quickly as it began. Both man and boy take up the litter
and continue in silence. I cannot see his face anymore, but I feel
Nanyawyn's anger still cooking behind me and hear its undertone
among the trees.

"Thank you for helping me," I say. I want to say more, to
apologize for the harm done to his tribe, but I fear this will only
torch his anger once more.

I struggle silently with the pain that threatens to make me sick again. I try not to think of the danger I have brought to the Miwok.

Soon the sound of rushing water reaches through the trees; we have come to the spot where the deer trail and the creek meet. I know where I am and I know that the Sonoran Camp is near. I am anxious to be home, to be away from the angry Indian.

Suddenly Kalelenu stops. With a glance between them, he and Nanyawyn lower the litter to the ground, more gently this time.

"What is it?" I ask, "why are we stopping?"

The boy points to the forest and whispers briefly to the man. Both of them cock their heads, listening to the woods just as Mr. Boyle used to listen to *The Pelican*. Then Nanyawyn disappears into the brush. I am glad it is he who goes to investigate whatever has caught their attention; I feel safer with Kalelenu.

There are raised voices from the forest and soon I hear the crash and snap of someone running through the underbrush. "Quinn?" I draw air into my lungs to respond, barely able to gasp "Here!"

Jack is first to reach the trail, nearly falling into the path behind me, pushing the last of the brush aside. After him are Nanyawyn, Papa, then Aldridge and his father, and Mr. Ellison.

Papa dashes forward, stopping short of the litter. "You're hurt," he acknowledges. "He said you were hurt."

"I fell, Papa. The Miwok helped me. I may have broken ribs and I know my arm is broken. But they helped me, Papa. They are my friends. They did not hurt me." I say this very fast as I do not want Nanyawyn to be right about white men. Mr. Turner and

Mr. Ellison both have their rifles raised.

"Tell me how to help you."

I struggle to my knees and then to my feet, waving Papa away as he reaches to help. Once I am standing, he examines my legs and hips and back, my ribs and arms, the gash on my chin. "Where are your clothes?"

Nanyawyn gruffly speaks to the boy who pulls my shirt and coat from a pack he has slung over his shoulder.

"They are wet," Papa notes, fingering the garments. "Did you fall into the creek?"

"No, I fell from the rocks. I do not know how they got wet."

"Blood," Nanyawyn says, his voice wary. "Blood was washed from them."

His back to Nanyawyn, the Miwok boy moves close and slips my little pistol and bag of shot into the pocket of the wet jacket. He then reaches once more into his pack and pulls out a leather pouch, opening it to reveal a thick dark paste. Pantomiming that I am to apply this to the wounds on my face and scratches on my arms, he says "*Nem Tykwakome.*" He speaks slowly, but I still do not know what he means.

"Here take my coat," Papa says, removing his jacket. "Give the fur back to them."

I reluctantly remove the rabbit blanket from my shoulders as I have grown accustomed to its warmth in the chill of the darkening forest. I offer it to Kalelenu, but he backs away, shakes his head and pulls on the older Miwok's arm.

"A gift," Nanyawyn says after a brief exchange with the boy, pointing to the blanket. "From 'Miss Moon,'" he mocks.

"Thank you," I say, choosing to ignore the Miwok's tone.

CHAPTER 15

May 7, 1849

"I CAN'T BELIEVE IT. I've lived here all my life and I've never been to an Indian village." Jack frowns, fingering the edges of my rabbit-skin blanket. It is not made of whole rabbit pelts, but strips of the fur woven together like a basket. Jack has been stroking the blanket since his arrival. I often do the same, thinking of the fur muff of Mama's Christmas-morning story.

"I did not mean to be there," I reply, shifting my weight to ease the throbbing of my ribs. Jimmy Fassberg's father, the blacksmith, made a metal-and-canvas contraption that fits on my cot and keeps me sitting upright even while I sleep. Still, I am not comfortable. No position is comfortable for long. "What happened to your eye?"

Jack paws at the purple bruise on his cheekbone. "I ran into a door."

For the third time since Aldridge and Jack arrived, Mrs. Ellison bustles into the tent house, this time with a plate of gingerbread. All week she has cared for me, asking if I want food, water, or extra blankets. She does not need to ask if anyone wants the gingerbread.

Upon our return from the Miwok camp, Papa found no new untended injuries. Finally resigned to the fact that he could do no more for me, he expressed his admiration for the way Miss Moon had dressed my wounds: the stitches along my chin and jaw were small and evenly spaced, closed precisely (or the best that could be done after an encounter with jagged rock). The wrap on my arm was fascinating: a thick woven mat curled and tied in such a way that did not slide and kept the bone in the right position for healing. He doubted that even splints would have been better. As for my ribs, nothing could be done about those, he said. The binding helped and would remind me to be still, but broken ribs are not easily treated and will heal in their own time. He admitted the Miwok woman knew what she was doing. However, he would not let me use the poultice, throwing it into our stove where it smoldered and belched a black smoke that made the tent smell like burning leaves (and worse) for three days. He cleaned my wounds with soap and water. I waited until he left the room to find my green Brazilian potion which I smeared on the cuts to soothing effect.

"What was it like?" Jack asks. I think he is disappointed not to have made it all the way to the Miwok village. He was the one who tracked me to the face of the waterfall (although he said I made it easy since I was slipping almost all of the way). There my prints ended at the base of the cliff, replaced by the tracks of moccasins. Only one pair, but Jack had seen the blood on the rocks. He ran all the way to the Sonoran Camp for help.

"There were dozens of cone-shaped huts gathered in a circle," I say, slipping into the story. "A large round hut like a cropped barn stood to one side, bigger than the rest. Each shelter was made from thousands of strips of bark. There were cook fires outside each hut just as in the Mexican encampment. The children were playing a game in the circle: rolling a willow hoop through which they threw a long stick like a spear as it was moving."

I cease telling the story when neither boy seems interested in the details of the village. If I could describe any of the weapons used, I might have kept their attention. I had seen nothing except bows and arrows and the rifle that Nanyawyn carried. I do not know what kind of rifle it was; it looked ancient.

"Are you comin' back to school?"

I shake my head. "Papa says that my ribs will hurt for another three or four weeks and I should remain in bed until they stop smarting."

"You could do that? Remain in bed that long?" Jack shoves the last of the gingerbread in his mouth and strokes the rabbit blanket once more. "I could maybe make a blanket like this from my rabbit skins."

Mrs. Ellison returns with three cups of milk. "You boys don't have school today?"

"School's over for the day, Mrs. Ellison. Thanks for the gingerbread. It was real good." Aldridge swallows his milk in one gulp. "You bake real good."

"Thank you, boys. Now, you shouldn't stay too long and tire Quinn out, you know. Just a little longer."

"Yes, ma'am."

"She's like a hen with new chicks." Jack shakes his head as Mrs. Ellison disappears into the store. "She must think we're gonna try to kiss you or jump on you or somethin'."

"Why would she think that?"

"Oh, you know. Older people act strange when boys and girls get together."

My mouth is dry. "What do you mean?"

"Come on, Quinn. We know you're a girl," Jack whispers. "We always thought you were peculiar, but we figured that was 'cause you were from Boston. Then when your pa kept saying we had to find 'her' and 'she' won't survive in the woods, well even Aldridge here figured it out." Jack chuckles softly, "I don't think he knew he was doin' it."

"You cannot tell anybody," I whimper, angry at myself for the sound. "Papa will send me back to San Francisco if you tell. Maybe back to Boston. He will not let me stay here if anybody knows I am a girl." My heart raps at my chest, the broken ribs aching even more from the pounding. "He says it is dangerous for a girl."

Jack nods. "Yeah. Beth tells Aileen that all the time. But, we won't say nothin', will we Ald? And we'll ask Mr. Ellison and Mr. Turner not to tell either. And Aldridge and me won't even tell Jimmy. We promise. We couldn't tell him no matter what, 'cause then all he'd want would be to see your bosoms."

I laugh and my ribs scream. I groan and clutch my side.

"Hey," Jack says, "can we see your ribs where they're broken?"

I nod and lean over before realizing that perhaps I should not. They know I am a girl now. While neither Aldridge nor Jack speak of breasts as much or as often as Jimmy does, I am not certain that they are entirely uninterested in girls' bodies. Cousin Alfred never tired of trying to sneak peeks. Plus I have noticed a difference in my friends today: they do not curse or insult each other as they normally do. They avert their eyes more. Something has changed.

Jack interprets my hesitation. "Ah, don't worry. We aren't tryin' to see your bosoms," he scoffs. "Besides, you don't have any yet."

I know that Jack is forthright with opinions and observations and rarely tempers his words, but the bluntness with which he acknowledges my lack of figure is irritating. Perhaps I should be grateful, as Papa would send me away if I looked too girlish. However, I am not grateful.

I turn so that Jack can lift a piece of my shirt.

"Holy Jesus. You look like you've been kicked by a horse."

They visit every Saturday before venturing into town with their apples and milk. One time they bring Jimmy Fassberg, but that is a vexation. Jimmy only wants to provide details about what he would do with five dollars to spend at the new whorehouse across the road from his father's blacksmithing business.

"They parade around nearly naked!"

"Stop it!" Jack roars, his face glowing red to the tips of his ears.

"Dammit, Jack. Are you gonna tell me I can't even talk about girls you *aren't* related to?"

"Don't mind Jimmy, Quinn. He hasn't been right since his ma ran off with that miner last Christmas."

As the weather improves, the Sonoran Camp is overrun with miners. Mr. Ellison has begun to call it "The Sonoran Town" because of the growing population. Mrs. Ellison estimates that the town's inhabitants would number five thousand if all of the men decide to visit at once. "Thank Heavens that only happens on the weekends," she laughs.

Mr. Ellison believes these numbers add to the urgency of

having a hospital ready in time for any unfortunate accidents or epidemics. My father has no comment on the subject.

For a couple of weeks following my injury Papa altered his routine, staying at his claim only two days before returning. It is mid-May when, confident of my recovery, he assumes his previous schedule. Mrs. Ellison assures him that she and her husband will keep an eye on me when he is gone.

During one of Papa's absences, Mr. Ellison rigs a curtain in the tent house to separate our cots from an over-sized anteroom. He furnishes the outer room with two large tables between which he places Papa's trunk of surgical instruments. He then builds free-standing shelves along one wall of the tent and transfers the medical supplies from Uncle James' most recent delivery to this new storage area.

Finding the accommodations so pointedly altered upon his return, Papa stands in silence. Then he mutters something about the tables making the place look more like a carnage house than a hospital before proceeding to inventory the new stores. I thought he would be upset at Mr. Ellison's blatant manipulation and I expected shouts of displeasure. Instead, I am surprised at his quiet resignation.

The days Papa spends away at his claim seem to bring him peace. The lines of his face and the wrinkles of his temper are smoothed upon his return. That does not fully explain his acceptance of Mr. Ellison's interference. He never says so, but since Mr. Ellison wants a hospital for the Sonoran Town I believe Papa surmises that playing the part of town doctor is to be the price of our room and board.

Early in my recovery, the ache in my side demands shallow

breathing, tiring me quickly and keeping me sequestered in the "room" behind the curtain. I am less bored when Papa is in town as I can overhear conversations with his patients beyond the canvas wall. Most of the discussions are baffling since Papa uses medical terms with which I am unfamiliar. I learn the names of a few bones, including the radius I broke, but I remember little else. I am mostly interested in stories about journeys to California.

Now more of the miners are American, having traveled from old and new states and even newer territories. Although the majority of immigrants are single males, whole families are coming as well. Those from New England and the coast of the Southern states still choose the dangers of sailing, but most of the immigrants travel by wagon across the rugged and barren land that lies between the Mississippi River and California. Many of these travelers are broken before they cross the Sierra Nevada: a great number of their companions have died along the way from hunger and thirst, accident and disease.

Their stories are as varied as their speech and I listen raptly, absorbing details so that I have tales to tell my friends. I refrain from retelling the stories that make me cry.

Even though more English is spoken now, my father resorts to any means of communication available. He uses hesitant Spanish for the Peruvians and Chileans, Californians and Mexicans; textbook French for the Canadians and Frenchmen; or shouting "SHOW—ME—WHERE—IT—HURTS" if nothing else works. Even those who speak English are sometimes difficult to understand as the regional accents and dialects are strong among the newcomers.

When his patients are less mobile (or too stubborn), Papa

makes trips to the heart of the Sonoran Town, the place he calls "the hell hole," carrying a valise of his essential tools and a bottle of something he calls *chlorine*, diluted and used for washing his hands after each patient.

"Dr. Holmes was a colleague of mine in Boston," Papa says. "He believed that touching a sick person and then touching another without cleansing one's hands was an almost certain way to spread whatever disease had sickened the first. I have no idea if it is effective, but Oliver had no doubts and he was brilliant. He was trained in France where he learned the latest methods." Uncle James keeps my father well stocked in bottled chlorine.

As spring progresses, Papa once again changes his schedule to spend five days at the claim followed by three days in the new "hospital" treating wounds, sniffles, the occasional bad tooth, and any number of other complaints. He still refuses to follow a regular week: he does not want to bow to the dictates of a trumped-up period of time, he says. God may have created the earth in seven days, but that did not mean Harold Walker had to live for Sundays. Despite his irregular schedule, word travels quickly about the availability of his services and there seems to be no end to the ailments.

I am once again able to accompany the boys on their marketing forays, the Turner's cow and a cheerful Guleesh with us. Except those times when Papa needed the mule to transport supplies to his claim, Jack borrowed Guleesh even when I was ill. Now the boy and creature are fast friends, if Guleesh's playful nips are any indication.

The Sonoran Town has changed during my convalescence. At least a dozen buildings stand where before there had been only canvas. The town looks more substantial and permanent now, although not nearly as solid as San Francisco and certainly nothing like Boston.

"...and so your pa just sawed it right off, like it was a tree trunk," Jack relates on our way to the town. "Ol' Ed Baldwin said that Mr. Bohannon would likely've died if he hadn't, 'cause his foot was all black and smelled bad. That's why they called on your pa—'cause none of them could stomach bein' around him, he stank so much. They poured whiskey down him 'til he passed out, then Dr. Walker went to work. He was real surprised when he came to; but now he's not sick anymore and he's even talkin' about gettin' a peg-leg, like a pirate."

I remain quiet. Papa never tells me anything about these trips into town. After hearing Jack's story I admit a preference for ignorance, thankful that Jack has not heard any more grisly details from Ol' Ed Baldwin. I suspect with each retelling the specifics will come.

"My pa said Bohannon cursed Dr. Walker for three straight days at first," Aldridge snickers, then turns to me. "When is your arm gonna be better?"

I glance at the wrap around my wrist. "Papa says it takes less time for ribs to heal than arms. He estimates I will have the wrap on for another two or three weeks." I stroke the slash on my jaw; Papa removed the stitches several weeks ago, but the wound still itches.

"Yesterday was the last day of school until September. I couldn't hardly wait for it to be summer!" Aldridge chirps. "I got more chores, but the days is longer too."

"The days are longer," I correct.

"Good Lord, Quinn. It's gonna be like bein' in school with you around," Jack complains.

"If you are going to speak English…"

"I know, 'you must speak it prahpahly.' Geez."

"You cannot tell me," I say, ignoring his parody of my accent, "that Miss Beth does not correct your grammar when you are at home."

"All the time." Jack scuffs his feet, choking our path with dust clouds. "But I'm not home much. Evgeny's home."

I recall Mr. Ellison's story about the Russian trapper Miss Beth married last year. "Oh, your stepfather."

"He's no father of mine." Jack's frown warns me not to pursue the subject. Talking with Jack lately has been like trying to pet a porcupine (one of Mr. Ellison's more colorful expressions which seems to apply perfectly to Jack).

"Quinn, we been gettin' 5 pennies each apple instead o' just one," Aldridge interrupts, "and I get a silver quarter for a little pitcher of milk in the Mexican camp. I've saved $24 since March.

"We don't go to the Saxon camp though, 'cause they don't want milk and they don't want to pay us for the apples. They tell us we need to start a 'tabulation' for 'em, but we aren't gonna do that 'cause Jack says it's money or nothin'. One of 'em tried to steal an apple once, but Jack kicked him in the stomach and ran like hell."

"How come you never correct us when we curse?" Jack asks.

"Papa curses. So I suppose if it is proper English no correction is necessary."

The boys find this amusing and spend the next few minutes

using their repertoire of swear words in proper sentences. I do not mind this really, but when they pepper their play with insincere apologies made through the laughter, my face begins to burn. I prefer the swearing to the on-going acknowledgment that they consider me different now.

The bargaining begins as soon as we enter the unmarked boundaries of the Mexican camp. We do not have to venture far along the road before our wares are depleted. Jack and Aldridge's pockets are well weighted with coins and all of us are sated from the generous helpings of rice and beans our customers urged upon us. Still, Aldridge is not ready to give up the chance for more income and runs home to fetch another cow even as Jack protests that he and I will be gone by the time he returns. Nothing we say deters him.

Jack and I turn for home with Guleesh in tow. Aldridge has already disappeared around the bend in the road.

"What's your real name? It can't be John Quincy."

I hesitate. "If you know my real name, will you be tempted to call me that instead of my boy name?"

"Nah. It would be hard to change now."

"It's Guinevere."

"Like King Arthur's queen?"

I would have thought nothing of the man who suddenly darts from the roadside brush, crossing the road to disappear inside a saloon tent twenty yards or more away. He is bandy-legged wearing a cap like those favored by the small band of army men whose claim is nearby. They are called dragoons and thus the site has been dubbed Dragoon's Gulch. Mr. Ellison suspects that these men are deserters. No one knows for certain. No one dares to ask.

Jack stares after the soldier, his knuckles whitening as he tightens his grip on Guleesh's lead.

"Jack, what is it?"

He shrugs then abruptly hands me the mule's reins before disappearing into the bushes where the man had first appeared.

"Jack!" The only response is the cracking of brush. I follow, pausing to tether the mule to a tree a few feet from the road. If the sounds from the forest are any indication, Jack is already far ahead. Applying the tracking skills that the boys constantly boast about, I follow him. I only hope their bragging comes to something.

To my surprise, I clearly see the broken branches and scuffed earth where Jack has gone further into the forest. "Jack!"

"Over here," he calls, not far from me now. He sounds strangely hoarse. "Slowly, Quinn, slowly."

I turn in the direction of Jack's voice until I see his faded shirt through the underbrush. Only as I push a branch from my path do I see the girl, sitting in a pile of pine needles, clutching her knees, head down, rocking. Jack is squatting beside her, smoothing her torn and dirty skirt over her knees. The girl whimpers and bats his hand away. At the sound of my approach, she lifts her head and I gasp: one eye is swollen shut and blackened, her face puffed, blue bruises on her cheeks.

"Rosa," Jack whispers, but the girl responds only with a frightened gaze that darts between us. "Rosa." He turns to me, "it's Rosa Barajas." Jack knows most of the inhabitants of the Mexican camp.

"How badly is she hurt?"

The girl groans and lowers her head again, drawing her knees even more tightly into her chest, continuing her urgent rocking.

"Bad, I'd guess." Whispering a few words to the girl, Jack uses her name like a caress and makes soft, repetitive sounds of calm much as Uncle John used the day I tried to fly my invisible horse to San Francisco. I think she is hurt very badly.

I squat beside them. "Did that man do this?"

Jack's body tenses. "I'll bet all the money in my pockets he did. He was tryin' to hide somethin'. If this was it, he had reason to hide. He's still got reason; he just doesn't know it." Jack gently places his hand on Rosa's shoulder and speaks to her again, assuring her in a mixture of Spanish and English and another language I have never heard before. Gaelic I guess. His father spoke Gaelic to them when he and Aileen were young.

Suddenly my own body tenses as I recall the warnings my father spoke of in San Francisco: men beat each other, he had said, but "....they do the same, and worse, to women." My hands tremble and a cold settles across my shoulders as visions of one dark corridor on *The Pelican* waver before me. This is what could happen to girls, to women. This is what my father meant. This is what Mrs. Reynolds and Mrs. Llewellyn had tried to tell me. I knew that now and imagined each of them pointing to Rosa and repeating "and worse." This is worse.

I am not certain if my tears are for Rosa or myself.

Jack finally coaxes the girl to her feet and we follow a faint trail that stretches along the forest floor toward the Mexican camp. Rosa shuffles between us as Jack and I support her.

"Jack, Guleesh is tied up there," I point a shaking finger up the steep slope. "Should I fetch him?"

"I doubt she's interested in riding any mule," he barks. Then he speaks again to Rosa. The girl groans a sharp "no" and backs away. She bends forward and clutches her hands to her belly. I am assaulted by a memory of Mama bent at the waist, clasping the swell of the baby. On that horrible night when Papa guided her back to bed, Mama's pain was different but she was as frightened as Rosa. I had banished this thought over time. I have refused to remember a lot of things until now.

"No riding," Jack announces, soothing Rosa again and coaxing her along the path. "This way is straight to the camp. It'll be faster and we can avoid bein' near the miners. We'll get the mule later. Are you gonna help me?"

I wipe my eyes and we brace the girl between us again, guiding her along the trail that rises toward the Mexican camp. My ribs ache at the exertion. I would not have made it up the steeper slope to the mule and I am thankful that Jack chose this kinder path. I am grateful I have my ribs to think about rather than this frightened girl and the memories that cling to her.

Wedged between us, Rosa walks with timid steps, stopping occasionally to bury her face into Jack's collar, soaking him with tears, panting with sobs. He says nothing, standing firm with arms wrapped around the taller girl, stroking her hair, waiting until she can take another step on her own.

We enter the road at the base of the Mexican camp, nearly carrying Rosa. She seems to have grown weaker as we walk. Jack turns decisively up the path, ignoring the stares and the whispers. Waves of people skitter before us to spread the news of our approach. Those who remain circle slowly in guarded silence, curious but distant.

A despairing wail pierces the air and a woman pushes her way through the circle of on-lookers, rushing to Rosa's side. Rosa collapses into the woman's outstretched arms and they crumple together to their knees, Rosa's tattered skirt billowing as she falls. A fist-sized stain mars the skirt. I had not seen the back of Rosa's garment before, but I have soaked and boiled the used linens from my father's hospital often enough to know what the rust-colored mark represents. My quaking begins anew.

A small man charges from behind the two kneeling women. He rushes forward and grabs Jack's shirtfront, pulling the boy close and screaming questions.

Breaking free of the man's grasp, Jack screams back first in English then Spanish: "I don't know. We found her, down that path. She told us nothin'."

The man angrily surveys the faces that have gathered around the scene, threatening to charge the onlookers, screaming questions to each in turn. When his gaze pauses on me, Jack yells again. "No, no. Quinn was with me."

The argument continues and I clench my fists, silently willing them to stop, wanting them to be calm and quiet, wanting the scene on the forest floor to have been a dream for both me and Rosa. This is the nightmare of a Poe tale, a story gone wrong.

"Come on," Jack is saying, grabbing my arm, pulling me away. "Let's go."

I allow him to pull me. I glance back at Rosa and the woman as they weep in the road, the man staring after us, anger pulsing from him like firelight. "He does not believe you, Jack. Why did you not tell him about that man?"

"I don't want him killed."

"But he hurt her!"

"No, I'm not talking about the soldier. He deserves to die."

Jack thrusts his chin forward. "If I was to point Senor Barajas to that man, if I was to take him into the miners' camp and show him the man that did that to his daughter, he'd kill that soldier for sure. Then there he'd be among all those white miners, havin' killed one of 'em. What do you think they would do to Senor Barajas, Quinn? You think they'd let some Mexican kill a white man and walk away?" He shakes with anger that nearly rivals that of Senor Barajas.

I am no longer able to contain my sobs.

"Oh don't cry for Chrissake. If you cry, everybody'll know you're a girl."

I find the idea terrifying. If they know I am a girl, I will be vulnerable like Rosa. I do not want to be like Rosa. I do not want to be touched like that soldier touched Rosa. I smear my tears across my face with a swipe of my sleeve. I cannot stop them flowing.

"Stop it, dammit. Just stop it." Jack's own voice shakes. "You just stay away from the miners' camp, you hear? I don't want that soldier to see you."

Would I recognize the soldier if I saw him again? Except for his cap, he looked like every other miner: disheveled, bearded, with clothes the color of dirt. Mining must be a filthy business.

Even my father returns from panning crusted in grime. Unlike the other miners returning to the Sonoran Town, Papa will not long tolerate the dirt beneath his fingernails, soil on his clothing, or hair greasy and uncombed. His first task is to bathe and throw his clothes into the kettle for boiling. There is relief in this cleansing, I think. Yet I see his calm wash away with the dust as he puts on his doctor face and leaves the solitude of the claim behind him. He is different from these other men. Papa does not belong here, I think, and the thought confuses me for I do not understand why I know this.

I recognize the spot in the road where we first saw the soldier. I turn to where I have left the mule tethered. "He is down here," I say. "I left Guleesh here."

The sound of the dull but rapid clomp of Jack's feet causes me to turn again. He is running up the hill toward the miners' camp, kicking dust behind him. He is headed for the tent into which the soldier disappeared.

"Jack!" I follow him, but he is faster than I. With each step, my ribs remind me that I am still injured. "Jack!"

He pauses at the entrance to the large saloon tent where the soldier went, peering inside. After a brief moment, Jack squares his shoulders and strides forward. However, he does not enter. Instead, he moves between that tent and its neighbor and disappears from view.

I near the aisle where Jack has gone and stop, panting. Jack is rummaging through a pile of wood, ultimately emerging with a stout branch. Hefting its weight between his hands he turns and smiles.

I want to call out, scream at him to drop the stick and the notion that he can fight the soldier by himself. As I draw breath to do so, the soldier emerges from the tent, fumbling with the buttons of his trousers. He is drunk; even in my panic I can see that. He turns and lurches down the aisle toward Jack.

Jack does not hesitate. Still smiling, he struts toward the soldier, swings the branch, and smashes it into the man's face, spinning him around and knocking his cap to the ground. The soldier drops to his knees. Blood pours from his nose and mouth.

"Shit!" the soldier yells, his words bubbling as he grabs his face. "You broke my nose, you son of a bitch! You broke my nose!"

Flinging his weapon aside, Jack steps over the crouching dragoon and marches toward me. He still sports that stupid grin, but only for a moment longer. He stops, the smile replaced by a grimace as he looks down the road. I do not have to turn around as I know that Senor Barajas is behind me. I knew he had not believed Jack and had followed us.

"No!" Jack yells, running toward the Mexican.

Senor Barajas walks slowly up the hill, ignoring Jack's frantic attempts to stop him, his face set in a grim smile. Jack paws at the man's shirt, begging him in two languages to turn around and go back. "I hurt him bad," he pleads. "I hurt him already for Rosa."

Senor Barajas' smile widens and he finally stops. Cradling Jack's face in both hands, Senor Barajas kisses the boy on the forehead before continuing on. There is no hurry in his stride, his eyes focused on the kneeling man who covers a broken face. He does not take his eyes from the soldier. His step does not waiver even as men emerge from the nearby tents in response to the dragoon's loud and garbled complaints.

The Mexican steps behind the kneeling soldier and entwines his fingers into the man's hair, slowly tilting his head toward the sky. At first it seems he intends to kiss this man too; bending forward, his lips touch the man's ear. He whispers something then strokes his hand across the dragoon's throat, the glint of his knife startling as it catches the sunlight that filters through the trees. The soldier blinks and slumps sideways.

Senor Barajas straightens, dropping his knife into the dirt and turning to face the half dozen men who have gathered before the tent. He holds his head high, his arms at his sides. No one moves.

Blood trickles from the new mouth Senor Barajas gave the soldier, much as his other mouth, his real mouth, trickles from the blow Jack rendered. I fear that one or the other of those ghastly openings will speak. His eyes stare at the tree tops and he seems to be listening to the sounds of the birds, enthralled by their twitters. Meadowlarks, Jack told me once. Or perhaps they are finches. I cannot remember. I cannot hear them clearly now as my heart thumps and the shouts of the other miners collide overhead. Soon, I no longer see the soldier on the ground for he is hidden by the gathering men.

Jack is in their midst, pulling at their coats and yelling. Even the growing roar of the men cannot completely drown the boy's objections. The mob knocks Jack to the ground more than once. He quickly rises to his feet each time, his face streaked with dirt, his black hair standing out like porcupine quills. His presence only serves to irritate the miners. Their purpose is clear. This gnat of a boy will not stop them.

Senor Barajas offers no resistance as the miners surround him and march him to a nearby grove of oaks where they slip a knotted rope around his neck. They toss the rope over a low branch and tie the other end to a saddled horse. The Mexican is hoisted from the ground where, at last, he begins to struggle. He kicks and writhes as he dangles in the air. The rope stretches and the tree branch creaks in shared protest. I put my hands over my ears. I cannot close my eyes.

"Come on." Jack is beside me, grabbing my arm and spinning me away from the spectacle. "And stop crying."

I wipe my sleeve across my face as Jack pulls me down the hill.

"Stop it," he barks, leading me quickly to the main road. I take a deep breath. Jack does not turn around but he knows that I am still sobbing. "Stop it."

We reach the road and cross quickly, entering the brush where we first saw the soldier, the man who is now dead in the gap between the filthy tents of the camp. The man with two mouths.

"Stop it," Jack growls and I fear I may have spoken my thoughts aloud. He pulls me further into the brush until we reach the tethered mule, where he finally stops and buries his face into the bristles of Guleesh's flank. Then he sinks to the earth, dragging me with him, wrapping his arms tightly around me, his sobs matching my own.

CHAPTER 16

June 30, 1849

HIS NAME WAS FRANK, but no one knows if that was his first or last name. Not even his fellow dragoons claim the body. So, after three days, Mr. Ellison decides that he should be buried quickly since he has begun to stink. The grave will be marked so that anyone who comes later will know where he is. Mr. Ellison doubts anybody will come; if his fellow soldiers did not retrieve him why would anyone else? He was alone the day he died and will probably stay that way. Some men simply do not invite camaraderie.

Mrs. Ellison hastily stitches a canvas shroud and the miner is buried without ceremony among the hundreds who died of scurvy the winter before. "Among the scurvy lot," I babble remembering that expression as one of the curses Mr. Sterbenc threw at *The Pelican's* crew. It is fitting that Frank will be buried in the Sonoran Town's new graveyard among the scurvy lot.

The identities of the men who hanged Senor Barajas remain as much a mystery as Frank's. No one claims to have witnessed the hanging let alone participated, although everyone seems to have intimate details. According to the stories, the Mexican threw the first punch which broke "poor Frank's" nose. Then he sliced Frank up badly before slitting his throat. Frank was unarmed and, therefore, it was no fair fight. All that over the favors of a Mexican whore, they said. That is what they had heard anyway even though they could not swear to it as they had not been there. Never was there mention of a Mexican child or any other children.

Senor Barajas' body was cut down and dumped in the road at the foot of the Mexican encampment by the same men who denied having hanged him or having witnessed the death of Frank, the soldier. Rosa's father is laid to rest on the same day as Frank in a little cemetery not far from the tent that serves as the Catholic church. Senor Barajas' grave is marked with a fine white cross and he has many mourners. Jack discouraged me from attending the funeral since I am not Catholic and I am white. Even had he not, I would not have gone. I did not want to look upon Rosa Barajas and her mother burdened by the heaviness of their loss.

Mr. Ellison is furious at the news of a murder and a hanging. He paces the kitchen floor and rants about justice and due process and other judge-like things, his face ruddy with indignation. He and the town elders conduct an investigation, thumping through the tents looking for evidence. However, the white miners and the Mexicans band into their separate camps of silence. The questioning finally ends with a frustrated pronouncement from Mr. Ellison to no one in particular: "There will never again be a hanging in this town without a fair trial. Do you hear me? Never. I'll lop off the ears of each and every man I suspect of lying if anything like this ever happens again."

Papa returns at the peak of the furor over the deaths to endure several evenings of Mr. Ellison's tirades. Though the tales surrounding the incident have taken on fantastic proportions, there is no hint that children were a part of it and I like it that way. The further from danger my father thinks I am, the more remote the chance that he will pack me off to San Francisco. I barely raise my head at mealtimes as Mr. Ellison's anger washes over the scene, overwhelming my desire to confess that I could identify some of the miners who dragged Senor Barajas to his death. No, not dragged, walked. Senor Barajas was calm as if he knew his fate when he walked up that hill. It was just as Jack had said it would be.

The night before he is to return to his claim, after another supper of wrath and rabbit stew, Papa and I retire to our tent. "When I was a lad," Papa begins, his voice a whisper in the dark, "my friend Graham and I stole a full bottle of whiskey from the parson's cottage then promptly retreated to his conservatory to drink it. We were about your age at the time. It had been a rather boring summer. I do not recall what gave us the notion to perform this wicked act but we did.

"It was a full bottle and a warm day. Despite complaining bitterly of the taste and finding it astounding that people could stomach its burn, we finished it off. Then we curled up under one of the raised bed and lost all semblance of consciousness. We awoke a few hours later with pounding heads made worse by the sounds of a rousing argument.

"The woman was the milliner's wife, Mrs. Parsons. Ironically, she worked for the parson cooking his meals and supervising the housecleaners. She was one of the most beautiful women in town.

"The man was a tinker who frequented the village at least twice a year. He was a tall and handsome man who had a way with women. Or so it was told.

"He was not having a way with Mrs. Parsons, however. In no uncertain terms she told him that her husband treated her well and she would never think to leave him, would never have looked twice at the tinker had he not caught her in a moment of weakness for which she would be eternally sorry.

"The tinker was furious, protesting his love for her and outlining plans to quit his trade, to take up a good solid business in a faraway town where they could live together. Even at my young age I remember thinking that his was a plan short on details and long on hopelessness.

"Graham and I remained quiet and hidden. I fervently wished they would just end their argument and depart so that we could leave. However, they continued their discourse for an excruciatingly long time. It may have been no more than two or three minutes but it certainly seemed longer.

"Well the disagreement became more and more heated. Then we heard a dull thwack and the crashing sound of splintering wood and falling debris. The din was horrible. Then there were shuffling sounds and finally the slap of the conservatory door closing; then a deep quiet."

Papa pauses in the darkness and I think the tale may have ended. I am confused as to its origin or purpose.

"She was dead, her neck broken from the fall into the raised tables. Beautiful still except for the horrible angle of her head and the dirt soiling her dress. She had died before her face could swell or form a bruise.

"We ran away of course, Graham and I, swearing to each other that we would say nothing of this to anyone. I am sure we left enough evidence, including puddles of vomit, for any official to have known there had been witnesses. However, no one approached us and we did not approach them.

"The tinker left town which caused no stir as he had always come and gone as he pleased. We never saw him again.

"Only once did we contemplate breaking our oath: when the constable arrested Mr. Parsons for the murder of his wife. Luckily the man had an undisputable alibi and my friend and I were free to remain silent. And miserable—how could we confess to knowing the identity of the murderer when, in doing so, we would have to reveal that we were nothing but common thieves?"

"I have stolen nothing, Papa," I murmur. "I have done nothing wrong. I am sad at Senor Barajas' death. That is all." I swallow hard at the half truth.

"But not the soldier's, I see." Papa did not press the issue and I did not explain the omission.

During the days that follow, I avoid the eastern part of the town and the miners. Unwanted images cross my mind frequently: Rosa's fearful eyes, the miner's second mouth, Senor Barajas writhing and kicking at the air. The visions are disturbing, made more so by new, disconnected thoughts of my father vomiting whiskey into flower beds and Dick Sterbenc with his nasty grin, the latter of which makes my heart pound and my limbs tremble.

It was simply too rude. I tried ignoring the insolence with which Mr. Sterbenc had walked away from me. Perhaps he was busy but that did not excuse his boorishness. Maybe he was just thick and did not realize the significance of getting word to the Dunsfords of my safety. I did not want them wandering in the strange town of Rio thinking I was lost forever. Without Mr.

Boyle or the captain around, it was Mr. Sterbenc's help I needed.

How often had Mr. Boyle warned me about being on the quarterdeck? I could not count the times he had stressed this, never explaining but never changing his emphasis. If I stepped there, I would be breaking an important rule of the ship. I had broken rules in the past of course but nothing major and nothing I could not justify were I to have been caught.

The ship was in port now and I hoped the rules changed in port, but had my doubts. This rule would have to be broken as there was no other way. I had to get Mr. Sterbenc's attention again. He was already far down the deck with his back to me. How very rude.

I searched one last time for someone other than the second mate to whom I could speak. There was no one else. It was the first shore leave the men had been granted in some time and it did look as if Mr. Sterbenc "had no one to spare" just as he had said.

Well there was nothing for it. I climbed the ladder, stomped my way to the helm, and placed myself firmly in front of *The Pelican's* second mate. He could not ignore me now.

Nor did he. I did not expect the smile. It was not the type of smile one could warm to but a smile nonetheless, showing uneven and crowded teeth. "Your protector isn't here, my girl, and I am surprised that he hasn't warned you against being on this deck."

"If you mean Mr. Boyle, then be assured that he has warned me, Mr. Sterbenc," I said. "However, this is important and you simply must help me. I am sure that the Dunsfords are wandering in town, a strange town to them, looking for me right now. They could get lost themselves and since I am safe and back on the ship they must be told."

Mr. Sterbenc crossed his arms and stared down at me, "They'll find out soon enough when they return. They won't stay out all day looking for a little orphan like you."

"I am not an orphan!"

"No matter." Then suddenly squaring his shoulders he surveyed the decks. "No one knows you're here do they." It should have been a question but was not.

"I suppose one or two of the crew may have seen me come aboard," I say quickly, startled at the tone of his voice and forgetting the sequence of events that lead me to seek his help.

His mirthless grin widened. Although I had earlier compared him to Jeremy Franklin I no longer thought that. Jeremy Franklin was a terrible boy but he did not frighten me as this man did. "You're not to be on this deck. Come with me." He grabbed me by the arm and headed toward the stern.

"No, no. You must help me find the Dunsfords. To tell them I am safe," I yelled, fighting against his grip.

He led me to the railing and pushed me hard against it. "I could toss you in the sea right now," he snarled, his face close to mine. "I'm bettin' you can't swim and will sink directly to the bottom of the bay. No one will know."

"Cook will know," I protested, finally remembering that it had been Cook who told me the captain and Mr. Boyle were ashore.

"Cook? Hell, Cook's a nigger. Who'll believe him over me?" Still, he pulled me from the railing and dragged me toward a hatch cover that rose mid-deck. I sat on my haunches but it did nothing to slow the man.

Wrenching the hatch open, Mr. Sterbenc slung his arm firmly around my waist and lifted me from my feet, swinging himself onto the ladder hidden beneath. I dangled over the gloom below unable to see to the bottom of the hole, a damp heat rising from the darkness. Were I to fall, what would I find? What was down there that breathed hot air and lived in perpetual night? I grappled for any hold I could find. Nothing.

"You're to do as you're told."

I wriggled and kicked. He said nothing and merely tightened his hold, hurting me more than before. I clawed at his arm, scrapping as hard as I could until I felt his skin tear. "You little bitch," he snarled into my ear. Then he dropped me.

I expected a prolonged plunge into the bowels of the ship, to land atop a lion pacing in the dark or to fall into boiling oil, tumbling into a sinister void and left to writhe among spiders or snakes. Instead, my feet hit a deck almost as soon as I fell and I toppled backwards against something solid, dropping to my rump with a thud, one short burst of air pushed from my body. There was nothing sinister below, except of course Mr. Sterbenc. I suspected that I was somewhere near the captain's own cabin.

I had no time to move before Mr. Sterbenc was in front of me, silhouetted against the light from the hatch, grabbing the front of my dress and pulling me to my feet. He brought his shadowed face close to mine. I could not discern his features in the dark, but I imagined them to be alarming. "You little bitch. Do that again and I'll knock your head off," he hissed.

I believed him. His awful breath chilled against my neck. My thoughts tumbled and scattered and regrouped heavily into an empty place in my stomach. Please let me go, please let me go.

"I'd rather it were the blonde girl," he jeered, stroking my cheek. "She's much more to my liking."

A pitiful squeal buzzed past my lips, belying any attempt at bravery. My ears throbbed in time with my heartbeat and I squeezed my eyes closed.

"Mr. Sterbenc?" A shadow darkened the hatchway. "Mr. Sterbenc, are you below?"

There was an immediate change in the confines of the gloomy passageway. I was still frightened but suddenly realized that I was not the only one. Mr. Sterbenc pulled me closer and slapped a rough hand over my mouth. "What do you want? I'm on my way to the head."

"Signal from shore, Mr. Sterbenc. Captain's on his way back. You told me to let you know."

"Fine. Get back to your post."

Above, my rescuer moved away from the hatch, feet slapping rhythmically on the deck. Perhaps it had not been my heartbeat I had heard after all.

"A word of this pet and I shall throw you overboard at the next storm." He pulled me further along the dark corridor and, opening a door at the end, flung me roughly into the light beyond. "No one will believe you anyway so keep your mouth shut. And stay off the quarterdeck." He slammed the door, his footfalls heavily retreating along the passage.

I leaned against the wall, sliding down its smooth surface until I sat on the deck, willing my breathing to calm and the trembling to cease. I silently thanked God and the stars and the man whose voice I did not know for my escape from the dark hallway and Mr. Sterbenc and his awful smell.

Finally looking round, I realized that I was now only a few feet from the main cabin; a short distance to true safety. I stood and wiped my hands on my ruined skirt, leaving streaks of blood. I surveyed my palms; the blood was not mine. At least I had hurt the man a little.

I decided to wait a short interval before asking the captain to help find the Dunsfords. Once he was on board I would no longer need Mr. Sterbenc.

Still I would do as the second mate had told me: no one would know about the hatch or the cramped corridor or his threat to throw me overboard. I would not needlessly worry my guardians about the filthy boy in the streets of Rio nor the filthy man in the bowels of *The Pelican*. The danger had passed and I did not want to fear the next storm.

The day after the hanging I beg Mrs. Ellison to cut my hair. It has been several months since Mrs. Llewellyn had shorn my locks and they curl around my face and into my eyes. I want them gone.

I retrieve the leather straps Miss Moon had tied around my ribs and use them again each day, moving them higher on my body to hide my budding breasts. Jack may not have noticed them yet but I have; I want to take no chances.

The mere act of rising from bed each day is a chore. I fall into an exhausted slumber at night, awaking well before dawn unable to return to sleep, unable to quiet my mind. By sunrise, I have slipped into a half-dead doze. I groan at any intrusion.

Jack does not care that he is intruding. He stops by daily to report that rumors about the murder and hanging continue to spread through the town. We are not yet tainted by them. Neither is Rosa, fortunately, as word of her evolution from rape victim to whore has not reached the Mexican camp.

The first day Jack brings eggs and borrows Mrs. Ellison's kitchen to fix breakfast before he runs off to church. The second morning he brings a wooden box with his barn cat and her four new kittens tucked safely inside, wrapped in an old shred of blanket. Unlike Uncle John's barn cat, this one seems to welcome human contact, allowing me to pet her and hold the kittens until Jack must return the family to the barn.

Jack's rule is that I have to get out of bed and dressed before I can eat anything he fixes or pet the kittens or join him in any of the other schemes he dreams up each visit.

By the fifth day I rise early and wash my face and pull on my boots in anticipation of Jack's visit. Usually he stomps his feet on the step below the tent flap to announce himself. Today I hear a soft scrape of feet on the treads; even Jack must realize how early it is.

I rub my eyes one last time and lift the tent flap. Jack stands outside, his head bowed, clutching his left arm close to his side, his shoulder slouched unnaturally low. When he raises his head, there are dark circles beneath his eyes as if he has not slept in a long time. A black bruise reaches across his chin. His breathing is shallow.

"I fell from the barn roof. I can't move my arm."

"What were you doing on the barn roof?" I motion him inside to sit on one of the small stools Papa keeps in the hospital tent.

"I was shooing the chickens off. They wouldn't come down on their own. They'd already tried to lay a couple of eggs there."

I do not believe him, but say nothing. I know better than to confront him in a lie, given his usual denials. Instead I reach for his shoulder. He cries out.

"Papa left yesterday. He will not be home for at least five days," I say watching the pain pass across Jack's face, "and you cannot wait that long. We are going to see Miss Moon."

"No!" he yells, clutching his arm more tightly as if to prevent the imagined Miss Moon from touching him. "I'm not goin' to see some Indian."

"Well that is just stupid. I cannot help you; Papa is not here. Miss Moon is the best chance you have. Papa was impressed with her skill when she set the bone in my arm and stitched my jaw and strapped my ribs."

The set of his chin is not encouraging. "No. I just need to get my arm back in place is all. I'm not bleedin' or anythin' so it can't be that bad. You try it. Try pushin' it so it looks like it's supposed to."

I survey the distortion of the shoulder that shows through his shirt. I place my hand softly on the wounded arm then step quickly away as Jack yells.

"No. Try again, Quinn, please. I'll be quiet."

It is no use. He tries not to scream; however, his squeal is worse than yelling. Sweat glistens on his brow and his face has lost its color.

When the Ellisons burst into the room, I realize that Jack and I have been making a lot of noise in the early morning hour. Mr. Ellison has his rifle at the ready. Upon seeing Jack and his distress, the rifle is forgotten and they each attempt to realign Jack's arm. They are met only with painful squawks.

"We are going to see Miss Moon," I announce again.

Although both Jack and the Ellisons argue, I countered their protests. Miss Moon is skilled, she is only an hour's walk away (whereas I have no idea how far or even where my father's claim is), she is not hostile, and seems to have the angry Nanyawyn in control despite his nature.

Finally, the Ellisons relent. However, if we are not back by two, Mr. Ellison will come hunting us. Stick to the deer trail, he says; no short cuts. He can follow us easily if we stay on the trail.

I assure them that we are in no danger and promise to stay on the known path and return quickly.

We walk slowly to avoid jarring Jack's shoulder. The terrain seems more rugged than I remember. Usually we have no trouble scrambling over the rocks and fording the creek.

It is some time before I realize that Jack is singing beside me. Well it is not singing really but something very like it. "What are you doing?" I ask.

"I'm prayin'," he responds. "I'm prayin' to the Blessed Virgin to get this over quick."

"You do not pray to God?"

"I'll bet he's busy with more important stuff."

"What do you say?"

"Holy Mary, Mother of God. Then I ask for what I'm askin' for."

"Does it work?"

"It makes me feel better. And the time goes faster."

It is late morning before we reach the Miwok village. By then Jack's pace is a shuffle, his shirt ringed with sweat, his face ashen.

The village is quiet in the midday sun, hazy through the clouds of dust kicked up by the children at their games. Our approach is heralded by dogs; I do not remember dogs from my first visit. The hair on the back of my neck rises just like the ridge of fur bristling down the backs of the snarling animals. I stop and step closer to Jack, well away from the invisible periphery of the campground which the dogs guard. I am dimly aware that the village games have ceased and that the children have joined the circle of dogs. Some of the older boys have raised bows, arrows readied in the strings.

Jack has his knife in hand, sweeping the circle of animals with both his eyes and the blade. I reach into my pocket and pull out the little pistol, pointing it at our furry guards, vainly trying to keep the gun steady, wishing that my heart would stop pounding.

"What is that?" Jack hisses. "Put it away. Just put it away. You can't know what you'll hit."

There are children standing behind the dogs, so I slip the pistol back into my pocket.

Miss Moon eases her way through the press of sentinels and the young men lower their arrows. The dogs stop barking, still wary but no longer vicious. Her presence has quelled the ferocity.

She walks straight to Jack, briefly surveying his injury. Urging him to sheath his knife, she leads us to a fire pit in the inner circle of the camp, bidding him sit on the woven mats that surround it. Her voice almost a whisper, she speaks to Jack, moving to his side and kneeling beside him. She motions for me to sit with my back against his back. We are surrounded by dogs and gawking children and women, a silent watchful circle.

Jack makes no sound as Miss Moon strokes his injured

shoulder. She pushes his elbow tightly against his ribs and clasps his hand. Shushing and soothing and gentling, she rocks his arm toward her, pressing his elbow into his side. The motion is opposite of what the Ellisons and I had done. Jack moans and pushes his back hard against mine but otherwise does not resist. Miss Moon moves the arm gently back and forth, coaxing it further and further each time, softly talking and humming.

There is a popping sound and Jack groans. The tension leaves his body, his full weight pressing against me, bending me forward. I cannot see his face and do not know what has happened. I can see Miss Moon sitting on her heels, hands on her thighs, looking pleased. Jack breathes deeply. Then he moans; a moan of relief.

"Get off of me please," I gasp from my crunched position. As Jack releases his weight, I uncurl and scramble to my knees. He is clutching his left elbow again but the shoulder is in place. "Are you all right now?"

He nods, watching the crowd warily as Miss Moon rises and walks to her hut. She returns with bowls and baskets filled with food which she lays on the mats at our feet. Jack surveys the contents. "She won't try to poison us, will she?"

"You say some of the stupidest things, Jack."

"You'd worry about that too, if that other Indian was here!"

I glance around the village for a sign of Nanyawyn, for Jack is right. We may not be welcome here. I have again put the Miwok village in danger and, when Nanyawyn returns, he may not hesitate to unleash his displeasure.

With a length of soft hide, Miss Moon fashions a sling and ties it firmly behind Jack's neck, cradling his arm in the loop. She holds up both hands, fingers spread, pointing to the sling and giving him instruction. Neither of us understand a word.

Jack does understand the language of his stomach, however, which is growling with discontent. He surveys the foods Miss Moon has placed before us and reaches for an item resembling corn cakes.

"These are awful," he whispers, not trying to hide his disgust at the taste of the cake. Miss Moon giggles and hands him a bowl, urging him to dip the cake into it. Honey. Jack wolfs the cake and licks his fingers. "Geez, Quinn, I think those are grasshoppers," he says, pointing to one of the baskets. "She *is* tryin' to poison us."

Again Miss Moon sees our reaction and, shaking her head, reaches into the basket, snatching one of the insects and crunching it between her teeth. She offers them to the children in the surrounding circle. One child smiles, grabs a handful, happily munching on the insects as he scampers away, passing some of the treats to the others. I sample the seeds and pine nuts and dried berries she offers as Jack reaches for another cake and the honey bowl. We leave the grasshopper basket alone.

The Miwok men arrive as Jack devours the last of the cakes. Kalelenu leads the party. Miss Moon rises, crossing the camp to greet her son and the others. Kalelenu carries one end of a litter on which a large deer lay. The litter is like the one on which I had been carried, not long ago.

Kalelenu sets the litter down, removes the bow slung over his shoulder, and joins Jack and me at the fire.

"Good," Jack nods, acknowledging the deer with a thrust of his chin.

The Miwok boy removes an arrow from his quiver, handing it to Jack. It is reed-thin with a long and slender arrowhead, feathers

neatly tied at the base. He points to the arrow then the deer then
to his own chest. This is meat for his family, like the rabbits from
Jack's traps. I recognize Kalelenu's pride for I have seen it in Jack
before.

As the two boys continue to admire the deer carcass and the
weapons, I am distracted by the drama unfolding at the periphery
of the camp. Miss Moon has met Nanyawyn at the outer edges
of the Miwok village. Even from a distance I know he has seen
Jack and me: his stance is defiant and he stares over the head of
the woman who dances in his path. I rise to my feet. Miss Moon
places a hand to his chest. She tilts her head to one side then the
other, stepping into Nanyawyn's path, swaying back then forward
with a tempered rhythm. It is not the dance of my parents in the
moonlight of the doorway in Boston: this is an exotic dance of
will and rage.

The dance lasts only a moment. Nanyawyn strides toward
us, shoulders squared and black hair swept behind like Guleesh's
mane. His anger has not been quelled.

"Leave now," he snarls. "She can do no more for the boy."
With a glance at Miss Moon who has come to his side, he adds:
"She says to keep the arm wrapped for ten days. It can happen
again."

We have been dismissed. As we walk from the encampment,
Jack glances over his shoulder every few paces as if expecting a rifle
shot. I am discouraged by this second encounter with Nanyawyn
as it has ended no more favorably than the first.

CHAPTER 17

August 10, 1849

PAPA INCREASES HIS HOSPITAL DAYS during the summer months because many new residents have moved into the town. There is probably business enough to keep the hospital open all week, although he does not do that. The ailments do not vary much but the number of people who need attention swells tenfold. Mr. Ellison now displays a sign in the store announcing the days until Papa's return from his claim and there are usually ten or more people waiting the morning of his homecoming.

Aldridge, Jack, Jimmy and I spend most of our time at the creek, soaking our feet in the cool water as the thermometer in the Ellisons' store tops 98°. When it comes time for the boys to strip and wade into the deeper water, I know the cues, make my excuses, and leave. Only once was I caught unaware of the custom: in the late spring before Jack and Aldridge discovered my secret. I had to think of a plausible excuse for not joining them even as they stood before me without a stitch on. I do not remember what I said (Jack later confessed it was mostly babble), but I do remember nearly breaking my ankle trying to get away, my face hot and burning. Certainly I had seen naked boys before but I had been related to them. According to Jack, this was one of the first times he and the others had noted how peculiar boys from Boston were.

The boys surprise me no longer. Either Aldridge or Jack will say: "It's really hot today, let's go swimmin'" or something equally obvious well before they start unbuttoning anything. They move more slowly too. Jimmy is usually in the water before the others have their shirts off. By August I am well acquainted with Jimmy's body and its irregular tan lines: his dark forearms, neck, and face, the bronze torso, and everything else that glows white in the shade of the forest. I no longer run away, but if I linger too long Jack casts me a private glower and silently threatens with a raised fist and a knowing grin. It is not that I want to see Jimmy's body, but I like making Jack scowl.

Jack's shoulder has healed well and it does not seem to hamper him. He is eager to climb rocks and swing from tree limbs once again.

He finally confronted me about the gun I carry. "When was the last time you cleaned that thing?" he asked, motioning for me to hand him the pistol.

"I have never used it so I have never cleaned it."

"All the more reason!" He turns the tiny weapon over and tries not to laugh. "Look at it. It's covered in pocket lint and crumbs. That thing could explode in your face. I'll teach you how to clean it. You got any shot for it?"

I do and we spend the afternoon wiping the gun clean and practicing how to load it (just as the Bear had taught me). We do not shoot as Jack is not sure I can get more of the right kind of shot. "I bet they don't even make guns like this anymore," he says. He never mentions its existence to the other boys, at least not within my hearing.

The latest shipment from Uncle James included several "new"

books and magazine publications (courtesy of Matthew's foraging) which add to my repertoire of yarns. The pages of one short story, "The Tell-Tale Heart," quickly become dog-eared with repeated readings. I have come to know the literary tastes of my friends. Because they like the gory things, I have even developed tales based on invented histories of the blood on the linens I boil and fold for my father.

I have plenty to tell them after this morning's patients: Papa treated two broken arms, three broken noses, and several toes lost during an impromptu axe-throwing contest. As I prepare to leave the hospital, anxious to meet up with the boys and catalogue the casualties of the day, the door leading from the Ellisons' store is kicked aside to reveal a sorry trio: a huge blond man and a boy of Matthew's age with dark curly hair. They are dragging the slumped body of a disheveled and unconscious man between them.

A strong wind of whiskey precedes them as they stagger into the room, the blond man bellowing: "Hey, Doc, can you give our friend here a hand. He's been cut." His words are slurred but the accent is clearly Australian. He is the man Mrs. Schwartzman threatened to shoot in Stockton. I do not recall his name. He is even more drunk than he was the evening I first met him. Perhaps he is always drunk.

The Australian and his friend lurch to the closest table and drop the limp body of their companion on top.

"Little row at Miss Weller's. Some sneaky bastard with a very sharp knife," the blond continues. "Accused our friend Dick here of cheating. Stupid sot. Couldn't tell Dick was too drunk to cheat, I suppose." He laughs, the sound grating over his teeth.

Papa surveys the damaged man. "Not very agile, was he? I see at least six wounds. This one," he points high on the man's thigh, "is probably the worse. One can only hope it did not cut the artery. Probably not, as he would have bled out already if it had." The man moans. Moving closer to look at him, my stomach lurches and my lips tingle. Even covered in dust and blood, sporting a grizzled beard, the man is unmistakable. He is Dick Sterbenc from *The Pelican*.

"He'll be out for a while. I conked him one for good measure to stop his bloody mewling," the blond man says, slinging an arm around the shoulders of the curly-haired boy, pulling him to the door. "We'll leave him to you, Doc. Be back in a couple of hours to pick him up if he's still alive."

"Now wait a minute," Papa protests. "I shall need your assistance."

It is too late. Cackling, the Australian stumbles through the store, weaving and leaning against the boy, leaving all doors open in his wake.

"Bloody bastards," Papa mumbles and turns to me. "Here take this cloth and press on his leg, right here, as hard as you can."

I follow the directions as Papa busies himself with removing Mr. Sterbenc's bloodied shirt, exposing the various wounds. I find the harder I press on Mr. Sterbenc's injured leg, the less I tremble.

Papa moves around the prone man assessing and cataloguing the wounds aloud. Papa often does this. His patients think he is speaking to them, giving them his diagnosis, even attempting to assure them. However, I have come to believe this is not true. The patients are specimens on his table, their circumstances triggering him to log the issue and then search for the page in his mind that holds the clue to their cure.

In addition to the leg wound, Mr. Sterbenc's ribs have been laid bare on one side and his arms are sliced in several places.

"Just as I suspected, that leg is the worst. Let us start there," my father murmurs, grabbing a knife from atop the trunk that serves as a platform for his medical tools. "Move your hands," he orders as he cuts Mr. Sterbenc's trousers from waist to boot top, laying the material open. "Now press again in the same spot."

I obey, looking away as Papa prepares for the surgery. I do not want to see the wound. Worse, I do not want to see what Papa's cutting has left exposed. My friends call it their cock (although only Jimmy says that word now as Jack and Aldridge ceased making any reference months ago). Cousin Alfred called it his "willy" those times he had waved it at me playfully. I do not want to look at the ugly shaft that is attached to Mr. Sterbenc, protruding from a thatch of dirt-colored hair; however, my eyes are drawn there nonetheless.

"Watch what you are doing! You need to press here. Hard."

"What is wrong with him, Papa?"

Papa has been gathering the tools and swabs and ointments he will need and only when I pose my question does he seem to realize who I am and what is on the table before me. He quickly grabs a cloth and covers Mr. Sterbenc's private parts. "I see this sort of thing every day and think nothing of it. I am truly sorry that this had to be your first look at a...um...a penis."

"It is not my first look," I mumble.

"I beg your pardon?"

"Alfred used to show me all the time." I avoid mention of the more recent viewings.

"Alfred. Yes, I might have guessed."

"But what is wrong with him? He has sores or something."

Papa moves quickly to take my place, directing me to Mr. Sterbenc's other side so that I may press against the gash over his ribs, just as I did to the leg. "Were I to hazard a guess, I would say he has a disease called syphilis."

Not wanting to catch a disease that causes such ugly, oozing sores, I back away. Papa chuckles. "You cannot contract it by touching him. Well not...not the way you or I are touching him. This disease is transmitted by...fornicating with others who are diseased." After a moment's hesitation, Papa says, "No questions? You are familiar with that word: fornication?"

"The Reverend spoke of it in some of his sermons. 'Thou shalt not fornicate with whores.'" Certainly not diseased whores I surmise, not if that earns you the glistening pustules that cover Mr. Sterbenc's (what had Papa called it?) penis.

"Such a refined education from the church," Papa says with disgust. "He has lost some blood but I do not think he will die of these wounds. Unless there is another knife-wielding gambler in his future, *that*," Papa nods his head toward the man's privates, "is what will kill him. If he lives long enough he'll eventually go mad, assuming he hasn't already." Mr. Sterbenc groans as my father begins to stitch the leg.

"Papa, I know this man. He was the second mate on *The Pelican*."

Papa pauses mid-stitch and grabs Mr. Sterbenc's chin, turning the man's head. "Mr...what was his name? Boyle? This cannot be Mr. Boyle."

"No Papa. Mr. Boyle was the first mate. This is Mr. Sterbenc.

He was the second mate."

Papa studies my face for a moment. "I take it you do not like the man."

I shake my head. "He frightens me." And he did. Even in his current oblivion, the memory of his grip and the stink of his breath make me tremble anew.

"Well I believe I will be finished here long before he regains consciousness. As soon as I begin on his ribs you may leave. I will not need your help any longer and you can safely make your escape." Papa nods. "He frightens me too."

With relief I press harder on Mr. Sterbenc's ribs. This stems the blood flow and I hope will make the process go more quickly.

"However," Papa says after a moment, "I do have one problem." Tying a bandage around the leg wound, he circles the table and nudges me aside, rethreading his needle and preparing to repair the ribs. "I need to find those reprobates who left him. Once he comes around he will be ready to leave. Sore, probably more from the blow on his head than the cuts on his body, but ready. His friends need to take him away. Do you think you and the Irish boy could look for them in town? I do not want you to go alone."

I race to the Moylan farm. Having to find the Australian and his friend is a more favorable alternative to being in the same room with Dick Sterbenc as far as I am concerned. Fortunately, Jack is only too glad to accompany me. Dropping his shovel and swatting dirt from his trousers, he declares that the muck in the barn will still be there when he returns.

"How do you know these men?" Jack asks as we race up the road toward the eastern part of the town. Our plan is to go to Miss Weller's tent, as that is where the Australian said the stabbing occurred. It will be a good starting point for our search even if the men have moved on.

I tell him a little of the incident on *The Pelican*, ending the story after Mr. Sterbenc's first threat to throw me overboard. I do not tell him everything as I fear Jack might return to the hospital and club Mr. Sterbenc if he knew more. "And the Australian was in Stockton. He did not do anything bad, but he scared me and Mrs. Schwartzman threatened him with her pistol."

Lifting the flap of canvas that covers the opening to Miss Weller's establishment, I smile despite my serious errand. This will be the first time I have ventured into the tent although I have been under it many times. Beneath the floorboards of this and any saloon in town is gold. On several occasions, the boys and I shimmied under the raised floors to scoop up gold dust accidentally spilled as the miners paid for their drink and gambling and other pleasures.

Despite the brightness of the morning, Miss Weller's tent is dark inside. Lanterns hang from every tent pole, their glass smeared with soot. The light must fight through the grime. There are few people inside at this hour, since it is a weekday and most of the miners are working their claims. One of the larger tents, it is the size of both the Ellisons' store and the hospital tent combined. It is divided by large sheets of canvas that create other rooms toward the back. Like the hells of San Francisco, Miss Weller's never closes.

As Jack and I enter, the Australian's exclamations and oaths shake the wooden floorboards and the canvas walls. He is engaged in an unruly hand of cards, the boy sitting beside him. Now that we are here, I am not sure of the wisdom of my errand, even accompanied by Jack: the blond man dwarfs the tables and chairs and people around him.

Regardless, I walk past the other tables to the big man's side, hoping he will not see me shaking in the half light.

"Excuse me," I say. I must repeat myself before he turns toward me. Even in the shadows, I see his unfocused eyes are rimmed in red.

"Well," he blinks, "what have we here? What can I do for you my fine young fellow?" It is evident that he has no recollection of me at all.

"Your friend is stitched and ready to leave the hospital."

"He ain't dead?" The Australian sounds surprised and a little disappointed.

"Quite the contrary."

He blinks several times as his head bobs dully. "Hmm. I reckoned he'd be dead by now. Well Danny and me'll just finish our card game and be along shortly, darlin'."

Jack steps in front of me. "You need to get him now. The doc needs the table for other patients."

This is clearly a challenge and I tense, glancing between Jack and the Australian in surprise. I did not tell Jack to say that; I do not even know if it is true.

Hissing sounds escape the Australian's lips. I take a step back before realizing that the man is chuckling. It is a throttled and eerie sound, but a chuckle all the same. "Well, cub's got stones, I'd say. I like that. C'mere, boy." More quickly than I would have guessed the drunken man could move, he grabs Jack's shirtfront pulling him forward.

Jack knocks the Australian's hand away. The huge blond rises, sending chairs crashing around him. As he reaches for Jack once more, the youth he has called Danny stands and steps in between them, encircling the Australian with both arms.

"Leave him, Colin," the dark-haired boy says firmly. He is not nearly as drunk as his companion.

Colin. Colin Hurley. I remember the name of the man Mrs. Schwartzman threatened. I pat the pocket of my coat, hoping for the protection of my little pistol. Except it is a hot day and I am not wearing my coat. A drop of sweat trickles down my back. Despite the heat, I shiver.

The murmurs of the tent fall silent as Danny and Hurley remain locked in their strange embrace, Hurley glaring over the boy's shoulder at Jack. Jack stands ready with fists clenched, breathing like an angry horse. The big man staggers, leaning into the boy who holds him, who whispers to him, who tries to settle him.

With a stifled snort Hurley's eyes once again lose their focus. His gaze shifts from Jack to the boy embracing him. Briskly entwining his fingers in the dark curls, he scowls into Danny's face and I fear he will pull the boy away, leaving the path to Jack unchecked.

Hurley weaves as he surveys the boy's face. He pulls him closer. Then, suddenly he smiles and musses Danny's hair roughly.

"No harm," he says before lunging to pick up one of the toppled chairs, falling heavily into the seat. Hurley unsteadily casts his eyes up and down Jack then does the same to me.

"We'll be along," Danny assures us as Hurley turns back to his card game. I release the breath I had not realized I was holding.

Jack is not placated. He stiffens and I imagine steam rising from his body. The air in the tent is hot and close and I want only to get outside. "He'll be along he says," I whisper, moving between Jack and Hurley, much as Danny had done. "We know where to find him if he lingers too long." The waving tent flap beckons and I push against Jack to move him toward it. It takes more of a push than I expect but he finally relents.

"Son of a bitch," Jack mumbles once we are clear of the tent.

"You could have gotten us killed!" I snarl as unbidden images of the soldier with two bloodied mouths flicker before me.

"I hate bullies like him." Jack stomps off in the direction of the hospital tent.

Outside the Ellisons' store, Mr. Sterbenc is seated on the steps, head bobbing as he struggles to remain upright. He is dressed in Papa's worn clothes with an old blanket slouching from his shoulders. His face is void of color except the dark sunken places beneath his bulging eyes and he clutches his ribs every time he sways, a grunt and an oath punctuating any sudden movement. I know of only two occasions when Papa turned people out of the surgery; both were when the men had been abusive and loud. I smile to think these are the reasons Mr. Sterbenc finds himself alone and in pain on the street. I am not surprised.

These days, every inch of the Ellisons' store is used to the fullest. Mobs of miners swarm into the Sonoran Town looking for the pans and pickaxes and shovels that will become essential tools in their lives. These wares crowd one corner of the store. Sacks of nails and other building materials lay scattered among twenty-pound bags of foodstuffs. Glass jars and steel cans of fruits and vegetables line the shelves beside tins of crackers and tobacco, bolts of cloth, and the universal red flannel shirts the miners wear. The variety reminds me of Uncle James' warehouse, only not as organized. Despite the jumble, Mrs. Ellison knows exactly where each item may be found if asked. It seems an impossible puzzle to me.

Several people have congregated in the store but none appear to be waiting for my father. Jack and I make our way through the kitchen to the hospital, so that we can tell Papa of our success finding the Australian.

Inside the hospital are two Mexican boys pulling shirts over chests and stomachs covered in a red rash. Papa is gesturing and stammering to the father and mother, his face pale like the linen bandage he wrings in his hands. He utters an incomprehensible sentence, a combination of Latin and English and Spanish roughly translating to "Wash the body for not hot."

"What are you trying to say to them, Dr. Walker?" Jack asks.

Papa is startled to find us in the room. "I want them to constantly bathe themselves in cool water to keep the fevers down."

Jack translates and the parents nod in understanding.

"And make sure they stay away from anyone else. All of them. They need to stay in bed until the rashes are gone and the fever has passed. They can have no visitors. Measles are highly contagious." Papa's voice cracks. "And her…" He points a trembling finger at the mother.

The woman's hand goes to her throat in response to Papa's attention and I see that her neck is covered in the same red rash.

She pulls her shawl closer around her shoulders to hide her throat, but is unable to cover the swelling of her belly. The beginnings of a knot pull at my stomach.

"When is the baby due?" my father asks, turning to Jack. "Ask her when the baby is due."

Jack obliges. "The end of next month, she says."

Papa clasps one hand across his forehead rubbing his temples. "Tell them if the baby comes while she is sick they must find me immediately. It is very important. *Muy importante.*"

The family nods their appreciation to Jack and leaves the hospital with wary eyes, astounded at the behavior of my father. Even Jack looks puzzled as he watches Papa pace the hospital floor. "I must go to the Mexican camp to see if there are more cases. I must tell them what they need to do if they catch it and warn them to stay away from others." He spins on Jack. "Have you had the measles?"

"I don't know. What are they?"

"Fever, red rash, coughing that lasts for three days or so. Perhaps if you ask your parents."

"My parents are dead."

Mice. The mice have found us. I back against the door jamb as furry, frightening things scurry through my thoughts: the stuffiness of the bedroom in Boston, the stickiness of fevered skin, the shadow of my parents looming across the walls.

"Sorry. I am sorry." Papa glances frantically around the room. "I cannot risk exposing you. Do you know anyone else who understands English and speaks Spanish as well as you?"

"My sister, Aileen."

My father shakes his head. "If you have not been exposed I

doubt she has either. Can you teach me the words to say just as you said to those people?"

"I can go."

"No. You could die from this disease," Papa yells. "Those little boys could die, their mother could die; the woman's baby could… die." Papa clenches his temples again. "Just teach me the words," he barks.

~

Papa slept fitfully for the next two days, tossing in the squeaky cot. I wanted to shut myself in the old storeroom to get some sleep. However, I doubt I would have found peace there for my father's apprehension was as contagious as the measles.

Jack had taught Papa well. Papa needed his notes only once during our visit to the Mexican camp. He found three other cases of the disease, all of them well past the worrisome stage. Using his own flawed Spanish plus the phrases learned from Jack, he convinced the Mexicans that their plight was serious, and he stressed the importance of voluntary quarantine. By the time Papa and I left the camp, every family knew what to do should rashes appear.

Jack was angry when he learned that I was to accompany my father on this mission. His temper was curbed only by Papa's patient explanation: once having had the disease a person cannot get it again. "Guine has already had measles," Papa said.

"It's Quinn, Dr. Walker," Jack corrected. Papa coughed and grumbled before thanking the boy.

Following the visit to the Mexican camp, I do not leave Papa's side. He goes about his work at the hospital, instructing me and talking to me of nothing in particular, our combined energy channeled into a frenzy of activity. Together we scrub the surgery and fold bandages and organize the shelves between patients. He does not speak of going to the claim. He listens to my stories although I am sure that he will never remember any details. I know he dreads a visit from the woman's husband, but we do not speak of that. I believe we both hope to avoid its occurrence by not mentioning it.

Three days after the visit from the Mexican family, as we gather for supper, there is a knock outside the kitchen. The woman's husband has come to fetch Senor Doctor. The baby is coming.

Papa rises to gather his tools from the hospital, ordering me to remain.

"I can help."

"You cannot. You are not old enough to witness a human birth. I want you here and safe, so stay where you are."

I kick the kitchen chair as I rise. "Why will you not let me go? How much more difficult can a human birth be than that of a cat with its multiple babies? Or a horse with those spindly legs jutting everywhere? I've seen those!" I want to yell more, but refrain. How dare he push me aside as if to protect me from the world. As if he could.

My father lunges at me so quickly that I back into the wall nearly toppling Mrs. Ellison's butter churn. "Where have you learnt your manners? You are never to speak to me in that tone of voice again, young lady. Do you understand?" He is shaking but I do not know if it is because of me or because of what he might find in the Mexican camp.

Regardless, I do not answer. Ducking under his arm, I flee from the kitchen, my heart racing and my face burning. I quickly leave the town and stomp past the Moylan farm, kicking dirt and pebbles before me on my way to the creek. I want to be near the creek and feel its coolness; it is the one place where my anger might be quelled. There I will not think of Papa and his strange moods, or if I do, I will have that place of sanctuary surrounding me and soothing me.

As I approach, I furiously recite the names of the plants and creatures along the way. Jack has taught me, as he seems to know them all. Some of the terms are so fanciful that I suspect he is inventing them; I like hearing them anyway. Just as I liked hearing the names of things on *The Pelican*.

I cross the stream to a small island of stones and lay on a flat rock that hangs over the flowing water, reaching for the minnows that swim just beneath the surface. I never catch any. They are always just out of my reach, like my thoughts sometimes.

"It's a water walker," Jack said, as I prodded at the long-legged insect that skirted the surface of the creek. Jack and I had gone to the creek immediately after Senor Barajas' death. Neither of us wanted to go home.

"A water walker? Like Jesus?"

"You're goin' to hell, Quinn Walker. You can't compare Jesus to a bug."

"I did not mean it that way. I meant only…well, I do not know what I meant. It just came into my head."

Then the image of the chained crucifix around the neck of the Brazilian priest came into my head too. I wanted only to change the subject and talk about anything except Jesus and death and Senor Barajas. Every few minutes, the face of the Mexican seemed to float before me, choked and red, the image overlaid with the Reverend's words: *For all have sinned and fall short of the glory of God.* The man with the second mouth was there as well. I shuddered.

"How did you know that Senor Barajas would be killed?" I was sorry I asked the moment the words left my mouth.

Jack lowered his head. "You won't tell the others that I cried, will you?"

"No. If I did, I would have to tell them that I cried too."

"But you're a girl so that's to be expected."

"Stop saying that. No one knows I am a girl except you and Aldridge. Well, and Mr. Turner and the Ellisons. The Miwok know too, but they will say nothing." I was appalled at how many people knew my secret. "You need to stop thinking of me as a girl."

"I can't think of anything else." He kicked at the water. "That could've been you we found in that gulch instead of Rosa."

I knew that. That could have been me in the depths of *The Pelican* too. I realized that as well. "You have to forget I am a girl."

"Just like everyone has to forget that your pa's a doctor, I suppose." Jack tossed a rock into the depths. "Why do you do that? You pretend you're a boy and he pretends he's not a doctor. Why can't you just be what you are?"

"Papa says he's not a doctor anymore."

"The hell he isn't. He's the best doctor we've ever had around here. Why would he want to stop bein' something he's good at?"

"I think he wanted to stop being a doctor when Mama died."

Jack hung his head again. "Yeah. My Da said there was a lot he wanted to stop doin' when my mother died too. He didn't stop, but he wanted to."

Jack removed his shoes and dangled his feet in the cool water, watching it surge over his toes. "It's my fault. I may as well have put a sign around that soldier's neck and pointed Senor Barajas right to him. I made it real bad."

I could think of nothing to say.

"I should've killed him myself. I just needed to swing a little harder and then run like hell and nobody would've seen. Or I could've just gone to get the mule and not run up that hill at all. There's lots of things I could've done that wouldn't have gotten Senor Barajas killed."

The sun sets well before I return to the hospital tent. I am calm now. Being near the creek has helped.

Papa is not yet home so I light the lantern by my bedside and open a book. I read the same page three times.

When my father returns, he enters through the side flap of the hospital tent, just as I had done, so as not to disturb the Ellisons. He drops his medical bag in its usual place by the trunk. Only then does he part the canvas curtain and enter our bedroom, bringing a stool from the surgery with him. He sets it beside my bed and sits, taking my hand in his. I watch him closely, but cannot tell what his thoughts might be. My own are speeding too quickly to catch: were they…did everything…what…how are…?

Papa opens my fingers to their full length then rolls my hand over and strokes my palm, examining the lines. He turns it once more to manipulate the bones and massage the tendons with his thumb. He gives my hand a gentle squeeze as the tent seems to close around the lantern light.

"Are they…are they alright?" I whisper.

He smiles and moves his head in a barely perceptible nod. "It is a boy," he says. "A very tiny boy. Both he and his mother are healthy. She is over her fever and the rash nearly gone."

Papa sits up straighter and sighs. "I may as well not have been there. It was the easiest birth I have ever attended. She labored for two, three hours at most. I have been walking in the town since then."

He looks around the tent as if assessing the canvas walls and the rickety cots for the first time, his eyes finally resting on the lantern. I am certain he does not see it. Crickets sing outside and the walls of the tent occasionally whisper as moths hit and flutter, guided by the light of the lamp.

"It was nothing to do with me," he murmurs then raises my hand to his lips, caressing it softly. He stands and kisses my forehead. Finally he turns and enters his surgery, taking the lantern with him, closing the canvas behind him. I hear the familiar rustling noises and the occasional *ting* of metal as he cleans his instruments and sets them in their proper places.

CHAPTER 18

September 26, 1849

I AM NOT CERTAIN that I trust this man who pretends to be my father, who greets me each morning with a smile, ushers patients into the hospital-tent with good cheer, and walks with a light step. I have never seen this man before and while I like the softness of him I wonder when Papa will return and tell this man to go away.

"School has been postponed for a week," he says. We stand side by side rolling bandages, stacking them neatly on the shelf. He clears his throat. "Miss Beth and Aileen are not well. I saw them yesterday. Stitched up your young friend too. He said that a cow had kicked him right above the eye."

"Did you believe him?"

"Do you have reason to believe he would lie to me?"

"It is just that he has a lot of accidents involving livestock," I say, thinking of the chickens on the roof of the barn. "I should think a blow to the head from a cow would have killed him."

Papa shrugs and says no more. He will tell me nothing of Miss Beth's and Aileen's illnesses, either. He refuses to say anything about his patients, even though I have overheard enough conversations to know about most of the ailments that travel through the Sonoran Town and who has them.

This new Papa is less annoyed when I question him further

about the Moylans. "My dear, a patient's disorder is only discussed between that patient and the doctor, like a priest hearing confession," he says, chuckling. The thought is odd coming from my father and I stare in disbelief. He does not seem to notice. "My colleague and friend, Oliver, believed that a physician was nearly like a clergyman: there to listen to the complaints and help the body (as opposed to the soul), but not to assume they can 'save.' Salvation is a decision that the patient alone must make. I believe Oliver was being a bit dramatic when he announced this. He was a poet when not studying medicine. Poets are a strange breed. However, I am beginning to believe that perhaps he was right."

"Will they be better next week?"

"Yes, I think so. As well as they can be. In the meantime, I thought you might want to accompany me to the claim. This shall be your last chance before school starts again."

I am amazed and excited, wanting the airy feeling in my chest to last forever.

We load Fuego with provisions. We are only to be gone two days, Papa says, so even the extra food and clean clothing the two of us must take will not burden the horse too much. Guleesh can stay behind and help Jack haul apples to the Mexican camp.

We leave at dawn, seeking the banks of an Estanislao River tamed by a dry summer. We ride until we reach a wide creek hiding among the green granite cliffs. This creek has no name that Papa knows and has escaped the notice of most other gold seekers although he cannot fathom why. "That is good," he says. "Otherwise we might have to dodge prospecting holes and worry about new dams diverting the stream, those beastly water cannons and all of the trouble the other creeks and rivers are struggling with these days. They may have overlooked this one because the terrain at the junction is too rugged. Whatever the reason, I am thankful."

As we climb into the mountains I am soothed by the gentle sway of the horse and the warmth of Papa's back as I press my cheek against it. The late September sun toasts the air. I am tempted to trill my tongue in imitation of a cat's purr, but decide against it. Even this new Papa may think me strange for doing so.

We reach Papa's campsite just after noon, the tent perched on a barren stretch of rocky dirt well back from the water's edge. Like all miners, Papa leaves his tent and belongings at his claim when he returns to town. The presence of tools and possessions warns others away, indicating a working claim. Papa says the miners have a code of ethics that prevents people from stealing one another's belongings. Since severe punishments are inflicted on any who break those rules, I suppose it is no surprise that Papa's camp is untouched.

The creek thunders by wildly, splashing over the boulders and rock piles that litter the banks. The ground shakes from the rumble. If this is a river tamed by summer drought, I believe I would tremble at its power in the wet season.

We unload our provisions and turn Fuego out to graze in a small meadow hidden behind a thrust of rocks at the far side of the camp. We munch on slabs of cornbread that Mrs. Ellison has packed for us. Then we set to work. Papa shows me how to use the sluice box he has anchored in the stream a few feet from the bank. He digs earth and stones from a pool where the flow eddies, shoveling the slurry into the sluice's tray. The silt is washed through the strange contraption by the creek's own power. Among the remaining stones, I pick out three large nuggets of gold. I am excited and request permission to do some of the digging.

We work all afternoon in this manner. I soon opt for the easier task of sifting through the sluice for the nuggets when the shoveling proves to be hard work and my arms begin to ache. By sunset, we have filled three pouches with golden stones and flakes and I am content and starving.

"I had a patient yesterday," Papa says, stirring the embers of our evening fire with a slender stick. We have eaten our meal and the night has robbed the warmth from our campsite except for the small circle where we huddle around the flames. "He was from Chicago where he worked in a small stockyard. He had a wife and three grown children there still. One day he decided to pack up with his two youngest boys and come to California to see the elephant."

I did not think I had heard Papa correctly. "I beg your pardon?"

"My reaction exactly," Papa chuckles. "I stopped in the middle of stitching his arm (he had come in with an infected cut from here to here)," he touches his elbow and then his wrist. "I was quite taken aback. 'I hope you are aware that there are no elephants in California,' I said to him.

"Well he laughed and said that of course he knew that. 'Going to see the elephant' was just a phrase that people were using to indicate they were going to California to dig their way to wealth and happiness, do something they had never done before. Something unexpected. Something grand, unique, and perhaps even frightening."

In the embers before me, I imagine the menagerie elephant swaying. She was something grand and unique and terrifying. The crackling sounds from the burning pine logs remind me of the whip used to subdue her. I do not smile at this memory.

"He was amazed that I had not heard the expression before. On his journey across the states he had seen deserted homes with 'Gone to see the elephant' painted across their doors, wagons with the phrase displayed on their sides: 'Going to see the elephant.' People from all over the nation, he said, are headed for the promise that is California."

Papa stares at the fire then leans back to survey the silhouettes of the trees against a diamond-crusted sky. The sigh that escapes him has weight; not like a breeze whispering among the trees, but like a salt-laden gust from the sea.

"Did he see the elephant?" I ask.

Papa breaks from his reverie. "Unfortunately, his was a sad tale, my sweet. I believe his elephant may have trampled him: his boys both dead now, his gold squandered, his health jeopardized. He would like to go home, but dreads facing his family."

"Have you seen the elephant, Papa?" I do not know what possesses me to ask. The question is more personal than any I have ever before asked my father.

He does not answer immediately. "I do believe I have. There is something wonderfully compelling here, like no other place I have ever been. It is grand and beautiful and…"

"Savage," I offer as his pause lengthens. I do not understand where the thought originated although it feels appropriate. I am unsure that Papa will have followed my reasoning, and I want to explain. "I feel as if I can touch the wildness here. Even in the Sonoran Town, even with thousands of people near, I can touch it. Little is hidden, as it is elsewhere. I did not feel like that in

Boston or Rio or even in San Francisco. I think the wild may be there, but there are…walls to keep the untamed things apart from us. Here, there are no walls."

"You are a curious child."

"But it is true."

"Do not begin a sentence with 'but.' *But* yours is a good observation. It is true." Papa smiles. "I think that here we see the true nature of people without the gloss of civilization. They obey rules, but only barely and only those most important for survival." Papa stokes the fire and we are silent for a long time. I am pleased that he understood. "I have had a letter from your Uncle James. I am sorry to tell you that your grandmother has passed on."

Passed on. Such nice words for something so final. "My parents are dead," Jack had said, and the shock of his bluntness had been cold and honest, reminding me of the horror and loneliness of what that word meant. "Passed on" was something civilized people wrote on the walls.

"Your Aunt Jessica will be moving to San Francisco," Papa says. "It will be good for you to have her there."

So there it is. I have been tricked. I mistook his proximity for intimacy. He continues to talk, but I do not hear him. I do not want to listen to his coaxing words and well-constructed arguments. Papa has lulled me into believing that he wanted to spend time with me. Instead, he announces that Aunt Jessica will be in San Francisco, bringing grace and love and a civilizing influence. Walls. All of which will enable me to live there. Require me to live there. I am to be bundled off again. He has planned my life without consulting me, again. Why had I ever thought my father might actually enjoy my company?

"Did you hear me?"

"Of course I heard you. I am not deaf. My constant chatter is a certain sign of that."

"Do not take that tone with me, young lady. I thought you would be happy."

"Why would I be happy? Why would you care if I were happy? When have you ever cared if I were happy?" My cheeks burn like embers in the fire. I kick dirt into the coals.

"Guine…"

"I am to live away from you, where you do not have to acknowledge my existence. How could I not be happy?"

"Guine! You have not…"

"Have you tired of me?"

"I am going with you!" He shouts. "You are not going alone. I have no plans to leave you."

I am stunned.

"James says San Francisco has grown tremendously. There is work for a doctor there now; a white doctor. So many more people are staying in the town, catering to the needs of the miners. Your uncle says they outnumber the miners now. I could be useful. I have…I have decided to return to my profession."

Because of Mr. Ellison I do not think Papa has ever left his profession, but I do not say that aloud. My heart stops pounding and my rage ebbs. He will return to San Francisco with me. I will live in safety with Papa by my side.

The joy I want to feel at this news is not there, and I am angry with myself. I am to live as I have wanted since leaving Boston and yet I am not happy. I do not say that aloud, either.

I opt to gather firewood the next morning while Papa cleans our breakfast plates. When I washed up last night, the creek water was so cold that I had to keep my hands between my thighs to warm them as I slept. I did not want that again. When he offers the choice, I do not hesitate.

"You will find the best firewood over there." He points to the place where Fuego grazes behind the rocks, among the wild grasses near the water's edge. "Be careful," he warns, "the bears are foraging. They hibernate in a month or two and until then will eat anything that comes their way. The meadow itself should be safe with the cliffs all around, but do be careful. If you see one, do not run. Walk at a normal pace away from it and back here."

There are no bears in the meadow. I see this as soon as I wade a few feet into the creek to get around the rocky outcrop. The horse stands peacefully, chewing crisp stalks of wild oats. The pasture itself is small, surrounded by sheer cliffs of gray-green stone which rise into the sky, topped with pine and hemlock. A vertical land, I say aloud.

Downed branches lay in broken heaps at the foot of the cliffs. Instead of rushing to gather them, I dawdle in the mist that clings to the creek's shore. I listen to the crunch of grass and the whipping sound of the horse's tail flicking at unseen taunting creatures. The rising sun has not yet touched here although the trees at the top of the cliff glow in its apricot light.

I find it difficult to think of leaving the Sonoran Town, leaving my friends, leaving Jack. I push the thoughts away before I feel that prickling sensation behind my nose that means I am about to cry. I could use a tail like Fuego has right now to thrash such ideas away.

Finally, I load my arms with firewood and head back to camp. There seems little point in lingering if I only end up crying.

I step carefully into the water, not as sure of my footing as I was when my arms were empty. Papa is crouched in the shallows, clean tin dishes stacked neatly on the beach behind him. He has removed his shirt and is splashing water on his face, over his head, under his arms. He ruffles his hair, beads of water showering around him, sparkling in the early morning light. He is thin, the shadow of his ribs striping his torso like the pattern on the fur of Uncle John's cat. The muscles of his arms are well defined, but his shoulders are stooped.

When he stands and clasps the top button of his trousers, I prepare to shout, to make my presence known. Then he turns. Perhaps he has sensed me, knows I stand near. However, I realize that is not the case as his gaze snaps toward the camp and he straightens, a frown creasing his forehead. He shouts something and takes a step closer to the shore.

The crack of a gunshot echoes along the canyon walls. Papa stumbles back into the stream. Firewood splashes into the water as I drop my arms and take a step toward him. Then, a second blast reverberates and he falls.

I crouch behind the rocks, out of sight of the camp, wanting to dash to Papa's side but unable to move. My hand trembles as I reach for the tiny gun in the dampened pocket of my coat (had I fallen in?). I clasp the handle and draw it forth. "Put it away," Jack had yelled, "you don't know what you'll hit." I do not want to think of that now. I want to hit something.

Papa's limp body is buoyed on the current, caught on the stones where he has fallen. I cannot distinguish the rise and fall of his chest from the wash of water that pulses over him. Let him be breathing, please let him be alive.

I peek around the rocky outcrop and strain to view the camp, to see whoever it is that caught Papa's attention just before...just before.

I see them. Men blur before me, indistinguishable from any other men through my tears. They are rummaging our campground, our tent. I see two of them; there may be more. One holds Fuego's saddlebags, another a burlap sack that is Papa's. The pick and shovel stand sentry at the tent's entrance, untouched. These men are not miners, for these objects are valuable to miners. Who are they?

I aim the gun at the nearest looter, cock the hammer, and pull the trigger. There is a snapping sound and that is all. Again and again I repeat these actions, but the gun does not fire.

Sitting back among the rocks, I stare at the little pistol. "Don't look down the barrel," Jack had yelled as we were cleaning it, "you'll blow your face off!" I check the flint. It looks right, but I cannot be sure and wipe it on my sleeve to clean and clear it of any water that may have splashed there. I distinctly remember loading the tiny ball and pellet of powder, tamping it into place with the little rod that lay in the powder pouch I carry. Just a light tamp, Jack had said, or the gun will explode. Dangerous. It is a dangerous thing yet useless to me now. I turn again and face the camp.

Only one man remains, the sack slung over his shoulder. He is walking away from the tent, away from Papa crumpled so silently by the shore. I wipe my eyes and aim the pistol again and pull the trigger. The explosion is sharp. The man stumbles, drops the sack, and clutches his arm. Then he runs, disappearing into the brush that surrounds the campground. I kick the dirt. I had been aiming at his head.

I reload: pellet then ball, tamp once lightly. Pellet then ball, tamp once lightly. My hands shake and I must retrieve the iron shot from among the rocks more than once. Still I manage, moving again into position to pull the trigger.

They are gone. All of them gone. The campsite is empty.

I run to Papa's side.

Mr. Ellison asks few questions. He recruits three other men and borrows a wagon and team while I down a pitcher of water. Mr. Ellison puts an old saddle on Fuego, frowning but accepting my refusal to ride in the wagon. "A saddle will make the trip easier," Mr. Ellison announces. I suppose he noticed my wobbling legs. "Take this too," he says, handing me a slouched hat. I have lost my own although I cannot remember when or where. "Can't fit any more blisters on that little nose of yours."

The ride is easier with a saddle. I allow Fuego a gallop since I no longer worry that I will slip from his back and fall and break something and be of no use to Papa at all. As a result, the journey back to Papa's claim is faster. I try not to think of the time I wasted before. Wasted because I was too small and weak and peculiar and all of those things my friends say I am (even Jimmy Fassberg, who does not know the whole story).

Papa is as I left him. One boot still dips into the water because

I could not drag him any further onto the shore. The lean-to I
erected to keep the sun from burning him has collapsed at one
end, but his face is still shaded. He is weaker. His eyes flutter, but
they are shut more often than they are open. He seems relieved
to see us, but has little breath to say so. The bandages I had
hastily fashioned are soaked scarlet and I replace them before
Mr. Ellison and the men carry him down the hill to the wagon
that sits on more level ground. I follow behind, holding Papa's hat
and medical bag, so that I do not have to watch my father's jaw
clench or hear his swallowed groans (which I hear anyway). He
loses consciousness before they reach the wagon.

Through all of this, I find myself repeating Jack's prayer:
"Holy Mary, Mother of God" so that I will not have to think
about the color of Papa's face and what that might mean. Without
much thought, I use the phrase over and over as I find it oddly
calming. Jack says I am not entitled to ask Mary for anything
being the heathen Protestant that I am. Still, if anything can be
done, it seems more appropriate to ask for help from a lesser deity
instead of vying for God's attention. Then I worry that she may
not be a lesser deity after all and, now that she knows I think of
her that way, she will not want to help me. I ask only that he live.
It is the same request I made all the way to the Sonoran Town
and back. Surely even I am entitled to ask for that. Holy Mary,
Mother of God.

The prayer leads me to thoughts of Miss Moon. I cannot
help it. I want to have a picture of Mary in my mind, this woman
whose help I seek. Yet all I conjure is the face of Miss Moon,
calm and concerned and gentle. Jack would thump me if he knew
I was thinking of a Miwok woman as the Madonna. That alone

would get me into hell faster than anything.

As soon as the road to the Sonoran Town comes into sight, I tell Mr. Ellison my thoughts (except the Madonna part). I need to seek Miss Moon. There is no one else.

"Foreman here will go with you," he says, but I shake my head.

"I do not think the Miwok will welcome a white man with a rifle riding into their village. They know me," I say. Then I imagine Nanyawyn's angry face. I might not be welcomed either. Instead of saying so, I turn onto the deer trail that hugs the familiar creek.

Fuego and I stop only for water as the day continues to warm and our energy to flag. It is nearly sunset as we approach the village, greeted by the dogs. My thighs hurt from the effort it has taken to stay on Fuego's back. The horse is skittish around the dogs and his hopping makes my discomfort worse. The dogs stay at a distance, barking their warning as the villagers crowd around us. Finally, one boy calls them off. I recognize him from the last trip and assume he knows me too.

"Please, you must help me," I say, slipping from the saddle and grasping at Miss Moon as she parts the on-lookers and comes to my side. She removes my hat and clicks her tongue at my blistered skin. "No, no. Not me. My father," I beg, my stomach tightening with dread. She does not understand and I do not know how to make her understand. I had not expected this.

She tries to direct me to her hut, but I drop to my knees. "No, no. Not me," I repeat. Desperate for her help, I wish the angry Nanyawyn were near. How else can she be made to understand? This is not for me and she must leave the village to help me. Now that I have come all this way, I am not certain she will do this.

I wipe the tears from my cheeks and reach into my pocket

for the little pistol. There is a gasp from the villagers as they step away, but I can think of nothing else to do. Holding it before me, I pantomime the shooting and clasp my breast as if I have been struck. I hold my hip where the other bullet entered Papa's flesh. Then I collapse into the dirt. I fear I have added to her confusion with this performance, but as I rise and look into her face I see that Miss Moon understands everything.

With a quick nod, she flees to her hut, emerging with a bulging shawl tied in a bundle and slung over her shoulder. I struggle into Fuego's saddle and beckon for her to follow. With a wary look at the horse and the help of the children, Miss Moon swings herself into the saddle behind me. She gives brief instructions to the young men then nods her head once more. She is ready to go and I urge Fuego forward.

I push the pace, increasing our speed until I feel Miss Moon's body stiffen with fright. I slow the horse until she relaxes; but each time I subtly increase Fuego's gait. We never manage a gallop and twilight darkens around us. I am terrified that we will reach the Sonoran Town too late.

When we arrive and enter the Ellison's store, Miss Moon sees Papa and her wariness and fear drop away. I recognize the determination and focus on her face. It is the same with Papa each time he tackles a new case. I was right to bring her here.

Papa is already laid in his cot, his boots and clothes stripped from him. Several lanterns have been lit and the stove is ablaze despite the lingering heat of the day. A large kettle of simmering water is waiting. Miss Moon lays her shawl beside the cot and opens it flat, revealing bowls and pouches, knives and needles. Rummaging through the hospital, she collects bandages and sniffs at the bottles that line the shelves, rejecting the latter with a grimace. Then she cleans Papa's wounds with warm water from the kettle and gently prods and pokes, her fingers exploring the edges of his wounds, turning him to inspect the other side where the bullets emerged. Only the bullet to his shoulder has exited. This does not please her and she keeps a hand at his hip, as if to divine where the errant bullet rests.

Papa has been slipping in and out of consciousness, Mr. Ellison says. I think this is for the best for he is only mildly troubled by Miss Moon's ministrations, groaning as he would in his sleep at a bad dream. I have heard this groan before and find it oddly comforting.

She cleans and stitches Papa's shoulder, applying her mysterious poultices and wrapping him tightly with strips of leather she pulls from the abundance of her shawl. I will gladly give her the straps that bind my chest and I show them to her. She shakes her head; I can keep my straps.

She works until the door to the hospital crashes open and Nanyawyn fills the room with his anger, followed closely by Mr. Ellison and Kalelenu. I block his path so that he does not disturb the woman who keeps my father alive.

"What have you done?" he snarls, grabbing my shirt and pulling me closer.

"Papa needs her," I say, untangling his fingers from my shirt. I am not afraid of him. I am more afraid of what lies in the cot just beyond the canvas curtain. There is room for nothing else.

"I tried to stop them," Mr. Ellison explains.

"That is alright, Mr. Ellison," I say. "This is her husband and her son. They want only to protect her."

"Why bring her here?" Nanyawyn is shaking with ire.

I pull the canvas curtain aside. "This is my Papa. He is a doctor, like Miss Moon, but he needed a doctor himself. I knew no other whom I would trust." For a moment, Nanyawyn watches the woman he calls stupid, the woman I believe he loves. Finally, he and the boy sit on the hospital floor and wait, as I do.

CHAPTER 19

September 30, 1849

MAMA IS HERE IN CALIFORNIA and she rides proudly on the elephant, her skirts tucked between her legs like blousy trousers. Her bare feet dangle behind the enormous ears. It is an African elephant; I have seen the illustrations, so I know. The ears are bigger than those of the menagerie elephant. Mama is so beautiful riding in sunshine, her dark hair floating loose upon her shoulders. The light catches strands of red and gold among the tresses, ringing her head like a halo.

The elephant walks in the river, stepping among the stones with amazing surety over the uneven footing and the rushing water. It trumpets; but it is not the mournful sound I remember from Boston—there is something like triumph in its blast.

Papa joins them, one hand on Mama's dainty foot as he walks beside her and the elephant. He talks to her although I cannot hear his words. He is barefoot too, but the stones and the riverbed and the current do not cause him to waver. He has a hole in his shoulder the size of my fist, but his stride is strong and he is smiling.

Then Mama slips from the elephant's back into my father's arms and they dance in the river to the pulse and gurgle of the water. It is the Estanislao at spring peak, tumbling down from the mountain in a cold torrent. Mama's dress billows on top of the water, busy at its own dance.

Papa lifts her suddenly and carries her to the shore, to the base of a tall digger pine. He sets her down on a patch of purple and yellow and white petals among the shaded roots of the tree. I frown, for crocus cannot grow among the roots. Yet there they are just as she would like them. She runs her hands over their faces and smiles, then points to the flowers that bloom in the sunshine a few feet away: lupine spears and golden poppies. There are thousands of them waving above the green grasses, a blanket of blue and gold that covers the field and the hillsides all around. Papa picks a bouquet, but as he presents them they are already withered. I am not surprised, for the lupine and the poppies and the other wild flowers always fade quickly when they are picked. I have tried before to build my own bouquets.

Mama is disappointed at the tiny deaths; however, she will not allow Papa to try again. She is content with the crocus and smiles and gently pulls my father to her, kissing him softly on the lips.

With a tender stroke to her cheek, Papa comes to take my hand. I try to speak, to request he bring Mama with him. The river is suddenly louder and I do not think words come from my mouth anyway. So I walk with him down the hill.

This is not the only dream I have, but it is the one I remember. I awaken to soft light seeping into the tent. I am on my cot. Nanyawyn led me to the cot last night, at Miss Moon's direction, when my body began to burn and my eyes lost focus and the sound of Miss Moon's voice began to fade into the distance even though she had not moved. She was digging into Papa's hip at the time, using the long silver bullet puller I fetched from the instrument pouch in Papa's medical bag. She intended to cut him to retrieve the bullet lodged in his hip; but I remembered the bullet pullers and stopped her hand before she used the knife. When I demonstrated how the instrument worked, clasping it so that the small cage at the bottom retracted, her face lit with delight.

I suspect that she was gentle as she inserted the device into the hole in my father's hip. However, as I watched it plunge into his flesh and heard the wet slurp as the wound swallowed the silver tool, she called to Nanyawyn and had him lead me away, to sit on the cot and put my head between my knees. He was gentler than I expected and when I thanked him, he nodded in place of his usual grunt. He handed me a cup of strange bitter tea, like the tea that Miss Moon had earlier urged my father to drink. Soon I dreamed.

Now, as I awaken, the tent is quiet and the lanterns are extinguished so that I know the soft light comes from the day. From my cot I see the covered limbs of the three Miwok who have made their beds on the floor around the tables in the hospital.

Papa is on his cot, a blanket pulled to his chin so I see none of the wounds that keep him there. His eyes are open and when I sit he smiles and motions me to his side. I think perhaps this must be the smile Mama saw in the North Church.

"Thank you," he says, his voice a whisper. "I have been waiting for you to awaken. You seemed so peaceful in your sleep."

"I had strange dreams," I answer, even though he has not asked a question.

"Me too. I think it was the tea she gave us."

He reaches one hand above the blanket and I hold it, just as in my dream. Papa dozes often, but I am not frightened by this as his lips are almost pink and his smile's shadow remains even in slumber. Perhaps he too sees Mama on her elephant when his eyes are closed.

The Miwok stir and the two men slip from the tent as Miss Moon pushes aside our canvas curtain. She kneels by the cot and tests Papa's forehead with her hand, then pulls the blanket down, revealing the straps that encase his shoulder and hips. There are boards bound to his sides and he chuckles when he sees them. "Very clever," he notes, then lets his head fall back onto the cot, exhausted by that little effort. Miss Moon gently lifts his various bandages and presses the skin underneath. Satisfied with what she finds, she pulls the blanket back into place and offers Papa a cup of tea. He nods enthusiastically.

Mr. Ellison is our next visitor. "Did you see who did this?" he asks my father.

"It was your friend," Papa says, his sleepy gaze turned to me. My stomach flops as I think he is referring to Jack. Jack is the only one he calls "your friend." "The man from *The Pelican*. The man whose leg I stitched. The one with the sores."

I am relieved and angered at once. It is not Jack to whom he refers, but it is someone I know, someone I have come to hate.

"He did not shoot me, but he was with the man that did. The big blond man."

Colin Hurley.

"...*blond man*. You know these men?" Mr. Ellison asks me. I nod. "Why would they want to shoot your dad?"

That I do not know. "They are mean drunkards," I say. "Especially the Australian. I think he is the worst of them."

"...*worst of them*. A big blond Australian?" Mr. Ellison asks. "Did he have a boy with him? A curly-haired boy?" We look at Papa who nods. "Harold, they came in looking for you yesterday. The boy had a bullet in his arm and they wanted the doc to fix him up. But you weren't here and Quinn hadn't come to fetch us yet. We didn't know you'd been hurt, so I sent them on their way. I told them you would be back by, well, by today. Holy Christ, they didn't even know who they'd shot.

"Did you shoot at them? Did you hit the boy?" Mr. Ellison asks of Papa.

"I did," I say. Papa and Mr. Ellison stare gape-mouthed, reminding me of the Reverend when I had uttered something rude. Their shock dissolves into a look of admiration. I want to say "I meant to kill him," but I do not.

"That means they could still be in town," Mr. Ellison says, his eagerness building. I forget sometimes that he is the *alcalde* here and his job is to maintain order in the Sonoran Town. "Would you be able to recognize them, Quinn?"

"No," Papa cries. "It is too dangerous."

"Yes," I say. "I know them. They may be at Miss Weller's, as that is where they were the last time."

We leave over more protests from my father. Mr. Ellison gathers his allies as we walk up the hill. His recruitment explanation is simple: the men we seek shot Doc and justice must be served. He does not need to say more and we become a band of fifteen before we reach Miss Weller's. I want to run to the Moylan farm to get Jack, as I suspect he will be angry when he learns he is not to be part of this; but we have no time or at least I do not believe there is time. They could escape, these men who have tried to kill my father.

Miss Weller has the sooty lanterns lit already.

Danny is slumped in a chair in the corner, his face gray and unhappy in the stuttering light of the lamps. I too would be unhappy with a bullet hole in my arm and no one to tend to it. I think there may be more to his demeanor—he is sullen perhaps.

Beside him slouches Mr. Sterbenc, dozing open-mouthed with his face on the barrel meant for card games. Colin Hurley is not with them and I whisper this to Mr. Ellison, pointing out the other men.

Mr. Ellison exchanges words with Miss Weller and she nods her head toward the back of her tent where the canvas curtains hang. "They had gold," I hear her whisper and my face begins to burn. Of course they had gold; they had Papa's gold.

Mr. Ellison directs his men to surround Mr. Sterbenc and Danny and stand guard at the entrance to the back rooms. He says nothing and I know the men have done this before, as hand signals are sufficient.

"What do *I* do?"

"You point out the Australian when he comes through that flap," Mr. Ellison whispers.

As I turn to start my watch, Colin Hurley is standing in the opening, nuzzling the hair of a lithe girl around whose neck his arm is draped. As he turns to his mates, he seems to sense something in the room and his charming smile fades to a frown before I can raise my arm in accusation. He pushes the woman-child into the nearest man and disappears behind the flap, back into the rooms. Two of Mr. Ellison's men follow him into the depths of Miss Weller's tent.

Danny is on his feet, shaking Mr. Sterbenc from his stupor. Neither of them tries to flee. Cocked and loaded rifles are pointed at them.

Mr. Ellison's men find a hole cut in the side of Miss Weller's tent through which Colin Hurley escaped. They do not find the man.

Regardless, Mr. Ellison says that we will put the remaining two criminals on trial. He insists on a swift trial, citing a guarantee in the American constitution. The Sonoran Town is an American town, he asserts, and the American constitution means something here. Besides there is no jail and he does not want to keep Mr. Sterbenc and Danny locked up in his storeroom overnight.

The kitchen table and all of the chairs and stools and barrels Mr. Ellison can find are moved into the hospital tent; Papa's surgery tables are shifted aside. Mr. Ellison says the proceedings must be conducted where his prime witness is: immobile in a cot. He swears-in his jury. They are mostly the same men who captured Danny and Mr. Sterbenc, although he will not recruit the Californians since he is unsure of their citizenship. He selects only men who have come to California from the United States. Then he directs them to leave their weapons with his wife in the store. It will not do to have weapons in an American courtroom.

Once these men are seated there is no room in the hospital tent for anyone else. Word has spread quickly of the captured criminals and I hear the murmur of a gathering crowd through the canvas. They sound like hornets.

Mr. Ellison says that I will be called as a witness too. I argue that I could not see the faces of the men who shot Papa; I was crying. He wants me there anyway. I am not looking forward to admitting to tears in his courtroom.

Mr. Ellison pounds a hammer on the kitchen table and calls for order, reading the three charges he has written in his ledger: attempted murder, accomplices to an attempt of murder, and theft. He is to be the defense attorney as no one else has stepped forward. There are many miners in town who used to call themselves lawyers, but they are quiet now. Mr. Ellison announces that he will also be the prosecutor for the same reasons.

There is a lot of talk and procedural business that I ignore, wishing that I were outside by the creek with my friends instead of in this tent which gets hotter and stuffier with each passing hour. I do not want to look at Mr. Sterbenc and the miserable Danny who are tied to chairs in the middle of the hospital room.

Mr. Sterbenc seems to be in pain and begs a drink more than once to "steady" himself. Mr. Ellison will not allow drinking in his court, so Mr. Sterbenc slouches against his bonds, sweat glossing his skin, his face gray and his look ugly. Danny is in pain as well, holding his injured arm close to his side, the color drained from his face. He weaves in his seat as if he has been drinking.

"Michael, the boy must be treated," Papa says, then turns to Nanyawyn who crouches in one corner with his son and wife. Miss Moon has refused to leave my father and Nanyawyn will not leave her. "Please ask Miss Moon to tend the boy."

"Why?" Nanyawyn barks.

"It is not civilized to let him suffer."

Nanyawyn snorts, but speaks to Miss Moon nonetheless. She approaches Danny hesitantly, examining and treating the wound as she casts wary glances at the jury and Mr. Ellison (who fidgets with his pocket watch every few minutes). As Miss Moon works on the boy, Nanyawyn stands by her side and glowers around the courtroom. He had to leave his rifle outside as the others had done, although it took a lot of persuasion. He needs no rifle to look lethal.

The jurors grow impatient, sweating in the heat of the tent. Finally, Miss Moon straps a poultice on Danny's wound. When she approaches the lad with tea Nanyawyn warns her off. If it is anything like the tea she served to Papa and me, I understand— the boy needs to be awake and aware of what is to follow.

Ministrations concluded, Mr. Ellison quickly calls his court to order and Papa to testify. The jury crowds around Papa's bed to hear the tale as the Miwok retreat to the opposite corner.

I know the story, but I still find it hard to hear when Papa tells of being in the creek unable to move, unable to keep water from washing over his mouth and nose, trying simply to breathe and not to die. At the end, Mr. Ellison asks if anyone involved in the shooting is in the court. Papa points to Mr. Sterbenc and Danny.

Once Papa has given his account, Mr. Ellison asks me to step forward, put my hand on the Bible, and swear to tell the truth. He asks me my full name, just as he asked Papa, and my mouth is suddenly dry. I glance in Papa's direction, but he is dozing again and I do not know how to proceed. I have sworn to tell the truth and, if I do, I must reveal that my name is not John Quincy Walker. Mr. Ellison repeats his request: please give the court your full name.

"Guinevere Elizabeth Walker," I say, expecting to hear gasps from the jury. There are none. They are smiling, some nodding their heads. I have surprised no one. I have fooled no one except maybe Jimmy Fassberg (although I suspect that even he will say he knew I was a girl all along, mostly to avoid having Jack and Aldridge tease and laugh at him).

Despite my previous concern, I do not hesitate to say that tears obscured my vision and I could not identify the men who were there when Papa as shot. Still, Mr. Ellison asks me questions and urges me to respond in detail: Did you shoot at the men? Where is the gun you used?

I rise to retrieve my coat from the peg on which it hangs in our bedroom, removing the tiny pistol from the pocket. I forgot it was there and feel guilty that I did not leave my weapon outside as the others had done. Mr. Ellison does not seem to notice or chooses not to say anything as I place the gun on the table before him. There are several chuckles in the courtroom, as it looks very small there.

Then the questions continue: Did you know you hit the man? Yes, I say. How did you know? He dropped the bag and grabbed his arm. Which arm did he grab? His left, I say, reenacting the scene in my mind, clasping my own arm as the man in my memory had done.

Mr. Ellison points to Danny, drawing attention to the arm that has just been treated for the bullet wound: his left arm. The back of his left arm.

With nothing more to say, I am dismissed. I am hot and thirsty and my stomach is churning and I do not wish to be sick in front of Dick Sterbenc, who is now staring at me. I think he has remembered me from *The Pelican*. I ask permission to leave the hospital-tent, calling it court to be polite to Mr. Ellison.

When I rush through the tent flap, I find a few dozen people waiting outside for the verdict. Their upturned faces float before me as my stomach spasms and bile rises in my throat.

Jack is at my side, grabbing my arm and leading me around to the front of the store, to shade and a place to sit.

"Did you eat breakfast?" he asks. I shake my head which I hang between my knees, much as Nanyawyn had demanded I do the night before. I hardly know Jack is gone before he returns with an orange and cold biscuits and a cup of cider. He has raided the Ellison's kitchen and I am grateful.

"How is your pa?" he asks, munching on a biscuit himself.

"Bad," I say. Then I repeat what Miss Moon told Nanyawyn, trying to keep the tremble from my voice: the first bullet passed through his shoulder, missing bones and lungs and heart and important blood vessels. When Nanyawyn translated this I whispered that it is a miracle, but he looked at me strangely. Perhaps he does not believe in miracles.

Papa was not as fortunate with the second bullet: his hip bone was broken and the bullet shattered. Miss Moon retrieved all of the bullet fragments, she believes. I do not describe for Jack the way the bullet puller gouged into Papa's flesh, but I see it still and am tempted to lower my head once more.

My father can wiggle his fingers and toes. Movement of his arm will be limited only a little, I say. We must wait for the bones of his hip to knit before we can know if he will walk again. It will be many moons before the hip is strong, Miss Moon says. I snort cider through my nose when I say this. At least two moons per

Miss Moon. I find this hysterical. My tears sting and I cannot tell if they are from the cider or the multiple moons or something else.

"I was listening at the tent flap," Jack says. "You shot the bastard."

"I missed the bastard," I correct.

I tell Jack what I did not say in the hospital tent: "My shot hit a rock. The bullet must have bounced into the boy's arm. I could barely drag Papa away from the water. I could not lift the saddle to put it onto Fuego. I had to climb onto a rock before I could get on the horse at all. And I almost missed the wrong man."

Jack slings his arm across my shoulders. "You shot the bastard," he repeats, then suggests we go to the creek to cool our feet in the water and escape the heat of the afternoon. It is oppressively hot, although not the sticky hot of Boston. It is just the early autumn of California, Jack tells me. The nights get cold, but the days are like summer. This weather could last into October.

When I glance up to give him my answer about the creek, it is my first look at the laces of stitching through his eyebrow and the purple bruising that rings his eye. He bows his head and opens his mouth. "I know," I interrupt. "A cow."

"You be back in an hour, you hear?" Mr. Ellison comes behind us from the store, hearing as we once again discuss a trip to the creek. "They just got finished defending themselves and now the jury's talking it over. I expect we'll know shortly what they decide to do about those two."

"What could they say to defend themselves?" Jack asks.

"...*themselves*. Oh, how they didn't do the shooting and they kept urging this Hurley fellow to return to help Harold, but he refused. Claim they're scared of him because of what he might do. According to them he's a real bad sort and it wasn't their fault at all. They didn't even know your father was there until he stood up from the creek. Didn't see him. So murder was not the intent."

"Do you believe 'em?"

"...*believe 'em?*" Mr. Ellison shrugs. "I guess I can see it in the boy, but I don't think that Sterbenc character is much better than Hurley. No matter. I don't make the decision. We'll see what the others think about it.

"Your dad's sleeping again. And I don't think your Miwok friend is too happy about us being there disturbing him. So I hope they decide quickly or else we'll have one mad Injun lady to contend with," Mr. Ellison says. "Be back in an hour."

We agree, but do not go to the creek. An hour would not be enough time.

The jury does not take the full hour anyway and when Mr. Ellison summons me back to the hospital-tent, Jack sneaks in as well and we sit quietly on the floor near the canvas curtain. Papa is behind us and Miss Moon continues to tend him. Nanyawyn and Kalelenu crouch in the opposite corner. I am not surprised that the men will not leave while Miss Moon stays, but Nanyawyn looks none too happy.

Mr. Ellison bangs his hammer for quiet, then asks for the verdict as I hold my breath. "Not guilty," the foreman says of the first charge. My heart jumps.

"Not guilty of attempted murder," Mr. Ellison repeats, writing in his ledger. "And of the second charge as accomplices?"

"Guilty." Danny and Mr. Sterbenc are found guilty of theft as well.

"So what do we do about these criminals, gentlemen? Have

you…has the jury decided on the punishment?"

"We have, Mike. We want 'em hanged."

Mr. Ellison appears to be as stunned as I. "Hanged?"

"Yes, sir. They left the doc to die and stole his gold. If word gets 'round that a man can get away with woundin' a body and takin' his hard-earned money, well who knows what kind of lawlessness we'd have in this town. We talked about just whippin' 'em, but that leaves 'em alive to do it again. Maybe meet up with their friend and go to Mariposa or maybe up north someplace. And when those towns hear that we let 'em go with a warnin', why Sonora'd be the laughingstock of the territory. We don't want no trouble."

"Not the boy," Papa says from his cot. "You cannot hang the boy." His voice is raspy and his words slurred. I think perhaps Miss Moon has given him more tea.

Mr. Ellison faces his jury and, one at a time, asks for their concurrence with the sentence. In turn they each agree, some voicing firm conviction, some glancing between the two condemned men with a look of pity before grimly nodding their heads. None of them demur, although it is clear they are not all enthusiastic. "The jury has decided, Harold. It was a fair trial."

"Fair?" Mr. Sterbenc spits. For a moment, I think he is going to stand and fight with the ropes that strap him to the chair. His face is purple and hate glares from his eyes as he sweeps them over the jury and Mr. Ellison and me. It is only a brief outburst, however, and he sinks back into the chair, head bowed to his chest as if in defeat.

Jack and I rise to leave as two men from the jury untie Mr. Sterbenc and Danny in preparation for leading them from the tent.

Bonds released, Mr. Sterbenc springs forward and seizes me by the neck, slinging Jack aside with one blow. He grabs my little pistol from Mr. Ellison's table and holds it to my head. I hear the snap of the hammer as he cocks the gun.

"I'll kill her," he shouts. "You come after me and I'll kill her." He wrenches my head sidewise and my breath is reduced to short gasps. My heart pounds until I hear nothing else. Mr. Sterbenc is still speaking, but I cannot hear the words. He drags me toward the tent flap.

Suddenly he screams something loud and horrible, relaxing his grip. I take a deep breath and jab my elbow at his ribs, then lunge toward the nearest juror who stands among the others, shock washing their faces.

When I turn, Mr. Sterbenc is on his side, clasping his thigh and writhing in pain on the floor, screaming obscenities. He brings one hand forward and stares at the blood that is smeared there.

Behind him stands Nanyawyn holding a bloodied blade.

"Damn you!" Mr. Sterbenc shouts. "Did you see that?" he screams to the jury, who stand mesmerized at the scene before them. "That black savage stabbed me! Right in the back of my leg! You gonna let him get away with that? You gonna let some fucking Indian cut a white man? He could've killed me!"

Perhaps my ears have not yet recovered from the pounding my heart gave them. Perhaps I am not really seeing the hospital tent as it is. I expect action or protest from the men that crowd the room. Instead, the jury remains fixed. The only movement is Mr. Sterbenc who rolls to his knees, then collapses again on his side. He clasps his injured leg, his mouth repeating accusations and oaths that sicken me. The jury members stare at Nanyawyn, their eyes darting between the Miwok man and the knife in his hand. I am astounded at their silence.

Nanyawyn is defiant in his stance and does not sheath his knife nor wipe Mr. Sterbenc's blood from the blade.

"Oh, he'd have killed you if that's what he had in mind, Mr. Sterbenc," Mr. Ellison says at last. His words are not aimed at Mr. Sterbenc, however—his eyes are fixed on the jury. "I don't think there was ever any chance of that. He just laid you low so we could have you. Now, boys, take ahold of the prisoner and do it right this time. Tie off that leg too. Don't want him bleeding to death before we hang him."

The men shake their stupor and cautiously step to the man on the floor, casting their eyes warily at Nanyawyn who does not move.

"I don't want the hangings within the town limits," Mr. Ellison says as he directs the group through the tent flap, both prisoners once again bound. "Take them…" I do not hear the rest. I move quietly to Papa's side.

Papa is pale and his face shines with sweat. His eyes are closed, his breathing shallow but steady. I doubt he is aware of anything that has happened in the tent for a while.

"Come on, Quinn. I know a shortcut," Jack says, peeking around the tent flap. "We'll be there first." He had followed the jury from the hospital, but returned for me. "Hurry."

Papa's eyes flutter open. "Do not go, please." I was wrong; he was aware.

What can I say to him? I do not want to see another hanging, but I want Mr. Sterbenc punished for harm he caused the sailors under his command, for the terror I felt in *The Pelican's* dark passageway, for his association with the man who nearly killed Papa.

"I will be back," I say. Then I turn to face Nanyawyn. "I am sorry. I am sorry that I put you and Miss Moon in danger." The small dark man before me says nothing. "Thank you."

"Come on," Jack urges, motioning me to follow him. I let him pull me along as I do not know what else to do. I do not know where we are going, but Jack seems to know. He runs and I stumble behind him.

We arrive at a small clearing in the woods only moments before the jury enters, dragging the prisoners with them. As the townspeople appear, ropes are thrown over the branches of two stout oaks. There is plenty of room for the jury and the judge and the gallery who have come to witness the conclusion of this trial. Everyone calmly does their part as if they always knew how this would end. It is like watching Senor Barajas and his quiet acceptance of the fate Jack had predicted. There is even laughter from among these spectators. I did not expect this. I expected the verdict, but I had not imagined what might come after.

Mr. Sterbenc will be hanged first. He is placed on a horse with the rope around his neck. He snarls and snaps and struggles like the menagerie bear, roaring his loathing and fright. When the horse is pulled away, he falls and swings and kicks. His body thrashes and contorts. Wet sounds sputter through his lips and his face reddens. Only when the choking stops do I turn away. The throes of this death were not much different from those of Senor Barajas and that does not seem right. The truly evil should suffer more than others; but that is not the case here.

Someday I will tell Mr. Boyle that his second mate got what

he deserved although maybe for the wrong reasons. He was strung up, I will say, but my heart will not be in the telling.

I leave before the silent, shaking Danny can be lifted onto a saddle, his face shiny with tears and slime from his nose. He did not avert his eyes from the convulsions of his companion, even though it was clear he wanted to. I have the choice and I take it.

"Wait, why are you leavin'?" Jack has discovered my absence and run after me.

I do not answer as I have no words.

I want Jack to continue walking by my side, but I am not surprised when he drops back and returns to see Danny hang. I wish Jack had stayed with me. I would have liked his company today. Today, I am thirteen.

CHAPTER 20

December 15, 1849

THE BROTHERS Sverre and Brynjar Skjeggestad are two of the biggest men I have ever seen; they are almost as big as the Australian. For two years they have delivered provisions throughout the deep valley of central California and into the foothills of the Sierra. They are strong and willing to haul any load. Uncle James trusts them. According to Uncle James' letters, they are very good with the rifles they carry too.

Countless times during their visits to the town, I watched the brothers lift huge bags of flour, coffee, and beans like weightless children. The loads were carried from the backs of mules into the Ellisons' store to be set in their haphazard places. The mules were then loaded with boxes of gold to be hauled back to Stockton and then on to San Francisco. Papa had shipped his gold every other week with the Skjeggestads, receiving return confirmation from Uncle James that all was as expected on the other end.

Today, they have brought their ox cart. Usually they leave the rig in Stockton, after transferring the goods to the mules, as it is too difficult to get the wagon safely over the rough terrain. However, this time the load is different and there is no choice; the cart must weather the soggy hills and rutted roads into Sonora.

The brothers appear unflustered by the request to transport

Papa. Papa is to ride on the camp cot which will be secured to the bed of the wagon. Papa himself will be strapped to the cot to keep from being toppled. I have already fashioned straps to ensure he stays in place; they are like those *The Pelican's* sail maker made for our Cape Horn rounding. The backrest that Jimmy Fassberg's father crafted when my ribs were broken will be fastened to the cot too. Papa will ride as if on a chaise lounge through the foothills. I wager that the Sierra Nevada have never seen a chaise lounge before. I will ride Fuego.

Papa delayed the trip as long as he could, garnering his strength for the long journey. He hoped to leave by Thanksgiving, to ensure that the snows would not hamper us, but his body would not let him. Now, although the snows have not yet come to Sonora, the mountains above are already covered and he does not want to wait any longer.

The approach of winter did nothing to slow Sonora's growth. Autumn passed and more trees were cleared to make way for new homes, the fallen timbers evolving into the houses themselves. The push for gold continued and with it great stretches of the river beds were laid bare, slashes scarring the cliff faces. I fear this place will be unrecognizable within months. The village of fireflies will be no longer, but not because I am leaving: the glowing tents are rapidly being replaced by hard-walled structures that rise among the remaining trees.

Today the sun has not yet risen over the mountain tops. The town is quiet as we say our goodbyes to the Ellisons. For the first time in days, the skies are clear; it has rained almost continuously since mid-November. The brothers have covered the ox cart with the lean-to to keep Papa and his odd chaise and the shipped goods reasonably dry should the weather revert. My oilskin covers me from neck to boot heels, just in case. We are an odd sight, I am certain.

"The town elders voted in favor of the hospital, Harold," Mr. Ellison says, standing alongside the wagon. "We've instituted a gold fee and will start collecting taxes in the new year for construction. We'll need a real doctor too."

"You will need a doctor who can withstand the rigors of mountain life, Michael. I fear that is no longer *this* doctor," Papa says, running a hand down his hip. "There is always Miss Moon."

Mr. Ellison shakes his head. "...*Miss Moon*. If it was up to me, I'd have her as the doctor here. But most of the people don't trust Indians and that husband of hers has made it plenty clear he isn't fond of white people. I fear we may have to settle for a lesser-skilled physician. Truth be told, the missus and I may visit her if ever we're ailing. I plan to learn a little Miwok in the meantime, however I can manage that."

Miss Moon and her family left Sonora during the hangings. I could not blame them, having witnessed what I had. She returned every few days with Nanyawyn to check on Papa's progress and refresh the poultices. They came only at night and did not bring Kalelenu again. After a few weeks, once she saw that Papa was doing well, even those visits ceased.

In thanks for her skills and kindness Papa presented her with his bundle of surgical tools, including the bullet puller. He will order new instruments through Uncle James, he says, certain that they will arrive in San Francisco well before he begins practicing again. He would not let the want of a Miwok word for "thank you" stop him from expressing his appreciation for what the woman had done.

Last week, once news spread that we were leaving, townspeople wanted their health checked again by "Doc." I suspect it may have been that they wished to say goodbye.

Hundreds came. With each visit, the people describe to Papa the illness he had treated. They lead the weakened doctor to a chair to sit as they talked. He nodded good-naturedly and re-examined wounds, if there were any, assuring both himself and his patient that they would suffer no more from that account. The Mexican family whose baby he helped deliver brought their infant, boldly handing the boy to my father. I had never seen Papa hold a child before—he was hesitant at first, but then cradled the tiny head to his chest and closed his eyes.

I delayed telling Jack of our return to San Francisco. I wanted him to hear from me, not from rumor, but I knew my goodbye would be difficult and did not want to rush it. When I finally mentioned it, he set his jaw and said it was probably for the best because I would not pass for a boy much longer. Miss Moon's leather straps were already failing to flatten me, he declared. He was not sure he could keep Jimmy Fassberg from noticing and he did not want to be beating up his friends to stop their blathering. Then he abruptly turned and ran to his farm, not pausing or waving or doing anything that I hoped he would. I thought he was being thick-headed, as I did not think anybody in Sonora believed I was a boy anymore, including Jimmy Fassberg. Jack did not come again to see me and I packed Papa's and my belongings in solitude.

"I'll make sure Miss Beth gets that mule," Mr. Ellison says, as he helps me onto Fuego's saddle. Papa has given Guleesh to the Moylans although he does not say why. There would be plenty of work for the creature in San Francisco, but I like that he will stay to help Jack distribute apples. Guleesh will be happier, I think, as he really likes Jack.

The road away from Sonora is barely passable. Still, the oxen and cart and Fuego seem to have little trouble. We pass the schoolhouse, but it is Saturday and nothing stirs there. Behind are the orchards, winter dormant. Then the Moylan barn and their farmhouse come into view and I lift in the saddle in search of any movement there. At first I see nothing. Then Jack emerges from the barn, pausing at the entrance. I wave, struggling to control the prickling sensation just behind my nose.

Jack remains still for some time then waves briefly before dropping his arm to his side. He does not move again, watching as Papa and I continue on the road until we round a bend to the other side of a stand of gnarled oaks. I do not stop watching him either.

I was anxious to get away from Boston and New York. Rio was a wistful farewell; leaving San Francisco had been easy. However, Sonora is different. I will miss the firefly town and the voices of the pines and the oaks and the coddling creek. I will miss the Ellisons and Miss Beth and the schoolhouse and my schoolmates. And my Miwok friends. I will miss them all. Mostly I will miss Jack, even though he can behave like a mule sometimes.

Stockton is a sloppy stew of mud and people, horses and cattle. The usual noise is trounced by a constant downpour:

raindrops drum on tents, hats, saddles, and roofs in a steady tattoo. Yes, there are roofs for there are many wooden buildings in Stockton now.

We stop at Mrs. Schwartzmann's, only mildly surprised to see she is now among those whose businesses have hard walls. Her hotel is a two-storied wooden block with a bold sign announcing its purpose. She offers us a private room on the second floor, no extra cost, before realizing that Papa cannot manage the stairs.

"Hell, you two take my room," she declares. "I won't have you bunkin' with them rabble, you two bein' gentlemen and all. No reason I can't cart this fat rump up the stairs if'n I put my mind to it. I'll just bunk up there tonight, never you mind."

The room where the rabble stay is just like the hotels of San Francisco. Two "shelves" are tacked the full length of the walls, their struts acting as the demarcation between beds. Sixty men could be accommodated. A man might choose to sleep on the floorboards or one of the shelves above. Most of the men bring their own "linens," but Mrs. Schwartmann rents mattresses and blankets if needed. She tries to put the drunks on the floor she says, so that they will not get sick on any men below them. That is not always successful.

"You are doing well, I see," Papa says as she shows us to her room: a purple cloud of odd furniture and ruffles.

"Business has been great!" she says. "There's regular steamer service from San Fran to here every day. The fleet's in Vallejo and the army's in Benicia, so the boys is always coming into town on their leaves to sample what Stockton's got. It's a sight closer to get here than to San Francisco and we got almost as many saloons and hells and whorehouses, beggin' your pardon son, as the big city's got anyway. Our gamblers hain't as crooked I hear; but that might not be certain.

"Why, Mr. Walker, you could take one of them steamers back yourself. Trim the trip down to one day, it would, an' you wouldn't have to ride in no ox cart, gentleman like you. Keep you a lot dryer too, 'cause they got rooms below the decks."

Papa thanks her for her suggestion and explains that he and ships do not get along very well.

"Suit yourself, Mr. Walker, but I think I'd take one day of sickness over three or four days of drownin' in that ox cart."

She leaves us then and I fall into bed with a sigh. It is the first feather mattress I have slept on in nearly two years and I remember nothing until Papa pulls the curtains to let in the weak light of noon the next day.

The setting sun is poised to dive into the fog that creeps over the hills and into San Francisco. The circle of its face is shrouded in high clouds and it hangs like a silver coin above the hills.

Papa has endured the voyage from Contra Costa as he does every time: not well. He stands most of the way, leaning on his new cane, free hand gripping the railing until his knuckles are white. We caught the last ship before sunset, the most popular time, and it is crowded. There is no place to sit (and Papa is seldom comfortable sitting anyway). I blame this on Dick Sterbenc although I know this is not correct, as Sterbenc was not the shooter. Why I continue to think of him as the villain is a mystery. I try to shake the thought as we clear the balding isle that hides Yerba Buena Cove from view.

As we round the island, I think perhaps we have made a wrong turn somewhere for I see only a forest of leafless trees floating upon the waters and swaying with the tidal wind—the masts of the abandoned ships. When last we sailed, there were less than a dozen ships discarded here. Now, hundreds of vessels flounder in the water, sails furled, and decks empty. Timbers scream as the hollow hulls scrape against one another. Loose rigging rattles like the chains of Marley's ghost. The ships are lifeless and going nowhere in their massive graveyard.

Beyond the cove, rising from the beach and stretching up the coast toward the strait of The Golden Gate are thousands of buildings and tents. I blink my eyes and hold my breath in wonder: the sandy hills are barely visible beneath masses of wood and brick and canvas. Where a village once stood is now a solid city, rising from the dunes. Sunlight is trapped in the lowering fog and the new city looks oddly flattened and distorted in the strange light, like a thick gray tapestry has been laid across the flank of some great prone beast.

ACKNOWLEDGMENTS

My deepest gratitude to:

The historians, enthusiasts, and redactors who meticulously researched this time and people and set that knowledge in a form that I could understand: Malcolm E. Barker, H.W. Brands, JoAnn Chartier, Eugene L. Controtto, Chris Enss, June E. Hahner, Robert Fleming Heizer, JoAnn Levy, C. Hart Merriam, Devon Mihesuah, Dallas Murphy.

The chroniclers, letter writers, and diarists who lived this time and had the foresight to keep records: Joseph Perkins Beach, Henry Bigler, Ann Eliza Brannan, John Henry Brown, Richard Henry Dana, Joseph T. Downey (that rascal), Mary Ann Elliott, Jesse Benton Fremont, William Jones, William Perkins, Steve Richardson, Vicente Perez Rosales, Adele Toussaint-Samson, William Shaw, James Horace Skinner, Mary Holland Sparks, Bayard Taylor, Henry Bulls Watson, William F. White, and so many more brave souls.

Tom Boriolo who urged me to find Guine's true voice.

Megan Casey who exposed the publishing world to this novice and whose friendship guided and encouraged me along the way.

Sumant Pendharkar for his publishing advice.

Tiffany O'Brian (Butterfly and a Dog Photography) for a gorgeous cover photo, and to Anda Beninger (abeninger.com) for her remarkable re-imagining of the image.

My editor, Richard Biegel, whose friendship and encouragement were as crucial as his editorial guidance.

The children who inspire me: Billy and Katy Moylan (my godchildren) and Katie, Isabella, and Avalon (my granddaughters).

The women who inspire me, keep me laughing, keep me honest, and dry my tears: Julie Moylan, Harriet Newbold, and Rita Wells.

Matthew: my husband, lover, partner and friend. Enough said; he knows how I feel about him.

My deepest apologies to:

The crew of *The British Isles* whose harrowing experience off of Cape Horn was stolen for *The Pelican*. I fear I have not adequately described the terror of those events.

The anonymous Presbyterian minister of San Francisco who preceded Reverends Woodbridge and Woods and Williams in that city and whose purported existence I have hijacked for Donald Dunsford.

Mr. James Fraser, the real *alcalde* of the Sonoran Town during the time Guine and her father were there. He was a store-owner as well, but left no evidence of a wife or a trial or a hanging having disturbed his tenure. I plead poetic license.

The Sonoran Miwok tribe. I tried my best to find a native speaker of the Sonoran Miwok dialect so that I could give precise names (and their translations) to my beloved Miwok characters. I had only mystifying dictionaries of the Northern and Central Sierra Miwok. I hope I have come close.

CPSIA information can be obtained at www.ICGtesting.com
Printed in the USA
LVOW050257230213

321407LV00003B/333/P